Courting *Morrow Little*

Books by Laura Frantz

The Frontiersman's Daughter
Courting Morrow Little

Courting *Morrow Little*

A Novel

LAURA FRANTZ

a division of Baker Publishing Group
Grand Rapids, Michigan

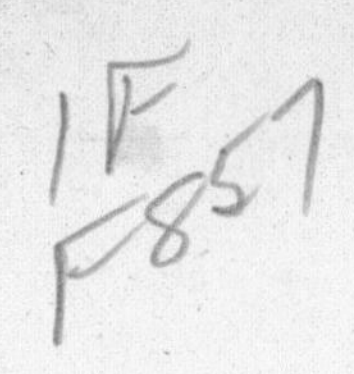

Published by Revell
a division of Baker Publishing Group
P.O. Box 6287, Grand Rapids, MI 49516-6287
www.revellbooks.com

Printed in the United States of America

Library of Congress Cataloging-in-Publication Data

Frantz, Laura.
Courting Morrow Little : a novel / Laura Frantz.
p. cm.
ISBN 978-0-8007-3340-7 (pbk.)
1. Single women—Fiction. 2. Frontier and pioneer life—Kentucky—Fiction.
I. Title.
PS3606.R4226C68 2010
813′.6—dc22 2010004279

Scripture is taken from the King James Version of the Bible.

This book is a work of fiction. Names, characters, places, and incidents are the product of the author's imagination or are used fictitiously. Any resemblance to actual events, locales, or persons, living or dead, is coincidental.

10 11 12 13 14 15 16 7 6 5 4 3 2 1

To my brother, Chris, who has Christ's
heart for a hurting world.

Prologue

Red River, Kentucke

July 1765

Morrow paused on the river trail to wipe her brow with the hem of her linsey shift. It was a true Kentucke July, and the woods were hot as a hearth, the leaves of the elms and oaks and sycamores curling for lack of water, the dust beneath her bare feet fine as flour. Even the river seemed like bathwater, its surface still and unbroken as green glass. She'd been following her brother Jessamyn to swim, but a treasure trove of wild grapes along the river's edge slowed her.

"Morrow, quit your dawdlin'," Jess yelled over his shoulder.

She stuffed the grapes into her mouth till it wouldn't close then filled her pockets for him. His quick grin was thanks enough.

"Why, them's big as marbles—or trade beads," he exclaimed, filling his own cheeks. "Reckon Ma would want some to make jelly?"

"We can pick her some after we swim," she said, shucking off her shift and hanging it from a sticker bush.

At the sight of her, Jess began to snicker. "Morrow Mary Little, you're fat as a grape yourself. And so white you hurt my eyes."

Truly, she was as plump as she could be. Stout, Pa called her, like most of the Little clan. Though five years old, she'd still not lost her baby fat, and only her face and feet and hands were tan. The rest of her was white as milk.

She grinned, bubbling with glee at his teasing. "You're so skinny I can see right through you. And you're brown as bacon."

Only ten, he worked the fields alongside Pa like a man, tending tobacco and corn while she mostly toted her baby sister around and helped Ma spin. Joining hands now, they jumped off their favorite rock, shattering the river's calm. Cool at last, they surfaced, smiling, glad to be free of the fields and Euphemia's fussing.

Morrow twirled in the water. "Ain't it fine—" she began.

But the smile had slipped off Jess's face. He held up a hand as Pa sometimes did, forbidding further talk. Bewildered, she looked about. But her brother wasn't looking, he was listening. Beyond the noisy jays and flighty cardinals and whisper of wind, past the heat shimmers of midsummer and the wall of woods, came a startling sound. The humid air was threaded with shrieking and screaming.

All at once Jess began to wade to shore. Morrow followed, but he turned, his freckled face suffused with a strange heat. "You stay put—don't even twitch—till I come back."

She watched the woods swallow him up as she sat in the shallow water, unable to stand up any longer on her trembling legs, unable to listen to the shrieking and screaming out there somewhere. With her hands over her ears she waited, and then when the water turned cold she started up the trail to their cabin, forgetting her dress. Naked as a jaybird, she flew into the quiet cabin clearing. The slant of the sun told her it was nearly time for supper. But where was Ma calling her to come in? Or the ring of Pa's ax as he split wood? Or Jess reminding her to bell the cow before he turned her loose in the meadow? For once she even missed her baby sister's wailing.

Her bare feet ate up the dry, dun-colored grass leading to the cabin porch. There on the steps, like a discarded doll, lay Euphemia. The dying sun lit her baby sister's wide blue eyes, only Euphemia didn't blink or cry. Had she fallen down and hurt herself? Morrow looked around. Where was Ma? Her breathing was a bit ragged now as she surveyed the toppled churn and water bucket by the cabin door. Some unseen hand seemed to tug her ever nearer, but she saw she'd have to step over Euphemia to get there, and she couldn't do it.

Sweat trickled down her face, yet she started to shiver like it was winter, eyes on the open door. Frantic, she looked around for Ma and Jess and Pa. Digger should have been here too, alerting them with his bark, welcoming them home. As soon as she thought it, she saw his furry body beneath the rosebush to one side of the cabin, an arrow through his middle.

An Indian arrow.

With a cry she jumped over Euphemia and ran into the ransacked cabin. Ma was slumped over her spinning wheel, but Morrow couldn't get to her past the splintered furniture and broken glass and scattered clothes and quilts. A flurry of feathers from the tick that had been Ma's pride were dancing in the draft coming through the cabin door. They rained down around Morrow restlessly, soft as a snowfall, almost as white. Standing there, her heart hurt so fiercely she felt it would burst.

"Morrow!"

Behind her, hard hands scooped her up and tore her away from the sickening sight. Pa carried her to the barn, away from the blood and the smell of death and their torn-up things. But he couldn't remove the gruesome memory. And he couldn't explain why the Almighty had let it happen in the first place.

1

Fort Pitt, Pennsylvania

June 1778

Morrow took out a painted paper fan, her gloved hands trembling, and recalled the look of horror on her aunt's face moments before when she'd embarked, as if she'd stepped into a coffin instead of a keelboat. Or perhaps Aunt Etta was ruing that she'd smothered her niece in silk, given the tobacco-chewing boatmen at the oars.

Beneath the wide brim of her straw hat, Morrow's eyes timorously swept the deck. Was she to be the only female on board? And what of her escort?

Up and down the rickety dock she looked, searching for the man her father had hired to bring her safely from Fort Pitt to Kentucke. Even with the summer sun in her eyes, it didn't take long to find him. Amidst all the folks lining the waterfront, one man stood out and was making straight for her. Although his attire was the same as almost every other settler in sight, he moved with an air of authority that nullified the need for any introduction. Only Ezekial Click could cause the crowd to part as decisively as the Red Sea.

"Captain Click!" someone shouted.

With a dismissive wave of his hand, the frontiersman turned toward her, his moccasins making short work of the long plank that dangled over green water smooth as a ballroom floor. He soon stood before her, his long rifle pointed toward the summer sky. He was leaner and more weathered than she remembered and wore a fringed linen shirt that fell to buckskin breeches. His long yellow hair and eyebrows were streaked white from the sun, and his fur felt hat was angled jauntily to one side, a turkey feather atop it. Brilliant blue eyes peered out of a brown face, instantly taking her measure. "Would you be Miss Morrow Mary Little?"

"I am." Charmed by his use of her whole name, she dropped a small curtsy, which seemed only to amuse him.

"It's been some years since I've seen you." His voice was deep and mellow yet held a hint of command. She tried not to stare but couldn't help herself. It was this man who had wooed them into the wilds of Kentucke so many years before. Being a Quaker and a frontiersman, he seemed to have a fondness for preachers like her pa. Among all the rogues and ruffians who followed him onto the frontier, the new Kentucke settlements could stand a preacher's civilizing influence, he'd said. And so they'd followed him west and, she reflected, seemed to be following him still.

"I reckon you remember little of that trip," he mused, shifting his rifle to his other arm.

She flushed, eyes returning to the river. "Just the horseflies and the heat."

But even as she said it, a bittersweet wave washed over her. She recalled her mother packing wafer-thin china plates into straw-lined barrels outside their summer kitchen in Virginia. Tearful goodbyes to neighbors and the fine brick home she'd been born in. And then the memory blurred to deep green woods so suffocating the sun never shone. One sweltering day atop a rocky precipice called Cumberland Gap, their wagon had tipped its load and sent those fine china dishes flying like pigeons into a shady chasm so deep they'd never see daylight again. Her genteel mother, she remembered, had been pregnant and burst into tears. Was he remembering it too? The smile on his face told her he just might be, but then it slipped away.

Was he also thinking of that simmering summer years before when her family's life had been torn asunder? He'd not speak of it, she guessed. 'Twas far safer to ponder what she knew of him. The man standing before her was a bit of a riddle, both revered and reviled in the Kentucke settlements. Rumor was he had a daughter so wild he'd had to carry her to finishing school in Virginia and was just returning from doing that. Morrow supposed Lael Click was nearly as well known as her father, what with her fair hair hanging to her feet. Though they'd never met, she'd heard enough to make her ears burn.

"This won't be a pleasure trip," he told her, adjusting the brim of his hat.

The warning in his words made her tense. Once again she was mindful of her fancy dress and ashamed she'd not had the sense to wear homespun. Did he think she was all lace and ribbons, not fit for rigorous travel? She noticed that he'd already dismissed her and was now perusing the polemen . . . who were perusing her. With a flick of her wrist, she snapped open her fan so she could hide behind its feminine folds. Feeling flushed, she turned her attention to the rough wood of the boat, which was little more than a raft with a crude cabin atop it, the sides peppered with loopholes that bespoke danger. A floating fort, no less. Perhaps this was why the frontiersman looked so at home on it.

His voice shifted to a more soothing tone. "You should see the Red River in two weeks."

Two weeks. A fortnight and she'd be home. But would they ever make it? Aunt Etta's parting look told her they might not. Indians were known to lie in wait along the north shore of the Ohio River, intent on killing settlers who dared venture down that vast watery road. Her father was well aware of the danger and had hired the famed frontiersman as a hedge against trouble. If anyone could bring her safely home, it was he.

But no matter how capable he was, Ezekial Click couldn't take away the fear she felt as the keelboat shuddered and left the dock, dodging a sandbar as it moved into the sluggish current. He led her to a barrel to sit on, the dark lettering on the side telling her it held rum. A morning mist hung over the three rivers that intertwined here, and an eternal wind set the ribbons of her hat aflutter like the fort flag high above. Softly she recited the waters' names to test her memory. The Monongahela, the Allegheny, and the Ohio—Indian words, all.

As she pressed her back against the sun-warmed wood of the cabin, her eyes stayed true to the north shore, the Shawnee shore. She heard Captain Click remind the polemen to keep to the middle of the mile-wide river, well out of rifle range. Her gaze fastened on the place known as Fort Pitt. Its wooden walls were receding now, a brown bulwark atop a high hill overshadowing a scattering of Indian lodges encamped on the plain beneath. She squinted in the sunlight, remembering Fort Pitt was a place for treaties and trade goods. A gateway to the west.

How safe was she? The grim set of Ezekial Click's jaw assured her she'd have been better off staying in Philadelphia. Unbidden, a Scripture learned at her father's knee rushed to mind. *I will call on the Lord, who is worthy to be praised: so shall I be saved from mine enemies.* The words wove through her head like a song. But solace her they did not.

Captain Click served her a wooden trencher of greasy beans and bacon before joining the steersman, who held the tiller of a wide-bladed oar aft of the cabin. Night was falling fast, the stars winking at her like the jewels that adorned the gowns of the belles back in Philadelphia. But the evening air was still steamy, and the mosquitoes seemed more intent on her supper than she was. How she wished the Redcoats had evacuated the city in April instead of the heat of June!

She slapped at a particularly large insect, thankful the army had finally evacuated at all. What was supposed to have been a simple six-month visit to her father's sister in Pennsylvania when she turned sixteen had stretched to two years. Morrow had arrived in that great city with the Redcoats on her heels, and the cozy visit she'd envisioned had changed into one of near servitude as the British took Philadelphia. Aunt Etta's humble dress shop in Elfreth's Alley had become an astounding success as officers' wives and the local ladies flocked to have gowns made for the weekly balls, horse races, and theatrical events.

Remembering, she smiled wryly and looked down at the dress she wore. When the English ladies had left the city, they'd neither paid their bills nor collected their dresses, so Morrow was the beneficiary of this entrancing gown and a good many more. Aunt Etta's fine hand could be seen in all the feminine details of the ecru silk she now wore, from its silver thread to the blue sash about her waist. A veritable garden of flowers in full bloom adorned the hem of the full skirt, sewn with such stunning detail that Aunt Etta had been forced to make a half dozen of them. Morrow had soon been pressed into service, her humble sewing skills transformed as she assisted her aunt in catering to the high-minded women of the scarlet and gold regimentals.

Dazzled at first by all the finery and fuss, she soon grew tired of the wearisome work. But it was more than this, truly. While Sir William Howe and his mistress led the unending gaiety in the city that first winter, General Washington's ragtag army was freezing and starving not twenty miles away at Valley Forge.

Now, amidst the monotony of the boat, snippets of her life in the city returned to her like scenes from a play, full of color and drama in retrospect. Was it just a fortnight ago that Aunt Etta had all but begged her to stay?

She'd been minding the shop when her aunt returned from the printer, her face a deep poppy red beneath the lace veil of her hat. 'Twas the heat, Morrow guessed, as June had bloomed so hot one could cook an egg on the cobblestone walk.

After shutting the door so hard the shop bell jingled for half a minute after, Aunt Etta removed her hat, an elaborate concoction of raspberry silk and faux pearls and flowers, and arranged it on a wooden stand in the storefront window. Impeccably dressed, she was as much an advertisement for her services as the shingle embellished with the image of a needle and thread outside her door.

"There's a new mantua maker six doors down," she said, shedding her lace mitts and dropping them onto the countertop. "This woman is boasting she can sew a gown in one day! The printer showed me her advertisement himself, though I scarcely believed it."

"One day?" Morrow echoed. "Perhaps a child's dress or an infant's christening robe. Certainly nothing like the gowns you turn out."

"Not *I*, Morrow. *We*. The gowns *we* turn out. Just this morning Lady Richmond stopped me on the street and asked if you would embroider the hem and sleeves of her sacque gown for the coming officers' ball. I didn't dare tell her you'd be on some sinkable contraption halfway down the Ohio River by then." She began walking about the shop, stopping to straighten a stack of ladies' magazines on a tilt-top table. "Though there *is* still time, you know."

Morrow paused in placing some silk masks on a shelf. "Time?"

"To change your mind about . . ." She hesitated, lips pursed sourly as if the very word was lemonlike. "Kentucke."

Morrow expelled a little breath. "But the plan is in place. Pa's expecting me."

"I daresay my need of you exceeds his need of you."

Biting back a reply, Morrow turned to the shelf and tried to change the subject. "Captain Keene and Mr. Marcum came in while you were away and purchased some things."

Etta rounded the counter, eyeing the shelves of fabric. "My, but those two are running up quite an account. They're here nearly every day. I wish one of them would ask for your hand and be done with it. Then you'd have to stay on."

Morrow tried to soften her aunt's agitation with a smile. "Mr. Marcum is more interested in shoe buckles and sleeve ruffs than me. And Captain Keene is said to be betrothed to a lady in England. Besides, I told them I was leaving."

"And?" Etta paused, green eyes sharp.

"Mr. Marcum bade me farewell. And Captain Keene . . ." She felt herself go pink at Etta's probing stare. "The captain said he'd not frequent Elfreth's Alley quite so often once the sunlight of my presence had left this place."

"Ah, I knew he was smitten!"

"For all his pretty poetry, Aunt, the man is twice my age."

"At four and thirty he's quite a catch. And a respected officer in the king's army, to boot. What prospects have you once you return to the wilderness?"

"Prospects?"

"Lice-ridden frontiersmen? Rum-soaked trappers and traders? Your father should be ashamed calling you home at such a marriageable age."

As she remembered it afresh, Morrow's stomach clenched tight. What if Aunt Etta was right? What if she was making a terrible mistake returning to Kentucke? Sighing, she set down her half-finished plate and let the steersman's dog finish her supper, her thoughts turning toward home. She'd not seen her father in two years. *Two years.* Though her homesickness had been acute, the British occupation had kept her rooted to the little shop and house on Elfreth's Alley until today. But now she was free. *Free!* The stench of the city was fading away, and she could draw an easy breath. *If not for . . .*

Shutting the thought away, she lay down on a pallet in a corner of the keelboat's cabin behind a muslin curtain. Captain Click was never far away, his gun trained on more than Indians. He'd let no one take liberties with her, she knew. Perhaps he was thinking of his own daughter tucked safely away in one of the finest finishing schools in the colonies. Morrow wished he'd talk about her and ease the boredom that hung between them. But she'd heard that the frontiersman was a man of few words. Besides, he had little time for idle chatter. Though he lounged against the house of the keelboat like the most indolent loafer, his beaver felt hat pulled low over his astonishing blue eyes, his surveillance never ceased.

The next morning, beneath the brim of her own hat, she stole a discreet look at him in the brilliant sunshine. Not a twig snapped along the north shore or a leaf stirred in the gentle wind that he wasn't unraveling its source. Sighing, she took out the volume of poetry Aunt Etta had packed and turned her attention to a bit of lighthearted verse. Only she wasn't lighthearted.

Moments before, Captain Click had escorted her to a crate, its top softened by a beaver pelt. Here she sat and partook of breakfast—some cold journey cake and lukewarm coffee. The rising sun skimmed off the water with an emerald shimmer, and she peered over the rim of her pewter cup, watching a heron take flight. The land was beginning to assume a familiar shape, like an old friend she'd been missing and was coming to know once more. They were rounding a bend in the river, slipping toward the southern shore, and it seemed she could reach out and touch the brush-laden bank.

So lost was she in its wild beauty she started when Captain Click sat down nearby, rifle at the ready. But what was one gun against a canoe full of Indians? Though the polemen had pistols in their belts, she felt taut with tension, eyes returning to the north shore—the Shawnee shore—again and again.

"I don't recollect putting you on watch this morning."

The quiet comment took her by surprise. Did he miss nothing? "I'm just . . . remembering, I guess." She read kindness and concern in his face and blinked to keep the sudden welling in her eyes from spilling over.

He settled his gun across his knees. "Best think of the future, not the past."

"Yes," she said, looking to the book in her lap. But how was she to do that when the past cast such a shadow?

Last night she'd dreamed about Ma and Euphemia and Jess. The closer they drew to the Kentucke settlements, the more vivid were her memories, as wide and deep and dark as the river they now ventured down. They seemed to take her by the shoulders and shake her, making her recall every single detail she tried so hard to forget.

It seemed her life had just begun when the warring Shawnee had come on their killing and kidnapping spree. She'd been but five then; now she was nearly eighteen. During those barren years, something else had occurred that continued to upend her. Something so frightening and memorable it had marked her like ink upon paper. She had been ten, and it was just her and Pa then, and Jess's shadow. A blizzard had been busy burying the cabin, and every so often she'd peer past the shutter and wish it would stop. It reminded her of the day her family died, when the fluffy tick had been torn open and feathers whirled like snow in the ransacked cabin.

This night Pa was hunched over his Bible at the trestle table near the fire, preparing the Sabbath sermon. With Ma's apron wrapped twice around her, she worked near him, humming a little tune, setting out some salt and three pewter spoons badly in need of recasting. Venison stew bubbled over the fire, and she stirred it with a careful eye, thinking she'd made too much yet knowing why. For Jess, in case he came. Surely after just a few years he would not have forgotten the way home. Each night, she set a third place at the table, and when supper was done, she put his unused cup and plate away. If her brother did come home, she wanted him to feel welcome and see his place waiting, reassuring him they'd not forgotten.

"Heavenly Father, we beseech Thee to forgive our sins as we forgive those who have sinned against us. Bless this food to our bodies. And please bring our boy home. Amen." Pa finished with a shine in his eyes, and she was glad he didn't look at her lest she bubble over herself.

They ate in silence as the snow and wind worked to bury them. At least, Morrow thought, there'd be no Indians about on such a night, and she could rest easy for once. She was glad to see Pa eating heartily, helping his thin frame flesh out a bit.

"You're getting to be a fine cook, Morrow," he said, taking more bread.

Smiling, she refilled his bowl, but before she sat down, something thudded on the porch. Had the wind toppled the churn? She lit another taper, surprised to find her hands shaking. A second thud caused Pa to pause, his spoon suspended in midair. Their eyes locked as they weighed what to do. A third thud sounded, and they both stood.

She scooted into the shadow of the corner hutch as he cracked open the cabin door. There, as if frozen to the porch, was a tall figure in a buffalo robe, the thick fur edged with ice. A trapper caught in the storm? A lost settler just shy of the fort? *Not Jess.* Disappointment covered her like a cloud. Pa welcomed the stranger in, then wrestled with the wind to shut the door.

Through the stingy light of three candles, she stared as the man shed his wrap and let it drop, the heavy hide looking like a bison just felled in a hunt.

Her lips parted, but she couldn't make a sound. A blur of beads and buckskin assaulted her, and she backed up further. In the tall Indian's arms was a smaller Indian. She watched as Pa took the boy and laid him across the clean feather tick of his own bed in a cabin corner. Dismay trickled through her dread. She'd just opened that tick and cleaned every feather before sewing it shut again. And now this dark and dirty boy . . .

"Morrow, get this man some stew and cider and I'll see to his son," he called to her.

His son? How did he know? Not a word had been exchanged. But the boy on the bed did look like the man who came to sit cross-legged by the fire. She served him, and he ate her thick stew with his fingers like he was starved to death.

"Bring some clean rags—and put on a kettle to boil," Pa said next.

She did so, and then, without being asked, she went to the medicine chest mounted on a far wall. Truly, no words were needed to see that the boy was sick. His feverish face was the color of dried blood, and she could see small spots, like a hundred bee stings, covering his flesh when Pa removed his buckskin shirt.

Standing over him, she finally found her voice, but it was as shaky as a windblown leaf. "Boneset tea will break a fever."

"Aye, Morrow, so it will."

"Is he bad sick, Pa?"

"I'm afraid so."

What if he died in their care? She cast a look at the fierce Indian again. Would he hack them to pieces with the tomahawk hanging from his belt? Fear chewed a hole in her stomach, and she thought she might be ill herself.

Beside her, Pa ran a hand over his sandy beard. "Empty the water bucket and fill it with snow. We've got to pack him in it to bring the fever down. Then we'll try to break it with boneset."

The wind had driven a foot of snow against the cabin steps, and she scooped some of it up, filling the bucket. She heaved it to the bed, so addled she left the door open. Finished with the stew, the tall Indian shut the door for her, then stood at the foot of the bed watching them, his face like brown granite. Under his scrutiny they worked, packing the boy in new snow, the icy shards shining like broken glass against his dusky skin.

"Strain the tea and we'll ease it down," Pa told her.

She worked carefully, efficiently, trying to still her shaking. Using a small spoon, they slowly fed the boy the tea, only to have it come up again. She remembered Aunt Sally, the settlement midwife, saying, "Boneset tea will nearly always break a fever, but makes you ill when taken hot." In her befuddlement, Morrow had forgotten. She surveyed the mess, about to burst into tears.

"Let's pray," Pa said when they'd cleaned things up, as if it was the Sabbath and he was finishing a sermon. Only this time he got down on his knees. She darted a glance at the Indian at the foot of the bed. Would he pray too? Did Indians pray?

She knelt down beside Pa, folding her small, cold hands. Only the Almighty could help them now, and revive the sodden feather tick twice ruined by Indians. She hardly heard what Pa prayed. When he finished, he attempted to talk to the tall man while Morrow stood by the strange boy and watched the snow melt against his feverish skin.

He looked to be older than she, perhaps the same age as Jess would be now. His hair was almost as long as hers but stick-straight where hers curled a bit. It was the first time in her life she'd seen an Indian up close. Some of the settlement women said the savages had black hearts. She wished he'd open his eyes so she could see if his eyes were black as well.

"What kind of Indian do you reckon he is?" she whispered when Pa returned to the bed.

He eyed her thoughtfully. "Shawnee, I think."

She looked up at him, mouth agape, fresh fear in her heart.

"If it were Jess lying there so ill among the Shawnee, I hope someone would care for him," he said.

She bit her lip. There was no use arguing with Pa, as he always had the right answers straight from Scripture. She said before he could, "Love your enemies, bless them that curse you, do good to them that hate you, and pray for them which despitefully use you, and persecute you."

He smiled. "Well done, Morrow."

The Shawnee stayed for four days. As she and Pa tended to the boy, the tall Indian would go hunting in deep snow, bringing in all manner of meat. Rabbit, deer, even buffalo.

When the boy's spots receded and Morrow's began, the Indians finally went away. She lay on the filthy feather tick and wanted to die, but Pa and the Almighty kept her alive.

"You're meant to live, Morrow," Pa told her, rocking her by the fire. "Just like the Shawnee we helped save, God has a plan for your life."

Morrow shot upright like a loosened spring, the thin sheet beneath her damp with sweat. The creak of the keelboat and the scuttling of a mouse were a welcome reprieve from her nightmare. In one dim corner a single grease lamp smoked, reminding her she was afloat and almost eighteen, not desperately ill and only ten. Pa wasn't here holding her, telling her everything would be all right, and she wasn't covered with spots, just sweat.

Through the makeshift curtain that gave her some semblance of privacy, she could make out Captain Click's sturdy shadow like a locked gate barring harm's way. They were camped for the night on the safer south shore of the river while the polemen slept or stood watch. Groggily she ticked off how many days of travel they'd made. Seven. And seven or so to go. She lay down again, wide-awake, knowing dawn was near. Reaching out, she fumbled with the drawstrings of her brocade purse, searching for a vial of rose cologne. Taking a bracing breath, she tried to summon good sense.

She was a woman now. A woman who simply must master her emotions before setting foot on Kentucke soil again. Yet her feelings were as fresh as the day she'd stood in the river and listened to her life being torn asunder. In her heart she was still five years old, watching her brother's retreating back as he told her to stay still, returning to the cabin empty of her mother's comforting presence, watching Pa erect a fence around two fresh graves. Nothing seemed able to cut the painful tether that bound her to the past, and the river was hurtling her forward, making her face it once again. Ready or not.

2

Not one Shawnee did they see, at least outside of her dreams. The late June sun was making heat shimmers all around, and the land was giving off the rich, ripe scent that she loved. When the keelboat rounded a sharp bend in the river, Morrow spied a man waiting in the shade of a sycamore at the mouth of Limestone Creek. *Pa?* How had he known the very day she'd be back?

At her elbow Captain Click said quietly, "I'll wager he's been here every day the past week waiting."

She didn't doubt it. *Two years.* What had time wrought? For all she knew, she could be coming home to a stepmother and a new brother or sister. Though they'd written, their letters to each other had been few and far between with the war on. She'd changed so much from the girl of sixteen he'd sent East. Had he changed too?

Captain Click came to stand near the gangplank, feet firmly planted between the cleats affixed to the deck. She could smell the cargo in the sweltering heat—ginseng and maple sugar, gunpowder and whiskey—in myriad kegs and barrels just behind them. It took all her nerve not to wrinkle her nose. She'd worn a more sensible dress today, gladly shedding her foolish Philadelphia finery, afraid her father wouldn't be able to tell who she was. But she'd kept on her gloves and straw hat, lowering the lace veil a little to hide her brimming emotions.

"Daughter, is that you?"

The voice calling from shore was warm and beloved yet strangely unfamiliar. Hearing it after so long made her burst into tears, right before Ezekial Click and the sunburned boatmen. She hardly heard the slap of the gangplank as it came down or felt the hard hand that helped her onto shore, sending her straight into her father's open arms. They enveloped her with all the warmth and strength she remembered, mingled with sweat and the tobacco he so loved to smoke.

She looked up at him, trying to smile. "'Tis me, Pa," she said through her tears. *But it's not you.* The man before her seemed a shadow of his former self. Leaner. More lined. Even his green eyes seemed faded to gray.

Captain Click thrust a hand forward to grasp her father's, cutting the emotion of the moment as he did so. "You've a fine daughter, Elias Little."

"I have you to thank for seeing her home," he answered with difficulty, his face grave beneath his sandy beard. "I trust you saw your own daughter safely to Virginia."

"Aye, Briar Hill," he answered, looking almost grieved. "And I wager I'll be as glad to get her back again."

With that, Captain Click turned and gave a sign for the polemen to bring her trunk ashore and heave it into the waiting wagon before continuing downstream where the river was the most dangerous. They'd travel another two hundred miles, he said, before delivering supplies to the settlements. Morrow felt her father's arm drape around her shoulders, snug as a shawl, and he waved with his free hand until they were out of sight. It was only then that he turned to her, amazement in every line and shadow of his aging face.

"I think Aunt Etta has sent someone in your place," he finally said, lifting her veil to better study her. There was stark wonder in his eyes, as if he was seeing someone else entirely.

At his scrutiny she almost squirmed, eyes flooding again.

"Two years is too long, Pa. We can thank the Redcoats for that, I suppose."

"We can thank the good Lord for bringing you back," he said, his smile surfacing. "Come along now. I've got to get you home before nightfall."

He helped her up into the wagon, and she nearly gasped at the sight of the gun leaning against the seat. Since when did he carry a gun? He was a preacher—a man of peace . . .

"There's been some trouble of late," he said, hopping up beside her and tucking the rifle out of sight.

Despite his sobering words, her soul seemed to reel with relief and wonder. *Home!* Her eyes fastened on the surrounding woods, lush and green, and the rutted ribbon of road that divided dense thickets of oak and elm and maple. A hot wind skimmed over them, spreading the heady scent of honeysuckle. She breathed deeply, shutting her eyes, so thankful she felt she would burst.

"Oh Pa, 'tis just as I remember," she said, turning to take a last look at the river. "I was afraid—being gone so long—that everything would be different somehow."

He smiled. "Your room's just like you left it. And I've planted a few more fruit trees. Some fine apples—goldens and Normandys and russets—outside your window."

She sighed with pleasure. She'd nearly forgotten the winsome view from her upstairs room and the way it took in the sunset as it lay like a golden benediction at dusk. In Philadelphia she'd looked out on brick buildings that blocked all God's green earth and left her to wonder if there was any.

"Aunt Etta was wonderful, Pa. But I'm so glad to be home." Even as she said the words, her conscience nipped at her.

Glad to be home, yes, but still afraid.

He nodded a bit absently, his attention fixed on the team that pulled them over the rutted road, darting occasional glances at the woods. There was an unusual wariness about him, a carefulness she'd not seen before, and it shook her to her calamanco slippers.

Taking a deep breath, she began to chatter as she'd not done for days. "I'd nearly given up coming home, truth be told. The British seemed to enjoy the city so much they showed little heart for war. At least General Howe. Sir Billy, they call him. He much preferred the dancing and the races. I was invited to a few of the festivities but declined to go."

"Your aunt wrote that you caught the eye of more than one British officer. I was afraid, from all she told me, you'd not return to me, or return a bride."

An officer's wife? Surely not. Not a Redcoat's bride.

Turning her head slightly, she studied his profile as she bounced about on the seat. Her absence had gone hard on him. He was a bit grayer at the temples, his once smooth face as lined as the cracked earth beneath the wagon wheels. "My heart is here with you, Pa, on the Red River. Not Philadelphia."

"Perhaps it was wrong of me to send you there, but I wanted—" He began to cough, his ruddy color changing to a wan hue. "I wanted you to have some peace. Forget."

Forget? But I'll never forget.

She swallowed down the words before she said them, remembering Ma's and Euphemia's lonesome graves. Lifting a gloved hand, she swiped at a tear as it left the corner of her eye. Dare she ask him the question that had dogged her all the way downriver? It took another half mile before she summoned the courage. "Pa . . . have the Shawnee come back? The Indian and his son, I mean?"

He nodded, face grim. "They come, as sure as the seasons. But I don't blame them. We're squatting on the sacred hunting grounds God gave them."

She paused, thinking of the settlers pouring into the Kentucke territory overland or coming downriver. It was all the men had talked about on the keelboat. "Seems like we could all just abide together in peace. Isn't there land enough for the both of us?"

"The Almighty only made so much land, Morrow, and the white man wants it all, so Captain Click says. The Shawnee know that and fight to keep the settlers out." He tugged his hat lower to shade his eyes. "I don't know why the Shawnee keep coming to our cabin. They just come, smoking or eating with me, sometimes saying a few words."

Startled, she lifted her veil. "But they don't speak English. And you don't speak Shawnee."

He cast a triumphant look her way. "I can communicate a bit."

Stunned, she nearly fell off the wagon seat with the next lurch. "How?"

"Trapper Joe."

Surprise seemed to seep into her very bones at the mention of their nearest neighbor. Half savage himself, the wily woodsman spoke a dozen different Indian dialects and knew the way of the woods as well as any Shawnee. Why, she'd nearly forgotten all about him. Or that Pa had entrusted him with the memory of Jess. Trapper Joe was faithful to bring back any news of white captives, though not once had he led them to believe that what they'd lost might one day be returned to them.

She looked toward the woods, the sun warm upon her back. Unbidden, the image of the two Shawnee hovered and refused to budge. The old fear she'd felt at last seeing them resurfaced. She recalled with crystal clarity the day they'd come to the cabin that stifling afternoon shortly before she left for Philadelphia. She'd been busy packing her trunk and Pa was cleaning his rifle when their sturdy shadows filled the open doorway.

They'd entered the cabin like they owned it, and she'd backed into a corner, the rough wood of the wall digging into her back.

The tall Indian was turning toward Pa, and as he did so, his hand fell to the tomahawk at his waist. Before he could pull it free, she let out a high, girlish scream, and Pa swung round and faced her.

"Morrow!" His stern voice seemed sharp as an ax.

The sound died in her throat, and the Shawnee laid their weapons on the table. Pa was motioning her forward, and soon, despite her trembling hands, she was serving fried grouse, new potatoes, green beans, gravy, and corn bread. The Indians ate by the fire with their fingers, shunning utensils and the trestle table, their eyes on her as she moved to serve them. The younger man—the son—upended her completely, his painted physique a rainbow of red and black.

Afterward, she listened to their lilting voices on the porch, finding their tongue strangely melodic, coming as it was from the mouths of men painted for war. She'd carried the bitter memory clear to Philadelphia, and it had increased the fervency of her prayers for her vulnerable father left alone on the Red River.

Pa coughed again, the persistent sound startling her out of her reverie. "I've not seen the two Shawnee since winter. It's a dangerous time to be about, whether Indian or white. There's been some raiding—horse stealing and such. A family was burned out over on Drowning Creek. And Captain Click just told me the colony of Virginia is sending soldiers to Kentucke to try to quell the trouble."

Pondering his worrisome words, she fell silent and tried to take in all the loveliness that had so long been denied her. A cardinal flew by with a flash of red as they moved into the shade and took a westward turn. *Home.* This was her home, no matter what, no matter the memories. She lifted her chin and smiled at the sky.

Thank You, Lord, for bringing me back.

3

There was no place on earth more like Eden than their home on the Red River, Morrow thought. In certain seasons, the stately two-story cabin couldn't be seen, smothered as it was by trees. But it was a peculiar place, the house only half lived in. She and Pa occupied the west side while the east side was kept shuttered and shadowed. A dogtrot divided the two, joining twin porches at front and back. Two fine chimneys of river rock adorned each end, one nearly continually puffing smoke, the other banked for a decade or better. To her knowledge, Pa had never entered the east side since that tragic summer's day all those years before, though her own footprints had mingled with those of the mice, marring the dusty floor.

All was chaos within, just as the Shawnee had left it. The spinning wheel where Ma had slumped sat untouched, the wool she'd been working mere spiderwebbing. Splintered furniture was strewn about—a chair leg here, a hatchet-marked cradle there. All the prized glass from the broken front window had been swept up by someone, sometime, and replaced with oiled paper. But a few stray feathers from the shredded tick remained, having escaped a brisk broom, and startled her anew each time she entered. With the door ajar, they danced in the draft, and she felt she was five years old again, fresh grief spilling into her heart.

Their side of the cabin was feather-free and tidy as could be. Bright rag rugs lay like pressed flowers on the clean pine planks, and a huge hutch bore plates of pewter and what remained of the fine English china. From spring to fall, fresh flowers graced the trestle table, and winter boasted bittersweet. A staircase hugged the west wall, its hickory steps and handrail worn smooth with time.

Today she hurried to her room at the top of the stairs, standing in the doorway and surveying the plate-glass windows she'd just cleaned that bubbled and streaked in the sun. Her eyes were drawn to her bed, bigger than a girl's had any right to be, its counterpane immaculate, the pillows fluffed, the chamber pot out of sight beneath. Her old dolls sat primly on a shelf, and her fine Philadelphia clothes were hidden in a corner wardrobe painted with a fleur-de-lis. When she'd left for Aunt Etta's, the room had seemed just right. Now, two years later, why did it have a childish feel?

Although she'd been home less than a week, it seemed longer somehow, and she'd resumed her old routine with nary a blink. Still weary from the trip, she sank down atop the soft bed, her thoughts far upriver. To Fort Pitt and beyond to the bustle of Philadelphia. She missed it a bit. She'd forgotten how quiet the cabin was . . . how lonesome she felt. Pa was mending fences in the far pasture and likely wouldn't be home till supper.

She looked through the shiny windows, suddenly aware of a door groaning open below. The ensuing silence sent an icy finger of alarm down her spine. Pa always called to her when he entered, as if he knew it would ease her. She tried to swallow down her fear, but it had followed her for so long she felt nearly suffocated by it.

If it wasn't Pa . . . who?

Isolated as they were, company rarely came. A reassuring rumble of voices sent her scurrying to the landing, where she leaned over the stair rail. As she peered down, surprise lit her face. Standing below was an Indian girl scarcely older than she herself, clutching a bundle. Good Robe? She'd nearly forgotten the wife of Trapper Joe, who lived downriver. A stocky shadow appeared in the open doorway behind the tawny figure, voice booming.

"Miz Morrow, where are you?"

"Right here, Joe," she answered, hurrying down the steps.

He took her in head to toe with a surprised grin, as if making up for the time they'd been apart. "Well, I doubt I'd know you if you hadn't answered to your name. The fort's all abuzzel with news that you've come back. But I had to come over here and see for myself."

"I've not been home long," she said with a smile, hovering on the last step.

He pulled on his unkempt beard, eyes alight. "Well, it's high time I showed you my son," he told her. "We're calling him Elias, or Little Eli, after your pa."

She came forward, eyeing the bundle. "Pa told me the happy news. He's hardly a month old, is that right?"

Even before Morrow asked, Good Robe was offering her treasure. "You like?"

Touched, Morrow took the baby, thinking him no heavier than a feather pillow. The sight of his tiny face, eyes shuttered in sleep, wee fists curled tightly beneath his chin, filled her with wonder. "He's . . . beautiful."

"Good Robe was a mite skittish about comin' over here, seein' as how Aunt Sally turned her away," Joe said. "But I told her you ain't nothin' like them other settlement women."

Morrow flushed. Just yesterday Pa had related in the most genteel terms how Good Robe had walked miles to the fort while laboring only to have the settlement midwife shun her. She'd given birth on the trail going home, and after a frantic hunt Joe had found her, alone but having safely delivered their son. Morrow's heart twisted at the telling, yet she could hardly blame Aunt Sally either. The woman had lost a child in an Indian raid and had worn her unforgiveness like a badge of bitterness ever since.

"Please sit down and I'll make you some coffee," she told them, passing the baby back to Good Robe and showing her to a rocking chair. As she filled a small kettle with water and measured coffee at the hearth, she heard the scrape of boots on the porch.

Pa came in, mouth curving warmly at the sight of them. "Glad to see you, Joe, Good Robe. Is that my namesake there?"

"Sure is," Joe answered. "I was just showin' him off to Miz Morrow. But I got other business to discuss with you once we've had some coffee."

Hearing the somber edge to his voice, Morrow felt a touch of dread. Often, fresh from his forays into the woods, Joe would bring back news of what was truly happening on the western fringe of the frontier—not the slanted, tainted tales often told by British and American officers and the local militia, but the honest-to-goodness truth.

She served Good Robe first, then took the men their coffee on the back porch, where they sat with their pipes, enjoying a rare rain. Even the birdsong had stilled, giving way to the gentle slurring sound as the midsummer dust was dampened down. Standing in the dogtrot and looking toward the river, Morrow fancied she could smell honeysuckle, its sweet scent banishing the lingering supper smells.

She felt a bit awkward left alone with Good Robe. The Indian girl spoke little English that she knew of, though Joe spoke her tongue like he was born to it. They'd wed right before she'd left for Philadelphia, Morrow remembered. Joe had supposedly swapped five horses for her in some Indian town across the Ohio River. As the story circulated through the settlement, its baseness hurt her somehow. The Almighty had created man and woman and called it good, Pa said, and a woman's worth wasn't measured in horses. But to his credit, Joe did seem to care for her.

The sight of Good Robe rocking her baby was a welcome distraction, given the intense if hushed tones of the men outside. A sudden lull in their voices made her turn and look beyond the back door. Fireflies winged about with tiny lanterns on their backs, resurrecting a memory she'd rather forget. She sighed and tried to put it down, but it came on anyway.

When she and Jess were small, they'd catch a dozen or so fireflies and imprison them in glass jars, but he'd cry after mere minutes and beg to release them. Did he, wherever he was, remember her calling him lily-livered and stomping upstairs to the room they shared? It seemed he'd always given in to her whims, letting her use the fireflies like a night-light by their bed. But by morning they were mere bugs in a jar, hardly the ethereal creatures they'd been the night before.

Joe's voice seemed to saw into the silence, ending her reverie. "There's been some talk of a prisoner exchange," he was saying, pausing at intervals to puff on his pipe. "Some chiefs and soldiers at Fort Pitt are hammerin' out the details."

Listening, Morrow felt the same bewilderment she always did when they discussed her long-lost brother, torn between covering her ears and eavesdropping. She finally succumbed to the latter. Returning to the hearth, she sat down opposite Good Robe, nearly drowning out the men's voices by the creak of Ma's old chair as it pitched to and fro. But her foot came down at Joe's next question, and her rocking ceased. "Seen them two Shawanoe lately?"

Pa seemed to take his time with the answer, but already Morrow was straining for it, a deep dread knotting her insides.

"Not since last winter," Pa said.

"They been comin' for years now and I still ain't seen 'em."

"You're always away hunting or on some other business, Joe, otherwise I'd send for you."

"Well, somethin' tells me they ain't no ordinary Indians."

Pa leaned back in his chair—she could tell by the squeak and the grunt of it. His voice was thoughtful. "What makes you think so?"

"Them fancy gifts they bring. That horse they give you last fall's the finest I've seen this side of the Cumberland."

"I nearly refused it," Pa admitted. "With all the horse stealing between here and the Ohio, I'm still a bit befuddled as to whose horse I have."

Joe chuckled. "Only a fool would refuse such a prize. Besides, the Shawnee don't take kindly to bein' told no."

Pa paused a moment. "I've often wondered who they are myself, why they keep coming back. I didn't see the son for a long while and feared he might be dead given all the trouble. But then last winter he was with his father again. I don't think they mean us any harm, though they rattle poor Morrow considerably."

Joe chuckled. "She's rattlin' age, I reckon. One thing I can say for the Shawanoe, once you've done 'em a good turn, they ain't likely to repay it with evil. You've likely befriended the whole Shawnee nation and don't know it."

"Humph." Pa's doubt could be felt clear into the cabin.

"I ain't just speculatin' either. I got reason to believe the Shawnee whose son you saved years ago is a chief of the Kispokos. That's the warrior sect of the tribe." He paused as if to give Pa ample time to take it all in. "The past couple of years I've been hearin' about one of their headmen crossing into Kentucke to rendezvous with a white man. I believe that white man is you."

"Have any idea what his name is, Joe?"

"Matter of fact, I do."

Morrow leaned forward in her chair as Joe mumbled something unintelligible and commandeered the conversation once more. “But just so you don’t think he’s payin’ a social call, I hear he’s keepin’ an eye on the settlements. Either way, you’ve earned his respect, and that means a lot in these troubled times.”

Joe’s reassuring words did little to ease her. Morrow glanced at Good Robe, whose dark head was tilted toward her chest, eyes closed, the baby tucked to her breast. Was she still weary from the birth? Morrow hoped Joe had sense enough to canoe her downriver today and not make her walk all the way.

As the conversation on the porch wound down, Joe came in and roused his wife. Morrow gathered up the coffee cups and banked the fire for breakfast while Pa stood at the door and saw the couple off.

“The rain’s a welcome change,” he said. “I think I’ll leave the doors open for a spell.”

At his words, the flicker of fear in her heart seemed to flame. Holding back a sigh, she wandered to the front porch and looked at the dense wall of woods, then crossed to the back and did the same. The rain had eased, and everything was green and lush and wet. Almost peaceful.

How, she wondered, would it feel to be free? Free of fear? Free of the past? Free from all the hurt hidden in her heart?

Lord, are You there? she wondered.

Fear not, for I am with thee . . .

4

Morrow had nearly forgotten her birthday, but Pa reminded her of its coming. 'Twas a fine time to celebrate, he said, with summer humming all around, the days long and sultry. Since coming home, she'd yet to see her friends, and so she'd sent two invitations to Red River Station by Joe, asking them to join her for a little party. Several miles upriver, the sprawling station was fortified with blockhouses and stuffed with settlers fearful of wild animals and Indians. Sometimes it seemed to Morrow that she and Pa were the only ones not in residence, save the Sabbaths when Pa preached there. Would Lizzy and Jemima even leave its secure confines to come?

Her thoughts wandered back to Philadelphia where she and Aunt Etta had celebrated by taking a post chaise to a tea shop, where they'd eaten one too many scones, and then gone to the theater to see *The Prince of Parthia*. Despite all this civility, she'd been homesick and dreamed of having a tea party all her own under the giant elm near the orchard.

The last of July dawned bright, with red roses crowding the cabin steps and phlox and cockscomb blooming along the porch rail. Coming down from her attic room at dawn, Morrow noticed that both front and back doors were open again. Likely Pa was trying to air out the bitter odor of bacon she'd burned the night before, as well as woo any willing breeze.

Hastening to the trestle table, she surveyed the platter of queen's cakes she'd made, each confection dusted with sugar and looking far too tempting. Just recently she'd found the faded receipt written in her mother's flowing hand and had nearly gasped at the two dozen eggs called for. Forging ahead, she'd hung about the henhouse and coaxed the birds to lay, then gathered and cracked every one. Her mouth watered as she added a heaping helping of flour and sugar and two pounds of butter. Perhaps this was why she'd once been so round and Jess had teased her.

Taking a bite of cake, she looked down at the gown pinching her waist. The blueberry chintz was shot through with silver thread, the faux-pearl buttons down the bodice framed with exquisite ivory lace. The same lace formed a fichu about her shoulders before peeking out again from the hem. Her birthday dress, compliments of some officer's lady. She took a slow turn, liking how the glossy skirt rustled and swirled around her. Eighteen seemed a momentous age. Ma had married Pa at eighteen and birthed Jess the year after.

She passed to the porch, pleased to see Pa had placed a small table and three chairs in the shade of the elm near the orchard. Snatching up a tablecloth, she fairly danced across the yard in anticipation of her party. The breeze teased the damask cloth, threatening to whisk it off the table, so she anchored it with a pitcher of roses. In the distance she heard the rumble of a wagon. Lizzy and Jemima already?

Turning, she ran back into the cabin and returned with a tray of cups and saucers and the coveted queen's cakes. It was too hot for tea, truly, but she was anxious to air the porcelain teapot and fancy cups and saucers Aunt Etta had packed in her trunk before leaving the city.

By the time Pa had deposited the young women near the porch, Morrow had everything in order. Jemima was the first out of the wagon, her rotund figure wrapped in her best Irish linen dress, her bonnet festooned with a clump of wilted daisies. No plain homespun today, Morrow mused. This was a tea party, after all, betwixt friends who'd been apart far too long. Next came Lizzy, as lean as Jemima was generous. Her dress was just as fine, if wrinkled from riding, the airy muslin sprigged with tiny periwinkle flowers. She wore a simple bonnet, her fair face flushed from coming all the way from the fort.

Morrow hid behind the elm, watching them wander toward the porch. Pa spied her and chuckled as he unhitched the team by the barn. When the girls reached the cabin steps, she sat down at the table as gracefully as she'd seen the ladies do in Philadelphia, spreading her skirts over her slippers and tucking in a tendril of hair that had come free of her chignon. Taking hold of a silver sugar spoon, she clinked it gently against a china cup to get their attention. Both turned at once, but it was Lizzy who ran pell-mell toward her, nearly overturning the table in her glee.

"Morrow, is it truly you?" Lizzy's expression was all joy, green eyes wide with wonder. She caught Morrow's soft hands in her callused ones, reminding Morrow of the hard work that awaited now that she'd returned home. "What has your Aunt Etta done? You're hardly the friend I remember."

"We've all grown up, Lizzy," she answered, turning to Jemima, who'd stopped a short distance away.

Jemima's eyes were wide, not from welcome as Morrow had hoped, but from a sort of strained dismay. She held out her hands anyway, accustomed to Jemima's moods. They'd been friends for nigh on ten years and would likely stay that way, fractious though Jemima was.

At last her friend sidled forward, green eyes assessing her in one sweep. "I see you've picked up some fine Philadelphia airs. Best shed that fancy dress and remember where you're at."

"'Tis my birthday, Jemima. I wouldn't make a fuss otherwise," Morrow replied with a smile.

Jemima hugged her briefly, though Lizzy clung to her the longest. "I thought you'd not come back, Morrow, what with all the trouble here and there. Maybe marry a British officer and stay in the city."

"The only British officer I fancied was already taken," she said, sitting down between them.

"And who might that be?" Jemima demanded, removing her hat.

"John Andre," she said, toying with a spoon. "He fell in love with a Philadelphia belle named Peggy Shippen. I merely had the privilege of sewing her dresses."

"I've heard of John Andre," Jemima said as she eyed the queen's cakes. "He's a spy, according to the *Virginia Gazette*."

"If so, he's a very handsome one," Morrow replied, remembering Jemima was a voracious reader. "But I'm no loyalist, remember. Nor do I care to discuss matters of war on my birthday." She raised the porcelain pot and began pouring the fragrant tea. Lizzy leaned forward and took an appreciative whiff, her smile widening when Morrow said, "Labrador."

"Not British tea, then?" Jemima asked.

Morrow shook her head and passed the cream as the wind fluttered the edges of the tablecloth like a flag, reminding her strangely of Fort Pitt and its ominous walls. "I've had quite enough of all things English, truth be told." But her eyes lingered on the lovely Spode blue pattern of the china nonetheless. "Now, I want to hear some settlement news for a change. All the good news, that is."

Jemima's mouth took a downward turn. "There's little of that to be had, though some regiments from Virginia should arrive any day."

Lizzy chuckled, stirring her tea. "I've seen you at your window waitin'."

"There are some advantages to living at the fort," Jemima said, taking not one cake but two. "I get my pick of the soldiering men, if there are any worth having."

Lizzy took a sip of tea, voice soft. "I'm anxious for Morrow to meet my Abe. We're to be married in spring once he finishes his cabin over on Tate's Creek."

"Lizzy, that's fine news!" Morrow exclaimed. "Abe is a good man—the best, Pa says."

"Well, it's your pa who's agreed to marry us. And I want you to stand up with me," she said between bites of cake. "Will you?"

"I'd be honored," Morrow replied with a smile. "You needn't even ask."

Jemima looked her over reprovingly, dabbing the perspiration beading her lip with a napkin. "I'd think twice about any bridesmaid who'll likely outshine the bride."

But Lizzy merely winked and said, "Maybe we'll have a double wedding. Or a triple. I'll wager your pa never wedded three couples at once."

"Nay, nor wanted to," Pa said as he passed behind them.

Morrow stood up and took a cake off the platter, placing it in his outstretched hand.

"I'd best be on my way if you're talking men," he said. "Keep in mind that I'll not marry you three to just anyone, especially my Morrow."

"No need to worry," Morrow said when he'd passed out of earshot. "I'm eighteen now—nearly an old maid."

Jemima snorted, her mouth pursing scornfully. "You won't be for long, what with all the buzzel at the fort about your coming back home."

Morrow felt the heat bloom in her face. She kept her eyes down, studying the crumbs on her plate. "Seeing as how women are so scarce here, 'tis no surprise."

"'Tis true enough," Lizzy murmured between sips of tea. "There's been more than one man askin' after you, wonderin' when you'd be back."

Jemima leaned forward, conspiratorial. "I bet it's those Clays.

Though I can't figure out which one's the most smitten. My guess is Lysander. Though I remember Robbie moping about you at the last frolic before you left."

Morrow nearly winced. The memory was hardly pleasant. She'd felt like a fool with all the male attention and vowed she'd never attend a settlement frolic again. Jemima hadn't spoken to her for a month after, sweet as she was on Lysander. Even now her plump face was pinched with displeasure, as if resurrecting every detail.

Morrow took a steadying breath, wanting to steer the conversation in a safer direction, and gestured to the gifts atop the tablecloth. "I've brought you both a little something from the city."

Lizzy's face softened. "But it's your birthday, Morrow. I thought these presents were for you."

"I'm wearing mine," she said, fingering the lace fichu of her dress.

Jemima finished her tea, her fingers plucking at the shiny ribbon on her package. "I didn't bring you a thing, Morrow Mary."

"I don't need anything but your company," she said, pushing the presents closer. "Now go ahead and open them. Or do you want to guess?"

"Mine's mighty small," Jemima mused, toying with the ribbon.

Looking at her dark features, Morrow stifled a sigh. She'd almost forgotten how hard Jemima was to please—and how easy Lizzy.

Flushing with pleasure, Lizzy opened hers first, exclaiming over the soft, sepia-toned gloves within, the wrists cinched with tiny glass buttons that winked like diamonds. "Perfect for my weddin' day." With a little sigh, she looked back into the box and withdrew a tiny lace cap, silk ribbons dangling.

"I know you've always loved babies," Morrow told her, her

voice a touch wistful. "I hope you and Abe are blessed with a son or daughter real soon."

Jemima snorted. "I'm sure Abe won't waste any time commencing that. Now, what do we have here?" It was the first genuine smile Morrow had seen all day. Looking about for Pa first, Jemima pulled a pair of silk stockings from the box and held them aloft, admiring the scarlet garters. "You do have some sense, Morrow. I've had a hankering for silk stockings since I was eight years old."

"They're all the rage in Philadelphia," Morrow said, taking another queen's cake. "Looks like you'll have something to wear to Lizzy's wedding."

Jemima chortled and stroked the silk. "Maybe I'll catch Lysander's eye after all."

Reaching beneath the table, Morrow drew out two large bundles tied with ribbon. "Aunt Etta was kind enough to give me some scraps of fabric to sew you both something." At this, both friends leaned forward at once, reaching out eager hands as if the offerings might vanish before their very eyes.

Jemima tore hers open and shook out the gift, watching with delight as it unfurled like a flag into a lovely gown of bronze silk. Wide-eyed, she sputtered, "Why, I never . . ."

"Why, indeed, Jemima Talbot, I never saw you speechless before now," Morrow teased.

Across from them, Lizzy's thin, work-hardened hands caressed the rich rose brocade in her lap, and she looked up with tears in her eyes. "How'd you do it, Morrow? How'd you make us such fine things with nary a fitting?"

"There were plenty of Philadelphia belles just your size, Lizzy. 'Twas a good guess, truly."

"Fits like a glove, I reckon," Jemima exclaimed, holding her gown close. "Maybe you should think of setting up shop at the fort. Folks would come miles for such as these, though I daresay nobody could afford a one."

But Morrow simply shook her head. She'd lost her hankering to sew after so much time spent doing it, though she appreciated their pleasure. Her delight deepened when they insisted they change into their new gowns, bustling up the stairs to her room and coming back down looking badly in need of an ironing.

They passed a pleasant afternoon, talking and laughing and erasing the time and events two years had wrought. As the afternoon sun tilted further west, Pa hovered between the barn and pasture, seeing to the horses and waiting to return the young women to the fort. Morrow pondered whether to go with him, then pushed down her uneasiness. She'd promised Aunt Etta a letter and needed to see to supper.

Jemima's strident voice cut into her wandering thoughts. "Morrow, it must be hard on you leaving the city and coming back into the wilderness. You're so far from anybody here on the Red River. Maybe you and your pa should come to the fort for a spell till the trouble's quelled."

The trouble. Morrow looked up and felt a sudden chill. Years before, Jemima's family had been touched with tragedy, much as Morrow's own. Her eldest brother had gone hunting one fall and never came back. His bones were discovered later in some distant cave, identified solely by the initials on his powder horn.

Lizzy set down her cup and looked toward the wall of woods. "My pa didn't want me comin' out here today, given all the fuss over at Fort Click." At Morrow's startled look, she said, "Two girls went out to get water from the spring early one mornin' and never came back."

Morrow set down her empty cup. "Shawnee?"

Lizzy nodded, fingering the tiny lace cap in her lap. "A search party went after them, but it was little help. The Indians took off into the cane and the militia lost their trail, though they did find some bloody shoes and a bonnet."

The words fell flat, the silence tense. Morrow knotted the napkin in her lap, glad when Jemima stood suddenly and said, "Best be getting home. We'll see you on the Sabbath, I reckon."

Nodding absently, Morrow got up, walking with them to the wagon where Pa waited. They hugged her goodbye, and she breathed a silent prayer for them. 'Twas far safer to stay behind than risk the distance to the fort. Ignoring the tiny arrows of alarm that pricked her, she hurried to the cabin and placed the heavy bars across each oaken door with a decisive thud. Though the heat was intense, she drew the shutters and locked them, her gaze swiveling to the mantel where Pa's rifle hung. It was primed and ready for hunting, she knew, but she doubted she could use it. From end to end it stood as tall as she.

It felt strange to leave the party dishes beneath the elm, but common sense told her she'd best stay inside till Pa returned. Leaving her party dress on, she set about making supper, keeping an ear tuned for trouble. Lumbering so slow in the wagon, Pa surely wouldn't be home till after dusk.

As the mantel clock chimed four times, her hand gripped the wooden spoon. Suppose the two Shawnee came? The thought was so troubling she sat down hard on the bench at the trestle table, the spoon plopping out of the bowl and spraying batter onto her lovely dress. She dabbed it clean, remembering Pa's words at breakfast. Since the tragedy that had befallen them years ago, he'd been saying one verse in particular, and the Scripture now wended through her mind like a melody, the words lofty and noble and reassuring.

And we know that all things work together for good to them that love God, to them who are the called according to His purpose.

All things? Even visits by Indians? Even the death of a mother and a sister she hardly remembered? Or the disappearance of a brother, whose puzzling absence left them forever wondering what had befallen him? She'd rather have found his body and known he wasn't coming back, like Jemima's kin—the act final and complete—instead of this infernal, forever-after wondering.

Tears stung her eyes. She'd memorized the beautiful words Pa quoted by heart and ached to believe them. But another Scripture seemed to trump them just the same.

Oh Lord, help mine unbelief.

Half-asleep, Morrow sat in her rocking chair by the hearth, thinking of baby Eli and planning to sew him some under things, when the welcome sound of the wagon made her leap up. Night had fallen like a curtain half an hour before, and she felt keen relief when she unbarred the door and Pa's comforting shadow crossed the threshold. But sapped as he was from the heat and lurching wagon, he was in no mood to eat the supper she'd made. He simply took his worn chair across from her and brought out his pipe. Emptying the cold ashes into the fire, he looked tired but satisfied.

"I was afraid you'd gone to bed after all the fuss," he said, stuffing the bowl full of tobacco crumbles. "It's a pleasure to come home to a lovely daughter and a fine pipe."

She took a little shovel and retrieved a live coal for him from the fading fire, then sniffed the air, perplexed. "I've been gone a long while, Pa, and forgotten a good many things. But that's the queerest tobacco I ever did smell."

Studying her, he chuckled and leaned back in his chair. "You're not smelling settlement tobacco, Morrow. It's *kinnikinnik* our Shawnee brethren brought last winter."

Shawnee brethren, indeed. She wouldn't admit it smelled far finer than the crude tobacco consumed in the settlement. A cloud of dried roots and herbs perfumed the air between them, creating wispy spirals of smoke. She smelled dogwood and willow and inhaled appreciatively despite his troubling words.

"It's mighty fine," he added, drawing deeply and giving her a wink. "I've been thinking of what to give you for your birthday. Maybe I'll whittle you a pipe."

At this she smiled, remembering how little amusement she and Aunt Etta had shared in the dress shop on Elfreth's Alley. There simply hadn't been time to be lighthearted, and her dear aunt was always so concerned with appeasing her hard-to-please customers.

Morrow looked about the tidy cabin, lingering on an unopened gift atop the trestle table. She'd nearly forgotten the package from Aunt Etta, hidden away in her trunk until today. Untying the leather string, she peeled back several layers of brown paper, enjoying the rustle of anticipation. A sewing chest was nestled inside, the mahogany polished to a rich brown sheen. Carefully she lifted the lid. Within the silk-lined space was an assortment of sewing needles, a box of buttons, spools of colorful thread, and several lengths of bright ribbon.

"A fine gift," Pa exclaimed.

"Aunt Etta is nothing if not generous," she said, pleased beyond measure. But it was the letter at the very bottom that piqued her curiosity. She opened it quickly, and the very first line set her heart to pounding.

Dearest Morrow,
I've dreamed that you're to marry a man of rank . . .

She nearly sighed. Aunt Etta was always dreaming of a great many things. The price of tea . . . the status of the war with England . . . whether or not the popular sacque gown would be replaced by the *robe a l'Anglaise*. With a quick look at Pa, Morrow folded the letter and put it in her pocket, hoping he wouldn't ask her to read it aloud. Best savor it later, she decided, in the privacy of her room. Besides, there were no men of rank that she knew of in the settlement, busy as they were fighting in the East. Just roughshod militiamen. And one too many Indians.

5

’Twas an easy paddle to Trapper Joe’s cabin further down the Red River. With Pa’s help, Morrow uncovered a canoe buried in a thick stand of mountain laurel along the rocky shore. As she tugged on the hemp rope to launch it, she tried not to think of whose hands had held the paddles or crafted the boat to begin with. Made of elm, it was smooth and sleek, its bulk taking to the water like some woodland fowl. A gift from the Shawnee, Pa had told her, when she’d been in Philadelphia.

She sat at the boat’s center, a willow basket behind her. What, she wondered, would Lizzy and Jemima think of this little excursion? She was hardly a fine Philadelphia lady today, tucked in an Indian canoe, wearing simple, scratchy homespun. She imagined their raised brows should they learn of her outing, especially in light of the news from Fort Click. But lately there’d been a lull in the trouble. Nary a horse had been stolen from the settlements in the week since her birthday. Pa had deemed it safe to ride the river, though he’d prayed for her as she got into the boat. She’d been a bit reluctant to go alone, as he wasn’t feeling well and couldn’t accompany her as usual.

Her eyes roamed the wooded ridgetops and ravines high above, every craggy edge the color of dried blood. The river was low now at summer’s peak, the little idling pools along its banks rimmed with red rock. Tilting her head back, she opened her mouth in a sort of wonder. Sunlight and water spilled off ledges smothered with ferns and meadow rue, drenching the river bottom in a rainbow of warm greens and golds. She'd nearly forgotten the beauty—why they'd settled here in the first place. Was it any wonder the Shawnee kept coming back?

Summoning her courage, she gripped the paddle harder, trying to push aside any unsettling thoughts as easily as she parted the water, eyes grazing the opposite shore. Despite the rich, ripe scent of brush along the banks and the peculiar odor of river water, she could smell the still-warm pie in the basket, wrapped in a clean cloth alongside the undergarments she'd made for Little Eli.

A few more bends and twists of the watery road and she was there, a sharp bark making her start. Trapper Joe's mongrel waded into the water, wagging its mangy tail in welcome. She smelled the smoke from their chimney before she saw the cabin's rough rectangle situated in the small, stump-littered clearing. To one side was a small garden but little else. Trapping and hunting as he did from fall to spring, Joe hadn't had the time or the inclination to put in a corn crop and prove up his own four hundred acres, so Pa let him live on a corner of their land. They'd been friends ever since coming into Kentucke together, though a more unlikely pair couldn't be found.

"Howdy do!" Joe's voice boomed like a cannon, only to be followed by Good Robe's echoing, "How do!"

Morrow smiled and waved, spying them in the shade of a giant sycamore not far from shore. Careful not to stand too soon and spill herself into the waiting water, she dug her paddle into the shallows and got out. Surprised by the lightness of the canoe, she pulled it partly up on the sand and collected her basket, making a beeline for the tree. Little Eli's cradle board was propped up against the trunk, and she longed to release him from his tight lacing, anxious to see how much he'd grown. But his eyes were shuttered in sleep, so she simply dropped down beside him in the sun-scorched grass, passing the basket to Good Robe.

"I've brought you a pie, some things for the baby," she said.

Trapper Joe lifted the linen and peered inside before reaching for his hunting knife. The steel blade dissected the flaky crust, and he cradled a generous wedge in one callused hand. Taking the knife, Good Robe cut her own slice, smiling at the first bite.

"*Oui-sah*," she said.

"That's Shawnee for 'good'," Joe said, wiping the steel blade clean in the grass and returning it to its worn sheath. He turned to take her in. "Seen them two Shawanoe lately?"

She darted a look at him and almost sighed aloud. Not once in Philadelphia had people talked of Indians. Now that she'd returned home, it seemed they talked of nothing else. "No sign of them since I've come back," she murmured.

He grunted and finished his pie in three bites, wiping his mouth with a loose linen sleeve. "You're liable to see them again shortly, once huntin' and trappin' commence."

Tamping down her dismay, she removed her bonnet and used the limp brim to fan herself. "I keep thinking they'll stop coming."

"This is still their territory, remember," he said, gaze sharp. "There's an abandoned Shawanoe village near here called *Eskippakithiki*." At this, Good Robe looked up, her eyes fixed on his face. "Word is they have a silver mine where the Red River empties into Kettle Creek." Morrow stopped her fanning and he shrugged. "'Course, I ain't seen any evidence of such, just hearsay, mostly what Good Robe told me. The big silver mines are up north near the Indian towns."

Morrow shot an apologetic glance at the Indian girl, but she seemed content to be left out of the conversation, examining the tiny clothes Morrow had made and smiling her appreciation.

Joe was studying her again, his eyes needle sharp. "Somethin' the matter with your pa? He ain't one to let you out of his sight."

"Pa's feeling poorly," she said, a bit embarrassed at the admission, accurate though it was. She was almost ashamed to say he'd caught another cold, as if it was somehow her doing.

"He ain't been well since you left. I keep hopin', now that you're back, he'll right himself."

"I'd best not stay overlong lest he come looking for me." She stood up, a bit light-headed from the heat. Sweat beaded her brow and upper lip, and she pulled an embroidered handkerchief from her sleeve and dabbed her face. The subtle scent of rose water clung to the sultry air and then vanished when she tucked the handkerchief away.

"Don't be a stranger," she said with a smile, catching up her empty basket. "Our door's always open."

"Much obliged for the pie," Trapper Joe said. "Give my regards to Elias."

Good Robe raised a hand. *"Paselo."*

"Thank you"? Morrow wondered. *Or "farewell"?*

As she pushed the canoe into the current, holding her shoes and skirts above the cool water, she half expected to see Pa waiting. He liked to ferry her about, admiring the fine lines and buoyancy of the boat and the smooth curve of the oak paddle. But he was resting as needs be, and she felt an inexplicable urge to get back to him.

Joe's booming voice called after her. "Best fetch me next time them Shawnee come callin'. I've got a terrible hankerin' to meet 'em."

She merely nodded, anxious to get away from his unwelcome words, glad when the blue water separated them. As the wind brushed her back and pushed her upriver, she shivered, her thoughts on the Shawnee and Joe's prediction of their coming. Each slap of the paddle on the still water seemed to stir her emotions until they became a breathless, desperate prayer.

Please, Lord. No more visits. No more kinnikinnik *or canoes or horses. Let the Shawnee leave us alone.*

As soon as she stepped through the open cabin door, Morrow realized something was amiss. The air was thick with the scent of Indian tobacco, its peculiar bluish white smoke stinging her eyes. For a fleeting moment she felt she'd walked into a trap. Pa and the Indian she remembered all too well stood near the hearth, backs to her. She started to turn away, words of welcome dying in her throat.

Pa swung round to face her, stopping her before she slipped out the door. "Morrow, if you remember, this is Surrounded by the Enemy, a principal chief of the Shawnee."

Surrounded by the Enemy. Why, she supposed she was indeed. The irony of it stung her. Her timid gaze trailed from the deeply lined face of the chief to the bear claws strung about his tawny neck. She didn't know which was more intimidating, the frightening jewelry or the man who wore it. Though she'd been away for more than two years, time and distance had not dulled his grandeur. Tall as a tree he was, and proud.

She marveled at Pa's composure—and the lack of her own. Beneath her linsey dress, her body began to tremble, and she could feel her face empty of all color. What had Pa told Trapper Joe? *I don't think they mean us any harm, but they rattle poor Morrow considerably.* Truly, *considerably* was kind. Hadn't she just prayed the Lord would keep them away?

She cast a desperate glance about the cabin. Her prayer was half answered, at least, for the chief had come without his son. She began backing out the door, mumbling something about milking, the striking of the mantel clock a blessed reminder it was time for this chore. Once in the safe haven of the barn, she breathed in the comforting scent of hay and horses, aging wood and tobacco. The afternoon shadows were lengthening, and she shut the heavy door, increasing the gloom. For a moment she leaned against the crossbar till her shaking subsided, wondering how long the Indian would stay. She'd tarry here till he'd gone. From her stall, Tansy bawled a protest, and Morrow reached for the milk pail hanging from a nail.

She took but three steps toward the back of the barn when she saw a shadow dance on the far wall. A trick of the light? She shut her eyes briefly as if to clear them, rooted to the hay-strewn floor, the milk bucket hanging heavy in her hands. *Oh no . . .* She wasn't alone—she could sense it now. Terror rose up and snatched all good sense, and she gave a sharp cry, holding the bucket in front of her like a piece of armor.

Not three feet away stood a man. He drew himself to his full height, and their eyes locked in mutual surprise. Above his loincloth and leggings was a loose linen shirt that fell a little below his hips. Even in the dim light she could tell it was some of the finest fabric she'd ever seen. Her seamstress's eye discerned it was English-made, without buttons at the neck or wrists, and it seemed to stretch taut as it ran the width of his shoulders. Every creamy fold was a striking contrast to his inky, shoulder-length hair. A trio of eagle feathers angled over one ear, affixed by a small silver medallion.

She was nearly slack-jawed with shock. Was this the chief's son? The boyishness that had once defined him was gone. He'd grown even taller since she'd last seen him, and his lithe form had fleshed out, filling his clothes with an understated elegance. There was something remarkable about him—an aura of barely restrained strength, like a panther about to pounce. She took a small step backward, but his dark eyes seemed to prevent her from taking a second.

In that instant she realized he was taking her measure as well, from the loose curls pinned atop her head to the impractical slippers showing beneath the hem of her petticoat. Heat fanned across her face, staining her neck and the square of pale skin above her snug bodice. The trembling that had begun to ebb started anew and her heart raced. Had she been penned up in the barn with a wild animal, her fright could have been no greater.

"I'm not going to hurt you."

The quiet words, so well articulated, so very English, knocked the wind out of her. She simply stared at him, unable to move. All her wrong assumptions rose up and left her breathless. Shame topped them all as she realized she'd thought an Indian incapable of speaking English. But this was quickly smothered by anger that he'd let her think so—let her and Pa make fools of themselves . . .

Dropping the milk pail, she pushed at the barn door, and it clamored shut as she fled. The pasture opened up before her, drenched a deep gold in the setting sun. She didn't stop running till she was at the paling fence that hemmed in Ma's and Euphemia's graves. Since coming back from Philadelphia, she'd not been here once. She hadn't meant to come now. Chest heaving, she began to cry, feeling five again and not eighteen.

Whether minutes or hours passed, she didn't know. Pa found her sitting there amidst a tangle of honeysuckle vine, head in her hands.

"Morrow, you all right?" His voice reached out to her, solicitous as always.

But she couldn't answer. He sat down beside her, and she looked up with a heavy heart, eyes awash. He seemed to be aging overnight, his russet hair going not gray but white. Years of being a widower and losing a beloved son and daughter continued to take a toll on him, and nothing she did could erase it.

She knew better than to give way to her turmoil, but it bubbled forth like a pent-up spring, every syllable soft but threaded with heat. "I wish you'd told me the son was here—before I went out to milk—"

"He means you no harm, Morrow."

She dashed a hand across her damp face, having lost her

handkerchief in the field as she'd fled. "You might have warned me he was in the barn."

"His father wanted to borrow a horse."

"A horse? Why?"

"I didn't ask—just gave him one."

"He's not who we think he is, Pa. He speaks English."

"What's that?"

"He said he wasn't going to hurt me. But I don't believe him. Even if he's as well-spoken as a white man, he's still a savage." She shook her head in dismay. "We've opened our door to them and made fools of ourselves, believing he spoke only Shawnee. All this time he's been misleading us—making us think—"

"Slow yourself down, Daughter. I can hardly follow you." He turned solemn eyes on her like she was a schoolgirl who'd failed to mind her tongue. "Do you blame him for his reticence? I suspect he's not sure whom he can trust. I see wisdom in his silence given these troubled times. It puts me in mind of the Scripture, 'He that keepeth his mouth keepeth his life.' Besides, he seldom comes. And when he does he says but little. His father does the talking."

The quoted verse did nothing to assuage her anger. He'd ever been slow to take offense, quick to forgive. And she understood it no more now than she did when he'd first taken the Shawnee in. Turning her head away, she set her jaw, ashamed to let him see her tears.

His tone was thoughtful if grave. "Perhaps the Almighty sent the Shawnee to our door."

At this, the tempest inside her erupted all over again. "Did the Almighty also send them the first time, Pa? To kill Ma and Euphemia and take Jess?"

He seemed to wilt at her hasty words, though his voice held firm. "We're coming closer, Morrow. Now that we know Surrounded's son speaks English, we can ask about Jess. You might help, you know."

"Help?"

"Talk to him. Ask about your brother. It seems like a God-given opportunity."

His urging grieved her, though she worked to keep her dismay down. "It's been a long time, Pa. Jess would be twenty-three now, a man. And you know what Joe said. Some captives don't want to come back."

"The Shawnee nation is large and spreads far," he conceded. "Jess could be with any of their bands scattered from Ohio to d'Etroit. Or he might have been traded to another tribe and moved further west."

She heard the regret in his voice and saw how his shoulders sagged as if bowed by the weight of it. He'd omitted but one thing. Jess could be dead. She didn't dare say so, but surely he'd thought of it himself.

"There's one thing that gives me comfort. God knows where Jess is, even if we don't. I believe we'll be reunited one day. If not here, heaven." Slowly he got to his feet, helping her up after him, his eyes scanning the woods. "Best not mention our visits with the Shawnee. Not even to Lizzy. We wouldn't want to court trouble."

She looked at him, a bit stung that he thought her so glib. Of course she'd not mention their visits. She was so ashamed of their coming, so fearful her father's friendship with them would be misinterpreted, she'd keep it a secret till her dying breath.

"Think no more of it," he told her as they walked across the darkening ground toward home. "We've other things to ponder. Tomorrow's the Sabbath and we must go to the fort. You've not been there since your homecoming. I imagine Lizzy and Jemima will be glad to see you again."

Would they, she wondered? If they knew about the Shawnee coming, would they even count her as a friend?

6

Morrow took a seat on the first blockhouse bench, untying the strings of her bonnet and placing it in her lap. She could feel the stares given her by the Red River congregation as they shuffled in. Perhaps she'd gone too far wearing her Philadelphia finery. The purple cloth of the bonnet was decidedly elegant, a far cry from simple settlement standards, with its silken cluster of lilacs hugging the brim. She'd worn it thinking no one would notice, or care. The bright summer's day seemed to call for it. But the unspoken consensus seemed to say it was too fine for a preacher's daughter. And it was creating a stir she'd not reckoned with.

Jemima turned into her row, Lizzy in her wake. Jemima's face was a stew of displeasure, her voice a hiss. "Morrow Mary, I wish you'd hurry up and get hitched so the rest of us could have a chance to do the same. As it is, you keep the men so stirred up with your coming and going they won't light and look elsewhere." As if to prove her point, she turned and skewered the unmarried men along the back row with glittering green eyes.

Morrow shrank down a bit on the bench, solaced that she'd given the men no encouraging glances. Still, their steadfast stares seemed to bore a hole in her back and embarrassed her as much as Jemima's harshness. She looked at the small watch pinned to her bodice. Would Pa never appear?

Once she'd counted the Sabbath her favorite day. For years she'd been at home on the front row, squeezed between Ma and Jess. In the shadowy corners of her mind, she could still see their silhouettes and hear baby Euphemia's fussing during the lengthy sermons. But being here today amidst all the male attention was something of a chore. Since she'd returned from Philadelphia, folks seemed to regard her in a new, bewildering way, and she couldn't quite fathom why.

With a glance her direction, Pa passed in front of his congregants and took his place behind the pulpit near the fire. Clearing his throat, he announced, "Now that the harvest is near, the start of singing school is at hand."

Morrow felt a flicker of delight. There had been no singing school that she knew of in Philadelphia, no gathering of folks like-minded about music, singing the winter away. The fact that the meetings were little more than an excuse for courting made them all the more worthwhile. She couldn't count the couples Pa had married since its humble beginnings years before.

As soon as he'd spoken, he removed his Bible from the pulpit and took a seat beside her. *What? No sermon?* She didn't need to look at him to know something was amiss. To her right, Jemima seemed to titter as a stranger in uniform took his place behind the hickory pulpit. The stale air in the blockhouse suddenly seemed warmer, the press of people more unpleasant. Morrow took in the striking figure in buff and blue, and the telling line of Aunt Etta's letter struck her like lightning.

The uniformed man cleared his throat and removed his tricorn hat, resting it on the pulpit. "To those of you who don't know, I'm Nathaniel McKie—Major McKie of the Virginia colony. My regiment has been sent here expressly for your protection. Red River Station will serve as the base of military operations as we plan our first foray into Indian territory."

He paused as if to let the weight of his words have their full effect. All around her, people began to murmur amongst themselves till the sound was a small roar in the large room. He held up a hand to still the din. "We Virginians have heard of the degradations this settlement and others have suffered at the hands of the British and Shawnee. By the authority of Governor Henry and the Virginia legislature, we mean to stop the hostilities—by any means necessary."

Morrow kept her eyes down as he went on to talk about the artillery they'd brought, the heavy cannon, the fresh supplies of shot and powder. Truly, this man liked the sound of his own voice. He smacked of civilization from the polished brass buttons of his fine blue coat to his shiny black boots.

"We know that the British are agitating the Indians, supplying them with guns and trade goods, goading them into reclaiming the Kentucke territory as their own." He paused and leaned into the pulpit, his finely modulated drawl that of a seasoned orator. "Surely a land like this is worth contending for."

There was a ripple of assent and several shouted "ayes" from the men. Morrow flexed her gloved hands, noting the fingertips were soiled. Beside her, Pa sat still as stone. When Major McKie's speech ended, Pa stood to pray. For peace. For God's will to be done in the settlement and to the ends of the earth. When he finished, he moved to the pulpit to give his sermon, but she hardly noticed.

There seemed to be a small collective gasp from the women present as Major McKie turned in her row. He took the seat Pa had just vacated, and his knee brushed the folds of her dress and stayed there. Prickles of heat climbed from her bare neck to her face. Even the tips of her ears felt on fire. He was entirely too close. She could smell his perspiring beneath the confines of his Continental coat. The fine lines of his uniform were striking but unfamiliar, accustomed as she was to the British scarlet and white. Jabbing Morrow with a sharp elbow, Jemima gave a murmur of disapproval. Or jealousy. Morrow didn't dare look at her.

By sermon's end, her face and neck still felt overwarm as

the officer beside her turned to her straightaway. "I'd heard the preacher had a beautiful daughter, but I find the praise somewhat . . . restrained."

She raised her eyes to look up at him, extending a gloved hand in her befuddlement. He took it firmly, not letting go. Jemima stood just behind her, a heavy shadow in the dim light. "Well, Morrow Mary, aren't you going to introduce me to the major? Or have you forgotten your fine Philadelphia manners?"

"Why, yes . . . of course," Morrow murmured, taking back her hand.

He let go reluctantly, his eyes never leaving her face. Was this what was meant by being instantly smitten? She feared so but couldn't fathom why. She was simply a settlement girl in a too-fancy hat . . .

Pa came to stand between them, a welcome buffer. Never in her life had she felt so glad to have him near. "I see you've met my daughter," he said.

Major McKie shook his outstretched hand. "Met her? I'm afraid I can't take my eyes off her."

The heavy-handed compliment only upended her further. She turned to find Jemima still hovering and made introductions softly without looking at him again. "These are my friends Jemima Talbot and Lizzy Freeman."

An awkward silence followed their greetings. Pa cleared his throat, taking her arm and squeezing it as if well aware of her unease. He cast a look at the open blockhouse door as people exited. "We'd best be starting for home, given the heat. The dog days of August are upon us."

"So it seems," the major said tersely, finally looking away from her. "I admit I was reluctant to take a post on the frontier, but I'm beginning to find the aggravation well worth it."

"Good Sabbath," Pa said, putting on his hat.

Morrow turned to go, forgetting to bid Lizzy and Jemima

goodbye. Outside on the fort common, settlement folk and soldiers were milling about despite the suffocating heat and dust, lingering by the artillery and admiring the small cannon and corral full of military mounts. Pa helped her into the wagon, and they soon passed through the fort's postern gates, waving as the sentries doffed their hats. She expelled a relieved breath and looked over her shoulder at the fading pickets. Major McKie stood stalwart beneath the oak beam that bore the name Red River Station, but she didn't raise her hand in farewell.

Pa pulled the brim of his hat down over his eyes. "Daughter, I'm afraid your return has garnered attention from every quarter."

"I don't know why," she said softly. "Except that there are so few women here—and an abundance of men."

The wind was so brisk it seemed to devour her every word. He gave no indication he'd heard her and appeared locked in serious thought. Was he, like she, trying to dismiss the ominous sight of so many munitions and uniformed men? The silence made the ride even longer, and halfway home a wagon wheel began to wobble. He jumped down to tighten it, but the effort seemed to unleash his deep cough. The summer cold he'd taken wouldn't budge, so stubborn that all the tonics she'd tried didn't help. Aunt Sally had just given her some cherry bark. Perhaps she'd make a tea of that once they got home.

Despite the beauty of the day and the dance of the wind all around her, she felt a new uneasiness. When Pa was well again, she'd not feel so unsettled, she reasoned. Singing school would soon commence, and she might even have a sweetheart. Most importantly, now that the soldiers had come, Kentucke would cease to be a battleground. Surely with McKie's Virginians to defend their settlement, the Shawnee would leave them alone.

Morrow leaned over the letter, quill pen suspended.

Dear Aunt Etta,

Forgive me for not writing to you sooner. Since I've returned to the Red River, there seem a thousand things that keep me from ink and paper. Each time I sit down, I am called away. Pa needs my help as never before. Please pray for him, as he's come down with a racking cough that even Aunt Sally cannot mend.

The sewing chest you gave me for my birthday is beautiful and a reminder of our happy times together. I'm sure the dress shop is a bit lonesome. I doubt you miss my singeing ribbons with the goffer iron or forgetting to order enough fabric, though you might still covet my help with the ledgers. Hopefully Lady Richmond is easier to please than when I left.

I must tell you that your dream of my marrying a man of rank may come to pass. A Virginian has arrived at Red River Station with a regiment of his own. Now there are dozens of soldiers to choose from. But Bluecoats, not Redcoats . . .

She dipped the quill in the ink pot again, a half smile playing across her face. Somehow Major McKie and Aunt Etta's letter seemed an interesting coincidence. Though he did seem a bit bold, she almost preferred this to the awkward, uncouth settlement men. And he *was* handsome in a worldly sort of way, all shine and polish and fine manners—

"Morrow, I'm in need of you." Pa stood in the cabin doorway, his perspiring face apologetic.

Flushed, she got up from his writing desk, ashamed of her romantic notions. "My letter can wait, Pa. I'm only writing Aunt Etta."

Despite her reassuring words, he still looked pained. She knew how hard it was for him to ask for her help. Doing so was a reminder of his own lack, the cough that wouldn't quit . . . and Jess. She was little good being a daughter—and a small, weak one at that—but he seemed intent on keeping her that way, forever reminding her to wear gloves or her bonnet as if trying to preserve her for that day he could hand her to a man with far better prospects than he had. A man like McKie . . .

Following him to the barn loft, she watched alongside the barn swallows as he balanced on a high-timbered beam, hanging tobacco from a long pole suspended between oak rafters. *One racking cough*, she thought, *and he might come crashing down.*

"Careful, Morrow, don't step too near the edge. Just hand me another sheaf."

She did as he bid, aware of the tobacco's pungent leaf, a painful reminder of pipes and *kinnikinnik* and unwelcome visitors. She didn't like coming to the barn now. Doing so brought back her meeting with the Shawnee. Her eyes drifted to the hay-strewn floor where she'd faced him, and she nearly winced. Hindsight made her rue she'd not stayed stalwart but had run like a rat for cover. How much better it would have been if she'd mastered her angst and spoken to him instead. Pa would have been spared her tears, and their questions about Jess might have been answered.

Half an hour later, with tobacco dust in her hair and sweat streaming, Morrow descended the loft ladder in dire need of a bath. Dismissing the copper hip tub half hidden by the corncrib, she considered the river. Beyond the open barn door, summer itself seemed to issue an invitation. With a quick word to Pa, she made her way down the trail with soft soap and clean towels, fighting trepidation all the way. The water was at its warmest in late August, a beguiling sapphire blue that looked like the sky turned upside down. Everything else was dry and dusty, the brown earth wrinkled from lack of rain, a few trees already turning a pale gold.

She paused at a fork in the trail, torn. The path she usually took led to the laurel and the half-hidden canoe and Trapper Joe's. The other was overgrown, a tangle of brush and vines and abandonment. *Perhaps . . .* She shut the thought away, only to take it up again when she was partway down the familiar trail. *Perhaps one has to face one's fears in order to banish them.* Should she return to the place where it had all began? A place not even Pa would go?

She battled a full five minutes, the shadows of the giant elms and oaks lengthening all around her, her eyes on the old trail that begged to be taken. With a tentative step, she started making her way as best she could, the hum of insects all around her. Briars and thornbushes scratched her bare arms and ankles, but she kept on, thirsty with curiosity. The old way wandered around a towering sycamore and a thick stand of laurel, as if testing her memory, before expending itself on the broad riverbank.

This was the place she'd last been with Jess all those years ago. Only it looked nothing like she remembered. Since then the river had cut a different path, and the boulders along its banks, once big as cabins to her childish mind, now seemed impossibly small. Her eyes lingered on the far shore, breathtakingly beautiful in the reddish-gold light. An abundance of grapevine wended its way with abandon, following the course of the river. It beckoned to her like something out of Eden, forbidden fruit, as if taunting her inability to swim. But how hard could it be?

Jessamyn had been a fine swimmer, and it had been Pa who'd taught him. She remembered how they'd frolicked on this very spot. Both of them had teased her and tried to pull her under back then, but she preferred to watch them from the sandy shallows. Sometimes she'd hold her breath as they disappeared under the calm face of the river for long periods, only to resurface and tease her further. The memory saddened her . . . made her bold.

She stood unsteadily and stripped to her shift, the river rock slippery beneath her bare feet as she waded forward. The sun touched the water with a final golden finger before hiding behind the treetops. She was up to her shoulders now, the water cold, the current moving past her arms and legs with a pulsing rhythm. She looked back to see her clothes lying where she'd left them, a small, insignificant pile of linen and a limp hair ribbon.

She kept on, her feet soon leaving bottom. Jess had taught her to dog-paddle, and the jerky movements came back to her now. She was almost halfway across but frightfully out of breath. She didn't remember it being this hard, being so winded. The river was no longer blue but black, more enemy than friend. A fierce current lashed her legs and pulled at her. Eyes wide-open, she went down. In seconds the enormity of her predicament washed over her. *Oh, Pa! Pa! Where are you?* Till now he'd always been near when she needed him. The thought of him all alone, buckled with the weight of another loss, deepened the darkness. Panic forced the last bit of air out of her lungs and she thrashed about wildly in the water. But the world beneath was cold as winter and seemed to pin her beneath its weight.

Weary, she stopped struggling. Memories of Ma surrounded her, warming her, easing her panic. Welcoming her home. For one fleeting moment she could see Euphemia just as she'd been back then—fair hair, mouth like a rosebud, eyes like blue buttons.

I'm dying . . . Lord, help me!

But there was no flash of light, no miraculous parting of the waters. She let go then, of her life and her breath, eyes shut against the darkness. Once she surrendered, she felt someone else fighting for her. Arms like hanks of rope encircled her, tugging her upward, freeing her from the current. When she opened her eyes, she thought she was dreaming. A man had hold of her, and she was floating on top of the water, choking and gasping, the thin muslin of her shift hovering around her as he swam her to shore.

He laid her on the bank, the sand a welcome bed. He bent over, chest heaving, hands on his knees, his dark form dripping water. It rained down on her, and she stared up into the last face she expected to see.

Surrounded by the Enemy's son.

Rolling over, she did the most unladylike thing she knew. She threw up all her supper, and a bucket of water, besides. He crouched next to her, his face clouded with concern. "Lie still till all the water's gone—and you can breathe again."

Shutting her eyes, she took a deep, shuddering breath and obeyed. But her mind reeled in confusion. The rich precision of his words, his tawny features, and the clothing that was a confusing medley of both Indian and white made her all the more wary. Who was he? Looking at him now, she saw things she'd not noticed before. His eyes . . . were they golden brown? Almost amber?

"You shouldn't come here alone," he said tersely. "There's trouble upriver."

She tried to sit up, but he pushed her back. He gathered up her clothes and hair ribbon farther down the bank before picking her up like she was little more than a corn-husk doll. She lay limp in his arms, feeling his grace of movement despite the burden of her wet body. The lights of the cabin came into view, and he climbed the steps, thrusting open the cabin door with one moccasin.

Pa's chair overturned with a thud as he stood. Before he said a word, she could sense his shock. Her unlikely rescuer stood her gently on her feet, his bulk supporting her while she faced her father and his. Surrounded obviously surmised what had happened in one sweep, but Pa struggled to make sense of the poignant silence.

"Daughter . . . did you nearly drown?" He came forward, eyes wet.

"I . . . I . . ." Her teeth were chattering now, not from the cold but from sheer emotion.

Face ashen, Pa eased her into a chair by the hearth, wrapping a blanket around her shaking shoulders. She wanted to cry—out of thankfulness and relief. Perhaps this was how the chief had felt when they'd saved his son. And now his son had saved her. The debt was paid in full. Each of them seemed to be thinking the same thing at once, the silence brimming despite their speechlessness.

Pa cleared his throat and went to the corner cupboard for a jug, then poured himself some whiskey. He offered it to the Indians, who declined, and then downed it in one gulp. Morrow's eyes widened at the sight. She glanced at the man who'd saved her life and was now dripping water onto the plank floor, his wet buckskins darkened to black. But he wasn't looking at her. He kept a wary eye on the open door as if expecting the trouble upriver to materialize on their threshold at any moment.

She took a measured breath, trying to summon enough decency to thank him, but the words wouldn't come. Instead she pulled her eyes from him, afraid her unwillingness was plain. But Pa more than made up for her lack, thanking them in English and Shawnee, his gratitude apparent. When they left, she sank into her seat by the fire, hugging the blanket closer, too tired to talk yet riddled with questions.

As if sensing her curiosity, Pa said, "They came right after you went to the river. Surrounded warned of a party of Cherokee near here. His son seemed restless when I told them you'd gone to the river. I tried to keep him here. I didn't want him to surprise you—or you him, half dressed." His face took on a reddish tint. "Surrounded said something about the water spirits drawing people to the bottom of the river. Some Shawnee superstition, I suppose. Being the young buck he is, his son soon disappeared, and by heaven, I'm glad he did."

She swallowed, still feeling she had a bucket of water inside her. "I didn't mean to cause any trouble, Pa . . . just saw some grapes on the other side of the river."

He shook his head in disbelief. "I can't bear the thought of losing you, Morrow. Don't ever try anything so foolish again."

The tears in his eyes made her more contrite, and she was suddenly exhausted. Standing on shaky legs, she turned toward the stairs, but he stopped her, putting an arm around her, hugging her like he'd not done since her childhood. She hugged him back, dampening his shirt, surprised when he seemed reluctant to release her.

"Tonight, while you were at the river, when Surrounded came with Red Shirt . . ."

Red Shirt. Was that his name? She felt a strange disappointment. She'd expected something else. Something strong and Indian-like. Not this. Drawing the blanket closer, she waited for him to finish.

"I found out a few things about our English-speaking Shawnee. He's a half blood. His mother was a white captive."

What? The startling words seemed only to skim the surface of conscious thought and left her staring at him, unable to speak.

"He was sent to the Brafferton School for Indians as a boy."

"Brafferton?" she echoed. She'd read about the school in the *Virginia Gazette*. It had a rich if controversial history. Had he been part of that?

"Apparently he did well there. A family in Williamsburg wanted to adopt him. But after a time he left and found his way back to his father."

She held her breath, trying to grasp all that he'd just told her, letting the words soften and reshape the misconceptions she'd had about him. Was he truly half white? She wondered why she hadn't suspected as much. His skin was too light for a true

Indian, as were his hazel eyes, though his dress and manner were convincing enough.

He swallowed and said, "We talked some about Jess. I tried to describe him as I remember him. But it's been so long . . ."

His eyes were a shimmer of gray green. She extended a hand to him, but he'd turned away, clearly too weary for more conversation. Bidding him good night, she climbed the stairs to her room, her own heart sore. Exhausted, she combed out her tangled hair and dressed in her warmest nightgown, drawing the bedcovers around her shivering form. Remembering she'd failed to say her prayers, she dropped to her knees, feeling more unworthy than she had in her whole life.

Father, forgive me. For holding a grudge. For hating the Shawnee. Thank You for sending Red Shirt to spare my life.

7

Since her near-drowning, Pa seemed to hover as if afraid she'd get herself into trouble again. She couldn't tell him how nearly losing her life had inexplicably shaken loose some of her fears. The place that had haunted her for so long was now nothing more than sand and red rock and rushing water. She wanted to go back again, if only to make sure it no longer had any hold on her, but all the chores of autumn waited. Joe came to help with the harvest, joining Pa in the field and cutting the roasting ears from the towering stalks, then the stalks themselves for fodder. It was blistering, backbreaking work, and she toted piggin after piggin of cold water from the spring to quiet their thirst. She was glad to return to the cabin, where she sat and ground hard-shelled corn with a hand mill. But before she'd filled a single sack with meal, she was spent.

Wiping her brow with a handkerchief, she considered other pleasures to be had beyond the stifling porch. Pa wouldn't quit working till dusk, so she had ample time to slip away, not so far as to miss his call, but just beyond sight of the cabin's sturdy, two-story shadow. The woods were alive with thimbleberries, and she had a basket on each arm, delighted when she found a patch thick and sweet. A handful left the taste of summer on her tongue.

Mouth and fingers stained purple, she straightened from stripping a vine and saw a flicker of movement deeper in the woods. At once she went still. He made not a sound, but there was no disguising the great height of him. A dozen discordant thoughts galloped through her head as she followed him with curious eyes.

He's half white but moves like an Indian. He's half Indian but educated like a white man. His English seems as fine as my own, yet I spent years thinking otherwise. What other secrets might he have?

Deliberately she stepped on a stick. Its crisp snap seemed to echo in the stillness, shushing even the birdsong. The realization that she'd seen him before he'd seen her gave her an inexplicable little thrill. But suddenly she lost sight of him. Within moments the fine hair on the back of her neck tingled, and she whirled, nearly upsetting her baskets. He stood behind her, rifle in hand, expression stoic. His eyes were so piercing they looked black, not brown. Something skittered across their depths that made her feel infinitely foolish.

She said in a little rush, "I thought you didn't see me."

"I saw you and purposed to avoid you."

"Why?"

"You're easily frightened."

"Do you blame me?" Even as she said it, her eyes roamed the woods, and she thought of soldiers and Indians and the panther tracks Joe had warned them about. When he didn't answer, she looked back at him, feeling bolder than she ever had in her life. "Why are you called Red Shirt?"

The forthright if softly spoken question seemed to amuse him. He regarded her in that thoughtful way he had, as if sifting his every word before he spoke. "I scout for the British—the Redcoats. But I refuse to wear their uniform coat, so they made me a red shirt instead. It's something of a private joke."

"Don't you have an Indian name?"

"I do."

But you're not going to tell me.

Their eyes met and held, and she sensed his resistance. Heat seeped into her cheeks, and she lowered her eyes, taking in every aspect of his dress as she did so. Today he looked more frontier scout than Indian. In a loose tow linen shirt that fell to buckskin leggings held up by colored garters, inky hair caught back in a queue, he might have been any man in the settlement—but for that bit of wildness about him. A shot pouch and powder horn were slung over his left shoulder, and a tomahawk and sheathed knife hung from his handwoven belt. A far cry from flashing silver and fine linen.

He inclined his head to the left, bringing a halt to the conversation. "There's an abundance of berries beyond that big maple."

She turned in that direction and began to walk, stepping over brush and briars, mind whirling. When she looked back, he'd gone. To see Pa again, she guessed. Her stomach knotted with the notion that he came and went at will and put them all in danger. Or perhaps he felt he could get away with it, isolated as they were.

Why was she so befuddled in his presence, forgetting to ask the only questions that mattered? If she didn't speak to him now, she might never. Abandoning her baskets, she hurried down the path he'd traveled moments before, hoping Pa was still in the field.

As she rounded the cabin, she found Red Shirt filling up the doorway, looking at her as if he lived there and not she. The idea filled her with cold fury, and she climbed the steps and faced him, her back against a porch post for support. But he spoke before she could untie her tongue.

"Where is your father?"

She swallowed, unwilling to answer. "Why do you keep coming back here?"

"That's not what I asked you."

His pointed calm blunted some of her anger. She looked down, eyes on her berry-stained apron, feeling a sting of conscience.

This man had kept her from drowning, yet she couldn't summon a speck of kindness for him.

She said a bit more softly, "I—I don't know where he is. That's not your concern. You shouldn't be here. 'Tis as dangerous for you as it is for us."

"I'm well aware of the danger."

Taking a deep breath, she darted a look at him again. "I'm concerned for my father. He isn't well. If you have any feeling—any decency—you'll leave us alone—"

"Your father asked me to come. I wouldn't be here otherwise."

"That's right, Daughter."

She whirled and saw Pa standing behind her, Joe at his elbow. Humiliation covered her like a cloud. Pa's eyes held a stern rebuke, and he passed inside the cabin, calling for her to bring some cider from the springhouse. She noticed Joe eyeing Red Shirt warily and remembered he'd never seen him before. Grudgingly, she went to fetch the cider, wanting to hide in the cool dimness of the stone walls till they'd finished talking. But she did as Pa bid and served them, fleeing to her room afterward and not coming out till Pa stood at the bottom of the steps and called to her.

She hovered on the landing, looking down at him, and he said, "I don't want you to discourage Red Shirt from coming, Morrow."

Exasperation pricked her. "But Pa, that puts you in a terrible predicament. You could be accused of spying for the Shawnee—or the British."

"No one knows of our meetings."

"Not yet, you mean. Suppose someone sees them here and—"

"I'll not bar the door to them, Daughter," he said sternly. "Strange as it sounds, I consider them friends. Besides, I have my own reasons for wanting them here."

Because of Jess. She sighed, spirits plummeting. In her haste to be rid of Red Shirt, she'd not thought to ask about Jess. "Did you tell him about Major McKie?"

His smile was tight. "I'm sure he knows more about McKie than we do. He's likely tracked McKie's every move since he and his men came into this territory. Telling him about military matters would be pointless—and would make me a spy as well. Wouldn't it?"

Chagrined, she fell silent. She'd not tell him of the hope kindling in her heart. Perhaps the coming of McKie's Virginians meant the Shawnee visits would stop. Soon the woods would be overrun with spies, ferreting out trouble, looking for Indian sign. Surely that would keep them away.

Slowly she came down the steps, upended anew when he said, "Red Shirt brought us both something."

He took a package off the trestle table and held it out to her. Startled by Red Shirt's unexpected gesture, she took it reluctantly, noting the heavy paper and string. She felt Pa's eyes on her, as if weighing her reaction. Did Red Shirt think he could curry her favor, her forgiveness?

A rush of resistance rose up within her. Setting the gift aside, she went out, bent on retrieving her berry baskets and finishing her task. Nay, forgiveness couldn't be curried or cajoled or bought. It had to be given freely from a Christ-filled heart absent of all hate.

Like Pa's. Not hers.

The next morning she placed her package on the bench by the dogtrot door, wondering if Pa had opened his. But he wasn't near enough to ask, having left the cabin before dawn to finish cribbing the corn before the heat set in. She'd overslept this morning, thanks to a fitful night, and hadn't heard him go. The previous day had been altogether too stimulating, and she was worn out, so weary on wakening she'd wished it was dusk instead of daylight.

Dutifully, she made a kettle of mush. As she worked, she eyed the package, drawn yet repelled by its presence, thinking she'd better bury it somewhere out of sight. Its presence gnawed at her, tempting her to untie its string and unravel the mystery of its bulk and weight. Perhaps it was an animal skin or pelt—or some Indian trinket. Whatever it was, she wanted to be rid of it and knew just the place.

Slowly she opened the door to the dogtrot. It groaned in protest, the hinges rusty from disuse. Snatching up the package, she hurried across to the east side of the cabin, pushing open the heavy door for the first time since coming back from Philadelphia. For a moment she nearly forgot why she came, lost in the bewildering disarray. Why, thirteen years later, did Pa still refuse to right the furniture, sweep up the stray feathers, clean up the mess? She'd hoped, during her time away, he'd have done so. Or let her do it in his stead now that she'd come home. But she knew the past was too painful. By shutting the door on the life he'd lived with her mother, he hoped to heal.

A copper kettle sat by the hearth, tinted green from age. She dropped the package into it, satisfied as it was swallowed up and hidden from view. As she turned to go, a shaft of sunlight came through a grimy windowpane high above, striking a floor-length mirror and catching her reflection. Snatching up an old curtain, she rubbed a section of glass clean and peered closer, wondering why McKie paid her any attention at all.

At the sound of a footfall on the porch, she hurried outside. She drew the door shut as quietly as she could and came in the front door to fool Pa. He was sitting at the table when she entered, wearing a new beaver felt hat set at a slightly rakish angle. It made him look years younger, covering his silver-threaded hair. Was this what Red Shirt had brought him? She studied him as she poured him a cup of coffee and passed the sugar.

"You needn't remove your hat," she said softly. "Considering that it's new and all."

Pa touched the felt brim as if he'd forgotten and watched as she dished up the mush. Thus far he hadn't asked what she'd done with her own package, but she sensed he understood her reasons for shunning the gift. And she tried to be courteous, though she was hard-pressed to hide her dismay at his obvious delight. The comfortable silence they shared soon began fraying, and she knew he had something on his mind that had little to do with felt hats and unopened packages.

When she took his empty dish away, he cleared his throat. "I've already milked this morning. Thought I'd spare you the trouble."

"I didn't mean to oversleep," she said, pouring him more coffee. "Now that you're done with the harvest, you can stay abed a bit longer yourself."

Pa sighed, a strange utterance coming from him. Was it her imagination, or was he flushing beneath his sandy beard? He swallowed and said, "Did Lizzy speak with you at the last Sabbath service?"

His face was so hopeful she hated to shake her head no. He had something womanly to tell her, she guessed, and it went hard on him. "There was hardly time, remember? We were a bit late, and then there was Major McKie . . ."

"Well, you'll need to ready your dress if you're to stand up with her," he murmured.

She kept busy, putting beans in a kettle to soak and fussing with the fire. "But I thought she had her heart set on a spring wedding."

"Well, Lizzy and Abe have got things a bit backward . . ." His voice trailed off, and she straightened and looked at him. He avoided her eyes, reddening further beneath his fine hat. "For heaven's sake, Daughter. Do I have to spell it out for you?"

Still befuddled, she said nothing.

He coughed. "We'll be blessing their baby come spring, understand. I cannot be any plainer than that."

Lizzy . . . expecting? It was Morrow's turn to redden. The lace christening cap came to mind, along with her innocent words over tea. *I hope you and Abe are blessed with a son or daughter real soon.* Well, perhaps not *this* soon. Flustered, she made a sudden move, overturning her cup. Hot coffee gushed onto the table and dripped onto the pine planks below. She was only too glad to get down on the floor and clean it up, hiding from his aggravated gaze.

First Good Robe and now Lizzy. Morrow felt a fierce rush of what could only be called covetousness. She'd always loved babies . . .

"They've asked to be married in a fortnight," he said, standing and wiping his brow with a handkerchief. "In the meantime, maybe I'd better send you to see Aunt Sally. I'd hoped that my dear sister had time enough to discuss these matters given the two years you spent with her in the city. But I can see that she taught you to sew and little else."

She stood up, perplexed. "Discuss what matters, Pa?"

"Matters of the heart. Falling in love with the right man. Waiting to bed till you're wed." He took off his hat then jammed it back on his head, turning toward the door.

She stood speechless at this indelicate outburst. Rarely had she seen him so addled. Since her homecoming, he seemed to treat her differently, almost with a sort of awe, even dread, as if he didn't know quite what to do with her.

Lizzy and Abe . . . and a baby?

She felt slightly hurt that Lizzy hadn't confided the happy news, ill-timed though it was. Well, there was little to be done except ready her dress, like Pa said, and pray for good weather. There was no finer frolic than a wedding, she mused. No matter the season or circumstance.

8

Once again Morrow stood before the dusty mirror on the east side of the dogtrot, the chaotic remains of the cabin all around her. Spiderwebs glinted silver in the morning light, and the huge stone hearth gaped empty like the mouth of a cave. She'd come over to peer into the full-length looking glass and didn't mean to tarry, just linger long enough to check for any stray strings or buttons she might have missed when dressing for Lizzy's wedding.

She'd shunned her Philadelphia finery, Jemima's dark face hovering in her mind. No doubt she'd accuse Morrow of trying to outshine Lizzy if she wore such. With this in mind, she'd remade one of Ma's old dresses, adding lace to the sleeves and bodice and embroidering tiny rosebuds on the pale lavender skirt. The gown was fetching but looked somewhat incomplete. Spying a dusty trunk, Morrow knelt down and lifted the heavy lid. It opened with a groan, the interior musty, but in moments she'd come up with some ivory combs. A smile stole over her pale face, and she murmured, "Thank you," feeling her mother had given her a gift.

When she met Pa on the porch—the combs holding up her weight of hair, the remade dress falling in graceful lines to the porch—something passed over his face that she couldn't fathom. Was he remembering the dress had been Ma's? Or about to rebuke her for trespassing to the east side of the cabin?

"We'll have to take the wagon, Morrow," he finally said. "I'm afraid your horse will soil you."

"But Pa, I'm only the bridesmaid, not the bride."

"You might be by day's end," he murmured.

She felt slightly sick at his scrutiny and started into the cabin. "I'll go change. I have another dress if this one's too fancy . . ."

"It's not the dress, Daughter." He paused and smiled slightly at her confusion. "You have no idea how lovely you are. That's part of your charm. You are so like . . ."

Adele? The near mention of her mother's name turned her melancholy. Did he know she'd been missing a mother more of late? Wishing she had a sister, at least? There were so many questions she couldn't ask him, fine father that he was. Womanly things. Heartfelt things. Things a man might laugh at. Lately the lack of a close confidante left an unmistakable ache deep inside her.

Her voice turned plaintive. "Pa, please don't worry with the wagon, or we'll be late. I like riding Belle as she's so gentle."

He finally nodded and went to fetch the mare. All the miles to the fort she tried not to imagine Ma riding beside Pa, dressed in the gown she now wore, still lovely in midlife, untouched by tragedy. Jess would be there—and Euphemia, all grown up, sixteen to her eighteen. A fine family, whole and unbroken. Yet in such turbulent times, who on the frontier could boast of this?

She was, she reminded herself, on the way to a wedding and wouldn't give quarter to melancholy. Self-pity was of the devil, Pa said. So she simply looked around, letting the wonders of the wilderness rush in and fill all the lonesome places inside her. A warm autumn wind bent the tall timothy and bluegrass, and the sky was aswirl with wispy clouds. Her prayers for fine weather this day had been answered.

The fort's front gates were open wide, overseen by soldiers

bearing muskets, and revelers were already rolling kegs of cider across the common in anticipation of the dancing. In the midst of the melee was Major McKie in full dress uniform. The certainty that he was waiting for them seemed to release a bevy of butterflies inside her. When he spied them trotting through the gate, he hurried over to help her down, holding tightly to her gloved hand just as he'd done on the Sabbath.

"I'm a bit late . . . Lizzy might need me," she said with a beguiling half smile.

For just a moment their eyes met, his astonishingly blue—a different hue than her own, but equally startling in his deeply tanned face. She read a dozen different things in his gaze—all admiring. Murmuring an apology, she excused herself, leaving Pa alone with him.

The Freemans' cabin was tucked in a corner beside the northeast blockhouse, the door open. She hurried there now beneath a sun that foretold ten o'clock, an hour ahead of the nuptials.

"Morrow, I feared you weren't comin'," Lizzy exclaimed, standing on the threshold and catching sight of her. "Hurry and help me dress. Aunt Hannah is tendin' to the food and I can't find Alice."

Alice was often missing, Morrow mused, feeling a fondness for Lizzy's wayward younger sister. The cabin's interior was dim, and the grease lamps smoked miserably. Morrow worked hard not to wrinkle her nose at the smell of burned bacon. Since Lizzy's mother had died two years before, the family had yet to manage her absence well, and Morrow saw reminders of her everywhere about the cramped cabin.

As she helped her friend into the heavy gown, she tried not to eye her waist. "Lizzy, you look beautiful. I know Abe will agree."

Lizzy smoothed the just-pressed rose brocade with rough hands. "I can't thank you enough for the dress. It's just right for a wedding . . . makes me feel like a bride. Now, can you help me pin the veil in place?"

Standing before a cracked mirror, Morrow arranged the delicate lace around the knot of curls atop her friend's fair head, letting it fall about her shoulders. Even yellowed with age and torn in one corner, its fragile lines were full of grace.

"It was Ma's veil," Lizzy told her.

"It goes with the gown like it was made for it," Morrow said, securing the last pin. "Oh, Lizzy, 'tis a lovely day to be a bride. Seems like everyone in the settlement is here to wish you well."

Pressing her hands to her flushed cheeks, Lizzy stole another look at herself in the mirror. "I reckon your pa told you Abe and I couldn't wait."

Morrow lowered her head and fussed with the veil. "I wish you'd told me, Lizzy. You're my dearest friend, remember."

"I wanted to but didn't know how. Guess I'll get to use that christening cap you brought me soon enough. I do wish we'd waited, though. I'm about to bust out of this dress!"

Morrow fingered some posies in a vase atop a bureau. "You can hold these flowers in front of you, like this." Taking them, she wrapped the stems in a handkerchief she'd brought and passed them to Lizzy, angling her hands down in front of her waist. But on Lizzy's thin frame, the baby was already showing, and no bouquet could hide it. Morrow wondered how far along she was.

"I reckon folks'll laugh to see me waddle to the river," she lamented. "I'll be bearin' in spring. March . . . April maybe."

"What's done is done, Lizzy," Morrow said softly. "Best think of your baby now. There's nothing finer than a family. Now, what else do you need before we walk to the river?"

"I need to sit down and rest a spell. This heavy dress makes me feel a mite woozy."

Morrow reached for a pitcher of water and a cup. "You're not going to faint, I hope."

Lizzy chuckled. "You're better at that than I am. Remember that last frolic right before you left for Philadelphia?"

Morrow flushed. "'Twas the heat."

"More than not it was all that male attention," Lizzy said with a knowing smile, taking a sip of water. "And now Abe tells me you've caught the eye of several settlement men . . . and one too many soldiers."

At this, Morrow looked up, surprise swirling inside her. One too many? Did she mean McKie? Was it already being bandied about the fort? Sitting down across from her friend, she shook her head. "I never meant to catch their eyes."

"You can't help it, I reckon," Lizzy acknowledged. "Folks say you take after your mother, that she turned the head of every man from Virginia to Kentucke when your father brought her over Cumberland Gap."

Morrow bit her lip. It seemed odd that mere strangers could recall what she could not. Her own meager memories of her mother seemed in tatters. "I remember so little, Lizzy."

"Pa said your ma was the prettiest woman he ever saw and you're just like her."

"Truly, I don't see what all the fuss is about. When I look in the mirror, I see plain Morrow Mary Little, too short and too stout, who's afraid of her own shadow."

Lizzy chuckled and shook her head. "You know why Jemima just about spits every time she sees you, don't you? She can hardly catch a beau, yet you don't seem to want one and could have any man you please, even Major McKie."

Morrow exhaled in a little rush, glancing at the open door. "He's quite bold. I—I don't know what to make of him."

A sudden wariness etched across Lizzy's features, and her voice faded to a whisper. "I'd hoped he might be the man for you, Yankee Doodle Dandy that he is. But Abe said you'd best be careful, Morrow."

Morrow tensed. "Careful? But I've not encouraged him."

"I'm glad of that. Abe told me somethin' about McKie forcin' his attentions on a woman at another post. And then there was that ugly business with the Shawnee."

Morrow looked at her blankly, her bright opinion of the major beginning to tarnish. Lizzy darted another glance at the cabin door. "Shortly before McKie came here, he was stationed at Fort Randolph. That's the fort up the Kanawha about a hundred miles from here. A few months ago, Cornstalk, the principal chief of all the Shawnee, rode in there with his son and another Indian, carryin' a white flag. They wanted to warn the soldiers that because the whites were breakin' the latest treaty made there, Cornstalk could no longer control all his warriors from raidin' the Kentucke settlements."

"But why would the Shawnee come near a fort and put themselves in danger?"

"Abe said it was a matter of honor. Cornstalk promised during the treaty that he would report any trouble, be it Indian or white. But instead of dealin' with them fairly and lettin' them go, the soldiers took the three Indians prisoner." Her expression tightened. "McKie broke into the blockhouse where the three Shawnee were being held. A group of soldiers came with him, and they started shootin' and clubbin' the Indians till—"

Morrow stood up, nearly overturning her chair. "Don't, Lizzy—please . . ."

Lizzy paused, her revulsion plain. "Neither he nor any of the other men were arrested. McKie was moved here and then promoted."

"What? Are you sure?"

"Abe was at Fort Randolph when it happened. He was in charge of the detail that buried the Shawnee."

Stunned, Morrow stared at the cold hearth. Lizzy swallowed hard, looking sickened by the retelling. "Only a butcher could do what was done. You'd be smart to stay clear of the major, though Abe says he's already so besotted with you he speaks of you before his men."

The beautiful day had turned black. Morrow hardly heard Alice enter, her girlish chatter filling the quiet cabin. "Oh, Morrow, let me look at you! The bride's in rose and you're in purple—must be one of your ma's remade gowns. I wish I had your way with a needle." She leaned into the mirror behind them, her fair features so like Lizzy's, and pinned a cameo to her bodice. "Preacher Little says to come anytime you're ready. Abe's already at the river."

Slowly the three of them walked across the common, holding their skirts out of the dust. The sloping bank beyond the gates was matted with dun-colored grass, and the river was shrunken and shallow from lack of rain. Spring did seem a better season for a wedding, Morrow mused. There was something about autumn that spoke of endings, not beginnings.

As the waiting crowd parted to let them pass, Morrow tried not to look at the man who stood at the front of the throng. But McKie was looking at her, as eagerly as if he was the bridegroom and she was the bride, and for a few agonizing moments she thought she might fulfill Lizzy's words and faint again. The tale of his misdeeds hovered round her like a dark shadow in the autumn air, and she felt a bit sick. She tried to concentrate on Pa's heartfelt words, spoken in the sonorous tone he saved for such occasions. "Dearly beloved, we are gathered together . . ." But the beauty seemed washed out of them today, stolen by the man who stood near her, who wasn't honorable or good or true as she'd thought an officer and a gentleman should be.

A warm breeze lifted Lizzy's veil, and Abe lifted his hand to keep it in place. The solemn cadence of Pa's benediction was broken by a horse's staccato hoofbeats, and every eye present seemed to swivel west. Morrow surmised trouble in one sweep of the lathered bay horse and its distraught rider before he'd come within fifty yards of them. As Major McKie broke away to meet him, a ripple of unrest passed over the crowd. The men surrounding them began checking their rifles, some reloading where they stood. Other folks began fleeing into the fort without waiting to hear the rider's news.

"Hinkley's Station has been burned to the ground," the man rasped, so winded he could barely speak. "There's more than a hundred Shawnee and half a hundred Redcoats headed our way. I have to ride to Asaph's to warn 'em."

Major McKie took hold of the horse's bridle. "You'll need a fresh mount or you'll never make it."

The rider wiped a sleeve across his damp brow. "Most of the men were out in the fields when they struck. The women and children were taken captive along with a few old-timers inside the stockade."

The major's countenance hardened. "That won't be the case here. We've more than enough guns on account of my men and the militia. Are you sure of the enemy's numbers?"

"Click and Kenton both agree. Fifty Redcoats and a hundred Shawnee—maybe more."

Morrow could sense the unraveling of those all around her. She soon lost sight of Lizzy and Abe in the press of people. Had Pa even pronounced them man and wife?

Without waiting to hear more, Pa took her arm and they headed toward the fort. Raindrops started to pelt them, and she glanced at the sky now thick with thunderclouds and threaded with lightning. Even the weather seemed to call out a warning.

Major McKie's shout could be heard far and wide as he commanded the sentries to shut and secure both front and postern gates. As Pa readied their horses to go, McKie approached from behind. "You seem to be in a hurry, Pastor Little, yet I have need of every gun in this fort."

Pa swung round and faced him. "I'll not take up arms against any man, red or white. As a preacher, I'm neutral in this conflict, as you know."

The major's eyes rested on Morrow, his tone barely civil. "Even so, I can't imagine why you'd subject your daughter to danger, especially in light of what I heard the savages once did to your family."

Pained, she looked away. His mentioning Ma and Euphemia seemed only to sully their memory somehow. There was an awkward pause, and then she felt a little start at the mettle in Pa's voice when he answered. "The call to stay or leave is mine to make, Major McKie. If I feel Morrow is safer on the Red River, then that's where I'll take her."

The answering fire in the major's eyes sent a chill clean through her. "I'm within my rights to order you to remain." As if to prove it, he moved to stand in front of Pa's stallion and grasped the bridle with one hand, holding a saber-tipped musket in the other. The horse whinnied shrilly and jerked its head away.

Pa put on his hat. "Kindly step aside, Major McKie. I'm sure you have other matters to attend to than keeping us here against our will."

Morrow's legs nearly gave way as Pa helped her atop the mare and then turned to his horse. He had never made an enemy in his life that she knew of, but the realization that he'd just done so left her queasy. Just ahead the gates loomed, locked tight. One of the sentries approached them, his bristled face intractable.

"Are you allowed to exit, Pastor Little?"

Pa opened his mouth to speak, but McKie's hard voice sounded behind them, heavy with sarcasm. "The Littles rarely grace fort walls except for Sabbath services, I'm told. I suppose they invoke divine protection in times of trouble." He gestured to the sentries to allow them to pass, along with a few other folks who'd chosen to weather the conflict in their own cabins. Morrow looked over her shoulder before the gates swung shut, sorry Lizzy's lovely day had been spoiled.

Pa flicked the reins, urging his horse on faster. She wondered if he felt any fear . . . if he knew what McKie had done. Any hopes for peace that she'd cherished when the soldiers came now turned to ashes. Would the Kentucke forts fall as payment for the major's treachery against the murdered Shawnee?

She could think of but one thing. Cornstalk and his men might well have been Surrounded by the Enemy and his son.

9

"Looks like the British and Shawnee made one last strike before fall slips away," Trapper Joe surmised, drawing hard on his pipe as he sat with Pa at the hearth. "Soon they'll start movin' to their winter camps. I'd wager Kentucke won't see any more trouble till spring."

A fortnight had passed since the fright that had broken up Lizzy's wedding. Since then it seemed the settlement hovered on extinction, that they might be wiped from the surveyor's maps at any moment. But just as Joe predicted, the British and Indians seemed to melt away. A search party made up of the Red River militia had gone out after them in hopes of recovering the captives from Hinkley's Station, but the enemy seemed to have vanished just beyond the Falls of the Ohio.

As she lay in bed that night pondering it all, Morrow's mind kept circling back to Surrounded by the Enemy and his son. Red Shirt was a British scout, his father a Kispoko war chief. Had they been part of the raid? Were they responsible for rounding up defenseless women and children when the fort fell? She thought of all the captives—families who had been destroyed like her own. The events were so disturbing she pushed back the coverlet and dropped to her knees on the hard floor, hands folded like a child's.

Oh Lord, wherever they are, keep the captives safe. Please bring them back.

"Morrow, you all right?"

Pa's voice seemed to boom on the other side of her closed door, startling her off her knees. She bounded back into bed. "I'm fine, Pa—just can't sleep." She heard him shuffle back down the steps and wondered if his own ponderings kept him wide-awake as well.

Near dawn a heavy wind began to blow, adding an exclamation point to all her turmoil. Glad for daylight, she dressed and hurried to the barn to milk with unsteady hands, watching the first leaves of fall swirl through the cracks in the barn's timber. There'd be no Sabbath service or singing school till the trouble stilled. Her initial pang of disappointment faded to stark relief. At least she'd be spared the attentions of Major McKie.

She churned inside the cabin rather than on the porch, glad when the butter came and she could carry it to the springhouse. Stomach rumbling, she gleaned a few apples from a barrel just inside the door. Carrying them in her apron, she returned to the house, darting a quick look about the clearing and orchard. 'Twas best to keep occupied, she thought, and clear her mind of dangerous matters.

"Apple dumpling time already?" Pa asked with a wink when he came in.

She smiled at his attempt at lightheartedness, wondering if he was as distracted by the turn of events as she.

"I need to go out and cut some cane for the horses," Pa told her. "Best bar the door behind me."

She looked at him, wiping her hands on her apron, wondering if this was as unsafe as it sounded. His gun rested over the mantel, yet it did nothing to allay her fears. Should she ask him how to use it—or urge him to take it instead? But she stayed silent, and he went back outside, his reassuring footfall fading as she slipped the crossbar into place. Now that she was alone, her mind began making frantic leaps, entertaining wild speculations as fear knotted her stomach.

What if Red Shirt came and wondered about the gift he'd given her? Would she fling open the dogtrot door and point to the copper pot? Suppose her ingratitude raised his ire? She put a hand to her carefully pinned chignon. 'Twould make a fine scalp. And what little hair Pa had left—white as it was becoming—would suffice as well. The British were paying dearly for settlement scalps, goading the Indians into taking them, so McKie said. And Red Shirt was a British scout . . .

She pushed such ponderings aside and kept busy about the hearth, soaking some hominy in lye and polishing a few pieces of pewter, but her thoughts kept straying to the other side of the dogtrot.

With a sigh she finally gave way, unbarring the door and hurrying to the opposite room to retrieve the package hidden in the copper kettle. Its mystery had gnawed a hole in her ever since Red Shirt had left it behind, and she could stand it no longer. With a shivering breath, she blew off the dust, forehead furrowing as she tore at the paper wrapping and string, unprepared for the delight and confusion that swept through her.

I must be dreaming.

She bent over the gift in her lap, fearful it might dissolve if she so much as touched it. Never had she beheld such astonishing fabric. It lay cradled in the heavy wrapping like a blue violet cloud, shimmering like silk, plush and deep as snow. Where could he have gotten such an extravagance? The same place he'd procured his exquisite linen shirt? She'd expected beads and buckskin. Not this.

Leaving the disarray behind, she crossed the dogtrot again and stepped back inside the cabin. There she succumbed to its wonder and buried her face in its softness.

From behind her, Pa said, "It's the color of your eyes."

Whirling, she faced him, feeling she'd been caught in a trespass. He'd come through the side door she'd forgotten to shut and bar, surprising her with his stealth. Or had she been so caught up in the gift she hadn't heard him? She brought the fabric down and tried to look at it dispassionately. The exquisite velvet was a rich periwinkle blue, the hue of hepaticas hiding in the Red River woods. 'Twas indeed the same shade of her eyes.

"'Twould make a fine wedding dress," he told her.

She gave him a shy smile. "Are you trying to marry me off, Pa?"

"Strange that you'd say that." He cleared his throat and pulled a letter from his pocket. "Yesterday Joe brought this from the fort—which is still standing, by the way. Your Aunt Etta tells me she's had a dream about you. That you're to marry a man of rank. The trouble is, there's so many men of that description around, I'm a bit befuddled as to who it could be."

Flushing, she began folding the fabric. "Oh, you know Aunt Etta, Pa. Always putting such stock in dreams. If she'd had her way, I would have stayed in Philadelphia and married a Redcoat."

"I was thinking of a Bluecoat," he said, setting his damp hat on the hearthstones. "Maybe along the lines of Major McKie."

She felt herself stiffen but tried to school her features. "McKie, Pa?"

"It's obvious he's set his sights on you. But at present he's a bit too distracted for courting, given the Indian trouble."

She hugged the fabric closer. "Why, I—I just got home and there's so much to be done. I can't be thinking of courting and leaving home. Not now . . . not yet."

Saying no more, he sat and resumed whittling on a pipe while she set the fabric aside. But later, after they'd eaten, she cleared the table and sharpened her scissors, assembling all her sewing supplies. Using an old dress as a pattern, she opened the sewing chest from Aunt Etta and hunted for her silver thimble and some silk thread. Pa watched her as he whittled, as if wondering if she had the nerve to cut the fine fabric.

She breathed a silent prayer as the sharp scissors bit into the blueness, the lantern quick to catch the slightest mistake. Each slice seemed to raise successive questions. Red Shirt and his father had seen her sewing in years past, when she'd sought to stay busy and avoid them. Was it mere coincidence that the velvet matched her eyes? Should she wear it or save it? If she saved it, it must be for her wedding day. If she wore it, Jemima would swear she was putting on airs.

The bodice was nearly cut when Pa leaned back in his chair. "I'd best read you the letter from Etta."

She looked up, glad to take a rest and let go of the shears. He began slowly, his voice a bit husky from the cold he seemed to keep. He was working too hard, she thought. Now that the harvest was in, he needed to rest, but there always seemed to be something left undone. Studying him, she thought again how he needed a son to aid him—not a helpless daughter. As he turned to the second page, she found her eyes drifting to the velvet.

"Morrow, did you hear?" Pa's gruffness broke the spell, and she looked up. "My persistent sister has extended you an invitation again."

She withheld a grimace. "Perhaps Aunt Etta could come here when things settle down."

His smile was wry. "Silk and buckskin rarely mix, Morrow. I've invited her often enough, but she merely counters my offer with her offer, which is to have you to herself again. I think life as a spinster must be lonely. And with a war on . . ."

"Perhaps I'll go back . . . one day." *One day.* It had a lovely, noncommittal sound, far-off and evasive as it was. But for now she'd had her fill of Philadelphia.

He folded the letter, his eyes still on her. "She says the city is calm now that the British have departed. You could attend finishing school, enjoy the theater, do all the things you couldn't do last time, and—"

"No, Pa, please." She'd not tell him all that she didn't miss—

that the city was dirty and stank, that people threw the contents of chamber pots out second-story windows, that she'd been little more than a slave right along with Aunt Etta, catering to the British elite.

Shoulders stooped, he took up his pipe again, a pile of shavings at his feet. "There's another reason Philadelphia appeals to me. You'd be out of harm's way."

She fought down her dismay. *Not with chamber pots flying out of windows and a war on.*

In the still room, his voice seemed ominous. "There's a wilderness war coming, I'm afraid, the likes of which we've never seen. Sending you back to the city would be dangerous but seems a bit safer than keeping you here."

She sat down on the bench, forgetting her sewing, grieved by the deep lines of weariness in his once handsome face. *Perhaps we should both leave,* she almost said. She thought it each time she ventured into the east side of the cabin and stood among the shattered remnants of their lives. She thought it now, beset with worries about McKie and the British and Shawnee. Yet they stayed on. Because of Jess.

She wasn't supposed to see the letter, Morrow realized. All the Mondays of her life she'd spent dusting Pa's desk—save the two years she'd spent in Philadelphia—never lifting the hinged lid to trespass to the contents beneath. But life was full of firsts, and so today she did. Night after night she'd seen him at work composing on crisp foolscap and longed to ask who the letter was for. She sensed it concerned her, and that is why she trespassed. That it was addressed to Aunt Etta nearly made her shut the desk but for one telling line.

> Morrow seems to have caught the eye of one too many men, both savage and civilized.

The savage was Major McKie, surely. The lid came crashing down, and she whirled about, certain Pa stood watching her. But both doors were open, untouched by his shadow. The plaintive call of a dove was the only sound that shattered the stillness, and she started dusting again, the stain of guilt shading her features. If he were to enter now, he'd know just by looking at her. She might as well finish the deed.

Dropping the crude duster, which was little more than a flurry of goose feathers attached to a stick, she went to the front door, eyeing the barn and field and pasture before passing to the back porch and returning to the desk. It took but a few minutes to scan the long letter for the most important points, and when she was done, dismay overlay her shame.

> Morrow is a woman now and in need of further feminine influence. Since she has returned from Philadelphia, I see things more clearly. As you stated in your last letter, the frontier is no place for a motherless daughter, and certainly not a fatherless one. I am, as you know, not well. The settlement men, most of whom are dishonorable, are paying her entirely too much attention, though she seems not to notice. There is but one man and only one to whom I would entrust her, but I shall save that for another post.

She reread that final line two, three times. Which man? Surely not McKie. Perhaps another soldier or settler? She favored none of them yet found the fact that he did intriguing. And his solution? Leaning on the open lid, she pored over the final paragraph.

> I have decided to return Morrow to Philadelphia—to your care—at the earliest convenience, barring further hostilities between Indians and whites.
>
> Your loving brother, Elias

Oh, Pa! She wished he would appear so she could spill out her angst, confess her spying, change his mind. 'Twas only a few months since she'd left the city. Now Philadelphia seemed as far-flung as England and twice the enemy. Would he take her there himself? No, he'd said he would send her at the earliest possible convenience. Did that mean tomorrow? Next week? With what escort? Captain Click?

The sound of boots scraping the porch steps made her nearly panic. She didn't want him to see her so, tears spilling down like a spoiled child. With furious haste, she disappeared through the dogtrot door into the east side of the cabin. Dust motes swirled like snow as a shaft of sunlight tried to penetrate the grimy panes of glass on the landing above.

Sinking onto a three-legged stool just inside the door, she put her head in her hands. Perhaps she could just pretend she'd never read the letter and pray that it would get lost between here and Pennsylvania. Or that the war—the wilderness one or otherwise—would move closer and the danger would prevent her from going to the city. She couldn't possibly leave Pa, unwell as he was.

In time she heard him pass onto the porch and go outside. Likely he thought she was upstairs in her room. The hum of cicadas rose shrilly in the Indian summer heat. Inside the ravaged room came the age-old smells of stagnant air, dust, and disuse. In her haste she'd left the door open, and a gust of wind whipped through the dogtrot, rifling her muslin skirt and pulling strands of her hair free of its pins.

She was so lost in recollecting every line of the grievous letter that she neither sensed nor saw anyone at first. Silent as a shadow, Red Shirt filled the dogtrot doorway, lowering his head to see inside. His lithe outline was reflected in the looking glass just across from her, and she went absolutely still. He was so close she could have reached out and touched the fringe of one beaded buckskin legging if she'd wanted to.

He looked down at her, and then his eyes roamed the room, taking in every desolate detail. But as she'd often observed, no emotion crossed his face. How, she wondered, was it possible to look at all the mess and be unmoved? Her own heart hurt anew each time she came here. His father's people had done this. *The Shawnee.* Not the Wyandot. Not the Cherokee. The Shawnee.

Without a word she hunkered further down on the stool and wrapped her arms about her knees, shutting her eyes. The wind gusted again, dancing with a flurry of stray feathers. Just like that final day. Thirteen years later she could still recall the feeling—the awesome bewilderment and finality of it all.

Would it never leave her?

"Morrow, is that you?" Pa's voice seemed to echo down the dogtrot.

She stood up slowly, knowing he'd stay well away from the door lest he see the shattered remnants of his old life just inside. Why did she feel like she was a hundred years old? She'd been sitting far too long. Her knees seemed to creak as she got up and shut the ugly sight away, joining him in the late afternoon sunlight.

"I've been looking everywhere for you," he told her, removing his hat and running an agitated hand through his hair. "I never figured you'd be over on this side."

For once she didn't hide it. He might as well know she came here as often as she could, to think, to try to remember, even as she ached to forget. She looked around, feeling a chill despite the warm wind. "Red Shirt was just here. Did you see him?"

He looked at her like she was addled. "I've not seen him this day, Daughter. Not since he came the last time and had words with you on the porch."

On the porch . . . when she'd all but begged him to stay away. Her face burned at the memory. "He was right here—standing in the dogtrot doorway. Looking inside."

"Did he speak with you?"

She shook her head, searching the orchard and the far meadow, the pasture where the horses roamed, and every outbuilding as if she could conjure him up and make Pa believe her. She felt the need to resurrect Red Shirt, to prove she wasn't dreaming. But it was just she and Pa, after all . . . and the grievous letter that stood between them.

"Perhaps he came by to see if we're all right, given the trouble," he said.

But she believed none of it. "I'm not feeling well," she said softly. "I'd best go lay down."

He nodded and began coughing again, and her heart sank at the sound. Before crossing over the threshold, she took a last look over her shoulder, a sense of foreboding following her.

Where is he?

It troubled her that Red Shirt could see them yet stay hidden. How many times had he come by and watched them while keeping himself a secret? The thought was so unnerving she felt woozy. She climbed the stairs to her room, fighting for composure.

Did he stand and watch them from the woods . . . perhaps linger on her window? One moment he seemed like a friend, another he felt like an enemy. Which was he? Though he'd said he wouldn't hurt her—had even saved her life at the river—she couldn't quite shake the fear that he might turn on her, on Pa. She'd heard of whites befriending Indians to their everlasting regret. A half blood wouldn't be any different.

She climbed atop her bed and felt the feather tick deflate beneath her weight. At any moment Red Shirt could come up here and do what the Shawnee had done years before—slash the thick tick to ribbons and fill the room with feathers.

If it happened, she hoped he'd have the grace to tomahawk her first.

10

At week's end, Morrow stood at the edge of the apple orchard, dipping candles in the coolness of the morning. Wrinkling her nose at the smell of smoking tallow, she remembered the bayberry candles she and Aunt Etta had made. Nearly smokeless, they were a lovely green and filled a room with a pleasing spicy scent. She'd brought some home from Philadelphia in a candle box to save for a special occasion.

Carefully, she hung another rod from a branch of an apple tree, leaving them to cool and harden before dipping them again. It was wash day as well, and she'd nearly forgotten the clean laundry she'd strung across the fence just beyond the barn.

As she left the yard, a skiff of wind lifted her apron and teased the knot of hair at the nape of her neck. She could see Pa in the pasture with the horse the Shawnee had given him when she'd been in Philadelphia. The stallion pranced about as if his hooves were on fire, shaking his black mane and amusing her father. She heard him laugh out loud, and the merry sound made her smile. He spent an uncommon amount of attention on the animal, as if keeping it in prime condition in case Surrounded by the Enemy wanted it back.

He waved to her as she approached, then turned back to the high-spirited horse. Humming a hymn, she began rearranging the assortment of lye-scented petticoats and breeches and linen shirts on the fence, enjoying the feel of the sun on her back.

When she turned back around, she nearly dropped to her knees in the dry grass.

Two lithe shadows were approaching Pa, whose back was turned. They seemed to sweep across the sunlit pasture like a breath of wind, neither sensed nor seen, their hands resting on the tomahawks at their waists. She took a step toward Pa, words of warning dying in her throat as her fear was tamped down by their sudden familiarity. *Them . . . again.*

Heavy-hearted, she hurried back to the orchard and resumed dipping candles, acutely aware of Red Shirt as he passed behind her and headed toward the cabin porch. Once there he drank deeply from the water piggin, replacing the gourd dipper on the rusty nail above it when done. She prayed he'd merely quench his thirst and go. But his tall shadow soon fell across her as she hung another crossbar from a branch. Wary, she glanced at the rifle he cradled in the crook of one hard arm, its barrel pointing skyward. The stock was curly maple from the russet sheen of it, the coin silver engraving far finer than Pa's own.

Stiffening, she recalled his standing at the dogtrot door before he'd slipped away and left her amidst the disarray. And then she felt a sudden softening as the velvet fabric flashed to mind. Such a kindness he'd shown. Couldn't she respond in kind just once?

Smoothing her apron, she asked halfheartedly, "Would you like some meat? Bread?"

"No, I want to talk to you," he said quietly, even carefully, as if he thought she might fly away from him.

Still, she regarded him with doubt. Today his glossy hair fell loosely about his shoulders instead of being bound from behind with a leather tie. Worn so, it softened him somewhat, made him seem less fierce. This close she could see the stunning detail of his beaded belt and the intricate work along the fringed outer seam of his leggings. She'd hardly seen its equal in Philadelphia. Someone had taken care to craft him such fine things. Who was she?

"There's to be a prisoner exchange at Fort Pitt," he told her.

Her lips parted in surprise. "When?"

"Next spring. The Shawnee will bring their white captives to the fort, and the whites will release their Shawnee captives as well."

She took in the words, a bit disbelieving. "White people have captives?"

"A few. Sometimes Indian children are taken in raids by soldiers at the edges of the frontier and sent to schools like Brafferton."

Like you, she thought. "I'm surprised there's to be an exchange with so much trouble of late."

"The trouble at Hinkley's Station, you mean?" His eyes left her briefly to sweep the edges of the woods. "Those are the very captives the Indian commissioners want returned. Some of the Shawnee chiefs and American officers see it as a goodwill gesture—a way to promote peace, perhaps avoid outright war."

The news was welcome if surprising. Still, a nagging suspicion stung her. Had he and his father been part of the fort's fall? Yet why would he be promoting peace if he had been?

"Will you go?"

He nodded. "I've come to see if your father wants to go with me."

She looked away, her heart overfull. "Pa is unwell . . . coughing all the time. I wonder if he could even make the trip, or if we'd even know my brother if we found him."

He shifted his rifle to his other arm. "What do you remember?"

Color seeped into her cheeks at his scrutiny, and she focused on a forgotten apple dangling on a branch behind him. Could she entrust her memories to him? Suppose she did, and he was able to bring Jess back to them? What an irony that would be . . .

She took a deep breath, eyes falling to the tallow kettle. "I . . .

I remember my brother had red hair—bright as a flame. I can't remember the color of his eyes." This had troubled her over the years. Had they been a queer blue violet like hers? Or more gray green like Pa's? "He worked hard in the fields alongside my father. I recall Ma said his hair didn't match his temper. He was so loving and good. I've often thought . . ." She swallowed down the admission, throat tightening.

"You've often thought . . ." he echoed.

"I've often thought the Shawnee wouldn't kill him because he was so pleasing. Everyone favored him. Even the animals came to him. Birds and squirrels would eat out of his hand. He could make every birdcall that ever was." As she talked, a torrent of recollection seemed to unleash itself inside her, of things pressed down and denied, excruciatingly bittersweet. She fell silent, unable to look at him or say anything more.

She could see Pa and Surrounded walking toward them now and felt stark relief. Turning away, she abandoned her candle making and went inside the cabin. She stirred up the fire and reached for the biggest skillet to melt some bacon grease and fry hominy. On the porch, Pa and Surrounded were deep in conversation, their Shawnee words a wall that shut her out. She felt a little forlorn standing there listening, realizing he'd left her behind in his quest to find Jess. He was holding his own admirably, thanks to Trapper Joe's tutoring, though she sometimes wondered why he bothered with Red Shirt present to translate. But he'd said he wanted to be prepared if Jess came back, in case he'd forgotten his first language.

They sat at the table with Pa, surprising her, partaking of the meal in silence. It was almost a marvel to watch these tawny men eat without utensils, picking out chunks of meat and hominy with their fingers, then swiping the bowls clean with bread. She remained in her rocker, balancing her bowl in her lap, unable to take the first bite. When they passed outside to smoke, she drew an easy breath. But she'd not rest completely till they'd gone.

As she sat in a pale puddle of lamplight embroidering a handkerchief, she heard Pa preaching on the porch. Amazement washed through her. What did he hope to accomplish with that? Hadn't Trapper Joe just told them the Shawnee had a tangle of gods and deep-seated superstitions? Yet here Pa was sermonizing like it was a Sabbath morning.

When the Indians finally put away their pipes and left, Pa came inside and set his Bible on the table, smelling strongly of *kinnikinnik*. She hoped it had some medicinal properties to help heal his stubborn cough.

"I saw you speaking with Red Shirt in the orchard," he said, clearly pleased.

She nodded. "He told me there's to be a prisoner exchange."

"I plan to go, Lord willing, though spring seems a long time to wait."

"By then you'll be stronger," she said, forcing hopefulness into her tone. "I've seen how the harvest has worn you out. You need to rest and prepare for the trip."

"I'm thinking of having you go with us. Red Shirt is an able guide. 'Twould be a fine thing to kill two birds with one stone, getting to Fort Pitt and then Philadelphia."

Aunt Etta's letter flashed to mind, and she looked up in surprise, a retort on her tongue. But spring was too distant to stew about now. She said nothing and returned to examining her stitches.

He studied her, taking the chair opposite. "Have you come to terms with Surrounded and Red Shirt's coming, Morrow?"

Her needle stilled. Had she? Dare she lie to him? "No, Pa."

"Unforgiveness is a heavy burden to bear. I wish you had it in your heart to forgive."

"There's too much hurt."

"Red Shirt is trying to help us. He saved your life."

"You saved his long ago."

He leaned back, passing a hand over his beard. "I think he needs you to forgive him, befriend him. He's grieved at what the Shawnee have done. I think you could heal by accepting his friendship."

Her needle jabbed at the cloth like an exclamation point to her every word. "He's a British scout, Pa. The son of a Shawnee war chief. He puts us—and himself—at risk every time he sets foot on our land. Friendship seems contrary to all that."

"We've done nothing wrong, Morrow, in opening our home to them. Christ Himself would have done the same. And we don't talk war."

She looked up, surprise pulsing through her. "If not war, what do you talk about?"

"Personal matters. With Red Shirt, anyway. Like a father to a son. At the risk of betraying a confidence, I'll say no more."

She examined the tiny flowers she was making in the square of linen, a cluster of blue forget-me-nots amidst pale green leaves. "I heard you preaching to them on the porch."

He gave her a wry smile. "I find Red Shirt more responsive to spiritual matters than most pew sitters."

She looked up, alarm in her eyes. "I don't think your congregants would like to hear that."

"It's the plain truth, Daughter. Or do you, like they, think the Shawnee beyond the reach of God's grace?"

"I don't know," she said softly, putting her sewing away.

But I wish they were. I can't conscience the thought of Ma's and Euphemia's murderers abiding in heaven alongside them. Not even alongside a half-blood British scout.

11

Morrow continued to work on the velvet dress in the autumn evenings, her sewing suffused with the delight she always felt when creating something beautiful. Only the memory of Red Shirt's recent visit spoiled her satisfaction. Thoughts of the coming prisoner exchange and returning to Philadelphia seemed to line her soul with lead. She looked down at the half-finished dress and wondered what Red Shirt would think to see her plying this extravagance of fabric when she'd not even thanked him for the gift. Sighing, she cut more thread as Pa lowered his copy of the *Virginia Gazette* and looked at her.

"You nearly done with your dress, Morrow?"

She looked up and tried to smile, bringing the lamp nearer. "The bodice is giving me some trouble. I'm trying to edge it in lace but I'm nearly out of thread."

"We'll soon start Sabbath services again, if you can wait on your thread till then. Major McKie has deemed it safe to come to the fort, so Joe says."

Had he? Would McKie welcome them back? Or would he bear a grudge since Pa had refused to take up arms? She speculated silently, her hands smoothing the plush velvet, the firelight making it almost sparkle.

Once again her thoughts turned to Lizzy and Jemima. For the hundredth time she wondered what they would say if they knew of her and Pa's unusual visitors . . . this gift. She'd told no one their secret, and it seemed almost to fester inside her. Jemima was an inveterate Indian hater, given the loss of her brother. And Lizzy, so trustworthy, was now wed to a militiaman bent on defending the settlement. Morrow was glad she'd kept quiet. Here on the Red River, so far from kith or kin, it seemed they could do as they pleased . . . see whom they pleased.

Even the enemy.

As Pa finished leading the first hymn without so much as a sputter, Morrow felt a deep thankfulness take hold. Perhaps her prayers for his healing were being answered. For a few minutes, anyway, hope seemed to take wing inside her and chase away every shadow. There were many things to be thankful for this particular Sabbath. The day itself was pure Indian summer gold. Not a whit of trouble with the British and Indians had been mentioned. And no officer in buff and blue sat beside her on the hard hickory bench. Just Jemima, who'd whispered that Major McKie was away on a foray.

"Are you and your pa going to stay for the gathering?" Jemima asked Morrow at sermon's end.

Morrow looked at her, wondering if Jemima would rather they leave. "I believe so. Pa seems better today."

"With the harvest over, he's likely not so spent." Jemima turned and perused the unmarried men on the back row. "Might be a fine day for courting."

Morrow suppressed a smile. "Who takes your fancy?"

Her lips pursed in contemplation. "Lysander Clay, if he's not spoken for. And you?"

"I'm not sure . . ."

"That's the trouble, Morrow Mary. You ponder it all overmuch. Now just follow my lead."

Morrow watched Jemima sashay to the back of the blockhouse, eyes fixed on the waiting men. All had hats in hand and were standing at attention as if waiting to be examined like horses at auction. Amused at the thought, she smiled absently and realized several men were smiling back at her. Jemima took Lysander's arm and all but bolted out the blockhouse door, leaving Morrow to stand a bit helplessly before the remainder. A spasm of sympathy wrenched her as she looked at their hopeful faces. How could she choose but one and spurn the rest? Perhaps she should be a bit bolder for Pa's sake.

As she debated, Robbie Clay saved her the trouble, taking her arm just as two others stepped forward to do the same. She gave them an apologetic smile as he maneuvered her out the door into the sunlight and dust of the common, where they were among the first in line at the heavily laden tables.

"Seems like we've had an ample harvest," he said, eyeing the bounty. "What did you bring?"

"Apple cake," she said, aware of Pa's eye on her as he stood talking with Lizzy and Abe across the way.

"I had a mess of melons and would have brought some, but the deer ate them. I suppose your pa told you about my claim."

"He said your land borders Abe and Lizzy's over on Tate's Creek."

He nodded, pale eyes alight. "Once we drive the Indians out and I can live there instead of at the fort, it'll be as fine a place as any. Good bottomland for grazing. Plenty of cane. I intend to have lots of livestock."

"I've heard about your fine horses," she said, eyes on her gloved hands.

He grimaced. "The ones the Shawnee stole or the ones that were left?"

"I didn't know about that," she murmured, thankful when the line began to inch forward.

His fair face, a deep berry red, registered stark displeasure. "I aim to buy more once I work up the nerve to go all the way to Lexington."

The mention of Kentucke's largest settlement filled her with wonder. Lexington was a far distance—and fraught with danger. Some said the road there was lined with blood. Not even Pa would go. She suppressed a shudder and set her mind on the gathering.

As Robbie moved ahead of her, taking up a wooden trencher and filling it with fried chicken, her eyes roamed appreciatively over the abundance of wide platters and deep bowls. Roasted fowl and venison. Shucky beans and buttered roasting ears. Fried apples and thick wedges of watermelon. Assorted breads and jams and pies. Benches had been arranged in a circle of sorts with kegs of cider waiting beneath a blockhouse eave. She smiled her thanks when Robbie brought her a cup, and they took a seat near Jemima and Lysander. Taking a small bite of bread, she looked around her. With Major McKie away, she felt she had more breathing room and could enjoy the day.

She noticed Pa eating and talking with the men and read approval in his gaze when he glanced her way. Was he glad to see her behaving like a young woman should, with an admirer at her elbow and a full plate on her lap? Jemima seemed to be pleased with her escort, though Morrow couldn't say the same about Lysander. Robbie's younger brother regarded them with characteristic sullenness, though Jemima seemed not to notice.

Robbie downed the last of his cider, his voice falling to a whisper as if all too aware of his brother's scrutiny. "Looks like any courting will have to be done in full view of the fort. I'd come out your way if the Red River wasn't so far, but with all the trouble since Hinkley's Station, I'd best stay near at hand."

She looked down at her meal, suddenly queasy. What could she say to this? She hadn't meant to encourage him, nor have him court her. She'd only thought to keep his company for a meal.

He muttered around a bite of bread, "Of course I can't do any courting with McKie shadowing you like a hawk."

Setting her plate down on the bench between them, she tried

to think of a gentle way to discourage him and correct his wrong assumptions. "The major and I . . . we have no understanding," she began awkwardly.

"That's not what McKie says." He ran a hand through hair so light and fine it looked like spiderwebbing. She waited for him to elaborate, but he fell silent, face tight.

"I—I can't think of a suitor right now," she said, feeling pinched with embarrassment. "Not with Pa unwell . . . not with the trouble at hand."

He finished his cider and said, "I hear the major finds the frontier a wearisome place. I keep hoping his fancy leanings will take him back to Virginia."

She held back a sigh, letting the conversation dwindle. The sun shone in her eyes, foretelling two o'clock. Across from her, Pa was rising from the bench, alerting her it was time to go. She got to her feet, thanking Robbie for his company and hoping she sounded more sincere than she felt.

Before she could step away, he took her hand with uncommon brashness, tethering her to the spot. "Some folks say you're too soft for settlement life and I should look elsewhere for a bride. But I believe there are more important things to consider than a workhorse of a woman."

The slight stung. *So I'm too soft? More important things?* Though she was largely ignorant of such matters, his suggestive tone left little to the imagination. Overcome with embarrassment, she took back her hand and turned away, acutely aware of the eyes of Lysander and Jemima—and everyone else on the scattered benches—upon her.

He stood, and she realized with a start how small he was, only a bit taller than she. Tipping his hat to her, he began heading toward the table where her apple cake waited. "See you when singing school commences, Miss Little, provided McKie doesn't appear."

12

The afternoon following the Sabbath, Morrow finished churning and stood at the springhouse door. In the time it took her to heave a sigh, she spied Surrounded by the Enemy and Red Shirt emerge from the woods. The sight of them—of *him*—seemed to ignite every emotion inside her. Like a charge of powder, their coming kindled a host of bewildering things. Fear. Dismay. Curiosity. Shame.

Her first fleeting hope was that they hadn't seen her, but the one lesson she'd learned was they didn't miss much. She slipped back inside the dank darkness that smelled of pickled beans and buttermilk and waited till they passed to the porch. Pa was inside the cabin, having just finished stacking a rick of wood under the outside eave. With the cabin door wide-open, their voices soon drifted to her across the leaf-strewn clearing.

Catching up her heavy skirts with both hands, she fled into the far field, her carefully kept bun coming undone in her haste. Skirting the cornfield, she slowed to catch her breath, waist-high in the oatmeal-colored grasses. If she hoped to hide, she couldn't. She'd made a clear trail coming here so much of late, pulling weeds and cutting back blackberry vine so the stone markers could be seen. The plot was tidy now, looking nearly as new as when Pa had first fenced it.

She sank down against the paling fence that framed the mounded earth and wondered how long they would stay. Would Pa be displeased at her hiding? She sighed, feeling eight instead of eighteen.

A horsefly buzzed near her ear, and she swatted at it with a heavy hand. Her knotted emotions left her too tired to think clearly, and despite the brightness of the day, she was midnight weary.

She sat completely still, perplexed by her tangled feelings of wanting to return to the cabin and stay away. Looking at the grave markers, worn by time and weather, she felt a startling absence of anger, just a deep sadness. Tears trailed down her face and wet her bodice, turning the rose embroidery bloodred. She sank down further in the dry grass, letting the sun and wind dry her damp face. She wasn't quite asleep, yet it seemed she was already dreaming.

"Your father sent me to find you."

She shut her eyes as the deep voice overwhelmed her. Red Shirt's shadow fell across the grass and mounded earth, though he stayed a respectful distance behind the fence. She stood up slowly and smoothed her wrinkled skirt, not wanting to look at him. Still, she found herself staring. He was so tall, so lithe, a striking blend of linen and buckskin. The sun nearly blinded her but called out the glint of his hazel eyes and every lean, unbending line of him.

He was studying her as well, and his face had turned so pensive her throat tightened. Turning away, she sank down into the grass again, searching for her handkerchief. While she struggled to compose herself, she became aware of him sitting against the fence, nearly back-to-back with her, the wide sweep of his shoulder touching hers. When the rich timbre of his voice reached out to her again, she shut her eyes tight.

"Do you forgive me, Morrow? For my father's people?"

Never before had he said her name. It seemed to shorten the distance between them, bespeak some measure of peace. She clutched the hankie in her hands, aware of the sigh of the wind and her own thudding heart. Forgive him? Forgive them? For taking away all she held dear? The startling question bewildered her. Why would he ask? Or care about her answer?

When she opened her eyes, he was gone. All around her the spent grass was sunlit and serene and empty. But his heartfelt question seemed to linger.

She took her time returning to the cabin, pondering it all. Both front and back doors were open wide, and the familiar voices on the rear porch assured her they'd not left. She started up the steps, pulled toward the privacy of her bedroom, then backtracked to the washbasin. Her hair was as unkempt as her feelings, and she wound the loose strands into a coil, pinning them carefully at the nape of her neck. Next she splashed water on her face, removing every trace of tears. She returned to the hearth, but her movements seemed wooden as she began to work.

"Morrow, you there?" Pa's slender frame filled the doorway.

"Right here, Pa."

"Surrounded and Red Shirt are staying for supper," he said.

She nodded and he disappeared onto the porch, seemingly unaware of her struggle. She slowed down, took a deep breath, stoked the fire. By five o'clock the venison roast and new potatoes were fork-tender, and she'd even managed to make a pie with the last of the apples she'd picked that morning. As she set the table, she heard the growl of thunder in the distance and felt the heaviness of coming rain. The commotion seemed to drive the men indoors—she didn't even have to call them.

As they took their places, she sat down briefly while Pa prayed, then got back up again to put the food on the table and fill their cups. The silence was oddly comfortable, broken by the clink of cutlery and passing of the dishes. She was torn between joining them at the table or shunning them as she'd done in the past. Finally she sat down, Red Shirt across from her. His plate was full, but he made no move to eat. Instead his tan fingers toyed with the knife and fork, turning them over as if contemplating what to do next. He shot a glance at her, lingering on her hands as she draped a napkin across her lap and took up her own utensils. Was he trying to copy her . . . perhaps please her?

His hesitancy was so touching she swallowed down the ache in her throat with a forkful of potato. He followed with a forkful of his own and eyed her as she picked up her knife. He did the same, but slowly, cutting his meat by pinning it properly with his fork first. She could feel Pa's eyes on them both—no doubt he was enjoying their peculiar interaction. At the end of the table sat Surrounded, missing nothing, but shunning utensils as was his custom.

"A fine meal, Morrow," Pa said with a wink.

She gave him a half smile, accepting Surrounded's and Red Shirt's thanks with downcast eyes as they retired to the back porch to smoke. Tossing the dishwater over the front porch rail, she paused to study the sky. An angry black, its expanse was threaded with thunderheads as the sun set before the coming storm. Where, she wondered, were McKie's men on such a night? Nowhere near the Red River, she hoped.

Restless, she removed her apron, hanging it from the peg by the hearth. By the time she'd passed outside, the men were nowhere to be seen. Had they already gone?

Across the clearing, the barn door was ajar. Inside, a lantern hung from a beam, casting light on two beautiful horses—both stallions, one gray, one white. Pa was fretting over the gray, examining its leg and feeding it an occasional sugar lump to keep it quiet. Red Shirt stood to one side, back to her and arms folded, while Surrounded spoke in low tones to Pa in a mixture of Shawnee and broken English. Surprised, she turned away and took the river path, unmindful of the heavy clouds that looked about to burst.

Tonight the water was gunmetal gray, reflecting the surly sky. She stood on the bank she and Jess had played on years before. The trail here was becoming trammeled now, though the memory of that day was growing as cloudy as the sky. What she recalled most was the *feeling*—the fear and finality of it all. But it no longer haunted. Somehow, sometime, that part of her past had lost its power to wound her. Pondering it, she stood in the solitude, watching the sky struggle to stay light before giving way to the blackness of the stormy night.

"You shouldn't come here alone, *nekanoh*."

Startled, she turned. Red Shirt stood behind her, his hazel eyes on her and everything else at once. Was he remembering how she'd nearly drowned?

"*Nekanoh*?" She echoed the strange word back to him.

"It means 'friend' in Shawnee."

Did he say that to soothe her, in case she felt frightened alone with him? Standing on the bank beside him, she was struck by how tall he was. Why, she didn't even reach his shoulder. Even outdoors he was physically imposing, dominating the woods as well as the cabin.

"I didn't hear you," she said, then flushed at her foolishness. It was his habit *not* to be heard.

A flicker of amusement seemed to lighten his intensity. "I know. I've followed you since you left the barn."

She sat down on the nearest rock as thunder boomed a final warning. "I saw your horses—is one lame?"

"Snakebite."

She winced and turned her attention to the sky. The lack of lightning made her less skittish, and she felt the spatter of rain cool her flushed face. "I've rarely seen you here with horses. You must be going far."

He moved to sit near her. "We're traveling south to Tennessee."

Her gaze followed his across the river to the foothills now muted and misty with the coming rain, the mountains in back of them rife with black shadows. She said wistfully, "I've not even crossed this river, yet you're going beyond those mountains. I've been wondering what's on the other side."

"More mountains. And rivers. Some so beautiful they take your breath."

Her lips parted in a sort of wonder. He was always roaming, and she was always staying in one place. Did he ever want to stay put, or was he content to always stray? "How long will you be gone?"

"Three, four months."

She kept her eyes on the restive water. "Don't you miss home when you're away?"

He leaned down and picked up a stone, skimming it over the river's surface. "My mother died when I was a boy. Since then no particular place has seemed like home to me."

"Pa told me she was a captive."

He nodded. "She was taken as a girl along the Clinch River in Virginia."

She hesitated, a hundred questions in her head and heart. "What was she like?"

He grew thoughtful. "I remember her hair was yellow and she had eyes like yours."

Yellow hair. Blue eyes. *Precious little to hold on to*, she thought.

"She taught me the white words . . . English."

"What else do you remember?"

"Very little. The Shawnee don't speak of the dead."

Nor does my father, she almost said. She studied the strong, angular line of his jaw and the heavy fringe of his lashes as he looked down at the water. Did he ache to know more about his mother, just as she did, even though it was denied him? Did he feel there was a part of his life yawning empty, needing to be filled? She watched as he released another stone across the river's surface, face pensive.

"I remember she'd talk to God with her hands folded. Sometimes she'd take my hands in hers, and together we'd pray."

She took the words in, a bit disbelieving.

"She called God her Father, like your father does."

Her voice softened. "What happened to her?"

"She died of a fever when I was a boy."

The poignancy of his tone touched her. "You must miss her."

He shrugged slightly. "I have my father . . . others. It's enough for now."

For now. When, she wondered, would it cease to be enough? Would he ever want a wife, children? A home of his own? Being a half blood, what would he choose? The white way or the Indian? She shut the thought away, a sudden frustration overlaying her sadness. Whoever he was, or chose to be, he came and went as he pleased, revealing little, while their lives had been laid bare to him from the very beginning in all their dullness and simplicity.

"I know so little about you," she said suddenly.

"What do you want to know?"

Her forehead furrowed. "I . . ." She swallowed and looked at the ground. "Why do you keep coming back here?"

"Your father asks me to come. And your cabin sits near the path I often travel."

Though he hadn't said the name of it, she knew. The Warrior's Path. It cut through the heart of the Red River, across their very land. Perhaps that's why the Shawnee had done what they'd done that summer's day. Perhaps a settler's cabin was a desecration to them . . .

"I know you don't like my coming," he said, eyes on the river again. "And I don't blame you."

She shifted uncomfortably on the rain-slicked rock, his heartfelt question at the gravesite returning to her in a poignant rush. "I—I know you mean us no harm. But it seems dangerous for you. Your father."

"It's no more dangerous here than anywhere else."

"Aren't you still a British scout?"

"Not any longer." He sat beside her again, the damp linen of his shirt sagging against his broad shoulders, his buckskin leggings darkening to black. "I've begun to see that the Redcoats are using the Shawnee as a weapon to fight the Americans. And my father's people are suffering because of it. Their only hope is to break from the British and make peace with the Americans. Try to honor the treaty terms and hold on to their lands."

She thought of all she'd overheard Joe and Pa discuss of late, of McKie and his men, and her forehead furrowed. "But there are settlers—and soldiers—who violate the treaties being made at Fort Pitt."

He nodded. "And there are Shawnee who do the same by raiding the settlements."

"Is that why you're always on the move? Trying to keep the peace?"

"I travel to various tribes and frontier forts, sometimes acting as courier. Mostly I serve as interpreter and mediator for negotiations between the Shawnee and the British and Americans."

She shuddered, thinking he was in the very heart of the danger. She'd not wanted to talk war, yet here she was, trying to make sense of the turmoil swirling around them. Before she could mind her tongue, she said in a little rush, "I hope you stay away from Red River Station."

He turned thoughtful eyes on her, startling her with their intensity. "I'm well aware of the commander there. And I give that post wide berth."

She felt an inexplicable rush of relief at the words. 'Twas just as Pa had told her. He was, for better or worse, far more knowledgeable about McKie than they. "You're very brave to do what you do," she said quietly. "Or very foolish."

"Perhaps a bit of both." His eyes flickered over her through a haze of cold rain, his voice edged with concern. "You need to go back to the cabin. You're shaking."

But her trembling had less to do with the chill than her tumult of emotions. She opened her mouth to inquire why he'd asked for her forgiveness at the gravesites, but the words slipped away. Breathless, she stood, wanting to return to the cabin and the warmth of the hearth. She nearly fell on the slippery rocks lining the river's edge, but he caught her, steadying her with a hard hand all the way up the muddy trail and into the clearing. Pa was waiting on the porch with Surrounded, and the horses were now ready to go south. 'Twas a dismal night for travel, she thought. Dismal and dangerous.

Turning to Red Shirt, she said suddenly, "God be with you."

He let go of her arm, a telling surprise in his eyes. But it failed to match the astonishment she herself felt. For a fleeting moment he'd seemed almost like a friend. She'd seen him in a new light . . . had looked past his Indianness and nearly forgotten who he was.

And that she must never do again.

"We need to pray, Morrow," Pa said, surprising her with his abruptness.

Chilled, she stood by the hearth's fire as close as she dared without singeing her wool skirts, while he lingered at the table. "Pray for what, Pa?"

"While you were at the river, Surrounded told me the British and Indians are readying to strike the settlements again if McKie and his men cross the Ohio like they plan." His face assumed a gravity she'd rarely seen. "He wants Red Shirt to resume working for the British. Apparently he's the Redcoats' pick as lead scout and liaison. Even General Hamilton has asked for him by name."

"General Hamilton?" She spoke the name with a sort of revulsion. *Hair-buyer Hamilton?* The British commander who was goading the Shawnee into fighting their battles for them and paying dearly for settlement scalps?

"I'm afraid Surrounded expects—even demands—his son to do as he bids."

"But Red Shirt doesn't want to," she surmised. Although she'd overheard only the barest scraps of their private conversations, she'd gathered all was not well between Surrounded and his son.

"Red Shirt has come of age and must decide which road he will take. His heart is with the Shawnee, and he's served with their British allies in the past, but his white blood makes him reluctant to go against his mother's people. He's not made for war, he says, though he's fought many a white man already."

Had he? She'd suspected as much, but hearing it from Pa's own lips seemed to magnify her fears. "Were they with the war party that burned Hinkley's Station?"

He shook his head. "Surrounded says no, and I believe him. But he's going to join the fight to keep McKie out of the middle ground if it comes to that."

She struggled to stay calm, sensing they were being drawn deeper into a conflict they'd best stay clear of, and knotted her hands in her lap. "How should we pray, then?"

He set his pipe aside. "Let's pray that McKie and his men will abide by the latest treaty and keep to this side of the Ohio River, and Surrounded will see that peace is preferable to war—especially war with white men who seem to have no end, as Red Shirt says."

They joined hands across the table and bowed their heads. But as was so often the case, Morrow could not shape her wayward thoughts into any sort of petition. The Shawnee had simply taken too much. She could only say, "Amen."

13

Soon a heavy frost touched the land, and the time for singing school was at hand. Morrow sat beside a shivering Jemima, cupping a candle between her cold fingers. Blasts of bitter air swept through the loopholes in the thick blockhouse walls, and the room remained frigid despite the fire that greedily licked big burls of seasoned oak. She felt nearly numb beneath her scarlet cape, though Lizzy's fine kettle of soup warmed her insides during the lull between the Sabbath service and singing school.

She listened halfheartedly to Jemima's idle chatter as she relayed all the happenings Morrow had missed being absent from the fort. Jemima recounted courtships and illnesses and heartbreaks with such relish that she paused for breath only when the blockhouse door swung open to admit another member of the choir.

"Why, looks like the whole army's here," Jemima whispered with satisfaction as the rows behind them filled. She looked askance at Morrow. "Major McKie's back from his latest foray just in time. Might that have something to do with you?"

Unable to answer, Morrow looked at Pa as he stood at the front of the room and readied for the singing. Out of the corner of her eye, she saw Major McKie turn in her row to sit beside her. He was agonizingly near, so close that one wool-clad knee pressed against her cape. She gave a slight nod of acknowledgment but couldn't—wouldn't—look at him.

Jemima whispered a trifle loudly, "I hear the major has a mighty fine voice."

But Morrow hardly heard her, eyes on Pa. Behind the sturdy pulpit, he seemed shrunken, a shadow of the man he'd been in years past. Did anyone else notice—or care? In one gloved hand he clasped a clean linen handkerchief, not yet soiled with specks of blood. She looked down at her gloved hands, fighting fresh alarm.

He'll not be here another winter.

The realization took hold of her and seemed to shake her. As Pa tapped the tuning fork on the podium, then set it down on its stem to give a starting note, all that surfaced in her throat was a hard knot. If he died, what then? What was life without him?

The sweet strains of "Baloo Lammy" echoed around her, but she couldn't sing, nor could Pa for coughing. She opened her mouth to join in—once . . . twice . . . a third time. Heat pricked her neck and face, and she felt McKie's eyes on her as she struggled to start. But Jemima's soprano more than made up for her lack, and the major, though she hated to admit it, had as fine a voice as she'd ever heard. Robust. Perfectly pitched. Blending beautifully with Jemima's own. Morrow longed to follow along, but today her throat clenched tight as a fist as she watched Pa struggle to sing and pretend that nothing was the matter, perhaps for her benefit.

Before the music ended, she was on her feet, scooting past Jemima's bulk to turn out of her row. Head down, her profile hidden by the generous brim of her bonnet, she nevertheless noticed Robbie Clay seated on a bench by the door, eyes on her as she exited. Frantic he or McKie might follow, she headed toward the necessary at the other end of the common. A corral full of horses, mostly the Virginians', nickered as she passed. The sudden thud of a cabin door sent her scurrying into the narrow space behind the nearest wall.

"Morrow, is that you?"

Lizzy? The relief she felt was beyond measure. Her friend squeezed in beside her, slowed by her expanding waist. "I saw you come out of the blockhouse. I thought you'd be glad to start singin' again."

"I've no heart for it today," Morrow said.

"It's your pa, ain't it?" Lizzy's voice faded to a whisper. "I noticed he seemed poorly. At noon he hardly ate—couldn't for coughin.'"

"Oh, Lizzy, I feel lost. Pa's so sick, and my prayers go unanswered. There's no medicine to ease him. Even Aunt Sally has given up."

Lizzy moved nearer, voice soothing. "I remember when Ma took sick right before I met Abe. Seein' her so ill, bein' unable to help her, was the hardest thing I've ever known. But God was with me helpin' me to bear it. He brought Abe alongside me when I thought nothin' could ease the hurt of it."

"I know God is with me, Lizzy. But there's no Abe for me, and I don't know if there ever will be."

"Morrow," she said, a new firmness in her tone, "there's a dozen men in the settlement who'd marry you tomorrow if you'd just look their way. But that's the trouble—you won't."

"With Pa so sick, I can't think of such things. Besides, being a spinster doesn't scare me. Perhaps I could earn a living sewing—"

"Here?"

"In the city. Aunt Etta's shop . . ."

Lizzy shook her head. "You were little more than a slave there, sewin' night and day for those wealthy ladies. Would you trade all this"—she gestured to the far-flung stars and wide-open space behind their hiding place—"for the stench of the city? Is that what you want?"

"No." Her answer was flat, emphatic.

"Morrow, listen to good sense. You need to be thinkin' of what will make your pa rest easy. He's worried about leavin' you alone, surely. If he knew you were goin' to be taken care of, have a secure future, he could go in peace."

"But—"

"Now, we can rule out McKie. And I know you ain't fond of Lysander. But Robbie Clay is a right admirable man, and I've seen the way he watches you. He's got no bad habits to speak of, except bein' a bit afraid of the major."

Morrow listened halfheartedly, unable to tell her the true root of her turmoil. Lately she'd begun to feel she was living a sort of double life. The Morrow who came to the fort on the Sabbath was no longer the one who lived at the Red River with secrets she couldn't share. She needed a friend to reveal all that was on her heart, but the risk was too great. All she could utter was, "You'd best go inside, Lizzy. You shouldn't be out in the chill with a baby coming."

"Promise me," Lizzy said, squeezing her arm. "Promise me you'll think on it."

Morrow nodded and watched her go, wanting to call her back. A new heaviness weighted her as Lizzy left. She had little recourse but to return to the blockhouse, for there was nowhere else to go. Pa fixed a wary eye on her when she entered, as if trying to make sense of her unexplained absence. She could see he was merely mouthing the words to the song being sung. His rich baritone was missing but hardly needed; all she heard was Major McKie and the heavy drone of soldiers making a travesty of "O Tannenbaum." Even Jemima's piercing soprano was smothered by the swell of masculine voices.

Resuming her place on the bench, Morrow kept a respectful distance from McKie. His tricorn hat with its fancy cockade sat between them, resting atop pristine leather gloves. But it was more than this that divided them. The debacle at Fort Randolph pushed them apart, hurtful to her in ways she couldn't fathom. What evil was he planning next, she wondered? How could men do such things in the sight of God?

Pa was looking at them, his face cast in shadows. What, she thought numbly, did he think of McKie sitting beside her as if he had some sort of proprietary right to her? If she did change her mind and act on Lizzy's urgings, McKie barred the way. No man would approach her while he stood guard, certainly not Robbie Clay.

When the closing hymn was sung, the blockhouse seemed to fill with a resounding silence. Jemima got to her feet, smiling at the courting couples and soldiers on the bench behind them, but McKie's eyes were fixed on Morrow.

"Miss Little," the major began, putting on his hat, "I would ask you to walk about with me if the weather wasn't so chill. Perhaps another day."

"Yes, another day," she echoed, feeling caught in a lie. "I must go . . . my father . . ."

The sound of coughing was a welcome interruption, and she hurried outside toward the waiting wagon, relieved when McKie was detained by some settlement men. She laced her arm through Pa's, buoyed by a sweet feeling of deliverance.

He looked down at her, a telling concern in their depths. "Where'd you disappear to, Daughter?"

"I needed some room, Pa," she said quietly.

"McKie's crowding you a bit, I suppose."

She looked over her shoulder to make sure they were alone. "Something like that."

He drew her closer in a sort of wordless understanding, and her composure nearly crumbled again. She didn't dare tell him it was his own deathly appearance that sent her stumbling out the blockhouse door.

"Remember, Morrow," he said, a trace of wistfulness in his tone, "when you meet the man you want to be with for life, you'll want to run *to* him and not *away* from him."

The heartfelt words touched her. Is that how he'd felt about her ma? Would she, given time, feel the same? A deep melancholy stole over her. With all the turmoil in her heart, there seemed little room left for tender feelings.

14

They were sliding toward winter now, cold rain stealing every shred of Indian summer's brilliance. Morrow stood by her attic window, able to see the Red River through the woods' bare branches. In the early winter gloom, it looked like melted lead. Sometimes it seemed she'd always be here, watching and waiting, never changing. But then from somewhere in the cabin, Pa would start his coughing, and she'd be reminded that time was moving like the river in ways she couldn't see, working to turn her hair from cider to silver . . . have its way with her . . . leave her wanting.

In the dark days of early December, Lizzy's heartfelt plea seemed to make more sense. The names and faces of the suitors she might consider rumbled through her mind like a discordant melody. Robbie Clay. One of McKie's men. The smithy's son who was the most recently smitten. But trying to think of them in a romantic way made her skittish, and she shut her heart to the notion.

From below, Pa's voice, punctuated by bursts of coughing, ended her reverie. "Morrow, we'd best go see Good Robe and the baby."

She hurried down the steps, snatching up her cloak before following him over the rain-soaked ground toward the river. He pulled his felt hat lower against the weather, mumbling something about the sky looking like snow. She wanted it to snow—so hard they wouldn't be able to return to the fort till spring, so deep they could climb into the colonial cutter and sit back as it whisked them over ruts and rocks to Joe's. But today the canoe sufficed, partially exposed by a near-naked stand of laurel along the muddy bank.

With her help, Pa hefted the canoe into the shallows, holding it steady till she took her seat, then jumped in and pushed off almost at once. Despite his illness, he was still agile and maneuvered the vessel as expertly as his horse.

"How long will Joe be gone, Pa?" she asked, watching the river dimple in the rain.

"Oh, you know Joe. He tends to lose track of time out in the woods. Might not be back till spring."

"I'm surprised Good Robe didn't go with him."

"She wanted to, but it's a dangerous time to be about, and the winter promises to be a hard one. I assured Joe we'd keep an eye on them, help with whatever they need."

The little cabin soon came into view, its sturdy chimney puffing smoke. She'd meant to bring them a little something but had flown out of the house in such a hurry she'd forgotten all but her wits. Good Robe seemed as glad to see them as they were to see her, and Little Eli looked rounder and sturdier than before.

They visited all the dreary afternoon, Pa and Good Robe speaking a strange mishmash of English and Shawnee, as the four of them ate together around the crackling fire. Morrow marveled at Good Robe's economy, watching as she combined dried beans and corn and squash into a tasty medley. Holding up her wooden bowl for seconds, Morrow smiled as Little Eli waved his spoon as if asking for the same. But without Joe's joviality, it seemed a bit too quiet.

"I have a feeling Joe is missing your cooking about now," Pa told her.

Good Robe smiled at his praise, pointing to a beaver pelt drying in the corner. "Beaver tail his favorite, Pa Little. You too?"

At this Morrow stopped chewing, eyes flying to the corner pelt.

"I don't believe Morrow's ever made it," he replied. "But I'd be pleased if she did."

Good Robe nodded vigorously. "First you trap beaver and hang over fire. The heat makes skin split and peel back. Then you cut up and boil with vegetables. *Oui-sah*."

"*Oui-sah*," Pa said with relish. "Good, indeed."

Morrow discreetly removed her handkerchief from her sleeve and made a quick deposit, wondering how this succotash would taste with bacon instead of beaver tail. Little Eli looked up at her with wide green eyes, so startling beneath his fringe of inky hair. She fed him the rest of his gruel, amazed at his appetite. In the windowless cabin, the grease lamps smoked and their eyes stung, but they continued to talk, speculating on where Trapper Joe might have gone and when he might come back.

"And Surrounded? Red Shirt?" Good Robe asked. "You see them?"

Pa cleared his throat. "Not since fall. Last I heard they were headed south to Tennessee territory."

She nodded knowingly. "They go talk with the Cherokee about the soldiers."

Morrow felt her stomach knot. She rifled the baby's glossy hair as he sat in her lap chewing on a wooden spoon, relieved when the conversation took a turn and Pa began answering Good Robe's questions about the white man's God. Opening his Bible, he tried to translate some passages in Shawnee about sin and forgiveness, peace and prayer.

She listened absently, a bit startled as the rainy night at the river with Red Shirt returned to her. Looking down at Little Eli, Morrow tried to picture Red Shirt as a boy, inky-haired and amber-eyed as he prayed with his captive mother. Had Surrounded been tender with her? Had he minded that she clung to her beliefs and passed them on to their son?

The longer she lingered on the image, the more another memory flowered. She could recall soft whispered words and amens. Jess's short petitions and Euphemia's babyish jabber. Cold knees on the hard floor. Warm kisses afterward. She sat and let it assuage her hurt, surprised that it could soften and dispel some of the darkness. Her thoughts kept returning to Red Shirt's heartfelt question by the gravesites and her inability to answer. Why was forgiveness so hard to find? Why was it even harder to bestow?

When they got up to go, it was nearly twilight. Good Robe opened the door, and they gave a collective gasp. Snow swirled down over the expanse of soggy brown ground, the flakes big as English shillings. Icicles were already forming under the cabin eave, and Morrow nearly lost her footing in her fragile slippers.

She and Pa hurried to the river, the surface wind-whipped and edged in ice. Pa pushed off and paddled hard, but by the time their cabin came into view, he was spent. Morrow was so stiff from the cold she had trouble getting out of the canoe. He helped her to the bank and then beached the vessel upside down beneath the same snowy clump of laurel, urging her to go on without him. He had to see to the horses and bring them in from the pasture.

Hastened by a bitter wind, she hurried up the river path, marveling at the frozen world around her. It seemed to take an age to reach the front porch, and when she did the snow came up to her ankles. Just ahead she saw that the cabin chimney was belching considerable smoke, far more than their prolonged absence allowed. Her heart gave a queer lurch as she slowly pushed open the door. The familiar figures draped in buffalo coats weren't frightening now, just unexpected. Had they already returned from Tennessee?

She stepped nearer the hearth, no longer aware of her sodden slippers, and greeted them. "Pa's seeing to the horses," she said softly.

Surrounded swept past, leaving her alone with Red Shirt. In the ensuing silence, she removed her gloves and cape, busying herself at the fire. "You must be hungry, tired." She tied on an apron and bent to hang a kettle of leftover soup from the crane, nearly scorching her hand as she did so. "You're wise to come at night."

"We cannot stay," he said.

"But the snow . . ." she said, glancing at the ice-encrusted windows. "I've plenty of soup and bread." Turning, she brought out what was left of a black walnut cake from the hutch.

He made no reply, but his dark eyes glittered and took her in with an intensity that nearly made her forget where she was. Setting the cake on the table, she watched him take a seat on the opposite bench. He moved a bit stiffly, keeping his heavy coat about him, his handsome profile stoic in the firelight. Yet she sensed something grievously different about him.

Her hands stilled. "Would you like some cider while I warm supper?"

Oddly, he made no answer. She busied herself setting the table around him, trying to determine what made her so uneasy. Where was Surrounded? Pa? She glanced at him again—and forgot all about supper and her own growling stomach. Beneath the bench upon which he sat was a small but startling puddle of red. A suffocating sense of alarm shot through her.

What . . . ?

The sight made her inch her way down the table, slightly open-mouthed. He turned toward her as she approached, and his face held a strange heat. Dropping down beside him, she stepped on a corner of his buffalo robe and the heavy fur gave way, revealing a linen shirt stained scarlet. The sight of so much blood made her shut her eyes. Without thinking, she pressed a cold hand to his face, feeling she'd touched an andiron instead. He moved back slightly as if to get away from her, but in his fever-weakened state, she was faster. Turning to her sewing chest, she took out a pair of newly sharpened shears. In one swift motion she cut the back of his shirt from neck to hem, desperate to find out how badly he was hurt.

Oh, Pa . . . where are you, Pa?

His right shoulder was mangled, the wound packed with what looked to be buzzard down, but even that failed to stem the bleeding. Panic choked her, and she fumbled with the scraps of shirt, trying to staunch the flow. Woozy, she sank down onto the bench beside him.

"Morrow . . ." He seemed to grit his teeth as he said her name.

She didn't answer, just looked on helplessly as he leaned into her. In seconds her lovely wool dress was poppy red as his body sagged against her, his head against the lace of her kerchief. She lowered her face into the gloss of his hair, awe and pleasure piercing her pain.

"Morrow!" The clap of Pa's voice was like the coming of thunder in the cabin. "What in heaven's name is happening here?"

She looked up, feeling pale and shaken. Surrounded was behind Pa, clutching his medicine bag. She'd seen it dozens of times but hoped they'd never need it. Their long shadows hovered as they began moving Red Shirt, leaving her with the mess of her dress, her thoughts scattered.

In moments he was in Pa's bed again, just as he'd been as a boy. The distant memory pulled at her, and she began doing the same things she'd done then—boiling water, cutting strips of linen into bandages, praying silently. She kept looking over her shoulder to the bed, where Pa was examining the wound by lantern light. The mounting fear she felt was nauseating.

Face grim, Pa moved to the fire and thrust his hunting knife into the flames. "What happened out there?"

"Soldiers," Surrounded said tersely, then lapsed into Shawnee.

Pa paused briefly to examine the hot steel. "Was there a fight?"

Surrounded simply nodded, eyes on the barred door.

"Were they known to you?"

"*Mattah.* Bad men spring up like grass everywhere . . ."

Pa turned back to the bed, jaw clenched. "Hold the lantern for me, Morrow."

"Pa . . ." Her voice was fraying fast. "Can't you give him some medicine—anything—to ease him?"

"Look at him, Daughter," he said a tad sharply. "He's already unconscious."

She took up the lantern but couldn't look. The smell of blood sickened her, and the light swayed in her hand. Pa stifled a cough and reached out to steady the light. "I'll not have the both of you to tend, understand."

Shamed, she steadied herself, noting his own pallor was as sickly as Red Shirt's. Sweat beaded his wrinkled brow, but he kept on, at last extracting the ball. "Bring some water, and we'll clean the wound then mix some medicine."

Thankfully, his stomach was stronger than hers. She held the basin of steaming water, watching it redden before she replaced it. Red Shirt's eyes were still shut, his head turned away from them, his dark hair like spilled ink against the white bedding.

Pa looked from him to Surrounded. "He'll need to remain here while you go on to Fort Pitt. He's in no condition to travel."

Surrounded merely nodded, but Morrow's face clouded. "Shouldn't we move him upstairs? If someone comes—if there's trouble . . ."

"He'll be out of sight, protected," Pa finished for her. "Go up and ready your room. The sooner we move him, the better. I'll tend him through the night, and you can spell me come morning."

Lighting a candle, she climbed the stairs, seeing everything with new eyes. Opening her room to him was a little like opening her soul. She held the light high, assessing everything in one sweep. All within was clean, feminine, tidy. The bed was hardly big enough to hold him, though the linens were freshly washed. On a nearby table was a washbasin and porcelain pitcher full of water. She crossed to the shelf of dolls and gathered them up, burying them in the bottom of her wardrobe. Next she turned the bed down, folding the colorful quilt up at the bottom. He'd hardly need it with a fever.

She could hear the men coming up the steps, and she moved to hold the door open. Strong as they were, it was all they could do to carry Red Shirt. The move seemed to aggravate his shoulder further, sending sticky rivulets from his bare chest to the beaded belt at his waist. Slipping past them, Morrow went below and gathered up the weapons he'd left at the door, bringing them upstairs. Along one wall she placed his rifle and hunting knife and heavy trade tomahawk. She could feel Surrounded watching her, and she sensed approval in his gaze.

He looked down at his son a final time, his face graver than she'd ever seen. Then, without a word, he was gone, following Pa downstairs, leaving her behind with the lantern. She hesitated, knowing she should go. He lay peaceful, entirely still.

From the doorway, she heard a slight cough. "Morrow, go below to bed. I'll tend Red Shirt tonight."

How long had he stood at the door, watching her watching him? "Will he be all right?"

He came from behind and placed a bony hand on her shoulder. "He's strong. And the wound is clean. I believe all he needs is rest."

"But the fever—"

"I'll try to break the fever with boneset. We've other herbs besides. Surrounded has left some medicine."

This brought some comfort. The Shawnee were noted healers, even among the whites. Joe had often spoken of their skill. But sleep would be long in coming, if at all. She felt a sudden chill. What if he worsened in the night? What if she withheld what he asked of her? He might die without knowing her forgiveness . . .

"Pa, please, won't you let me stay and help?" Her plea was so poignant his own eyes glittered when he looked at her.

"No, Morrow, go below." His quiet words held a hint of rebuke.

Reluctantly, she turned away.

Sometime in the night, when the cabin was completely still, she heard her name. Pushing back the quilt that covered her, she climbed out of the trundle bed and paused on the first step, shivering in her thin nightgown. The stairs seemed to stretch to the heavens beneath her wobbly legs, and her heart slammed inside her chest. But she heard the call again nevertheless.

Morrow.

Dawn edged the landing window with pale yellow light as she passed by and entered her dark bedroom. Pa was sound asleep on a corner pallet, and the candle she'd left hours ago was spent. She could make out the shadowed figure in her bed, so distinct even in the darkness. Red Shirt was attempting to get up, and she ran to him, a small cry of alarm spilling out of her. Frantic, she pushed him back, but he caught her hands, entangling her in his bare arms. The heat of his skin shocked her.

"Don't—your shoulder . . ." she whispered as he unfolded to his full height, determination in every line of his striking face. The slats of the bed seemed to sigh with relief as he stood, then groaned as he sat back down again.

"You must rest," she whispered, glancing at Pa.

He took a deep, shuddering breath, and his forehead fell against the soft slope of her shoulder. Breathless, she watched him struggle to regain his bearings and finally sit upright. She could see the intense emotion in his expression, limned as it was by dawn's intrusion through the windows. Slowly she framed his flushed face with her hands, and their coldness seemed to help ground him.

"Olame ne tagh que loge," he muttered. "I am very sick."

"Yes, you are very sick," she echoed.

He looked past her to his weapons lining the wall. "I need water . . . then I will be on my way."

She shook her head. "No, you need someone to nurse you—to take care of your wound."

He looked down as if surprised to find his shoulder seeping, the bandages bloodied, but the sight seemed only to harden his resolve. "I can't stay here any longer . . . you know the danger."

She felt a sudden flash of sympathy. "If you go, you'll not make it to Fort Pitt. Your father left you with us for a reason. I—" She swallowed down the emotion that threatened to spill over, hardly believing what she was about to say. "I—I beg you to stay."

To hide her angst as much as to help him, she turned away and poured a cup of water. He drank it down and asked for another. Pa stirred on his pallet as Red Shirt stooped and began gathering his weapons, returning each to his belt, his movements sure and resolute. But when he stood, he staggered backward, straight into the older man's leanness, nearly toppling Pa in the process.

"You'll go nowhere this day," Pa said, struggling to right him and steer him back to bed.

Unwillingly, Red Shirt sat, one hand resting on the belt where his knife had been, the empty sheath digging into the soft feather tick. The blood was running again, creating tiny tributaries from his shoulder to his stomach.

She watched as Pa began to peel away the layers of soiled linen, her eyes entreating when she looked again at Red Shirt. "At least stay until I can sew you a shirt."

Pa cleared his throat and shot her a wilting look. "You'd do well to mind your own dress, Daughter."

Shamed, she crossed to her dresser for clean under things, then opened the wardrobe and rummaged for a gown. She went below to dress and start breakfast, trying to lose herself in the routine of making porridge and frying bacon. She saw Surrounded's medicine pouch on a table and began boiling water, wondering what could be done to break so high a fever. A cup on the table held the last bitter dregs of boneset, evidence of Pa's attempts the night before.

She hardly heard Pa behind her. He'd become so light in body the stairs no longer creaked to announce his coming. The corpse of a katydid, Aunt Sally called him. Weary, she turned to face him.

"He's in bed again, but I don't know how long he'll stay," he told her, washing his hands in a basin. "I've a good mind to knock him out with a double dose of whiskey."

The suggestion sent her hurrying to their medicine chest. With the dark jug in one hand, she rummaged for a small cup with the other.

He sat down, his beard covering a rueful smile. "You'll have to give it to him, Daughter. I doubt he'll take it from me, but from you he just might."

His wry amusement surprised her, but she hurried back upstairs, marveling at her eagerness to return to the sickroom—and Pa's allowing it.

Wary, Red Shirt leaned back against the headboard and watched her as she sat down by his side, the bed hardly giving beneath her weight. "You want me to drink the whiskey," he surmised. "If you bring me my buffalo coat and saddlebags, I will."

"You first," she said, extending the cup.

He obliged, trying to stay stoic despite several disagreeable swallows. Pa retrieved the saddlebags from the barn while she fulfilled her part of the bargain, lugging the heavy hide to her room. She found the smell of it oddly fragrant, reminiscent of the *kinnikkinnik* he smoked. His appreciation shone in his feverish eyes, and he took it from her with studied effort, spreading it flat on the floor with her help until it became a huge, dun-colored carpet.

"Your bed is making me soft," he said.

Perplexed, she looked down at the thick hide, wondering if he'd truly trade the feather tick for the cold, hard floor. But he was already upon it, exhaustion—or whiskey—slurring his speech. She studied him, concern tightening her features, and he studied her in turn.

"I think you're in need of your own medicine," he finally said.

Kneeling, she smoothed out one rumpled corner of the hide, nearly too weary to get back up. She'd hardly slept knowing he was under their roof, terrified he'd worsen in the night or leave them. The suspicion that he might yet still nettled her.

Suddenly the raucous bawling of the cow beyond the frozen window reminded her that no matter what was happening within cabin walls, their daily chores awaited.

He lay back slowly, favoring his wound. "When I wake up, I'll tell you about my trip south to Tennessee."

His eyes were already closing, and she breathed a plaintive prayer. Mindful of the frigid draft along the floor, she took the quilt off her bed and covered him. Reluctantly, she began backing out the door, wondering if his sleepiness was little more than a ruse to leave once she and Pa weren't looking.

15

It seemed he slept a solid three days, awakening only to eat and drink or have his shoulder bandaged. She rarely went upstairs, though sometimes when Pa was outside chopping wood or seeing to the horses, she crept up to the landing and peered through the crack in the door like a child of five, not a young woman of eighteen. Once she spied a book lying open on his bedding while he slept. Curiosity made her tiptoe nearer until she saw it plain. A Bible. Could he read? The notion was nearly as jarring as his speaking English. His time at Brafferton returned to her, stoking her growing curiosity about his past.

She kept busy below, but there was a heaviness edging all that she did. She expected to find him gone at any moment—or soldiers at their door. Perhaps he'd be well enough to travel by Christmas Eve. She'd nearly forgotten the party to be held for the singing school at their very own cabin. In years past she'd anticipated the event like no other, enjoying playing the hostess, preparing for the evening with a week's worth of baking. But now in just a fortnight, the group would gather, build a bonfire between the barn and cabin, roast chestnuts and dance and sing, drink cider and share supper. The coming event filled her with dread.

"We'll go on as before. If we didn't, we might be suspect," Pa told her as she began rolling out dough for apple tarts. "Red Shirt can stay upstairs, and no one will be the wiser."

"But some of the soldiers will be here, Major McKie among

them." She kept her voice soft, afraid of it drifting upstairs. Even now she looked around for any trace of Red Shirt's presence. Spying Surrounded's medicine bag, she wiped her hands on her apron and hid it away in a corner cupboard. By now, the wily chief was well on his way to Fort Pitt, some two hundred miles upriver. Who knew when he'd return?

Pa began to wheeze, a sure sign of his own agitation. "A great deal more is accomplished by prayer than by worry," he said, shrugging on his coat. "I need to go check the fence line. One of the horses is missing. But I'll be back by supper, Lord willing."

She looked up, surprised that he would leave her alone with Red Shirt, but he simply kissed her cheek and went out, the staccato hoofbeats of his horse growing fainter and fainter in the frozen air. The snow that had blustered with such fierceness two days past had dwindled, leaving a few scant inches upon the ground. But it was bone-chilling, the cold. She placed the heavy bar across the front door and replenished the fire, then returned to her baking.

The afternoon loomed long and lonesome, leaving little to do but sew the promised shirt. Thus far she'd stitched but one sleeve, relying on Red Shirt's measurements by sight alone. It had been easy enough to guess the breadth of his shoulders and chest by observing Pa dressing his wound. Recalling it now nearly made her miss a stitch and lose the thread altogether.

She held her wayward needle still, suddenly aware of the creak of the stairs and her own thudding heart. Red Shirt stood behind her on the last step, leaning against the railing, wearing leggings and Pa's largest nightshirt, his feet minus moccasins.

Relief washed over her like a wave. "I was beginning to think you were an old bear, hibernating in our attic all winter long."

Slowly he came and sat opposite her, taking Pa's chair. "How long have I been here?"

She held up five fingers. “Five sleeps,” she said, echoing something she’d heard Surrounded say.

His mouth crooked in amusement, and he looked about the spacious cabin as if getting his bearings before returning to the linen in her lap. “Is that my shirt?”

She took another stitch. “You can’t leave till I’m finished.”

“You’re sewing very slowly.”

She tried not to smile, but she felt her mouth tilt upward nonetheless. “I promise it will be a fine shirt. Better than the one I cut off you.”

He leaned back and put a hand to his hair, surprise skimming over his features. “You made me a braid.”

“Pa wanted your hair off your hurt shoulder,” she explained, a bit perplexed as she recalled her pleasure in the simple task. His hair had slipped through her hands like the finest black silk, but as she’d plaited it and tied it with black ribbon, he hadn’t so much as stirred, lost as he was in the grip of sickness.

“I feel stronger—the fever’s gone.”

“You’ll be weak yet as you lost so much blood,” she said. “But there’s another reason you can’t go. You still haven’t told me about your trip to Tennessee.”

A sudden spark seemed to light his keen eyes. “I wanted to tell you, but you didn’t come, even when I gave you back your bed.”

She looked up, full of wonder. “You wanted me to come upstairs?”

“You know I wouldn’t hurt you . . . dishonor you.”

“I—I know you wouldn’t . . . but . . . being alone with you . . . like that . . .” She faltered and looked away, a furious blush staining her face.

“It’s not the proper way,” he finished for her.

She merely nodded, trying to start sewing again, but instead making a knot of her thread.

He said quietly, "Sometimes I think you're still afraid of me."

She looked up at him again and wished she hadn't. His eyes held hers with a startling intensity, as if daring her to deny it. She got up abruptly, nearly spilling her sewing onto the floor.

"I made some broth," she said. "You'll need to regain your strength. And I'll have to see to your shoulder."

With Pa away, she had little choice. Standing beside his chair, she peeled back the bandages and began to clean the wound with warm water and clean rags. Red Shirt stared into the fire without so much as wincing. A nagging fear took hold of her. What if he could no longer use his arm? Hold a gun? Scare up his supper? Fight for his life?

Despite her gentleness, the blood began to flow again, and she swallowed down her dismay. The ointment Aunt Sally had given them long ago had a pleasant, lemonlike smell and braced her for a moment, but then the room tilted and began to spin. He was looking at her now, his eyes filled with sympathetic light. Gently yet firmly, his hand encircled her upper arm so that she was able to finish her task. But when he released her, she swayed like she was dancing and came down hard on his lap.

Oh Lord . . . how weak I am. 'Tis just as Robbie Clay said. I'm too soft.

Shame shot through her as he steadied her once again, standing her upright even as he got to his own feet. A perfect gentleman he was, giving her his chair. She took a deep breath as she sank down onto the hard hickory slats. He moved away from her and went to the hearth, taking up a black ladle and lifting the lid off the soup kettle. Turning back around, he hitched a stool closer with one foot, balancing a bowl of steaming broth in his good hand. Wincing, she turned her head away.

Amusement played across his handsome face. "What will I tell your father when he finds you on the floor?"

"I'll not faint . . . I should be spooning that soup to you."

His eyes narrowed. "That's the trouble. You take care of me—but not yourself."

She took the broth from him, glad to see him hungry as well. When had she last eaten? Yesterday?

They sat together in companionable silence, sharing a bowl, her senses alert to any trouble beyond the barred doors. She knew he was as wary as she, though there wasn't a trace of unease about him, at least that she could see. The sooner he healed and passed from beneath their roof, the safer both of them would be.

Red Shirt was on his feet now, helping Pa with the horses. Although his wound aggravated him, he made no complaint. She could sense his frustration with his slow recovery, his impatience at having to sit down and rest. He pushed himself, making daily strides toward some unspoken goal. One morning when she'd bundled up to do the milking, she found him leading Pa's prized black stallion out of the barn as she was about to go in. He seemed immune to the cold and wore no coat, just his usual buckskins and his new shirt. She, on the other hand, was nearly shaking as soon as she set foot on the porch.

Eyes on her, he held the bridle in one hand and the heavy barn door open with the other. The big horse nickered softly as if anticipating some pleasure. She wished she had a sugar lump to give him. He was so beautiful—and high-spirited. She'd never ridden him herself. Pa kept her confined to the mare. Wistfully, she looked at them both, wondering where they were going but hesitant to ask.

He took the bucket from her hand and set it down, shutting the barn door. When he turned back around, he mounted the stallion's bare back with tremendous grace and offered her his good arm. A bit clumsily she took hold, and he pulled her up behind him. Her wool skirt rode to her knees, revealing several layers of beribboned petticoats and snug wool stockings above worn black boots

Reaching behind, he took her arms and folded them about his supple waist. The simple gesture startled her . . . and turned her insides to jelly. She was glad he couldn't see her face. A quick glance toward the pasture reassured her Pa couldn't either. Nor had he given his approval, she was certain. Red Shirt had his own way of doing things, of asking and answering to no one.

He turned his head, his profile questioning. "Would you rather be in the barn?"

"No," she answered a bit breathlessly.

With that, he kicked gently at the horse's sides, and they turned away from the cabin, trotting briefly, then coming to a rolling gallop and clearing the first fence in the pasture, then the second. A queer exhilaration took hold of her, and she leaned into him, her wool hat flying off her head and lying like a blue puddle on the frozen ground.

He headed west, away from the fort, clear of danger. Or so she hoped. For a time they followed the river. It didn't take long for her to feel she was in a new land, a new life.

Sights she'd never seen unfolded all around her—a frozen falls, otters sliding down the icy banks of some nameless stream, sandstone cliffs set like a cougar's teeth in the side of a mountain. He was heading higher, through dense stands of pine, their redolence like some exotic spice.

"Are you cold, Morrow?"

His breath was a cloud, and in answer she wrapped her arms more tightly about him, urging him on. How could she possibly be cold, pressed against him, his warm body shielding her from the wind?

They climbed higher toward a circling eagle, and the trees seemed to fall away. Snow-slicked rocks scattered beneath the horse's hooves on the thin ribbon of trail. It seemed a bit hard to breathe, the air was so sharp and cold.

His gun was at hand, and the confidence with which he rode dispelled her fears. He'd been here before, perhaps many times, or so his purposeful stride assured her. Not once did she think about Pa or his alarm at finding both her and his finest horse missing. That was a world away, so dull and colorless she hardly missed its going. The present was all that mattered, and it was, in a word, divine.

When they could climb no further, he dismounted, taking her with him. She nearly slipped on an icy rock, but he caught her, his shoepacks sure on the frozen ground. He led her up a shaded path to a limestone wall, where they squeezed through an opening like a loophole. On the other side, the earth fell away, and it seemed they stepped into open sky.

She gave a little gasp, not of fear, but of awe. He turned to take her in, pressing his back against the cold cliff and drawing her in front of him. She looked down and found the toes of her boots in midair with only her heels on the ledge. But he had one hard arm around her, grounding her.

His breath was warm against her cold cheek. "I wanted to show you Cherokee territory, not just tell you about it."

She followed the sweep of his arm south, his finger pointing to distant snow-dusted mountains and a wide opal river. Small puffs of smoke revealed few campfires or cabins. The land lay before them like a disheveled white coverlet, uninhabited and without end, broken by more mountains and wending waterways. The unspoiled beauty of it took her breath. For a moment he relaxed his hold on her. With a cry, she reached for him again, fearing she might fall into nothingness.

"Careful," he murmured, steadying her. "Trust me."

She shut her eyes tight as his arms settled around her, anchoring her to the side of the cliff. Frightened as she was, she felt a tingling from her bare head to her feet. 'Twas altogether bewildering and frightening . . . yet pleasing. Gingerly, as if doing a slow dance, he led her off the ledge onto safe ground, where he released her and turned toward the stallion grazing on a tuft of grass.

His smile was tight. "We should return—soon, before your father thinks I took you captive."

Reluctantly she walked behind him, framing every part of him in her mind in those few, unguarded moments before he mounted. If he could ride to the top of a mountain and back, what was to stop him from reaching Fort Pitt?

He was quiet on the way down and, contrary to his concern about Pa, seemed to take his time returning her home. The sun foretold that it was nearly noon. They'd been away hours, though she felt they'd stepped outside of time.

A spasm of guilt shot through her. Not once had she thought of Pa—or missing the morning's milking. The cow would likely be bawling in complaint, and supper would be late. But as they came into the cabin clearing, all was quiet.

Red Shirt helped her down and then turned the stallion loose in the pasture. She peered into the barn, where she saw the cow had been milked and was bedded down in some straw. Together they walked up the cabin steps and through the front door. Morrow braced herself for the coming confrontation. They had violated Pa's unspoken code of conduct on several fronts, the least of which was being unchaperoned.

They found him sitting in his chair by the fire facing the door. Her wool hat—the one the wind had whisked off as they'd ridden away—was on the table. She kept her eyes down and murmured a muted hello. Red Shirt said nothing at all. Her hair was undone and her cheeks were raw from the wind and cold, but she'd never felt better in her life. Contentment suffused every part of her, disheveled as she was. Could Pa see that?

He looked to her, then Red Shirt. "Did you have a good ride?"

"Yes," Red Shirt answered, coming to stand beside her as she perched nervously on the edge of her chair. But the openness in Pa's features soon set her at ease. Why, he looked no more perturbed than if they'd gone to Sabbath meeting together.

He gestured toward the hearth. "It's bitter out. I've made some coffee."

She got up and poured two cups, adding sugar to Red Shirt's and taking cream herself before sitting down again. The silence wasn't stilted but strangely comfortable. Perhaps Pa was waiting till Red Shirt went upstairs—or outside—before taking her to task. They finished the coffee in silence as Pa loaded a large oak backlog onto the fire. When he turned back around, he looked toward the medicine pouch and said, "I'd best see to your shoulder."

She watched as Red Shirt shed his shirt without a hint of reserve, and caught Pa's eyes on her. Shamed, she looked into the fire, color creeping into her face. If he knew how he'd just held her . . . made her feel. That was why she found it so hard to look away from him. Yet they'd done nothing wrong . . . had they?

The wound was bleeding again. Perhaps their ride had simply been too much. Troubled, she turned back to them as Pa bound the shoulder with a long cloth strip. Feeling woozy, she went out onto the porch. Pa soon came to stand beside her, curiously silent.

"I'm sorry, Pa, for leaving without telling you," she said, eyes on her boots.

"I knew you'd come to no harm," he said quietly. "I knew you were in good hands."

Yes, she thought, still stunned that she'd just stood on the side of a mountain, one step away from death. Yet she'd felt like she was on the flattest plain, safe and sure-footed with Red Shirt beside her. She'd left her heart high up on that mountain, and it seemed she was there still, spirits soaring. She'd not felt so free—so fearless—in years. Could Pa tell just by looking at her?

The silence lengthened and turned tense. "I'd best see to supper," she finally said, glad to have something to do.

"Morrow . . ." He started to speak, then swallowed down a cough and motioned her inside the cabin. She went willingly, shutting the door on his tortured hacking. The sound made her eyes water and brought her none too gently down to earth.

Red Shirt sat by the fire, resting his shoulder and reading an old copy of the *Virginia Gazette*. She removed her cape and set about making supper. Though it had been a simple ride, and nothing significant had been said, there seemed a new understanding between them, a new tie. She couldn't shake the feeling that he would be there for her once Pa wasn't, that even now he sensed her sorrow and uncertainty about the future. The man who'd held her on the side of the mountain would continue to hold her in the valley.

If she'd let him.

16

Morrow had been missing the sanctuary of her room. Sleeping in the cramped trundle bed with Pa so near was making her something of a night owl. She heard all manner of things that never made it upstairs—his snoring, the scurrying of mice, the settling and shifting of the fire. Now, just as the mantel clock struck four, she came wide-awake at the opening of her bedroom door. She lay completely still, Pa's snoring finally giving way to coughing and masking the movement she so wanted to hear.

Red Shirt . . . leaving?

He was familiar enough with their cabin now that he knew where to step on the stairs to avoid their creaking. Silent as a cat he came down, his silhouette tall and dark in the firelight as he stopped briefly at the hearth and moved soundlessly through the cabin. A blast of icy air reached her in the few seconds it took for him to open and shut the front door. Perhaps he'd simply gone out to relieve himself. He had a natural sense of decorum that made him shun the chamber pot beneath her bed. Sometimes she sensed he felt her room was little more than a cage, that he was as confined as a bear in a trap. Little wonder he spent more and more time outside.

In seconds she was on her feet, her ruffled nightgown a tangle of linen and lace, long forgotten by some fancy Philadelphia lady. She nearly tripped over the hem but made it to the door, snatching up her shawl and draping it around her before tugging at the handle.

The sound of Pa's snoring made her bolder still, and she hardly minded the icy porch planks beneath her bare feet. Red Shirt was just an arm's reach away, his back to her as he sat on the edge of the porch. With his buffalo coat around him and his rifle near, he looked poised to leave just as she suspected. He was smoking the pipe Pa had made for him, and the aroma she was coming to appreciate enveloped her in a small white cloud. She sat down near him and watched as he inhaled and exhaled easily on the pipe, his handsome face a study of satisfaction.

He smiled down at her in the darkness. "You watch me so well I think you want to smoke."

"I've been wondering what it's like," she admitted. Thinking of Aunt Sally, she added, "Some of the settlement women smoke."

Still, she wrinkled her nose and drew back a bit as he reached for her hand and placed the warm bowl of the pipe in her palm, wrapping her fingers around it. Timidly she put the stem to her mouth. The pungent smoke seemed to race down her windpipe, creating a small storm. Gasping, she began to cough, sounding so much like Pa she thought Red Shirt might laugh. He thumped her on the back and gestured for her to be quiet at the same time, stopping just shy of clamping a hand over her mouth.

"Leave the smoking to me," he teased, taking the pipe back.

She tensed, wondering if Pa might appear. "I thought you were leaving."

"I had to see the sky. The stars."

She glanced up beyond the porch eave, awed. Tonight the heavens seemed near enough to touch. The bright trail of stardust she knew to be the Milky Way had never been brighter. No wonder he'd come downstairs. The view from her bedroom window was stingy indeed, but here on the porch, profound.

His own voice was touched with wonder. "The Shawnee believe that is the path to the Otherside world."

"The Otherside world," she echoed, drawn to an explosion of shooting stars to the south, like sparks from some heavenly fire.

"They say the stars are the souls of all the warriors from the beginning of time."

All those souls . . . What of his soul? she wondered. She thought of his Bible lying open upstairs. When he'd been in the barn helping Pa with the horses, she'd picked it up, surprised that it was so old and worn. The leather binding was fraying, a few pages missing. She could make out a signature inside, the fine writing so faded it was almost invisible. And she knew without asking that it was very dear to him.

Wrapping her arms around her knees, she looked skyward again. "When I consider thy heavens, the work of thy fingers, the moon and the stars, which thou hast ordained . . ."

"What is man, that thou art mindful of him? and the son of man, that thou visitest him?" he finished.

She turned to him, fresh wonder trickling through her.

"I spend a lot of time reading in your room," he said.

"I know. I saw your Bible."

"It was my mother's before me. That's all I have left of her."

"That's plenty," she said softly. "To know that she touched those pages . . . read those very words."

"I took it to Brafferton and asked them to teach me what it said. But I nearly lost it when I left Virginia."

"What happened?"

"A party of trappers robbed me along the Clinch River. The Bible fell into the water and I dove after it. I believe it saved my life."

"'Tis meant to save lives," she said with a little smile.

"You sound like your father."

"Do you mind?"

He took up his pipe again, face reflective. "He's different than any man I've ever known. I'm glad you're like him."

"But I'm not," she said, throat tight. "He's generous and kind and good . . . forgiving."

"You're different than you used to be. A few months ago you wouldn't have followed me onto this porch."

The compliment, if it was that, brought tears to her eyes. "I—I'm sorry for treating you so badly. I'm ashamed now of how I snubbed you—acted afraid of you—"

"It's common enough."

The admission startled her—made her feel grieved and defensive and tender toward him all at once. She longed to lay a reassuring hand on his sleeve but checked herself. There was no self-pity in his manner, only truth telling, and she sensed he didn't want her sympathy, just her friendship. And her forgiveness.

"A half blood belongs to no one, red or white," he said.

"You belong to God," she said softly.

The ensuing silence lengthened and turned tense. She was suddenly mindful of her cold feet and thin shawl and wondered if she shouldn't go inside. As she moved to stand, a sudden cry filled the clearing. A mockingbird?

He drew back as if bitten, moving between her and the sound so suddenly she nearly toppled backward. With a fierce gesture, he urged her into the cabin, his hands so fast upon his rifle that she gasped at the flash of moonlight on metal.

She fled inside, keeping the door cracked, and watched as he backed up, his rifle aimed at the clearing. The mockingbird failed to call again. He slipped in after her, and she shut the door with a thud, setting the crossbar in place. Across the room, Pa still slept through the commotion, though his snoring had ceased. Suddenly she realized they'd left Red Shirt's pipe and buffalo coat on the porch, but his expression told her it didn't matter. He'd stand watch and neither smoke nor sleep the remainder of the night.

"Go, Morrow," he whispered, nodding toward the trundle bed. "Sleep."

She shook her head. "What is happening out there?"

"Someone watches your cabin."

She felt a flicker of panic and glanced at the crossbar again to make sure it was in place. McKie had spies everywhere . . . but so did the Shawnee. He knew this as well as she. But his calm suggested such danger was a trifling thing hardly worth mentioning.

"Go. Sleep," he said again.

But she couldn't, stirred up as she was by what waited outside. Instead she took a candle and lit it at the low fire, shielding its flame against the draft with one cupped hand as she climbed the stairs to her room to better see the surrounding woods. Setting the candle on her dresser, she crossed to the smallest window and stood at its corner. Dawn was beginning to paint the frozen forest with sepia light. The mockingbird they'd heard moments before had sounded queer. She knew their call, and this particular one had not rung true. And he, far more familiar with these things than she, knew it too.

Morrow paced on the landing outside her room, hearing the creak of wagons and horses. It was early afternoon, and members of the singing school were already arriving in the winter gloom. A light skiff of snow graced the frozen ground, and a bonfire was already blazing down by the barn to warm the revelers. She could hear Jemima's harsh laugh, and it rankled her near-fractured nerves.

If only they could just skip to tomorrow—Christmas Day. It would be just she, Pa, and Red Shirt then. All week she'd been anticipating Pa's reading of Christ's birth in the Gospels and giving them the gifts she'd made. They'd share a special supper, and she'd wear the velvet dress. Red Shirt had not celebrated Christmas, he'd said, not since leaving Brafferton.

Taking a steadying breath, Morrow slipped into her darkened bedroom. He was standing by the window, arms crossed, looking down upon the bonfire and gathering wagons. She wondered how many frontier frolics he'd seen. The intensity of his expression told her he missed nothing, from the number of soldiers present to the caliber of weapons they carried, the condition of their mounts, and the uniforms they wore. Wary, she breathed another silent prayer.

"I wanted to check on you one last time . . . see if you needed anything," she whispered, stopping in the center of the room.

"Have you come to give me my orders?" There was a hint of a smile in his voice as he moved to stand before her, arms still crossed.

"Orders?" she echoed.

"Don't look out the window. Don't climb onto the roof. Don't go below."

She tried to smile, surprised at his easy manner, but her sense of impending disaster only deepened. "I have no heart for a frolic tonight. The soldiers are simply too close."

He looked down at her, studying her small form smothered in moss green wool. She pulled her scarlet shawl closer around her, chilled by the cold bedroom. She could hear Pa calling her but made no move to go. Distracted, her eyes fell to his feet. He wore the shoepacks he'd made as they'd sat together about the fire these long winter nights, just the three of them in a warm circle of firelight—she, he, and Pa. That was what she craved—quiet companionship about the fire, not the forced frivolity before her. She swallowed down a sigh, a bit startled when he put his hands on her shoulders.

In the dimness, his face held a rare pensiveness. "Do you forgive me, Morrow?"

The heartfelt words returned her to the autumn day he'd first asked. "Forgive you?" she echoed.

"Do you forgive me—for my father's people?"

The humble question, now thrice asked, seemed to resound to the far corners of the room. Her lips parted in answer, but no sound came. She had a keen awareness of her own thudding heart. The pressure of his hands. The warmth in his eyes. Below, the frolic seemed to fade away.

"Yes."

Before the word even left her lips, she felt an unburdening deep inside her, a telling softening and healing. Tears shimmered in her eyes, and she sensed he was as moved as she. But the poignancy of the moment was broken when a footfall on the stair sounded and Jemima's strident voice rang out. With a gasp, Morrow stepped away, fleeing the dark room and pulling the door shut behind her.

"Well, it's about time I found you!" Jemima lingered on the bottom step, bedecked in red calico and a poke bonnet. "Major McKie's asking for you."

The unwelcome words had a numbing effect, and Morrow blinked back tears before coming downstairs. Taking a deep breath, she ushered her friend outside while fighting the urge to look back, to make sure she'd shut the door to her room. She mustn't give anything away, no matter how rattled she felt.

"Morrow, you all right?"

She ignored Jemima's probing, greeting people as they arrived. Moments before, she'd decided to decline the dancing. Her excuse was that she felt a bit poorly, hardly an exaggeration. She must avoid McKie at all costs. She simply wanted to sit on a bench near the bonfire, her eye on the cabin to make sure no one entered.

Nearby the major was speaking with her father. Her attention shifted from them to a militiaman unloading a barrel of cider from a wagon and another hefting a large sack of chestnuts for roasting. The barn doors were open, and she could see the tables laden with food, hear the sweet strains of a fiddle. Soon the clearing between the cabin and barn was filled with folks, mostly couples, in high spirits despite the swirling snow. Absently Morrow watched the flakes shake down and lay like lace upon her shawl, her thoughts on the attic, far from the festivities.

"Miss Little, you're looking like a Christmas angel."

Distracted as she was, she hadn't noticed the major at her elbow. Why was it, she wondered, that he always managed to make a simple compliment sound excessive? She thanked him and threaded her arm through Jemima's, afraid to be alone with him.

"I'd like to be your partner for supper, if you've not been spoken for," he said.

She simply nodded, wondering if Red Shirt watched her from upstairs. Once she thought she saw his silhouette, but when she looked again, it was gone.

The evening passed in a sort of trance. She was mindful of saying and doing the expected things but enjoying nothing, watching the slant of the moon to judge the time, finding reasons to return to the cabin. The bitter weather seemed to cooperate, calling a halt to the festivities earlier than planned. Half a dozen wagons pulled out of the yard and groaned as their wheels crushed the powdery snow, and the soldiers went about fetching their horses.

Suddenly McKie was at her father's side, his ruddy face perplexed. "I'm afraid I'm missing my horse."

Pa studied him for a moment and coughed hard into his handkerchief. "Your fine gelding? Perhaps he simply came unhobbled."

Standing near, Morrow watched as Pa took a lantern and headed past the paddock, the major in his wake. She inched closer to the porch and waved goodbye to those leaving, wishing Lizzy had come. Her friend had been wise to stay put at the fort, heavy with child as she was. A few Clays were in attendance, Lysander and Robbie tarrying longest. The sight of them, a girl on each one's arm, was the one glad note of the night. Perhaps Robbie had finally given up on her and sought solace elsewhere. Not once all evening had he spoken to her.

"Morrow Mary, I thought you'd mind your manners and ask me to stay the night like last time," Jemima told her, a rebuke in her gaze. "Don't you remember? 'Twas that frolic right before you went to Philadelphia."

The mere suggestion engulfed her with panic. "B-but the weather . . ." she stammered. "You'd best make a start for the fort. The Tates have opened their cabin and barn to any who want to stay the night there, and it's only a few miles from here."

Jemima looked down at the gathering snow, her black boots dusted white. "Maybe you're right. I'd hate to be snowed in here till spring."

She turned away, leaving Morrow to breathe a thankful prayer. *If only the remainder would do the same,* she thought. The crowd dispersed slowly, most traveling in wagons and bearing pitch-pine torches to brighten the dusk—all but half a dozen officers who waited for Major McKie. The saber points of their rifles glinted harshly in the light of the fading fire, and she began backing away from them, shivering.

From the shadows McKie cursed and followed Pa into the barn to borrow a horse. Apparently his fine gelding was nowhere to be found.

At the cabin door Morrow waited till all was quiet, the yard bare, before going inside. She took the steps slowly, feeling an unmistakable emptiness even before she entered her room. The buffalo coat—gone. The weapons along the wall—gone. The far window—slightly ajar. Weary, she lay down on her bed, fully clothed, her head on the pillow where his had once lain. The masculine scent of him still lingered . . . made her feel lost.

In time she heard Pa's footfall on the stair, and his shadow filled the doorway. Long moments passed as he pieced together the obvious. Did he think she was sleeping? Or did he sense her heart was so full she couldn't speak? Coughing, he withdrew.

A bitter breeze wafted through the open window, but she didn't want to shut it, as if doing so would shut away the memory of what had happened here. She wanted to hold on to the sweet feeling of forgiveness a little longer.

Slowly she pulled the colorful quilt around her, curling up on her side, throat tight. She dashed her tears dry with a corner of the quilt. The realization that Red Shirt had taken McKie's fine horse almost made her smile.

17

Would McKie never look away from her? She'd worn her plainest dress—a chestnut wool gown and prim bonnet that made her look sallow, Pa said. She didn't dare tell him she did so in a desperate effort to stem the major's ardor, a bit amused when Jemima told her how fetching it was. 'Twas the first Sabbath of the New Year, and they'd sped through the snow in the colonial cutter to reach Red River Station. Every pew in the frigid blockhouse was filled with a great many coughing, sniffling congregants, but she hardly noticed. All she felt was McKie's eyes on her, conveying shameful things that couldn't be uttered. Stiff with embarrassment, she watched Pa remove his Bible from the pulpit and resume his tortured hacking.

As the service ended and folks shuffled out into the bitter winter's afternoon, Morrow noticed Robbie Clay along the back wall, hat in hand, tarrying as if waiting to speak to her. But McKie intervened, asking if she'd received an invitation to supper. Before she could answer, an officer came and whispered in his ear, and he excused himself, leaving her alone. When she looked up again, Robbie had gone, and it was Lizzy who stood by her side, issuing an invitation.

"Morrow, you and your pa should come eat with us," she urged.

Gratefully, Morrow accepted, knowing Pa needed a rest and a warm meal before going home.

Later, as Abe and Pa sat sipping cider and talking in low tones at the trestle table, she helped Lizzy with the meal, marveling at the change in her friend. Dear, devoted Lizzy was lean no longer. From the voluminous look of her, she'd not last till spring. Morrow's thoughts took a wistful turn. *How would it be,* she wondered, *to belong to someone? To have a child on the way? How would it be to live as Aunt Etta lives—alone and likely to stay that way?*

As Morrow stood at the hearth stirring a skillet of fried apples, she noticed three extra places had been set. But before she could ask who else would join them, a knock sounded and Jemima swept in, followed by Major McKie and an unfamiliar soldier. Morrow felt a sudden, sweeping dismay. She'd felt safe here—she'd thought McKie had other matters to attend to . . .

At once the major's eyes sought her out, and his penetrating gaze told her she was as helpless as a hare in a snare, without a single hope of escape. Pa greeted them as the men removed their heavy wool coats, and Jemima her cape and bonnet.

Lizzy cast an apologetic look at Morrow, bending to take the biscuits from the bake kettle, and whispered, "Those three invited themselves, and there wasn't a thing I could do about it."

Morrow sighed, easily believing it of Jemima. She tried to master her distaste as Major McKie sidled up to her, wearing a hint of a smile as if making some great joke. "Miss Little, it's been much too long."

Unwilling to play along, she glanced at the small clock on the mantel. "'Tis been but half an hour since we saw each other at service, sir."

Sir. She used the term freely when she saw him, as it seemed to keep some distance between them. Though she sensed it nettled him, she felt it her only defense against his unwanted attentions.

He sat down beside her on the bench. "Aye, as I said, *much* too long, Miss Little."

She cast a quick look at him, noting his blue silk waistcoat with its silver-gilded braid. He was a man of means, she'd heard, a Virginian who'd condescended to come to the frontier only after Governor Henry himself assigned him. But no amount of finery could convince her that he was other than who he was. The butcher of Fort Randolph. Her growing fear of him rivaled her revulsion.

"I'm beginning to think you have an uncommon fondness for children," he said quietly.

Had he seen her admiring the newborns at Sabbath service? Nodding slightly, she glanced at the empty oak cradle awaiting Lizzy's babe. "Yes, I do."

"Have you given any thought to having a family of your own?"

She nearly squirmed. The question seemed so intimate she could hardly answer. "Well . . . I . . . perhaps . . . "

He leaned nearer, and she felt a flicker of panic. Would he propose to her here and now, before a roomful of people? He was so besotted with her, Lizzy once warned, that he spoke of her freely before his men. She sensed his preoccupation bordered on obsession and that he was about to do something rash. But at least Pa was here, and Lizzy and Abe, if things were to take such a turn . . .

He was so close she could smell the sour tobacco on his breath. "Pardon my presumption, Miss Little, but you seem ill-suited for the frontier."

She looked at him, not wanting to, fearing his bold eyes. "I—what do you mean, sir?"

"You seem to have been made for some elegant Virginia drawing room, not this crude, roughshod cabin." His eyes traced her every feature, finally falling to the striped kerchief that clung to her shoulders and neck. "I have a farm in Caroline County, Virginia. A plantation, if you will. In my mind's eye I keep seeing you there—pampered, with servants, doing little more than being a mother."

The picture he painted made her feel ill. He continued, perhaps mistaking her silence for consent. "I could, if you would just give the word, remove you from this godforsaken wilderness once and for all."

Wilderness. Is that all Kentucke was to him? She looked away, remembering something Red Shirt had said—there was no word for *wilderness* in Shawnee.

He leaned nearer. "I could take you away from here—you could forget all this."

Forget? He meant Ma and Euphemia and Jess, surely. She kept her eyes on her lap, her voice soft but steel-edged. "I'll never forget, Major. And so long as I think my brother might be alive, I'll never leave this place."

He drew back, the thin line of his mouth pinched. "Well, if it's any consolation, I plan to avenge your losses and return your brother to you in the future. You have my word as an officer and a gentleman, Miss Little."

A gentleman, indeed. She bit her lip to curb a hasty retort, her thoughts full of Fort Randolph and the unwilling woman he'd had his way with there.

He opened his mouth to say more, but it was Jemima who saved her. She came up behind them, looking almost matronly in a heavy gown of butternut wool, a mobcap on her head. "If you aren't too cozy with Major McKie, Morrow, perhaps I might introduce you to Captain Kincaid."

Morrow stood up, smoothing her heavy skirts with nervous hands. She looked at the man Jemima held on to almost possessively, noting his dark hair and narrow eyes and robust build. Was Lysander a thing of the past, then? "Pleased to meet you, Captain."

"I've heard a great deal about you, Miss Little," he replied, his voice laden with an Irish brogue. He reached for her hand and brought it to his lips.

Jemima's smile held little warmth. "I wondered if I should make introductions since Morrow is such a charmer, John. But I believe," she said, looking straight at Major McKie, "that she's been spoken for."

There was an awkward silence, and McKie smiled a bit smugly. Morrow studied Jemima, a knot of alarm in her chest. There was something different about her tonight. She returned Morrow's gaze with a look of unmistakable triumph. Perhaps, Morrow mused, she was simply proud of winning Captain Kincaid over, if indeed she had.

Lizzy called them all for supper just then, presenting a fine elk roast and a huge kettle of vegetables, fried apples, biscuits, and gravy. Morrow sat between the major and Lizzy, mostly playing with her fork and pushing Lizzy's fine supper around her plate. In the stale air reeking of boiled turnips and threaded with the cold damp of a dreary day, she felt like fleeing, her thoughts suddenly full of Red Shirt. She knew these men she supped with would not hesitate to kill him, yet she realized with a start that they were his inferiors in every way.

She listened as they talked of banal matters, aware of Jemima's eyes upon her across the table. In the candlelight, their green depths were hard and cold as river rock, and Morrow felt chilled. Jemima had never been as affable as Lizzy, though she and Morrow had been friends for a long time. But today Morrow felt they were friends no longer.

"Pastor Little, I'd like my personal physician to attend you," Major McKie was saying as Pa began coughing again. "Dr. Clary has had some success with cases of consumption."

Consumption. The mention of the malady was as unsettling as Jemima's coldness. Morrow felt her eyes flood, and she fought down the desire to escape the crowded cabin, suddenly made more unbearable by her fickle friend's scrutiny. But she stayed and picked at her pumpkin pie for Lizzy's sake. Lizzy, who worked so hard and wanted to please. As if aware of her angst, she passed behind Morrow and gave her shoulder a squeeze as she served Major McKie.

Pa quieted his coughing and took a sip of coffee. "I appreciate the offer, Major, but I doubt even your fine physician would be able to do much for me."

His honest admission pained Morrow further. At her elbow, the major swallowed a bite of pie and looked across the table again. "I was hoping you'd ride in today with my fine gelding. I suppose you've seen no sign of him since your frolic Christmas Eve."

"No, Major, I have not," Pa answered quietly.

An awkward pause held the conversation captive, and Morrow felt a prickle of alarm. Did McKie suspect who had stolen his horse? Why was he regarding Pa as if he were to blame?

"I'll wager some savage has him by now," Captain Kincaid said. "You've surely heard about the recent fiasco at Bryan's Station. A party of Shawnees crept in at night and lured a whole herd of militia mounts out with sugar lumps. The regulars standing watch were scalped."

There was a low rumble of displeasure around the table. Slowly, warily, Morrow looked at Major McKie. In the flickering candlelight, his face seemed strained, almost ashen. There was a telling shadow of desperation there, and then it faded. Did the others see it too? She set her fork down, unable to take another bite.

"The commander there is a sluggard and a sot," McKie said coldly. "You'll not find that happening on my watch."

At this she nearly smiled. *Oh, Major, but it did, truly. Your fine gelding is gone.*

Pa resumed his coughing, and Morrow stood, trying not to

give the impression that she wanted to flee. "If you'll excuse us, I must see my father home."

Major McKie helped her with her cape, standing by as they thanked Lizzy and Abe for the meal and bid them all farewell. But Jemima hardly acknowledged them, her rigid stance almost defiant. *What has come over Jemima?* Morrow wondered. *Has Pa noticed it too?*

Numb, she got into the sleigh. As they passed through the fort's gates, the sun thrust through the clouds and shone feeble light on her face. Pa guided the bay over the brilliant expanse of snow, his features troubled.

"Is McKie pressuring you, Morrow?"

She fixed her eyes on the woods opening up ahead of them, the snow-laden branches silvery white in the cold light. "He was telling me about his home in Virginia."

"Telling you he sees you as its mistress, I suppose."

She gave a nod, glad the hood of her cape partially hid her tense face, wondering how he felt about it all. Though he was never one to besmirch a person or give way to gossip, she sensed he wasn't any fonder of McKie than she. "Do you know what happened at Fort Randolph, Pa? When McKie was there, I mean?"

His grim expression told her she didn't need to repeat the incident. "Joe told me."

"Then you know how I feel about his attentions. I'm afraid of him. And now I'm beginning to wonder about Jemima."

He grasped the reins tighter. "Jemima will make a fine soldier's wife."

She sensed this was no compliment. Truly, Jemima seemed right at home among the arrogant army men, her prejudices hard and deep. Morrow held on to her hood as a gust of cold wind tried to tear it free. "I was afraid—for a moment at table—McKie was going to accuse you of taking his horse."

"I'll handle McKie, Morrow," he reassured her. "Think no more about it. We'll not be back at the fort for a spell, anyway. I've decided to postpone Sabbath services and singing school for the time being. Even McKie agrees it's not safe for us to come so far with fresh trouble brewing."

"Trouble?" she echoed.

"The horse stealing at Bryan's Station, among other things."

Lizzy's fine supper sat uneasily in her stomach. Any trouble brewing was mostly of McKie's making. Hadn't Abe just confirmed McKie's planned foray into Shawnee territory come spring? Was this why the major had boldly boasted of returning Jess to them? She shivered despite the heavy blanket around her shoulders and the warming pan of coals beneath her feet. Each meeting with McKie left her more shaken. She'd begun to realize why he'd been sent from the Kanawha to the Red River. He was a brutal man who would take brutal measures in stemming the conflict with the British and Indians. And she and Pa, like every other settler in Kentucke, would be caught in the crossfire.

As the sleigh sped them along far faster than the jolting wagon, she found herself almost lulled to sleep by its whispering haste, one thought uppermost in her mind. Thankfully, Red Shirt had healed beneath their roof and was even now on his way to Fort Pitt. Whoever was watching their cabin that cold night hadn't made trouble for them yet. And McKie seemed none the wiser about who had taken his horse.

18

As winter crept toward spring, there was a new lightness in Morrow's spirit, a contentment she'd never known. Could it be God was healing the bitterness she'd borne for so long? She felt a deep relief as it did its healing work and wondered if Pa noticed the change in her too. She studied him as she hemmed a petticoat by the fire, pained by the somber lines of his lean face. Since Red Shirt's leaving, he'd slipped into a sort of despondency she could not right. Even the promise of spring, with arbutus blooming and sap running, failed to rouse him.

He was anxious for word of the prisoner exchange Red Shirt had spoken of, she knew. But it was more than this, truly. The constant tug-of-war between settlers and Indians was taking a toll. Perhaps he felt caught in the middle, befriending the Shawnee only to be privy to the soldiers who wanted to remove them. He'd become so fond of Red Shirt over the years, while her own heart had been hardened. Why hadn't she seen the bond between them?

"I have a feeling we might not see Red Shirt again," he said, folding his copy of the *Virginia Gazette* and setting it aside. At her questioning look, he added, "It's becoming too dangerous with McKie and his ilk about. Joe said the woods are thick with scouts and spies, and they've been ordered to shoot the enemy on sight. I'm not sure the prisoner exchange will ever materialize."

"But we've been praying about it all winter."

"We'll keep praying, of course. But sometimes the Lord, in

His wisdom, withholds the very things we pray about lest they harm us in the long run."

She looked down at the sewing in her lap, a bit shaken. Red Shirt's words—his poignant apology—took on new meaning in light of the fact she might not see him again. Yet wasn't this what she'd wanted all along? Hadn't she once nearly begged him to stay away?

As thunder grumbled a warning outside and the patter of rain struck the shingled roof, Pa rose from his chair near the fire with hardly a glance at her. "I'd best go to bed, Daughter. 'Tis time to finish readying the fields for plowing on the morrow."

She glanced at a window. Daylight still limned the shutters, and she had no desire to go upstairs to her chilly bedroom, but he needed rest. Her forehead furrowed as she put her sewing away. Shouldn't he have started plowing by now? 'Twas almost time to start planting, surely. But with Joe away on a long hunt, he'd had little help about the place.

The next day she rose early to take care of as many of his chores as she could manage, seeing to the horses and straightening his tools about the barn while he was in the field. Coming out of the henhouse before noon, she was surprised to find an unfamiliar horse hobbled near the orchard. *Please, Lord, not McKie.* As she stepped onto the porch, she smoothed her hair with nervous hands, fumbling with the pearl-headed pins that kept her chignon in place.

At the table Pa sat with Robbie Clay. A decided dread crept into her heart as Robbie stood up, hat in his hands. She gave him a half smile and took off her cape, hanging it on the peg by the door. She'd not spoken with Robbie since the harvest supper at the fort, though he kept the back bench of the blockhouse occupied on the rare Sabbaths Pa preached. Why had he risked coming so far, she wondered? Was McKie away on another foray?

"Good afternoon, Miss Little."

She murmured a greeting and plucked a piece of hay from her skirt hem. "Would you like something to drink? Eat?"

"Nay," he said. "I just came to see your pa . . . you."

At this, Pa slipped out the back door, leaving her to gesture to the fire where two chairs waited. Robbie took a seat, and the air turned so tense she sensed this was no simple call. For a few moments she felt she couldn't breathe. Panic seemed to take wing inside her ribcage and smother her. She sank into her chair and saw not Robbie Clay but Red Shirt, in his fine linen shirt and buckskins, his glossy hair caught back in a queue, his hazel eyes full of light and feeling.

"Are you all right, Miss Little?"

She pressed her back against the chair rungs and tried to pretend she was. "Fine . . . thank you."

Robbie knotted his hands together, leaning closer. "I thought I'd best have my say before . . ." He left off, reddening as he struggled for words. "I know your pa's feeling worse and needs help about your place."

There was no denying this. She simply nodded, wishing Pa would come back inside.

"I ain't one to press my suit so hastily, but under the circumstances, I thought it best."

Press his suit? She said nothing, her discomfort deepening. What about the girl she'd seen him with Christmas Eve? She'd never considered him a suitor herself, just a onetime supper companion . . .

He went on, voice low. "I figure I could help you here while you take care of your pa. Then, when he's passed on, we could continue to farm this place and my own. You'd not have to leave home."

Her eyes fell to her hands in her lap. "Are you asking me to . . . marry you?"

He colored, as if realizing his wording had gone awry. "I am."

"Why, I . . . think of you as a . . . a friend." She groped for words, wanting to let him down lightly, though there was no softening the plain truth. "But I don't love you. And you don't love me."

The flush suffusing his fair features was an unbecoming red. "Love seems a secondary concern out here, if you ask me. Secondary to survival, that is." His green eyes swept the cabin as if assessing the trade he offered before coming to rest on her once again. "What say you?"

Her eyes misted with mortification. "I say . . . nay."

He sat up straighter, a plea in his eyes. "I've already spoken with your pa, and he's willing if you are."

Willing? Willing to trade me for a man's work? She squirmed in her chair, trying to find something to say that would ease the sting of being caught in the middle of a business proposition. Robbie was, she guessed, trying to do the best he could and ease her present predicament. But he didn't love her. And any feeling she might have had for him had quickly eroded, given his fear of McKie. Folks were even beginning to make sport of him in the settlement.

As he leaned forward in his chair and reached for her hand, heat crawled up her neck and face. A lock of flaxen hair fell over his high forehead, emphasizing his earnest eyes.

"Say you'll consider it," he said.

She swallowed hard, some childish part of her wanting to shout a refusal. Instead she looked down at his hand as it covered hers. Square and smallish, it was only slightly larger than hers, the dirty nails sorely in need of a trimming. When he came closer and kissed her flushed cheek, it took all her will not to push him away. A flash of anger dawned in his face and then disappeared. Unsteadily she stood and murmured a goodbye while he let himself out and rode away hard into the early spring sunshine.

All the twilight sounds that she loved seemed to set up a chorus outside the door he'd left open in his hurry to leave.

The tree frogs were the boldest, nearly masking Pa's entry. She felt oddly hurt when he said, "Robbie spoke with you, I suppose?"

She simply nodded, eyes on the orange flames licking the charred logs behind the dog irons. He came and stood beside her, so close she was cast in his slender shadow.

"Out of all the men you've said no to, Daughter, Robbie seems the most persistent, other than Major McKie." He sat down across from her, eyes steadfast. "He's willing to live here, and you'd not have to leave home. He has plenty of kin in the settlement, so you'd have family. He says he wants to be baptized."

Hearing it so neatly stated sparked something new and dangerous inside her. Turning to him, she said softly, "I want to know why you married my mother, Pa. Did you love her—or was she simply a business proposition?"

"Morrow—"

"You never speak of her, yet I need to know. Do you never mention her because she meant so much—or so little?"

He stood up so suddenly he nearly overturned his chair. But he wasn't angry at her impudence, he was hurt—she saw and sensed it plain. In the firelight his tired eyes were all aglitter, the deep lines in his face aggrieved. And her own heart spilled over and seemed to break with his beaten look.

"I'm a dying man, Morrow, and I want to see you safely settled."

The knot in her throat wouldn't let her speak. She simply shook her head, as if doing so could somehow reverse things as they stood and take away his racking cough and Robbie Clay's barren proposal.

His voice held firm despite the tears that wet his weathered face. "I loved your mother, Morrow, more than my own life. When she died, I wanted to be with her, to face the Shawnee, to take every arrow that took her away from me. There's not one day that passes that I don't rue being in the field when the Indians came—"

"But you couldn't have stopped them."

"Nay, but I'd have welcomed dying with her."

The heartfelt words filled the tense air between them, rendering it unbearable. With a cry she covered her face with her hands and rushed past him, taking the stairs two at a time. Once in her room, she fell across the feather tick and tried to shut away the pain in his face. But it remained, as firmly planted in her consciousness as Ma's lifeless body slumped across her spinning wheel, as real as Red Shirt's poignant plea for forgiveness in her attic room.

If she loved her father, wouldn't she do this thing? He was so ill—dying—desperate for help about the farm. Truly, love was secondary to survival in the settlements. A man and a woman needed each other for practical reasons, sentiment aside. Yet she'd always hoped for more, abiding by the notion that love was a rare and precious thing, not to be squandered by second best. An enduring love helped weather the storms of life, was a shelter and a shade and a delight. She longed for a biblical love like Jacob had for Rachel. Like Solomon had for his Shulamite bride. She wanted a love she'd be willing to die for . . . like Pa.

Oh Lord, help Thou me.

In the following days, they spoke no more about Robbie Clay's visit, though Morrow continued to dwell on it. When she weighed her reasons for refusing him, hoping to cast them aside, she began to realize the true cause of her reluctance. Something far more disturbing was dawning in her heart. Something so terrifying and unthinkable she pushed it down time and again, only to have it rise like cream atop milk. The memory of Red Shirt suddenly seemed to shadow her wherever she went. His hands upon her shoulders. The rich timbre of his voice. The intensity and warmth in his hazel eyes when he looked at her.

Oh Lord, what have I done? In giving him my forgiveness, did I also give him my heart?

The terrifying realization had come to her slowly, not fully flowering till she'd been forced to take a hard look at her future. Since Robbie Clay had ridden away, she'd spent several restless nights, crying and praying and trying to summon the nerve to do what she dreaded. Finally, as dawn crept into her room on yellow feet, she worked at the washbasin to remove all traces of another fitful night. But there was nothing to be done for her bloodshot eyes. Pa had only to glance at her to see her turmoil. Yet she felt a blessed numbness, as if crying so hard had leeched all the life out of her and made what she was about to do both sensible and bearable.

She found him on the porch, looking out on the orchard now dressed like a bride with its profusion of blossoms. Their showy beauty hurt her, nearly made her change her mind. The sweet scent of spring wrapped round them on a warm wind, full of hope and promise, drawing her thoughts elsewhere.

Sinking down on the steps, the crisp calico of her dress settling around her, she said with forced calm, "Pa, please forgive me . . . for saying the things I did after Robbie Clay came."

He nodded slowly. "Of course I forgive you."

"I've been praying about his proposal." She swallowed, unable to look at him lest she start crying again. "I know how important it is for you to see me settled. It seems my reasons for saying no have been selfish . . . foolish. So I've decided . . . I've decided it would be best . . ."

"Go ahead, Morrow," he said quietly when she paused.

Did he suspect what she was about to do? As she opened her mouth to say more, he began coughing again, nearly masking the sudden whoop from behind the barn. The sight of a familiar figure startled her to her feet. Pa let out a low chuckle as Trapper Joe emerged from the trees and into the clearing. He approached the cabin porch in his lazy, loping stride, leading a gelding and packhorse. At the sight of him, Morrow felt a sweeping relief. Pa's wan face filled with color, and he stepped off the porch to hug the grizzled woodsman hard, which only started a fresh fit of coughing.

A shadow of concern creased Joe's face, but he blustered like usual, "I ain't in time for breakfast, am I?" which made Pa chuckle again. Morrow disappeared inside to fry bacon and eggs, pouring them coffee while they waited and traded news.

"Miz Morrow, you ailin'?" Trapper Joe asked her outright when she reappeared on the porch.

She passed him a steaming plate. "I'm fine, Joe, truly."

But his steady stare told her he thought otherwise. She toyed with her own breakfast, hardly able to eat, and was glad when he turned his attention to his meal.

"I wintered up north in Kekionga on account of the heavy snows," he said. "Beats all I ever seen. There's tradin' posts and stables and gambling dens and taverns on all sides. Even got boardwalks on the streets for them fancy ladies that come from d'Etroit to shop and attend balls them Redcoats put on."

"I thought Kekionga was the principal village of the Miami tribe," Pa said, taking a sip of coffee.

"So it is. There's hundreds of people there, and Indians from nearly every tribe. You should see Michikiniqua's place—that's Little Turtle, the principal Miami chief. He's got glass winders and paintings from Europe, fine china and goblets, even a harpsichord. But what beats all is the six-seater privy made of plankin' out back."

Morrow worked up a smile, glad to see Pa so amused. Joe held up his plate for seconds, and she served him her own uneaten breakfast before refilling his coffee. "There's a heap of British and Canadian soldiers there—and lots of war talk, none of it good."

"The British are taking a beating, I hear," Pa said. "It seems General Washington has learned to fight like an Indian."

Trapper Joe chuckled. "I don't care to stir you up with all the tomfoolery I heard. But I do have one piece of news. For Miz Morrow, anyway."

At this, she sank into her churning chair, heart overfull. He took another bite of his bread and chewed thoughtfully, leaving them all on tenterhooks.

Finally he flashed her a knowing look. "Right there in the heart of Kekionga, in William Burnett's fine tradin' establishment, I ran into Red Shirt."

Morrow simply stared at him, little eddies of disbelief welling inside her.

Pa looked up from his coffee. "When was that, Joe?"

Joe wiped his mouth with his sleeve. "Near the end of February. Had a mountain of furs he was tradin' before goin' on to Fort Pitt. Said he was hammerin' out the details with the Indian agent there about that prisoner exchange they've been promisin'."

She opened her mouth then closed it as Pa asked the question she couldn't. "Was he well?"

"Fit as a fiddle, seems to me. Said somethin' about his winterin' with you on account of a shot to his shoulder."

The beloved memory now seemed sharp as broken glass. He *had* been with them, bringing life and color into their cold cabin—and his absence still chafed. A bittersweet flood swept over her, so intense she had to bite her lip to keep herself in check.

"He was here for a few weeks and then disappeared right before Christmas," Pa told him with a rueful smile. "On Major McKie's fine gelding."

"You don't say." Trapper Joe looked as pleased as if he'd done the deed himself. He cast Morrow another look. "He sent a little somethin' to you."

She couldn't hide her surprise. "Me?"

He got up and went around the cabin where his horses were hobbled. She followed, hands clasped behind her back, heart in her throat. He seemed to take an interminable amount of time finding what he'd promised, finally presenting a parcel tied with leather string. "Comes clear from Kekionga. I told him I'd get it to you safe and sound."

"Thank you, Joe," she managed, wanting to open it in private so he wouldn't see her pleasure—or her tears. But his eyes were pinned on her expectantly . . . as were Pa's.

She sat down again, prepared to share the gift with them but afraid they could see her hands shaking. What had come over her? Her thoughts were just as wayward. *He wrapped this package . . . selected its contents.* It seemed almost sacred somehow, tethering them across the miles, strengthening their tie.

She tore at the heavy paper, revealing a wealth of otter fur beneath. The luxurious skins had been crafted into a short cape, deep and dark and sparkling, with a tie of black silk ribbon at the throat. Holding it close, she felt an overwhelming anguish that he wasn't there to give it to her himself.

"He trapped and made it with his own two hands," Joe told her. "I asked him. Best put it on so I can see how it looks on you in case he asks me."

She obliged, settling it over her shoulders and tying the silk strings in front, marveling at its exquisite softness. "Fit for royalty, I reckon," Joe announced. "Looks mighty fine on you, Miz Morrow."

Pa studied her, but she avoided his eyes, afraid he would see what was hidden in their depths. "I'd best put it away," she said with a tremulous smile, gathering up the paper and string and going inside.

They resumed their talking while she went upstairs. Opening her wardrobe, she hid the lovely fur away and shut the door on it, only to take it out again. Giving in to her growing need of Red Shirt, she buried her face in its soft, glistening folds, pleased—and grieved—beyond measure. For now she was certain of just what she had to do.

The next morning Pa rose early to begin plowing and putting in the corn crop with Joe's help. Knowing how the day would tax him, Morrow had baked his favorite breakfast, leaving the iron kettle overnight in the hot ashes of the hearth. Lifting the lid, she set the spoon bread on the table, its crusty top dripping with melted butter. To her relief, he took two helpings. But no matter how hard she worked to feed him, the flesh just fell off his slender frame.

He seemed preoccupied this morning, saying little as she sat opposite him and made a pretense of eating her own breakfast. Joe hadn't appeared yet, and her eyes were drawn to the ticking clock overhead. She must tell him today, *right now*. Setting her own untouched plate aside, she took a steadying breath. Though she'd practiced the words in the privacy of her bedroom, her heart twisted with such turmoil she wasn't sure she could stumble through them.

"Daughter, are you all right?"

His tender concern seemed the final straw that nearly sent her crumbling. "Pa, I've . . ." She swallowed hard, clasping her hands together, blinking back the tears that lined her lashes. The tense silence seemed to beg her to reconsider. He leaned forward as if expectant, perhaps hopeful. He'd known such heartache . . . he only wanted to see her settled. Couldn't she give him this?

"Pa, I—I've decided to marry Robbie Clay." He sat back and nodded, face awash with something she couldn't name.

She stumbled on. "I think it's best if we wed quietly, without delay."

Before I give way.

He cleared his throat and for a few moments seemed to be groping for words. When he found them, they sounded almost as stilted and forced as hers had been. "Very well, Morrow. I'll ride to the fort and tell him."

She nodded and turned away, hearing Joe on the porch. He appeared in the open doorway, voice booming as she reached the landing to her room. "Mornin', Elias, Miz Morrow. I just remembered the news I should have told you about when I was here yesterday. Abe says Lizzy has delivered a fine son and wants you and your pa to come see them."

She tried to smile, to speak, but the words wouldn't budge. The silence lengthened uncomfortably until Pa said, "Well, that's fine news, Joe. I was planning on going to the fort tomorrow, anyway." He looked up at Morrow hovering on the steps, as if waiting for her to announce their own tidings. When she merely looked at him mutely, he mumbled, "I believe we have some news of our own."

The grizzled woodsman scratched his beard and waited. Speaking past the knot in her throat, Morrow said, "I'm going to be married . . . to Robbie Clay."

Joe seemed to be trying to work up a smile, eyes sharp. "Well, that's news, all right. When?"

She looked at Pa, so shaken by what she'd just committed to she couldn't answer.

"We'll find out tomorrow when we go to the fort," Pa said as matter-of-factly as if they'd just been discussing the weather. He reached for his hat. "Best finish that plowing. We've other business afoot."

19

Morrow leaned over the low wooden cradle by Lizzy's bed, her face awash with wonder. Besides Little Eli, this was but the second newborn she'd held, and the same sense of awe wrapped round her heart. The other women in the room seemed more interested in visiting with Lizzy and hearing the details of the birth instead of paying the baby any attention. All but Morrow.

"Go ahead," Lizzy urged, leaning back against the headboard. "Pick him up. He won't break."

"I reckon not," Jemima drawled in the too warm room. "He's heavier than a sack of shot, though I don't know why. You and Abe ain't nothing but broomsticks."

Gently, Morrow scooped him up, tucking his head under her chin. His fair scalp was peeling a bit and he had red blotches on his face, but she found him beautiful. He smelled a sight better than Little Eli, given Good Robe's generous applications of bear oil. A Shawnee custom, she supposed. But this baby, whom they were calling Jordan Abraham, smelled sweet as spring. Cradling him, an overwhelming longing washed over her.

She turned back to the bed. "You did fine, Lizzy. He's just beautiful."

"Fine?" Jemima snorted, looking askance at the baby. "I heard her screaming clear down to my cabin. You would have thought she was giving birth to a buffalo."

Lizzy blanched, and Morrow felt a flash of irritation. "Childbirth isn't for cowards, Jemima. Just you wait and see."

"And how would you know?" she demanded, her gaze hard as river rock again. "You ain't even been kissed."

Aunt Sally chuckled and drew Jemima aside as if to quell a coming confrontation. They spoke in low tones, leaving Lizzy to finish her conversation with Abe's mother and sisters. Morrow moved toward the door, standing in the fresh air, well away from the smoking grease lamps. Surely the dirty interior of the cabin couldn't be good for a baby. An infant needed clean, fresh air. A shaft of sunlight hit them, and he mewled like a kitten, melting into her. The weight of him was so soft, so warm. Already she rued releasing him.

Since arriving but an hour before, she'd tried to strike a normal tone with Lizzy and keep peace with Jemima, but the secret she was hiding weighted her like stone. Moments ago she'd seen Pa disappear into the tiny cabin that was Robbie's and shut the door. While she waited, she tried not to think of all its implications. The newborn she now held seemed a promise of her own. What would it be like to live with a man . . . carry his child? The prospect of being tied to Robbie in such an intimate way filled her with a near-smothering dread.

Lord, help me honor my word and make Pa's last days easier to bear.

She clenched her jaw till it hurt and looked out over the long rectangular common, so busy now that warmer weather was here. She could hear snatches of conversation amidst the dust and confusion within fort walls. War talk . . . always war. Both the one in the East and the one on the frontier.

Morrow stepped into the shade of the cabin eave as a man striding toward her came sharply into focus. The sun struck each polished brass button, highlighting his epaulets and tailored coat. She shrank back, alarm filling every inch of her. She hadn't seen Major McKie since the awkward supper in Lizzy's cabin. She'd heard—hoped—he was away on a foray with his men.

She clutched the baby closer, a bit frantic. It wouldn't do to step back inside the cabin. As much as she disliked McKie, she couldn't be rude and cause a ruckus. She must keep the peace, be civil. She was afraid of what he might do if she didn't.

"Miss Little, you make a fetching sight with an infant in your arms."

His voice mellowed to a smooth timbre when he spoke to her. She didn't return his gaze but instead glanced past him to Robbie Clay's cabin. He removed his hat and tucked it under one arm so he was able to take her free hand. When his cold lips touched her skin, she wanted to shudder.

"Good afternoon, Major McKie. You've returned early from your foray." Could the collected voice be hers? She sounded like a Philadelphia lady exchanging pleasantries with some fawning officer.

He looked pleased. "Yes, and a successful venture it was, I must say. How are things with you and your father on the Red River?"

She merely smiled, or tried to, but words were denied her.

His gaze was steadfast. "Peaceful, I trust. Not a savage in sight?"

The question rattled her beyond all reasoning. She murmured, "No trouble to speak of, perhaps on account of your coming." The lie seemed to burn her lips. What on earth made her flatter him? Fear, she guessed.

He looked smug, moving nearer and making her want to take a step back. "Is this Abraham and Elizabeth's infant? Let me see."

To her surprise, he took the baby from her, holding him aloft so that his tiny head lopped to one side. Clearly, the major was more accustomed to drilling soldiers than holding babies. Was he trying to convince her otherwise, leave her with the impression that he was a family man, fond of children? She reached out to take the baby back, but Alice appeared, coming up behind them and fussing over her nephew.

"Here, let me have him," she said. "I've hardly had the chance to hold him with all these womenfolk about. And I'm his aunt!" She disappeared inside the cabin, leaving them alone in the dust and sunlight.

McKie wasted no time in coming to the point. "I must speak with your father. Is he within?"

"N-no, with Robbie Clay," Morrow blurted, adjusting her straw hat so that it shielded her face from his steady gaze.

His gaze was sharp. "Robbie Clay?"

"He . . . they have some business to discuss." Only then did she realize she'd misspoken.

His eyes swung to the far cabin Pa had entered, and his countenance seemed to harden. Did he suspect what their business was about? If he knew, would he try to stop them?

She saw Lysander Clay emerge from the blockhouse that served as McKie's quarters, his swagger evident in broad daylight. She'd heard Robbie's younger brother had recently joined the army, anxious to serve under McKie. Joe said he was a chief's man, though she didn't know what that meant. Light-headed, she excused herself and hurried back inside with Lizzy and the cluster of women as Lysander huddled with McKie.

In moments Pa appeared in the doorway, telling her it was time to go. Having admired the new baby when they'd first arrived, he now seemed anxious to return home. Or was his news for her making him hasty?

She mounted the gentle Dollie, while beside her Pa's black stallion snorted and stomped, making the mare shy away. Pa had some trouble bringing him round, but at last they rode out. Signs of the coming summer were everywhere, wending the season's spell in the honeysuckle and blackberry vine, in the thickly leafed trees and strengthening slant of the sun. But the beauty was lost to her as she waited to hear what it was Pa had to say.

"Robbie wants to wed you at week's end, Morrow. At our cabin."

Setting her jaw again, she simply nodded, eyes drifting to the rutted excuse of a road as they climbed a gentle swell of bluegrass and the fort disappeared from sight. He seemed to choose his words carefully as if knowing they would nettle her. "He wants no witnesses."

Beneath the brim of her straw hat, her pale face felt strained. "I . . . Major McKie shouldn't know."

He nodded. "There might be trouble, feeling as he does about you. I don't like wedding you under such circumstances. It's not as I hoped it would be . . ."

Not as you *hoped?* The bitter thought brought about a rush of emotion so intense she had to bite her tongue to stem her tears. Turning her face away, she felt for her handkerchief, grateful as they moved into the newly leafed shadow of an oak so he couldn't see her struggle. She was days away from being wed. Given this, why couldn't she put down these confusing feelings about Red Shirt? Why, as the days passed, was her heart so completely *his*?

"I'm glad of one thing," he told her. "When I see how you are with Little Eli and now Lizzy's babe, I know without a doubt you were meant to be a mother. A wife."

Shamed, she looked away. How could she give voice to the fact that she'd already given in to the sweetness of both? In her heart of hearts, she was already wed. And it wasn't Robbie Clay she'd surrendered to . . .

"With you married, I won't have to worry about returning you to Philadelphia should I go to the prisoner exchange with Red Shirt," Pa said. "Being on the trail in peaceful times is grueling. In times of war . . ." She glanced at his bearded profile beneath the shadow of his felt hat, knotting her hands in her lap, trying to stem her turmoil. "I'll say no more except that I'll be glad to see you settled."

He began to cough so hard she had to take his reins. His words washed over her, stirring up new worries instead of settling them. She was marrying to please him, to gain an extra hand about the farm. But he'd soon be gone, leaving her tethered to a man she didn't love. And pining for the man she did.

Her wedding day dawned clear, sunlight streaming in and waking her long before she wanted. Full of birdsong, it seemed to mock her with its bright beauty. She'd hardly slept, thinking it the last night alone in her bedroom. Sitting on the edge of the feather tick that had hardly held Red Shirt, she let her mind roam in shameless ways. *Perhaps tonight, my wedding night, if I shut my eyes . . . I could pretend . . .*

She eyed the chamber pot, thinking she might be sick again. How would she ever make it till four o'clock, the appointed time? Across the room her wardrobe yawned open as if awaiting her choice of a wedding dress. The day before, she'd tried to pick a gown, her reluctant hands avoiding the velvet. It hung unworn, a testament to things loved and lost. Perhaps she'd make her firstborn a little gown from it—a christening dress. But even the thought of that hurt her, and she shut it away.

She heard the closing of the door below as Pa went out. Was he as restless as she? They hadn't spoken of what would happen this day, but it seemed to be all they thought about, the prospect hovering like a storm cloud between them. Surely he sensed the upheaval in her heart. Over the years he'd wed so many couples—for all sorts of reasons. Perhaps he hoped that, given time, she'd grow to love Robbie. Or had he, like she, realized her true feelings and seen this as the only choice?

Lord, help me be a willing bride. Help me to forget about what I can't have and be thankful for what's before me.

"You look lovely, Morrow."

As she came down the stairs at half past three, Pa stood at the hearth in a pressed shirt and black breeches. The brocade waistcoat she'd made him at Christmas fit a bit loosely, but his linen stock was neatly folded in ivory lines, making him look every inch the earnest pastor. She tried to smile at him through her tears, taking a quick glance about the cabin to make sure Robbie hadn't come yet.

The front door was open, and a warm breeze stirred the fine yellow cloth of her dress. It cascaded around her, the hem a bit too long, but beribboned and lacy as a bride's dress should be. She'd wanted to wear a veil like Lizzy had done, if only to hide her distress. Beneath its lacy folds, Robbie wouldn't notice if she cried or trembled or was pale. But the east side of the cabin had turned up little in that way, so she'd remained bareheaded . . . and bare hearted.

"Don't you want some flowers, Morrow? There are some early roses budding around the side of the cabin," he told her.

But she simply shook her head, clutching an embroidered handkerchief.

"Did you speak to Lizzy—anyone—about this?" he asked.

"No, Pa."

Only Joe knew, and he was remarkably closemouthed where they were concerned. Going to the hearth, she sat down in her chair. He took his own seat across from her, and she realized they had no third place for Robbie. Perhaps he'd bring some of his own things from the fort. But the idea of him sitting there, breaking in on the circle she and Pa had shared for so many years, struck her as strange. Deep down she knew he didn't belong here, but what was she to do?

"Morrow, I need to talk to you . . . about a wife's duty to her husband."

Duty? His pained tone set off every alarm bell inside her. Heat flooded her face, and she felt she might be sick again. "Pa . . . *please*."

"I know it's a woman's place to tell you about such things." He reached up and loosened his too-tight stock, color high. "Since you're lacking a mother's influence, I'll have to do what I can."

Oh, why hadn't she asked Lizzy? She was woefully ignorant about these matters of the heart, yet having Pa tell her such things made matters worse, not better.

"A husband has certain—"

She shut her eyes, hearing the drum of horse hooves crossing the clearing. Pa was spared his sermonizing, at least. With a last look at her, he pulled himself out of his chair and went outside to meet Robbie while she stood on shaking legs. *Oh Lord, help me!* She felt she was sinking in a pit of despair and desire, longing for one man while giving herself to another. And she knew it was wrong—a lie, a cruel deception she wouldn't want inflicted on anyone. She felt sudden sympathy for Jacob, who'd mistakenly wed the unlovely Leah instead of his beloved Rachel. Had his grief been as great? Reaching out a hand, she clutched the arm of her chair.

Lord, help me do what pleases You. And Pa.

She braced herself for what she'd pledged to do, but it wasn't Robbie's voice she heard across the threshold, just Joe's. His gruffness reached clear inside the cabin, calling her out onto the porch. She stood in the doorway, looking out at them in the greening yard, trying to hear what it was they said.

Pa turned to her, face grim. "There's to be no wedding, Morrow, at least not today."

She leaned against the door frame, light-headed with shock. No wedding . . . no wedding night. No pretending to be willing. She started trembling again, this time out of profound gratitude.

Joe came to stand under the porch eave, one cheek swollen with tobacco. "Accordin' to Abe, Lysander got wind that Robbie was going to marry you and took it to the major. And McKie, smitten with you like he is, decided he needed a few more men on this next foray, so Robbie was pressed into service."

Pa stifled a cough. "Where's McKie headed, Joe?"

"Across the Ohio. Abe's been left in charge of the fort while they're away. He ain't sure how long this campaign's going to be. Months, maybe."

"Sounds like they're moving into Shawnee territory like McKie planned."

"That's what I suspect," Joe said.

Pa passed a hand over his beard. "I suppose this means the prisoner exchange is off."

Leaning over, Joe spat into the grass. "I wouldn't get your hopes up about anything peaceable happenin' once McKie crosses that river."

Morrow looked at Pa, saw him struggle to maintain his composure in the face of such crushing news, and her heart twisted. Turning away, she hurried inside and up the steps to her room to shed her dress. A dozen different thoughts rumbled through her mind, leaving her breathless and spent. She was stunned and sorry Robbie had been waylaid by McKie, yet so elated by the delay she felt ashamed. But she knew her gladness was to be short-lived. When Robbie returned . . . what then?

Opening her wardrobe, she reached into its shadowed corner and took out the fur wrap. With a prayer for forgiveness on her lips, she buried her face in its softness and wept, her feelings so tangled she couldn't begin to unravel them.

20

Where, Morrow wondered, had summer gone? To find her answer, she had only to take stock of the cribbed corn, the abundance of root vegetables stored in straw in the springhouse, the first kegs of cider and salted meat. With the harvest in, everything seemed to have ground to a halt. There were no more letters from Aunt Etta. No more news of McKie away on the foray that had halted her wedding to Robbie Clay. No word from Surrounded or Red Shirt. Everything on the Red River was sameness and stillness and peace. Though she remained calm on the surface, she was worn with worry underneath. Awaiting word of Robbie Clay's return seemed to strip away her joy bit by bit. Every day left her thinking the same thing. This could be the hour he came back. Any moment they might wed.

As she walked to the river to bathe, one bare foot skimming the water, she felt autumn in its cold rushing. She was careful to stay close to shore, recalling how the river had almost made her a watery grave. Thoughts of Red Shirt seemed to hover as she relived the moment he'd brought her out of the river. The memory was growing a bit dusty, as were his words to her in the attic before he'd disappeared. But the feeling he wrought—and she fought—remained.

Months had passed since he'd ridden away on McKie's fine horse. Not once had they seen so much as his shadow. His absence spelled something momentous, surely. Had he severed all ties with them, given the escalating conflict? Or had he taken up with the British again as Pa feared? Though they rarely spoke of him, she sensed he was often in Pa's thoughts, and it seemed they danced around the unspoken possibility he'd been wounded or even killed since seeing Joe at Kekionga last winter.

Oh Lord, wherever he is, please let no harm come to him.

Heartsore, she finished her bath and returned to the cabin to comb out her damp hair and secure it atop her head. But the heavy locks kept spilling down in wayward wisps about her face and neck despite an abundance of pins. As she rummaged through her wardrobe, she was careful not to stray to the fur shawl, instead picking the first dress her fingers touched. 'Twas a badly wrinkled sprigged muslin, light and airy and begging for the clothespress. She put it on anyway, liking the pale blue flowers that bloomed across the carnation-colored fabric and the way the rounded neckline was ruched with a deeper blue ribbon. She considered donning a kerchief to better cover up. But no one was about, save Pa.

"Morrow, I'm going out to the pasture to see to the horses," he called from the bottom of the stairs.

She called out an acknowledgment and then, feeling hemmed in by the shadows, went out into the orchard. There amidst the tangle of lush limbs and late apples where she hoped to find solace, she simply found a deeper sadness. Why was it that everywhere she went, Red Shirt's memory seemed to shadow her? Why was he even now so indelibly engraved on her heart? Here it was no different. She was cast back in time to the day he'd stood with her while she dipped candles, talking of Jess and sharing things she'd shared with no one, not even Pa.

In the lengthening shadows, the sweet sound of a dove calling for its mate carried on the wind. She paused, waiting for the answering call. The cooing came again, as lonesome and full of yearning as she herself felt. Still, no answer. Clasping her hands behind her back, she began walking slowly toward the depths of the orchard, wanting a look at the lonely dove. A sudden movement through the trees made her start, and she saw a telling flash of brown.

She swerved toward the shadow, but he was faster, the heavily laden branches swallowing him from sight. A bit dazed, she ran after him but within moments didn't know who was pursuing whom. They chased each other in dizzying circles till she wanted to fall to the ground, pleasure pumping through her, completely out of breath.

I must be dreaming . . .

She felt a sweet, bubbling relief that Red Shirt stood before her, hale and hearty, when she feared he'd never do so again. Without Pa's watchful presence, she took stock of him inch by inch, feeling she'd somehow earned the right after so much time apart. His hard jaw was clean shaven, the black silk of his hair damp from a washing and looking freshly combed, his amber eyes flickering warm as a hearth's fire. He was, she noticed, hardly winded.

Breathlessly, she said, "I heard a dove calling for its mate. But now I think that dove was you."

There was a hint of a smile in his eyes. "I was waiting for you to answer."

"I can't make birdcalls."

"I could teach you."

He seemed to be drinking in the sight of her as well, and she felt a certain shyness without her shawl. Yet she sensed he needed to see something soft and womanly and feminine. She was suddenly glad of her tumbled hair and bare shoulders and beribboned dress. And then a feeling of shame swept through her. No man had ever seen her so unkempt.

Her smile faded. "You must be tired—hungry."

"Mostly thirsty," he said, looking toward the cabin.

"Come in and I'll get you some cider. Pa's in the pasture but should be back soon."

"How is he?" The concern in his face was so telling, tears came to her eyes. He said quietly, "That's answer enough."

Shifting his rifle to his other arm, he took her elbow and walked with her to the cabin. The pressure of his callused hand seemed to steady her, and she felt a deep contentment. "I wasn't sure we'd see you again."

"I can't stay long. Overnight, perhaps. I need to talk to your father."

"He's been a bit downcast about the prisoner exchange."

He nodded in understanding, the lines about his eyes creasing as he squinted into the setting sun. "Everything is unraveling. From the war in the East to the trouble here in Kentucke and Ohio's middle ground. I'd not thought to see it come to this."

"Isn't there peace anywhere?" she wondered aloud.

"Here," he said, looking down at her.

For the briefest moment their eyes met. She'd not considered how welcome their cabin might look to him, hungry and tired as he surely was from a long journey. In a world where nothing seemed safe or peaceful or good, was their home on the Red River a refuge? Her eyes trailed to the shoulder Pa had tended so carefully last winter, wondering if it still ailed him.

"How is your wound?"

"Never better. I have you and your father to thank for that."

"I was afraid, when you didn't come back . . ."

He smiled and looked away from her, eyes scanning the clearing and woods before they passed inside. "I've lived a score or more years thus far. I intend to live another score or better."

Twenty or so to her nineteen. She'd been wondering just how old he was. Now she tucked the knowledge away like a keepsake to save. He lay his rifle on the trestle table alongside his powder horn and shot pouch while she fetched a crock of cold cider from the springhouse. By the time she'd returned, Pa was back, the pleasure on his face at seeing Red Shirt so heartening she found herself near tears again. They embraced, and she stood apart, surprised at how easily they took to being together again.

As she warmed leftovers from supper, they sat by the hearth and talked unceasingly in low tones, broken only by Pa's bursts of coughing. The contrast they made wrenched her heart. Red Shirt exuded strength and health and vitality, magnifying Pa's decrepit condition. *Not much longer now*, her soul seemed to whisper.

Toward nightfall she sensed Pa was growing weary. Before the mantel clock struck seven, he was asleep in his chair, head tipped to his chest, while Red Shirt sat across from him and quietly cleaned his rifle.

"I've made you a bed in the barn," she said, wishing he'd not insisted upon it. "But I'd rather you stay in the house with us."

"I'll not take your bed again," he replied, wiping down the barrel with a piece of tow linen she'd given him. "Feather ticks are for females. I prefer the hard ground."

She gave him a half smile, watching as he loaded his rifle. "I'm afraid Tansy isn't very good company. Not to mention all those horses."

"You should show me which stall is mine," he said, finishing his task.

Standing, he cast a long shadow in the last of the flickering firelight, and she moved toward the door ahead of him. The smell of rain was in the air, and they looked toward a surly sky thick with thunderheads. The wind was picking up, promising a stormy night. Her eyes roamed over the broad lines of the barn, a black silhouette in the gloom, and a new worry pricked her.

"I'm afraid Pa hasn't been able to fix the barn roof. You might spend a damp night."

He smiled, his teeth a flash of white in his tanned face. "Do I look like I mind a little rain, Morrow?"

The question seemed an invitation to look at him, and she

did just that, taking in his worn buckskins and clean if fraying frocked shirt. How many stormy nights had he spent in the weather, she wondered? She'd yet to spend one. Opening the barn door, she realized she'd forgotten a lantern, but she slipped into the shadows anyway, showing him the first stall in a gesture she now knew was completely unnecessary.

He leaned his rifle against a post before he turned back to her. "I wanted to talk to you away from the cabin. Your father . . ." He hesitated as if well aware how the mention hurt her. "Your father is concerned for you. What will you do when he's gone?"

She looked away, feeling small and uncertain standing there before him. "I—I don't know."

He asked quietly, "Will you marry?"

Her heart clenched in alarm. Had Pa told him of Robbie Clay? She felt a bit sick at the thought. "I can't think of marriage now, not with Pa so ill."

"Why not let him choose?"

She took a deep breath, daring a look at him, wanting to share her heart. "A husband, you mean?"

"Some practice it. Love comes in time."

In time . . . She didn't have much time. Robbie Clay would be back any day. She looked away, trying to tamp down her heartache, the intimate question on the tip of her tongue begging to be answered. "Do you have a . . . woman?"

For a moment she thought he might say yes, and she tensed.

"No," he finally said.

A bittersweet relief swept through her. Here and now, in the shadowed barn, nothing seemed to matter but the two of them. Every obstacle seemed to fade away. All the barriers between them turned to ashes with that one definitive *no*.

He leaned back against a post while she clasped her hands together and tried to summon the will to walk away. But the ensuing silence was rife with a hundred heartfelt things, each wooing her to stay. How different this was than the first time, when he'd surprised her in the barn and she'd run away from him. Was he remembering it too?

Looking down at the hay strewn about her feet, she felt his fingers graze her cheek and brush back the wisps of hair that had come free of her pins. She nearly shivered, yet the warmth of his hand seemed to reach clear to her heart. Was the sigh she heard his—or her own?

Slowly she looked up and his hand fell away. Without thinking, she reached for him again, needing his warmth and strength, and returned his callused palm to her flushed cheek. Despite the darkness, she sensed his surprise, and it matched her own as he ever so carefully closed the distance between them.

"Morrow . . ."

He was so close he could lower his face into her hair and breathe in the rose scent of her if he wanted to. He'd not dishonor her, he'd once said. She didn't rightly know what that meant, yet she almost wanted to find out. She was on dangerous ground, all her feelings tied in knots, her genteel ways fraying like silk thread. She felt the pressure of his other hand warm about her waist . . . his breath on her cheek . . . his fingers cradling her chin and drawing her in.

Oh Lord, I am lost.

She shut her eyes and waited for his mouth to meet hers. But in that achingly sweet instant, another sound rent the stillness. The barn door groaned open, and Pa's coughing filled the air with unwelcome fury. Red Shirt stepped away from her, and she whirled to face her father, so bereft she felt ill.

"Morrow, you all right?"

Had he seen their near embrace? "I—I was just coming back."

"It's going to storm," he said, leaning against the heavy door.

She went to him and, without another look back, shut the heavy door behind them with shaking hands. Walking across the dried grass of the clearing was an agony, for she'd left her heart in the barn. Pa took the porch steps slowly as if trying to get his breath, and she struggled for composure before the cabin lamp revealed her turmoil. Once inside, he didn't go straight to bed as she'd hoped but took a seat at the hearth and watched as she finished burying the coals for the morning's fire with a small shovel.

He passed a hand over his beard, voice solemn. "Are you in love with Red Shirt, Morrow?"

Stricken, she looked up, eyes awash. His face held a startling frankness that insisted she respond in kind. "Pa, I think you've misjudged us. We have a fine friendship, nothing more."

He hesitated, eyes grave. "I've seen the way he looks at you. I'd have to be blind as well as consumptive not to notice."

And just how does he look at me? She felt herself go hot and cold all over and fixed her eyes on the floor. Could he see what she tried so hard to hide? His curiosity—and questioning—seemed to strip her nearly naked and expose all her raw emotions.

"If I might be so bold, did Red Shirt ask for your hand?"

Setting the shovel aside, she said, "No, Pa. Why would he?"

"Why would he? Heaven has blessed you with a fine face and figure, and intelligence and grace besides. Nay, the question is, why wouldn't he?"

She sat down across from him, her hands twisting in her lap. "He merely asked if I'd given any thought to the future . . . to marriage." She swallowed hard. "He suggested I let you choose for me—a husband, I mean."

"And what did you say?"

"I . . ." What had she said? The memory only deepened her embarrassment. "I—I asked if he had a—a woman."

His eyebrows rose to sharp peaks, and she looked away, mortified at what she'd done. In the barn, the question seemed innocent enough, but now it seemed like she'd thrown herself at his feet in the asking. Was that what Red Shirt thought? Pa did, surely.

"Daughter, need I remind you that you're as good as betrothed?"

Betrothed. She smoothed her wrinkled skirt, grasping for words. "I . . . I . . ."

The clock ticked, and he began coughing again, bringing an end to their excruciating conversation. She helped him into bed before fleeing to the privacy of her room, where she knelt and tried to pray away her shame. But it remained, as did her wayward feelings for the man who was bedded down in the barn and would likely be gone come morning. Though she'd fought it, and would continue to do so, he'd become entrenched in her heart in ways she couldn't explain.

All she knew was this. Forgiveness was one thing. Falling in love was another.

21

She awoke to the sound of voices—Pa's low and broken by his rumbling cough, and the slower, measured cadence she was coming to know as Red Shirt's. For a few moments she lay lost between sleep and consciousness, thinking she'd only dreamed she'd heard him, and then their near embrace in the barn came rushing back. If Pa hadn't come in . . . what then? The shame she'd felt hours before had given way to an undeniable yearning in the night, and she'd finally surrendered to all its implications. She was deeply in love with him. Pa knew. And perhaps Red Shirt did too.

It was so early the light of day had only just begun to touch the treetops and her rain-streaked windowpane. The storm of the night before had been banished by a breathtaking swath of pink and gold sky. She lay abed till the voices ceased, then got up and dressed with such haste she could hardly manage her buttons. When she came down the steps, making a clean sweep of the empty cabin, she tried to not let her anticipation show.

"Morning, Morrow," Pa said as he came inside.

Her smile faded as she looked toward the door he'd left open.

"He's gone," Pa told her, "though he didn't say where he was headed. 'Tis probably safer left unsaid."

Safer, indeed. For my heart . . . and his. Near tears, she turned away. He cleared his throat as if about to speak, and she nearly winced. *Please, Pa, say no more about my being betrothed.* The very word was hateful to her now, as was her next anxious thought. Had he told Red Shirt about Robbie Clay? Could that be why he'd left without saying goodbye? Thinking he might have, her chest constricted so painfully she felt she couldn't breathe.

She held off going to the barn till after breakfast. Once there she collected the quilt atop the fresh hay that had made his bed, lingering near the wooden post he'd leaned against before he'd reached for her in the darkness. Oh, to cast back time and regain the feeling of his hand upon her cheek, his arm warm about her waist, the tender way he'd whispered her name . . .

She heard Pa's boots on the porch, and then his coughing grew more distant. He'd gone out to the field, she knew. She wanted to be as certain of Red Shirt. Not knowing where he was left her with an unfinished feeling that was nigh unbearable. Leaning against the rough barn wall, she wrapped the quilt around her as if it could keep his memory close, and wept.

Oh Lord, bless him, protect him. Please let no harm come to him.

By week's end, Joe brought word that McKie and his men had just returned from across the Ohio, having burned four Shawnee towns to the ground. The entire Kentucke territory, on tenterhooks for months, now seemed to be hurtling toward the long-dreaded wilderness war. As Joe related the grim news, Pa sat down on the porch step, looking spent.

"Red Shirt told me McKie had crossed into Shawnee lands, but he spared me the details. What really happened up north, Joe?"

"A trapper friend of mine just come from there and saw one of the villages firsthand—or what's left of it," Joe said tersely, leaning over to spit a stream of tobacco juice into the dirt. He looked at Morrow. "Maybe Miz Morrow should go inside."

But she stayed where she was, surprising them both when she said, "Fleeing from the ugliness won't change it any, Joe. I'd rather stay."

He took a deep breath and looked away as if envisioning the carnage. "McKie's men struck when most of the chiefs and warriors were away at a tribal council upriver. The soldiers shot down mostly women and children—them that couldn't get away. Scalped 'em too. I won't tell you what they did to the young squaws. Then they set fire to the village and destroyed all the crops they could. Cut down a couple hundred acres of corn, it's said."

Morrow looked toward the river, the sunlit water a blur of blue. Pa's voice sounded grieved. "What of Surrounded's town?"

"That'll be next, from what I hear. Sounds like McKie spent a lot of time up north scoutin' and surveyin'. No Indian town is safe."

Pa coughed into his handkerchief and worked to draw a breath. "Surely the Shawnee know what's to come. I've heard General Washington wants to award tracts of western land—Ohio, mostly—to veterans of the French and Indian War. McKie and his ilk are merely clearing the way."

"I heard the same," Joe said. "But don't think the Shawnee will lay down and let 'em. Some of these destroyed towns were something of an easy target, bein' the first Shawnee villages to come upon across the Ohio. The other ones are harder to find. Surrounded's is the farthest west, for good reason."

Was it? Far out of the reach of the whites? Was that where Red Shirt had gone? Morrow toyed with the hem of her apron, fingering the fine lace now fraying from repeated washings.

"You can bet Black Snake—their war chief—is headed this way. Surrounded is one of the Kispokos, remember. Won't take 'em long to gather their forces and come down, madder'n yeller jackets busted out of their hives." Joe turned and spat again as if to emphasize his words.

Morrow felt chilled. But it wasn't word of an impending attack that set her on edge. Joe's words, long dreaded, set her head to spinning. Robbie Clay was on his way home, as was Major McKie. She was still betrothed, about to wed. No matter that months had passed and she'd given her heart to another. Her commitments came rushing back, cast in stone, sickening her with all their implications.

She stood, her mind on anything but what she was about to say. "You'd best stay for supper, Joe. I've made a heap of chicken and dumplings, and you can take home what's left to Good Robe and Little Eli."

He shifted his rifle to his other arm. "Hungry as I am, there ain't gonna be any leftovers. But it's mighty kind of you, Miz Morrow, just the same."

The next day turned stormy. The air was heavy with the threat of a hard rain, and lightning split the expanse of black clouds above, reflecting Morrow's inner turmoil. Hardly able to keep her mind on her chores, she made a pretense of calm for Pa. Standing in what remained of her vegetable garden, pumpkin vines twisting around her feet, she absently took stock of late summer's bounty, her dress hem damp from a heavy dew. But her thoughts were tainted with the certainty that Robbie Clay would ride in at any moment.

She now felt she was in the midst of a dangerous game. No longer was it just she and Robbie Clay and Major McKie, but also Red Shirt. With McKie having pressed Robbie into service the first time, there was no telling what he might do next if their plans to wed went ahead. Her dilemma had kept her awake most of the night, and she now felt benumbed with weariness and worry.

Bending over, she picked up a small pumpkin for a pie, setting it outside the paling fence before searching the dewy ground for a gourd or two. When she straightened, she saw Joe standing with Pa in the pasture. From their slumped shoulders and the intensity of their expressions, she knew something was amiss. Her heart hammered harder, its cadence felt clear to her temples. Slowly they began to walk toward her, and it seemed an eternity before they reached the edge of the garden.

"Morrow, come inside the cabin," Pa said.

Forgetting her task, she did as he bid. Her first thought was of Red Shirt. *Oh Lord, whatever it is, please let it not be him.* The possibility was so terrifying she nearly broke down before she reached the porch. Beneath Pa's creased face was a telling shadow of alarm. Once inside, she turned to him, realizing Joe had slipped away.

"McKie and his men have returned to the fort," he told her. "But not everyone came back."

She took the words in, relieved that no mention had been made of Red Shirt, though her stomach still clenched with alarm. A fit of coughing shook Pa, and it was another agonizing minute before he finally said, "During the raid on one of the Shawnee towns, McKie put Robbie Clay at the front of the charge. He was shot down straightaway."

Shot down . . . dead? The words seemed to ring in her ears without end. Stunned, she sank down on the bench by the door. First the killing of the Shawnee along the Kanawha, and now this. "Oh, Pa, I'm to blame. If I'd not accepted him—agreed to marry him—"

"No, Morrow. You couldn't have known it would come to this."

Though she tried to stay stoic, she started to cry. "Why doesn't someone stop him? Why is McKie allowed to get away with murder and treaty violations and—"

"Red Shirt says McKie has approval from Congress to rid

Kentucke and the middle ground of Indians no matter what the treaties say. By any means necessary. Using whatever men necessary."

"So he can do whatever he pleases without punishment? Without fear of judgment? Robbie Clay was a farmer, not a soldier!"

"God will be his judge, Morrow." He sat down beside her, looking spent although the day had just begun. "McKie was wounded in the fighting—his arm, Joe said. He's recovering at the fort. I'm grieved things had to end this way. I know you didn't care for Robbie, though I'd hoped you would in time."

They sat in silence till the fire needed replenishing and his coughing called for more medicine. Thunder boomed a warning, and then the skies seemed to split open, pouring forth a heavy rain that cast the cabin in such deep shadows she scrambled to light candles.

"Pa, what do you suppose will happen next?" Her words were soft yet so full of angst he seemed almost to flinch.

He looked at her, his eyes grieved. "I don't know, Daughter. But I fear McKie will come here."

Sometime in the night Morrow was jerked awake by a single heart-stopping thought. McKie was coming. Perhaps today. When he did, what would she do? Say? She sensed that by accepting Robbie Clay's proposal, she'd earned the major's ire, shamed him in some way, and that was something she'd never meant to do.

Oh Lord, forgive me for my part in all this. Please protect us.

Mindlessly she performed her chores, eyes on the woods. How odd that the fear she'd once felt for the Shawnee was now embodied in the man she'd once hoped would be her salvation.

An officer and a gentleman from Virginia. The irony of it stung her afresh, as did the fact that her heart remained fixed on a half-blood scout who knew nothing of her turmoil and trouble.

The storm cleared, leaving everything muddy and unkempt. Toward dusk, while toting water from the spring, she heard a sudden commotion around the side of the cabin. Something dark and unspeakable came over her as she caught sight of the familiar figure in buff and blue. Watching him, she fought the urge to drop her water bucket and flee as he tied his stallion to the rail in front of the cabin. There was no hiding the dismay that blanketed her. She felt nearly smothered by it.

McKie turned suddenly, removing his tricorn, his hair the russet of an autumn leaf in the fading light. His eyes swept her from tip to toe. "Miss Little, I'd nearly forgotten how lovely you are."

She wore a striped muslin dress, hardly praiseworthy, she thought, unaware that its simplicity emphasized her every curve. There was something in his gaze that alarmed her, something behind his flattering words that put her instantly on edge, and all her fears came crashing down upon her.

Oh Pa, where are you?

As if hearing her heart's cry, he soon came out of the barn, his voice civil if strained. "What brings you so far from the fort, Major McKie?"

"I have business a bit north of here," he replied brusquely. "And since I've not seen your daughter in some time, I thought we might take a walk."

"Very well," Pa said after a moment's pause, beginning to wheeze.

Morrow set down her pail, her breath coming in labored little bursts, a prayer for deliverance dying in her throat as Pa passed into the cabin.

McKie was dressed in his officer's best, his uniform immaculate, an inky stock enfolding his thick neck, the linen of his shirt pristine. His sword belt was draped over his shoulder, and one hand rested on its hilt. As she glanced at it, a queasy wave threatened to unseat her supper. Had he used this very weapon when raiding the Indian towns? Had it cut down women and children? Babies like Little Eli? She felt weighted with the heavy silence that hung between them and all that he'd done. Her eyes drifted to the pasture and surrounding woods, and she saw one mounted soldier, then two. He'd come with a guard, she guessed, and then, when she looked again, they'd gone.

He led her into the orchard amidst the branches now picked clean of apples. Her thoughts whirled back to her meeting with Red Shirt. Robbie Clay had once stood here too . . .

"You must pardon me, Miss Little. I usually don't dress for war when I'm calling. 'Tis a sign of the times, I'm afraid."

She merely nodded, and he offered her his good arm, which she took reluctantly. He held his wounded arm a bit stiffly, and she could see the lump of bandaging beneath his uniform sleeve.

Deeper into the orchard they went, far from the eyes of Pa and McKie's men. Stopping abruptly, he looked down at her, his speech formal and clipped and cold. "Circumstances necessitate a speedy declaration, I'm afraid. Matters of war leave little time for courting, so I must cast aside conventions and ask you to become my wife."

She stepped back if he'd struck her. "Major McKie . . ."

He smiled, but it was hollow, almost haunting. "Why are you so surprised, Morrow? You are an astonishingly lovely woman. And I am in need of a wife."

"But we've hardly spoken—"

"Surely time spent sitting beside you at Sabbath services and singing school counts for something." His tight smile became a smirk. "I'm aware you're from fine Virginia stock. Botetourt

County, to be exact. I believe you to be of good breeding and intelligence. It's obvious you have an uncommon grace about you."

"B-but I hardly know you."

He looked a trifle irritated. "What is it you want to know?"

She said nothing, her angst so acute she looked down at her feet, feeling the woozy warning rush of unconsciousness.

Tossing his hat onto a stump, he took her arms, his fingers firm upon her thin sleeves. "Perhaps all you need to know is this. I'm aware that you're aiding and abetting the enemy, both Shawnee and British. The penalty for being a traitor is death, Miss Little, by hanging or firing squad. Would you wish this on your dying father? Yourself?"

The words sent her reeling. She took a step back, or tried to, but his hands shackled her, his fingernails puncturing the tender skin of her wrists.

"W-what do you speak of, sir? You have no proof—"

"Oh, but I do." The look he gave her was triumphant. "I have spies who've informed me of Indian sign about your cabin. And there seems to be more than a few people at the fort who are willing to believe the worst of you, including your dear friend Jemima."

Spies? Jemima? Sparks of disbelief kindled inside her. They'd been betrayed by friends? Settlement folk? And Lizzy? Had Lizzy and Abe been among them?

Morrow began to shake. She had to open her mouth to breathe. He was looking at her with such unabashed hunger she felt dirty. His hands gripped her arms, and his tobacco-tainted breath blew hot in her face as his mouth came down hard on hers. Frantic, she tried to push him away, but it was like felling a tree with her fists.

He shook her, face tight with fury. "It would grieve me to have to press the matter, Morrow. I could easily quell this traitorous talk . . . if you allow me the pleasure of calling you my wife."

Wife. For a moment she thought she would retch on his polished black boots. The woods seemed to tilt and spin, the cabin a mere pinprick of light.

With a little shove, he released her and she stumbled, nearly falling to the ground. He took time to straighten his stock, his mouth in a hard line. "I'll leave you for now, understand. But I shall return in a few days' time, and we'll announce our betrothal to your father and the settlement."

With that, he turned toward his horse and rode out. She started back to the cabin, but her legs wouldn't hold her. Falling to her knees in the grass, she sat shaking. Overhead, storm clouds were gathering again, and a chill seeped into her as the sky gave up its light. Unbidden, Aunt Etta's words returned to haunt her anew.

Dearest Morrow, I've dreamed that you're to marry a man of rank . . .

"You all right, Daughter?" Pa was waiting by the hearth, looking so old and vulnerable it made her heart ache.

From somewhere deep inside herself, she summoned the self-possession to say, "McKie's gone, Pa." *Dare she lie?* "He stopped by to see if we're well."

Silence. Could he see her turmoil in the candlelit shadows? Did he believe her? She wouldn't tell him the truth. Being branded a traitor—betrayed by supposed friends—would likely kill him sooner than the consumption.

Oh Father, help us . . . spare us . . . deliver us from evil.

22

In the days to come, Morrow's mind seemed bent beyond all reason as she agonized over McKie. The memory of his rough mouth, the bruises on her wrists she tried to hide from Pa, was nothing like the stain on her soul. Was he even now telling others about suspecting them as spies and traitors? Would he truly dismiss such allegations once they'd wed? Her desperate thoughts would center on running away and then would circle back to the man whose cough seemed to reach the rafters, tethering her to the cabin. She tried to disguise what lay so heavy on her heart, yet surely he sensed her distress.

"I'll not last till spring, Daughter," he said.

Spring was generous, she thought. It hurt her to look at him, scarecrow thin as he was. The medicine Aunt Sally had given them failed to ease him, and her own supply of herbs had dwindled. Thinking coltsfoot or mullein might help, she made preparations to go gathering. Whatever danger might befall her in the woods was far preferable to marrying Major McKie.

While Pa slept, she slipped out with a hoe and basket, wandering past red-rock cliffs and arches along the river's path, the call of warblers and woodpeckers her only company. Gold and crimson leaves, large as a man's hand, lay upon the surface of the still water. She walked slowly, thankful for the solitude if nothing else. Here among the hollows where the sun rose late and set early, she could cry unhindered.

As she went, the sigh of the wind seemed to whisper her

name. Sleepless as her nights had been, it was little wonder she imagined things. The trees stopped their rustling and she resumed her search, plucking a crimson leaf from her hair. When she'd finally found a patch of coltsfoot, she seemed to hear the call again, this time nearer. Slowly she turned, hoe in hand, nigh terrified. *McKie?*

Red Shirt stood in the shadows just behind her. The sight of him, so near when she'd thought him so far away, nearly proved her undoing. She turned her back on him for just a moment, fumbling for the handkerchief she'd misplaced. When she faced him once again, she spilled out her angst. "You shouldn't be here. Major McKie has spies everywhere—"

"Not here, Morrow."

She saw that he held the hankie she'd dropped somewhere along the way. The lace-edged cloth, trimmed with tiny yellow flowers, looked so fragile in his rough hand. Taking a step closer, he brought it to her face, carefully wiping her tears away. She wanted to tell him all that had happened with Robbie Clay and McKie, but her throat was so tight it seemed she'd swallowed shards of glass. She simply leaned into her hoe, feeling it was the only thing that kept her upright. Beneath her soiled muslin shift, she could feel a trickle of sweat brought on by her tumult of emotions.

He tucked the damp handkerchief in his hunting shirt, then caught the handle of the basket she held and led her deeper into the woods. Wordlessly, they climbed the side of the mountain for a full five minutes, far off the familiar trail. She soon felt the cool breath of a cave fanning the ferns and brush all around them. At its entrance, they sat on a cold slab of rock, and she shivered. Did he know every inch of this land? It had been the Shawnees' before hers. Would she ever stop feeling like a trespasser?

"Morrow, you need to go back to the cabin. I'll take you there, but you must promise not to wander so far again."

"But Pa—he needs something to ease him . . ." She broke off, her heartache rising, ready to spill over at the slightest provocation. Turning her head away, she studied the late-blooming laurel all about them. The bloodred blossoms reminded her of Pa's stained handkerchiefs about the cabin, too many to count, each like a banner declaring a life ebbing.

He said quietly, "Morrow, look at me."

She needed no such invitation and turned back to him, eyes wet. Oh, but he was so handsome it hurt her. This close, she felt drawn to him in ways that bewildered her. How could he both fascinate and frighten?

The intensity of his tone shook her further when he said, "Promise me you'll stay close to the cabin. There's a regiment of soldiers coming over the trace nearest your cabin. A Shawnee war party is in back of them. You'll come to no harm. But you need to bar the doors and stay inside."

"Will there be a fight?"

He lifted his shoulders in a shrug, and she knew he was trying not to scare her. Despite the danger pulsing all around them, she felt becalmed by his presence. Ever so gently he took her fingers in his, and they trembled like a bird's wing against the deep mahogany of his hand. He was looking down at the bruises that encircled her wrist like a dark bracelet, his expression inscrutable. But she was no longer thinking of McKie.

If the simple pressure of his hand fills me with such pleasure, what must it be like within the warm circle of his arms?

A gust of wind seemed to bring her to her senses, shooing her off the ledge. She wouldn't mention McKie. The risk was far too great. Doing so might endanger him just as it had Robbie Clay. Despite her desperation, she kept silent and started down the mountain ahead of him, clutching the hoe and basket, the herbs forgotten. As she walked, she had the uncanny sense they weren't alone and looked back. The sight of a dozen or more frontiersmen and Indians filled her with raw alarm.

"I'm traveling with a party in case of ambush," Red Shirt said.

Each Indian seemed dressed for war, skin glistening with oil and paint, British muskets in hand. Her eyes were drawn to their silver-embellished scalp locks and somber countenances before moving to the familiar garb of the frontiersmen. All bore rawhide belts hung with tomahawks and trade knives, powder horns and shot pouches slung over their shoulders. This was no hunting expedition, truly.

He took her elbow and propelled her past flaming oaks and maples while the party fanned out about them, ever watchful and stunningly silent. They moved quickly, their moccasins eating up the autumn ground. They had no horses, and she knew why. Horses left a plain trail and made too much noise and trouble, yet could move them to their destination far faster. They were on foot for good reason, she knew.

At the edge of the cabin clearing, Red Shirt paused while his party filed past. She looked to the porch but saw no sign of Pa. He was likely sleeping again, his only respite from the cough that racked him. Red Shirt's eyes swept the pasture and outbuildings warily and came to rest on her. Though he was but an arm's length away, she could no longer see him through her tears. If she wasn't so weary, she might have stood here as stoic as he, drawing strength from the forbidden bond of affection she felt between them. She wanted to smile, to give him something of herself, but there was no lightheartedness left in her.

"Stay close to the cabin," he said again, taking out the handkerchief and drying her tears a final time.

Her throat tightened as he turned away. Leaning on her hoe, she stood completely still and watched the men leave. Before the long column disappeared through the trees, the final brave turned back to her, the faintest glimmer of a smile on his unfamiliar face. At his waist, dangling from a willow hoop, was a fresh russet scalp.

The same color as Major McKie's.

It took some time for her to compose herself enough to return to the cabin. She didn't want to alarm Pa with her absence yet feared the shock she felt still strained her face. But truly, she didn't know whose scalp she'd seen dangling from that dark waist. There were bound to be a few settlers with that same shade of hair, though she knew of none offhand. She looked again at the woods where Red Shirt's party had just vanished. Her mind and emotions, sore from so much worry, now deepened to a sharp grief at his leaving. Returning the hoe to the barn, she walked woodenly to the cabin, empty basket in hand.

Pa was waiting, sitting by the hearth, worry creasing his face. "I wondered where you'd gone to, Daughter. It's not safe to be about in the woods, remember."

"I just wanted to find some medicine," she said.

Moving to the hearth, she hung the kettle from the crane over the fire and took some sassafras from a tin on the mantel. But she couldn't still her trembling hands and sent the roots and a pewter cup clanking to the floor. Mercifully, Pa made light of it and said no more. She worked around him, unable to be still. In time the kettle began to hiss, but it in no way muffled the thunder of hoofbeats outside their door. Going to a window, she saw half a dozen soldiers approaching, Lysander Clay among them.

Oh Lord, not soldiers.

Were they part of the regiment Red Shirt had told her was coming over the trace? She pressed a trembling hand to the windowpane, panic flooding her. They drew up just short of the porch and called for Pa to open the door. Retrieving his cane, she helped him up, then slowly opened the door. The late afternoon sun was in her eyes, but the stark unfriendliness in their faces was plain. Had Major McKie poisoned them with his traitorous talk? She took in the uniformed men and tried to master the fear and revulsion that swelled inside her. It seemed no one moved so much as a hairbreadth for a full minute.

"Good day, Pastor Little, Miss Little." The uniformed man who spoke was unknown to her. "I'm Captain Christie. We're conducting a search for Major McKie. We've word that he may have come to your cabin of late."

Pa stifled a cough then nodded. "McKie was here three days ago, Captain, speaking with my daughter."

"You've not seen him since?"

"No, sir. He stopped but briefly then left."

The captain turned to Morrow, his horse restlessly pawing the ground. "Did he give any indication of where he was headed, Miss Little?"

Straight to hell. She swallowed down the horrible thought, the bile rising in her throat, and made herself look at him. But it was the dangling scalp she saw, still bloody, a telltale russet. "He said he had business north of here and would be back to see me again," she said.

Some of the men smiled faintly and cast furtive glances at each other. Pa began to cough, and she moved toward him as if shielding him from their hard stares.

Finally the captain removed his hat and looked about the cabin clearing, lingering on the distant cornfield now turned to stubble. "We'll not trouble you further today."

Today. Morrow's heart turned to stone. Would they return tomorrow, then, with their sly glances and unspoken accusations? Would they accuse her and Pa not only of treason but of murder as well? She felt hunted, hemmed in, desperately afraid for herself and Pa—and Red Shirt.

At last they turned to go. As they rode away, Pa turned to her, looking more perplexed than she'd ever seen.

"What do you suppose has happened to Major McKie, Morrow?" he murmured, stifling a cough.

She passed him a clean handkerchief from her apron pocket, wanting to spill out what she suspected. "I—I'm not sure."

He sighed. "I have grave reservations about the major, particularly where you're concerned. But I never wished him ill. Or dead."

She looked north to the woods where Red Shirt had slipped away a mere half hour before. Already it seemed like a dream but for the memory of that dangling scalp.

"Did McKie say where he was going, by chance?"

She sat down unsteadily in her churning chair. "No, Pa."

"Perhaps he's still on business north of here. 'Tis strange he'd be missing."

When he passed inside, she shut her eyes tight, trying to empty her mind of Robbie Clay and McKie. *Oh, Red Shirt, what have you done?* In the gathering shadows of dusk, she felt the bond between them strengthen and her own confusion deepen.

Lord, I am lost.

23

Remembering Red Shirt's words to stay near the cabin, Morrow heeded his advice for several days, shuddering as Trapper Joe spoke with Pa about the search parties combing the woods for Major McKie. Listening, she felt privy to some horrible secret. Although the wilderness had swallowed more than a few men whole, his vanishing seemed more sinister, and the settlement was abuzz with alarm. Each tick of the mantel clock seemed to bring something dire and dangerous nearer, and her nerves grew raw. She tended to Pa, reading Scripture aloud to ease him, till her supply of tallow candles dwindled and she was too tired to climb the steps to her room. Holding on to his hand, she dozed in her chair between his bouts of coughing.

"Go upstairs to bed, Daughter," he urged, trying to smile in reassurance.

But she shook her head, afraid to leave him lest soldiers rush in.

His voice was a broken whisper in the tense air. "I can't have you by my side day and night. If you become sick, what will we do?"

Against her wishes, she moved to her room and sat on the edge of her bed, feet numb from the attic chill. Taking up her brush, she tried to find solace in routine things. The customary hundred strokes turned her hair into a silken curtain in the candlelight, but she hardly knew what she did. Worn with fatigue, she dropped the brush and it clattered to the cold floor.

As she bent to retrieve it, tears spotted the backs of her hands. The memory of Red Shirt drying her face then tucking her handkerchief into his hunting shirt rose to bedevil her. Did he take it to keep her memory close, to have something to remember her by in case he never saw her again?

She lay down and became aware of a telling silence. The absence of Pa's coughing turned the cabin into a tomb. Heart pumping wildly, she rushed downstairs to his side. His hand, his cheek—cold. He was too still, too peaceful . . .

Oh, Pa!

Dropping to her knees, she let out an anguished cry. He roused and turned. "I'm not dead yet, Daughter." Color filled his wan face. As he began coughing again, it seemed the most glorious sound she'd ever heard. Only she couldn't stop crying.

The lines in his face deepened. "Morrow, what's come over you?" He stroked her hair, and she cried till the candles were spent and the fire begged for wood. "I think it's more than me you're mourning. You're in need of a mother to discuss these matters of the heart. I've long forgotten what it's like to be in love."

She said nothing, her cheek pressed against the dampness of his nightshirt, thinking she'd misheard.

"I know you're in love with Red Shirt, Daughter. There's no use denying it."

Still, she couldn't speak.

He went on, a bit breathless, each word labored. "You need to take the happiness held out to you. Before it's too late."

When she heard hoofbeats long after dark, she feared the worst. Trembling, she glanced at Pa as he slept, his coughing quieted by a medicinal dose of whiskey. Moving to a shuttered window, she peered through the wooden slats at the clearing and outbuildings and saw a lone rider coming round the barn.

Her eyes fastened on the moonlit figure as he dismounted, hope rising. There was no mistaking the great height of him, the expert way he handled his horse, the agile manner in which he crossed the clearing toward the cabin.

Before he'd reached the steps, she'd unbarred and opened the door. He stood stalwart before her, the crown of his dark head touching the oak lintel as he entered, his broad shoulders filling up the emptiness.

Her voice was shaky, a bit disbelieving. "I thought you'd gone."

"I had to turn back."

"Why?"

"All that matters is right here."

She took the heartfelt words in, aware of the keen warmth in his eyes. He set his rifle by the door and barred it while she crossed to the hutch to get cider and bread. When she turned around, he was behind her in the shadows, well beyond the pale light of the lamps, making her forget why she was there in the first place.

"Morrow, I don't want to eat," he told her gently.

She set the cider down, tears lining her eyes, afraid to look at him lest she collapse crying in his arms. She was so tired—benumbed, even—her emotions scattered. Could he tell just by looking at her?

His own face bore weary lines as if he'd come a long distance, a few strands of charcoal hair escaping his loosely tied queue. He took her hands. "I know things have been hard for you."

Hard? No, nearly beyond endurance. But she couldn't say all that haunted her—McKie and his traitorous accusations, Pa losing his life by slow degrees before her very eyes, the depth of her feelings for a man she shouldn't love. She looked away briefly, throat tight, trying to stay calm. The seconds ticked by, and the sadness and confusion she'd pushed down for so long started to give way beneath his tender gaze. Taking back her hands, she covered her face and began to cry.

In moments she was overcome by his tobacco-laden scent and the warm, unyielding length of him, her head tucked in the hollow between his chest and shoulder, his arms tight around her. Behind them, Pa still slept, but it was an uneasy sleep, broken by an unsettling rattle in his chest.

Her voice was a whisper. "Why did you come back? 'Tis not safe."

"I came back to finish what we last started."

Did he mean their near embrace in the barn? Before Pa came in? His mouth was warm against her ear, his fingers stroking her hair, which frayed at the touch of his callused hand. "I came back to ask you to be my wife."

The words, so long wished for, were every bit as sweet as she'd hoped they'd be. But here in this shadowed corner, with Pa so ill . . . "Do you love me? Or do you feel pity for me, alone, almost fatherless?"

"Not pity, Morrow. Love. The love between a man and a woman."

Her lips parted in a sort of wonder. "Have you ever been in love?"

"Not till now . . . not till you."

"Then how can you be . . . sure?"

"I know my mind, my heart."

His quiet confidence—the intimacy of his words—kindled something deep inside her. All the months of hiding, of trying to deny him, began to erode like river sand. He was offering her what no man had ever done. His heart, an honorable proposal, a home.

Her thoughts began racing, grappling with the enormity of his asking. "Where would we go . . . where would we live?"

"There's new land west of the Mississippi. Few people have settled there. I want us to be among the first."

West. Far from bloodshed and betrayal and lonesome graves

behind a paling fence. He was looking down at her, his eyes lingering on her loosened hair. Was he already imagining her living alongside him, preparing his meals, sharing his bed? He'd never touched her in that way, yet someday she might bear his child. The thought filled her with a severe longing.

Reaching up, she touched his cheek, the silence between them brimming. She wanted to give an answer—to ease the pain and passion in his face—but the words lodged so tight in her throat she couldn't speak. It mattered little that she loved him. Did she love him *enough*?

"For a long time I put down my feelings for you . . . but I can't do so any longer," he said. He drew her nearer, touching her with his eyes and his hands in a wordless sort of lovemaking that stole her very breath. There were no barriers between them now, just this exquisite confession of feelings, heart to heart and soul to soul. "I'll walk away from you, if that's what you want. Yet I feel . . ." He swallowed hard, his voice a whisper. "I feel when I'm with you that you love me too."

Broken, she gave way, aware of the slightly wild, erratic rhythm of his heartbeat against her own. She clung to him, her fists full of the soft fringe of his frocked shirt, her need of him so overwhelming she started to cry all over again.

He smoothed her tumbled hair, his mouth brushing her ear and temple, his voice low and sweet and anguished. "Morrow . . . let me love you."

Yes, her heart cried. *Yes . . . yes . . . yes.*

He continued to hold her, pouring strength and comfort into her till her crying subsided. When his hands fell away, she felt a startling emptiness. "For now I'll say no more. In the morning I'll speak with your father. I won't go against his wishes. Or your own."

With that, he turned away, took up his rifle, and left the cabin.

She awoke to complete and utter stillness. Had Red Shirt gone? Or had Pa passed in the night? She hurried and dressed, crossing to her window half a dozen times in hopes of seeing them outside, not bothering to subdue her hair into its usual chignon. Stepping onto the landing, she waited for the welcome aroma of coffee, but all she smelled was wood smoke and tobacco. The hearth chairs were askew, and she wondered if they'd already spoken. Had he asked Pa for her hand while she slept unawares upstairs?

Heart in her throat, she stepped onto the front porch, finding the edges touched with frost, the remaining flowers bitten by the cold, their bright colors faded. Relief filled her when she saw them in the pasture—Pa working to keep upright with his cane but looking bent and rusty as an old nail beside the youthful, strapping Red Shirt. She sat down on the edge of her churning chair, but her eyes ran after them, hungry to hear what it was they said. Odd how they stood tall one moment, then knelt down the next. Even on his knees before a fallen log, Red Shirt's height was apparent. She stared in surprise as he bent his head.

Was he . . . *praying*?

Emotion flooded her. Half an hour passed before they came back, each moment making her more breathless and tense. Taking a shaky step off the porch, she smoothed the creases of her skirt. But he only glanced at her before walking away, leaving Pa to hobble toward her in the fragile morning's light.

"But I—he—" she half whispered into empty air.

"He'll be back," Pa reassured her, trying to get his breath. "He said he spoke to you last night and told you of his feelings."

She nodded, eyes lingering on him as he disappeared into the woods.

"This morning he asked me for your hand in marriage. But before I give my blessing, there are some things you need to understand." She felt a tremor of alarm and looked down at her feet. He continued quietly, eyes on the woods. "In the meadow there, while you waited, he asked if God would accept such a man as he."

She turned back to him, full of wonder.

"He spoke of those times in battle when he was a party to scalps taken and forts burned, and killing Major McKie—"

"No, Pa—please . . ." Her face turned entreating, and she held up a hand as if to stop the unwelcome words.

His eyes held a warning. "You need to listen, Morrow. There should be no secrets between the two of you, feeling as you do. Fortunately, God's grace is far greater than anything he's done. And Red Shirt's as sincere in his repentance as any man I've ever seen."

He began coughing again and turned to go into the cabin, leaving her alone on the porch. *Oh, Pa, what should I do?* Was God displeased with such a union? Was she willing to look beyond his past to the man he'd become, having given his life to God? By loving him—marrying him—was she betraying the memory of Ma and Euphemia and Jess?

A misting rain began to fall, erasing the blue sky and filling in the woods with gray. She was alone, truly alone, with her impossible decision. A flash of brown filled her vision as Red Shirt came back into the clearing. With as much composure as she could muster, she walked over the cold ground to meet him, rain pelting her face. He'd accept whatever decision she made, he'd said. He'd walk away from her if that was what she wanted.

Lord, what would You have me do?

Standing before him, she felt a sudden settling, a peace she couldn't explain.

You need to take the happiness held out to you. Before it's too late.

Reaching for his hand, she brought it to her cheek like she

had in the barn that stormy night, knowing that she'd loved him even then. His face was poignant, perhaps a bit disbelieving, touching her so deeply she found it hard to say what she was now sure of.

"I want to be your wife," she began a bit breathlessly. "I want to be yours . . . wholly and completely."

He didn't take her in his arms as she thought he might, but a look of pure pleasure shone in his eyes. Despite the stinging rain, they stood staring at each other as if weighing all the implications of what they'd just done, were about to do.

His hazel eyes were sharp. "You're sure?"

"Yes." Beneath her bodice, her heart swelled with a joy unknown to her before. Behind her, the cabin door opened and Pa appeared on the porch. They turned to face him, and Red Shirt's voice carried across the still clearing.

"Your daughter has agreed to become my wife."

Silence. Was Pa as pleased as she hoped he'd be?

"Well then," he said at last, "let's have a wedding."

Here and now? The suddenness of it stole her breath, but the satisfaction on Pa's face spurred her on. Now anxious to be out of the rain, she made a dash for the porch, her soon-to-be husband at her heels.

Up the cabin stairs she went without a word to anyone. Impatience pulsed through her as she rummaged through the dark wardrobe, fingertips seeking the lush velvet. Draping it across the bed, she shed her damp dress and left it puddling on the floor, not wanting to keep them waiting. The heavy gown fell into place, covering her embroidered under things. She didn't bother with a brush but left her hair unbound, liking the way the dampness curled and twisted the length of it.

Her hands felt a bit empty as she recalled Lizzy's bouquet. Coming down the stairs, she spied some bittersweet atop the mantel. Plucking it from its cracked jar, she brought it to her nose as if its peculiar scent could steady her. Though she longed for the roses of June, this would have to do.

Had it only been mere months ago that she stood by the hearth and waited for Robbie Clay? How different this was. Today she felt rushed but right and altogether eager. Like a bride should. But for the thought of soldiers at their door . . .

When Pa and Red Shirt came in from the porch where they'd gone to wait, she looked down at her bittersweet bouquet, tongue-tied. The three of them came together, a bit fumbling, even bashful. Pa stood before the flickering hearth, his Bible open in his hands, his heartfelt words broken by bursts of coughing.

"Dearly beloved . . ."

The poignant look on her father's face touched her. Was he remembering his own wedding day? How her mother looked? How he'd felt?

"With this ring I thee wed . . ."

She echoed the heartfelt words and watched Pa remove his own ring and pass it to her. Slipping it onto the fourth finger of Red Shirt's left hand, she found it wouldn't go past the knuckle. Taking a breath, she tried his little finger—a perfect fit. He looked down at the wide gold band with its distinctive Celtic cross as Pa reached into his pocket and produced a second ring, one she hadn't seen since childhood. It was her mother's own, the slender band reflecting all the rich, warm hues of the firelight. For a moment the heirloom in his hand was lost to her as she struggled with her emotions.

"With my body I thee worship . . ."

The intimate words seemed an open invitation to ponder what pleasures awaited them—how his hair would feel entangled in her fingers . . . the taste of his kiss. Till now she'd kept her mind swept clean of such notions. But today, her wedding day, she could think as she pleased of him. He was looking down at her, perhaps considering the same, and the realization made her heart pick up in rhythm.

"With all my worldly goods, I thee endow . . ."

At this, she almost smiled. Her earthly goods consisted of a few quilts and dresses and little else. And his? A fine horse and rifle, perhaps the clothes on his back. She didn't know and she didn't care.

As they bent their heads and Pa began to pray, she held her breath, waiting for the words, "You may kiss the bride." At all the settlement weddings over which he'd presided, not once had this been omitted. But instead his closing prayer was punctuated by a wheezing, thunderous blast. No call to kiss. She expelled her breath in a soft, disappointed little rush.

Pa sank into the nearest chair, wiping his brow with a square of cloth, utterly spent and still hacking. The day had been too much for him, truly. But before she could fetch him a cup of water, he got to his feet and passed onto the porch to give them some privacy. The fire's backlog rolled forward, sending a shower of sparks onto the hearthstones, the only commotion in the suddenly still room.

They stood motionless for a moment, locked in wonder. His warm eyes seemed to dance as he took in her gown and all its feminine details. Two dozen silk buttons. A froth of lace framing her bosom. Layer upon layer of lush velvet. Twin petticoats peeking out beneath the ankle-length hem. She looked like a bride.

She was his.

Slowly his arms went around her, and she held her breath. At last they could finish what they'd started in the barn . . .

All thoughts were blotted out as his mouth met hers—sweetly hesitant at first, then hungrily. Her senses began to swim in a woozy, melting rush. The unfamiliar feel of him beneath her tentative hands cast a strange spell. They drew apart only to melt back together again, kissing till they were breathless, till common sense prevailed. This was neither the time nor the place for lovemaking, not with Pa so ill and waiting on the porch.

"I must go," Red Shirt whispered. The sheen in his eyes told her all that time wouldn't allow him to say. His being here was as dangerous for her and Pa as it was for him.

"Your father . . ." he said. "He doesn't have long now. When he's gone, I'll come back for you."

"But when—how?" The plaintiveness in her voice seemed to wound him, and he brushed back a handful of her hair, entwining his fingers in it.

"Soon," he assured her. His eyes roamed her face as if engraving her every feature on his mind and heart. "Already I'm missing you."

He kissed her again, thoroughly and completely, till her knees nearly gave way. When he turned away, she faced the fire, unable to watch him go, clutching the bittersweet broken by their embrace. She pressed her fingertips to her lips where the passion of his kiss seemed to linger. Where, she wondered ruefully, would he spend their wedding night?

Behind her, Pa said, "I never thought I'd live to see this day. But I'm glad I did."

She turned toward him, feeling almost childlike in the hearth light. "Are we really wed, Pa, right and truly?"

"As a minister of the gospel, I can ascertain that you are, and it pleased me greatly to do it." Coughing again, he moved to lie down. "Now I'll try to oblige you by drawing my last breath so your husband can take you west like he wants, though I'd rather you just leave with him now and let an old man die in peace."

"Hush," she chided, helping him into bed. How he'd stood for the simple ceremony baffled her. She supposed prayer had propped him up.

"He'll make you a fine husband, brave and intelligent as he is.

His heart for spiritual matters says much about his character. I couldn't release you to a lesser man. And you'll make him a fine wife, like your mother before you."

She smiled at him through her tears, but his confident words failed to ease the sudden turmoil in her heart. With danger swirling all around them, there was no certainty of anything beyond this present moment. Already they'd been forced apart, though the most sacred vows had tied them together minutes before.

He studied her as if divining her thoughts. "Only God knows what the future holds. Best just pray and not ponder it overlong."

A fresh fit of coughing ended their conversation, and she got up to fetch him some whiskey and water. When he quieted, she took the empty cup and prayed it would settle him for the long night ahead.

His voice was fading fast. "You need only be the wife and mother God has called you to be, Morrow. Leave the rest to Him."

She kissed his brow and spread a second quilt over him, then blew out all the candles save the one that would take her upstairs. The velvet gown swished over the worn wooden steps without a sound, and she began to unbutton her bodice, wishing she could keep it on a little longer. Her bedroom was cold and drafty as a cave.

No need to worry about being a wife just yet. She looked toward her bed with its tidy counterpane, remembering how Red Shirt had dwarfed its sturdy frame. *Your bed is making me soft,* he'd said. He'd do things differently, she guessed, placing a hand to her heart as if to quell a sudden, yearning rush. He'd likely lay his buffalo coat down . . . and her down with it. The feather tick had hardly held her and Jess.

The memory stopped her cold.

Oh, Jess, where are you? Will I ever see you again?

24

Pa was gone within days. There was no last-minute warning, no final goodbye. He seemed to rally at the end, almost fooling her, making her leave his side for longer periods and sleep upstairs. And then she came down that final morning and found him gone, his shell of a body cold and slightly stiff. His hands were folded atop his chest—had he been praying?—and it seemed all the deep folds in his leathery face had been eased by some heavenly hand.

She sank down on her knees beside him, laying her damp cheek against his still shoulder, wishing he'd rise up and stroke her hair a final time. For a long time she stayed with him, unwilling to let him go. Such stillness there was. Such peace. The absence of his coughing ushered in light and birdsong and fresh air. He was free. Free of the past . . . free of pain and sickness . . . free of men like McKie. He was with Ma now, and Euphemia. Perhaps even Jess. How could she be sad when he was finally free?

Reluctantly she let go of him and turned to the hearth. Sometime in the night the fire had died, and she scratched about for a live coal to revive it, wondering numbly who to summon to help bury him. But no more than an hour had passed when Trapper Joe and Good Robe were at the door, the grizzled woodsman almost amused at her astonishment.

"Indian intuition," he said, nodding toward his wife. Their faces were grieved, reminding her that they'd lost a dear friend this day. Even Little Eli, tucked in his mother's arms, looked somber.

Morrow breathed a thankful prayer and felt a rush of affection for them. With Good Robe's help, she dressed Pa in his finest preaching clothes, tucked a bit of bittersweet in his hand, and combed his silvery hair while Joe brought in the coffin and winding cloth from the barn. The ground was forgiving, not frost-hardened but merely leaf-littered, and the big box slipped easily into place beside Ma and Euphemia behind the paling fence.

For one sharp, heartrending moment, she felt utterly forlorn. A cold wind whipped her wool cape as they huddled around the fresh mound in silence, locked in their own private thoughts. She couldn't bear to leave, as if turning her back on Pa would somehow take away his beloved memory. But the sun began to shine, warming their stooped shoulders, and they began a slow walk back to the cabin.

"We'll stay the night with you, Miz Morrow," Joe said, and Good Robe nodded in agreement.

She was touched by their concern but felt the call to be alone. "No need, Joe," she said. Dare she share her secret? "Red Shirt will be here soon. Pa married us a few days ago."

He simply stared at her in the cabin shadows and then said with a sudden grin, "You two sure took care of things in good time. Where you headed?"

"West. Missouri territory."

At the mention, Joe's face held a longing Morrow hadn't seen before. "Prime country for huntin'. Prime country for livin'."

Buoyed by the near reverence in his tone, Morrow almost smiled, then felt a deep dread knot her stomach when he added, "It's a good time to go with the settlements hunkered down for more trouble. I just heard there's a new officer comin' to Kentucke who makes McKie's command look like a Sabbath picnic. His name's Clark. George Rogers Clark."

She looked down at her wedding ring and stayed silent, wondering where Red Shirt was, if he was on his way back to her.

He stroked his beard, speculating. "I've been wantin' to head further west. If I do, I'll try to find you."

She blinked back tears. "I'd like that, Joe." Going to the mantel, she retrieved a dusty ledger and brought out a deed, handing it to him. He looked perplexed until she said, "Pa wanted you and Good Robe to have this place. For keeps."

He stood speechless, eyes wet and disbelieving. Good Robe's dusky face shone with pleasure, and she took a few tentative steps about the large room, looking over the rocking chairs and table, the overflowing hutch, and the big corner bed.

Spying the hastily written letter lying on the table, Morrow handed it to Joe. "Please post this to Aunt Etta for me. She should know about Pa—about my leaving . . ."

But even as she said it, she felt a twinge of conscience. Perhaps it was thoughtless to deliver such news in one blow—Pa's death and her decision to go west. But she couldn't leave her only kin to wonder what had befallen them. After living with the agonizing uncertainty of Jess, she wished that on no one.

He put the letter and the deed inside his hunting shirt, nodding in understanding when she said, "Don't mention Pa's passing at the fort yet, Joe. Not till I'm gone." Thoughts of McKie's accusations, of Jemima's betrayal, continued to haunt her. Might the soldiers yet arrest her for treason? Might they hunt down Red Shirt because of McKie?

Oh Lord, please bring him back to me so we can go west in peace.

When they took their leave, promising to return at week's end, she stood alone in the shadows, unable to bear the sudden emptiness. Going to the corner bed, she began stripping away the linens, tears spotting her hands as she worked. But she kept moving, rifling through this or that trunk or cupboard, trying to collect her scattered thoughts, working till she was exhausted. Time was lost to her altogether as she continued cleaning and sorting, getting things ready for Good Robe and Joe and Little Eli, while packing up a few of her own beloved things.

At day's end she stood on the porch, waiting and wondering and praying. The woods stared back at her, empty. *Oh Lord, did I dream it all?* The gold ring on her hand was a blessed reminder that she hadn't, yet her thoughts took a dark turn. What if, since his leaving, he'd run into trouble? What if he never returned? Their entwined lives now lay before her like a blank book, full of untold, pleasurable possibilities. Or page upon page of heartache.

The next morning she made coffee, unable to eat the biscuits she'd baked. As she looked around the tidy cabin, empty of Pa's comforting presence, she felt she no longer belonged to it, or it to her. Joe and his family would be happy here, and if Jess ever came back, they'd be waiting. The thought solaced her a bit, as did the memory of their gratitude when she'd given them the deed.

Shivering, she drew her cape closer about her as she huddled by the flickering hearth. There was little to do now but wait. And pray. And dream. Her head tipped forward to her chest in slumber, thoughts scattering. Through the cracked door at her back came a wintry breeze—and something else.

The call of a dove.

Coming awake, she looked over her shoulder to the open door, hope rising in her heart. Could it be? Slowly she made her way to the porch. The lonesome call came again, but the clearing was empty. She hugged a porch post, feeling it was the only thing that held her up, and scanned the edges of the woods. Shadows danced in the early dawn, golden light threading through the bare branches. Had she only dreamed it then?

But there to her left, through a break in the trees, stood a man. As soon as her eyes touched him, he was sprinting toward her across the leaf-strewn grass, and she was doing the same, so full of joy she felt weightless. They collided, breathless—she crying with gladness, he too moved to even speak. For long moments he held her, eyes roaming over the clearing and surrounding woods.

His mouth was warm against her ear. "You knew I'd come for you."

"I thought perhaps soldiers—"

He drew her closer and she clung to him, absorbing his warmth and strength. Taking her handkerchief from inside his frocked shirt, he dried her face and walked with her to the cabin. When they went inside, he looked toward the empty bed, sorrow etched across his face.

"Pa passed yesterday," Morrow said. "Joe and Good Robe came soon after . . ."

Even as she said it, she felt the need to leave and put the memory behind her. Danger seemed to hover, hurrying them into action. Although she was prepared to go, leaving everything behind was a hurdle she'd not reckoned with. She'd likely never see her home again.

He removed some garments from the haversack slung across his back and passed them to her. A bit shy, she disappeared up the stairs to her bedroom and shed her impractical dress, pleasure softening her grief. A calico shift, deep blue and figured with tiny yellow flowers, was soft to her touch. Along with this was a doeskin skirt bleached white, the blue beadwork and heavy fringe a marvel of artistry falling just past her knees. Donning both, she tied the leather belt around her waist and looked down at matching leggings and shoepacks. All she needed was her fur cape.

Going to her dresser, she peered into the small oval mirror, a bit bewildered by the young woman looking back at her. In her confusion and haste, she was hardly aware of Red Shirt on the stairs. He came to stand behind her, hands on her shoulders. Their eyes met in the mirror, and she sensed his urgency.

"I'm nearly ready," she said softly, tying the ribbon at her throat with trembling fingers.

The handsome lines of his face held something she'd not seen before. Deep concern . . . doubt. "I ask a hard thing of you."

She turned to face him, alarmed. Was he having second thoughts?

His jaw tensed. "I could take you East."

To Aunt Etta's? Tears shone in her eyes, and she looked at him entreatingly.

"No one need know what happened here."

"You mean our marriage."

"You could have an easier life—"

"A life without you?" She felt a twist of grief, hurt that he'd even considered such. "Are you . . . sorry?" And then she saw the sheen of pain in his own eyes.

"No, Morrow. I just want you to be sure." The tenderness in his tone returned, and she realized what weighted his mind and heart. Was she truly ready to leave her old life—everything she'd ever known—and go with him?

In answer she simply handed him the footwear she was unsure of. He knelt in front of her, slipping on a soft buckskin moccasin followed by a rougher over-moccasin tanned black to shed water. His long fingers made short work of the lacings, tying them off at her knees. When he stood, the shadow of doubt had left his face.

There was but one thing remaining. Crossing the dogtrot, she stood in the ghostly cabin and bade a silent goodbye to the hurtful memories of long ago. Red Shirt lingered in the doorway, a reminder that they were wasting daylight.

Soon her mare, Pa's black stallion, and a packhorse were loaded with quilts and sundry items, but most everything was left behind for Joe and Good Robe. Taking a last look around, she gathered up Pa's pipe and Bible where they rested on a table, tears blinding her. She said a final farewell to the home she'd known so long before passing over the threshold to where the horses waited, determined not to look back.

Danger seemed to nip at their heels as they slipped into the forest. He took her north, away from Red River Station, along the dreaded Warrior's Path. 'Twas a way unknown to her, and she sat atop Dollie, back and shoulders stiff beneath her fur cape. The landscape seemed skeletal and cold, the brittle leaves beneath their feet crackling loud as musket fire. Anyone within half a mile could hear them, she fretted. She didn't realize how skittish she was till they halted beneath a pine tree and he helped her down from the saddle.

She took the canteen he offered and brought it to her lips, trembling so that water spilled down the front of her. Retrieving a pewter cup from a saddlebag, Red Shirt filled it and covered her hands with his to steady them, bringing the water to her lips. The tender gesture settled her, and she gratefully took a few sips. But when he turned away, she began shaking again, ashamed when his eyes swept over her in quick appraisal and saw her fear for what it was.

"'Tis the cold," she said softly.

"More than the cold, Morrow."

Her eyes roamed the bleak woods till he gently turned her face back to his, cupping her chin with his fingers. "Keep your eyes on me. I'll watch the woods."

She managed a little smile. "'Twill not be hard to do—keeping my eyes on you."

The confession came out a bit breathlessly, surprising him as much as her, or so it seemed. He lifted her chin, lowering his head till his mouth hovered over hers at a delicious angle. Suddenly the danger around them was little more than mist. 'Twas the danger between them that set her to trembling again. Her thoughts were so full of their wedded kiss in the cabin her stomach swirled.

"Lovemaking in these woods is a perilous occupation," he murmured, and his hands fell away. But he looked every bit as disappointed as she felt.

He returned her to the saddle, taking care, she thought, not to look at her overlong again.

Back on the trail, she did as he bid and kept her eyes on him. Truly, studying him became her chief pleasure. When she grew saddle sore, she walked. Her new clothes lent her an ease of movement she'd never known, and she tried to imitate the innate grace with which he moved, seemingly at odds with his strength and stature.

The further they traveled, the more certain she was that she'd married a stranger. Their first hours together seemed to consist of a dozen different introductions into his heart and mind. The expert way he handled a horse. His staggering stamina. The disarming way he had of lapsing from English into Shawnee.

Sometimes he hardly seemed aware of her, and then he would suddenly turn to take her in, his eyes playful, almost roguish. She delighted in those looks—they eased all the discomfort of that first day when it seemed her body and bruised emotions could go no further. When they finally made camp long past twilight, she breathed a prayer of thanks.

Too tired to talk, she began mixing meal and water, pouring the batter in a small iron skillet near the heart of the fire he'd made, the orange flames licking skewers of salted venison, the juices hissing and spitting as they cooked. With a little creek beside them, there was plenty of water, its rushing making soothing music as the night settled in.

Side by side they ate, and then Morrow washed up while Red Shirt finished constructing a bark shelter between two sturdy trees, the roof and floor made of hemlock boughs cushioned by sundry blankets and quilts. Would this be their marriage bed, then? A woozy rush of something she couldn't name swept through her as she watched him work.

Never had she missed a mother's wisdom more than now. As she sat and tried to piece together what was supposed to happen this night and what was expected of her as a wife, the fire conspired to woo her, and she fell dead asleep, wrapped in its warmth rather than in the unfamiliarity of Red Shirt's arms. She didn't even remember him lifting her, removing her shoepacks, and putting her to bed.

In the morning, he had to shake her awake. When she saw him leaning over her, shirtless, his dark hair loose and disheveled, her first feeling was one of wonder. She'd dreamed she was asleep atop her feather tick, not the hard ground, and certainly not with a husband.

"You're beautiful awake," he said with a knowing smile. "But you're even more beautiful asleep."

Groggy, she watched him pull on his shirt against the cold dawn. She scrambled to do the same with her shoepacks, deciding to leave her hair down since it warmed her like a cloak. Already it was tangled as if she'd spent a fitful night, and every muscle she possessed cried out. Even her feet seemed scalded.

He helped her up, brushing back a hank of her hair. "How do you feel?"

Feel? She blinked and looked up at him. How was she supposed to feel? She didn't feel married. She just felt . . . bereaved. And bewildered.

His fingers skimmed her cheek. "Am I pushing you too hard, Morrow? I'm not used to traveling with a woman."

She shook her head, willing her emotions to behave, thinking he might kiss her. The taste of charred venison was still in her mouth from the night before, and she craved water—lots and lots of water. Turning, she left the shelter and hurried to the creek with a pewter cup. The frigid dampness sent shivers clean through her. She knelt and dipped the cup into the gurgling water as it splashed over cold stones, then downed three cups in rapid succession. Woozy, she stood, barely making it to the bushes before emptying her stomach into the grass.

Soon he was behind her, taking her in his arms. "Today we'll rest."

When she awoke hours later, he was gone. The wind in the treetops swept down and played with the fickle fire as she huddled beside it. Near her feet a small pot sat in the coals, its lid a clean piece of bark. It was her smallest cooking vessel, and she wondered what it held, if she should stir it. The wind whipped the aroma away from her yet blew smoke into her face. She felt a sudden pining for the cabin chimney but supposed she'd better get used to the smoke and the dirt. Already her traveling clothes were soiled in places, though she'd been careful as could be.

Shivering again, she felt a second blanket cover her shoulders as Red Shirt sat down beside her. His gaze was keen, almost dissecting, as if trying to judge how weary she was.

"I'm better now," she told him, pulling the blanket closer. "Come morning I'll be able to travel, and I promise not to slow you."

He lifted the bark lid off the kettle. "And I promise not to push you. As a husband, I have much to learn."

Taking a spoon, he stirred the pot's contents and offered her a taste. She grimaced and drew back, afraid of offending, yet he looked almost amused. Embarrassed, she blurted, "I feel so tired . . . so weak."

His gaze slid from her to the fire. "You're many things, Morrow, but not weak. I wouldn't take a weak woman as my wife."

Solaced, she reached for a bowl, filling it and passing it to him. He took a bite before returning it to her. She swallowed a spoonful, surprised the porridge was so good.

"*Takuwah-nepi*," he told her. "Bread water."

She tried to smile. It tasted like cornmeal mush but better, with dried berries and molasses mixed in. "I didn't know you could cook." Suddenly famished, she ate a second bowl and reached for a third, but he caught her wrist. "Too much will send you back to the bushes."

He was right, truly, but she felt chided like a child. In her confusion she tipped the pot over, and the rest of the porridge spilled out. He righted it without a word, but her humiliation was complete. Though she worked hard to stem her swirling emotions, her chest hurt so from the effort that she finally burst into tears.

He pulled her into his arms, his mouth warm against her hair. "You're missing your father."

She was, but it was more than this. How could she share her near constant fear of soldiers following them? "I—I am missing Pa, but I must be strong."

"Why? When your heart hurts, you weep. If you stop weeping, I will wonder." He leaned forward to place another stick of wood on the fire, his hold on her never lessening. "I know what it's like to grieve."

"Your mother, you mean?"

He nodded. "There have been others."

Many others. She knew without asking, reading the hard lines in his face. Her mind began leaping back across the long, lonesome months without him, their only tie the fur cape he'd sent by way of Trapper Joe. "I can't believe I'm here with you now after all that's happened. I thought—after you left last winter—you weren't coming back."

"I wasn't sure I should." He looked down at her, pensive. "I wanted your happiness—I wanted to see your father at peace. I wasn't sure I could give you either. I'm not sure I can now."

"What do you mean?"

"I live a hard life. Your father was concerned about how you would weather it. He asked me to be careful with you."

The honest admission grieved her. Pa always treated her like fine Philadelphia china. Now, away from the isolated life they led on the Red River, she sensed he'd been wrong in doing so. "I know I'm not strong. I've hardly been away from the cabin or Aunt Etta's dress shop. But you can't spend your life being careful with me. I'll be a burden, not your wife."

"Being careful suits me, Morrow, like being tender suits you."

She stared into the leaping flames, pondering it all. He'd always been so gentle with her, right from the very start. *Pa needn't have worried on that score*, she thought.

"Did your father tell you about the holy words . . . my promise?" he asked. Her forehead furrowed in question, and he said, "Deuteronomy 24:5."

She reached for a saddlebag and unearthed Pa's worn black Bible. The sight stirred her so much she nearly put it back. But the leather cover was warm in her hands, the printed page a familiar friend. *The holy words*, he'd called them. She leafed through the thin pages to the stated verse. "When a man hath taken a new wife, he shall not go out to war, neither shall he be charged with any business: but he shall be free at home one year, and shall cheer up his wife which he hath taken."

"I promised your father . . ." he began.

She looked up, a catch in her throat.

"I promised him I would do that very thing."

"Pa made you promise?"

"He didn't make me, Morrow. I gave my word willingly enough."

The silence deepened, and she found herself wishing he'd lie down with her and erase every cold, lonesome moment they'd spent away from each other. The starry beauty of the night seemed to call for it. But if he didn't do so soon, she'd be fast asleep and he'd have to carry her to bed again.

As the night deepened and the fire shifted and settled, he ended up doing just that.

25

As they traveled, Morrow began to see how sheltered she'd been. Shackles she didn't know she had seemed to fall away as the whole wide world opened up to her. Did Red Shirt purposefully take her on the most beautiful paths just to see her mouth hang open and her eyes grow wide? She sensed his pleasure as he introduced her to all he'd known since childhood, mountains and rivers and valleys new to her but as beloved to him as old friends. Sometimes she rode on the mare leading the packhorse, then she'd walk, her eyes on Red Shirt more than the woods. He steadfastly watched their surroundings, alert to any movement or sound.

When at last they came to the Ohio River rapids, Morrow felt a sense of awe unknown to her before. On its north bank, she felt small as an ant, the far shore like a distant star. This was the Falls of the Ohio—the spectacular run of rapids she'd heard about her whole life. Here the rushing water surged through slick shoots to the final falls where it poured like a giant pitcher into a wide, tranquil basin below. Perfect for swimming, Red Shirt said. Together they stood on a rock ledge some thirty feet above the water, with Morrow wishing it was June, not November.

She shivered and took a step back from the cliff's edge, watching as he dove off the ledge, straight and smooth as an arrow being released from a bow before being swallowed up by the waters below. She dropped to her hands and knees, awed and a bit dizzy. She'd spent her whole life *not* doing such things, while he'd spent his whole life doing them and doing them well.

Red Shirt waited below, arms open wide. She felt a frantic cry escape her as she jumped into sheer nothingness. The impact of the water was stinging, then bloodcurdling cold. But he was there, just like he said he'd be, and she relaxed in his warm arms.

"I can jump but I can't swim," she said, recalling her near drowning.

His half smile told her he didn't need the reminder. "I'll teach you."

She shivered as he straightened her shift about her shoulders. "Not in winter."

"The water's warm."

Her eyes widened. "Warm?"

"For November. Soon it will be ice."

"I suppose you swim in that too."

Longingly she looked to the south shore where smoke plumed. He'd wisely made a fire and shelter where their blankets and her clothes and shoes waited. They'd come to the falls just past noon, completing ten days of travel. But crossing the wide river in a canoe he'd hidden on a previous foray had nearly proved her undoing. If not for the confidence with which he managed the horses and their belongings, she'd have been terrified. Setting foot on the opposite shore brought a blessed relief.

For the first time since leaving the Red River, she felt somewhat safe. She no longer asked how much further they had to go, since the question seemed only to amuse him. "Counting your steps only makes the journey longer," he'd said.

Now he turned her around to face the river as it angled south, pointing out things she'd overlooked. An ambitious beaver dam sturdy as a bridge spanned the rushing water, and beyond it spilled yet another gentler falls. The beauty sent goose bumps all over her.

"The sky speaks of snow," he said, studying the gathering clouds.

She looked up, a little thrill filling her at the prospect of being snowed in with him in so pristine a place. "Seems like all the people in the world have fallen off and it's just us two. Like Adam and Eve," she said.

Despite the near-constant fear that shadowed her, not once had they seen any sign of another soul, either Indian or white, though the woods teemed with animals and the trees shook down their last stubborn leaves, making a colorful carpet for walking.

"At first light we head west," he said. "Soon you'll see the smoke from my father's camp."

The mention of Surrounded made her glad, yet the prospect of entering an Indian town for the first time filled her with dread. They would stop briefly for fresh horses and provisions, he said, but they'd not linger long, for it was necessary to cross the Mississippi before it froze and became impassable.

Morrow sat by the fire wrapped in a blanket, drowsy and content, and studied him. Red Shirt stood along the river's edge where large white rocks created shallow pools in which *sharla*—river trout—swam. In the afternoon he'd fashioned a fine hickory spear, securing a sharp flint tip to one end and binding it with sinew.

She found it hard to look away from him simply clad in buckskin breeches. Her eyes trailed from his thickly corded chest and smooth stomach to his bare feet. With one hard arm poised and ready to release the spear, he looked like a marble statue from one of Pa's history books. She couldn't take her eyes off him, couldn't tell how many fish he'd caught or how long he'd been trying. The twilight deepened as she studied him and wondered wistfully how many women he'd said no to.

"Morrow," he called over his shoulder.

She got to her feet and trod over frozen stones to see a fine catch of fish lying on a smooth rock. Pa had never liked to fish nor cared much for the taste, so they'd had little occasion to eat them, but Red Shirt showed her how to clean them and cook them in the coals, peeling the charred skin and backbone away when done. Of all the meals they'd shared, this one was the most spare. Just baked fish and little else. But somehow it seemed like the most sumptuous fare.

He met her eyes and said, "You're not so tired tonight. I think this side of the river agrees with you."

She smiled, wondering if he'd sensed how truly thankful she was. Getting up, she went to the river to drink, and he followed, the moon shiny as a pewter plate over their shoulders. She recollected only a few times in her life when she'd been out under the stars and not under the close eaves of the cabin. Free as a bird she felt, roofless and without walls.

He picked up a stone and skimmed it over the water's silvery surface. She watched him closely from the bank—she couldn't help it. Under Pa's watchful eye, she'd never had the privilege. Would she still be this smitten in ten years? Twenty? Here the privacy was profound. Almost hallowed. Yet he hadn't so much as kissed her since the ceremony at the cabin.

A second rock skimmed the river, and she sighed. His arm came down and he turned to her. "Are you missing home, Morrow?"

Thoughtful, she met his steady gaze. "No . . . I'm missing you."

He came to her and rested his hands on her shoulders, tipping her head back so that cold moonlight spilled into her eyes. "How can you miss me when I'm standing here beside you?"

"I—I don't rightly know," she said, feeling she'd stepped off a safe path onto perilous ground. "Aren't you . . . missing me?"

His handsome features turned perplexed. "You think I . . ."

The ensuing silence returned her shyness to her tenfold. A tiny knot of alarm bloomed in her chest, and she looked at her feet.

Perhaps she'd trod too far, but all she wanted was the comfort of his arms. Couldn't he sense that? Must she spell it out?

Gently he framed her face with his hands and brought her head up. "Morrow, you're mourning."

Mourning. A startling realization stole over her. He was telling her he wouldn't touch her so soon after Pa had passed, that she needed time to grieve. Tears shone in her eyes, and she blinked them back. How different he was from Robbie Clay and Major McKie. They would have had their way with her whether she was grieving or not.

"Yes, I'm mourning," she said softly. "I believe I'm mourning *you.*"

A flicker of surprise played over his handsome face, but his gaze remained steadfast. He stood stone still as if waiting for her to settle matters between them. Several breathless moments passed as she waged a startling battle, raw grief finally giving way to a deluge of desire. Without wavering, she inched her arms around his neck and threaded her fingers through his blue black hair.

"Morrow . . . are you sure?"

The tender question touched her. "Never surer," she answered.

Gently, like they were about to dance, he took her in his arms, and she felt a wall within him give way. He held her hungrily—even fiercely—his embrace erasing every fear she had as he buried his face in her freshly washed hair and murmured endearments she'd never heard. The stars and the river faded away, as did all her sorrow. She'd never forget the Falls of the Ohio on the night she became his bride in more than name.

They made poor time on the trail after that. The weather worked against them, snowing by day and turning their shelter to ice by night. Dense forest gave way to open prairie that she was only too willing to embrace after the unrelieved gloom of the woods. But it was so bitter she had trouble drawing an easy breath. The air seemed to turn to ice in her lungs, and her eyelashes froze together in a mournful moment over Pa. Red Shirt wrapped her in a blanket and his buffalo coat and helped her back on the mare. He seemed almost immune to the cold.

They sought shelter long before dusk. Soon a fire struggled to warm them, and she set about making supper from the provisions they had on hand. She was getting tired of jerked meat, remembering the hams hanging in the smokehouse back home. He left her alone in the shelter but quickly returned, carrying a skinned rabbit.

Her eyes widened as she took the meat. "You weren't gone long enough for me to put the kettle on."

"Hunting in the snow is for fools," he said, cleaning his knife. "There's no sport in it."

She began to make broth, then sat back and hugged the blanket closer. The wind was kicking up, almost animal-like, licking and biting the shelter with a keening wail. "I'd fear being out here with anyone but you."

"A new wife is supposed to say such things."

"I wish . . ." Her voice was soft, her eyes flickering over the snug bark and bough walls. "I wish we could be snowed in like this forever."

"Forever is a long time. Soon we come to the camp."

She tried to hide her disquiet, but he missed little. His eyes fastened on her face, warm from the fire, and he seemed almost as rueful as she.

"Once we ride in, I won't leave your side. Everyone will be curious about you. Many Shawnee have never seen a white woman. Some have never seen a white man."

The strangeness of it settled over her like a heavy blanket. He was taking her far out of reach of anything she'd ever known, so far she might be the first white woman to set foot in westernmost Indian territory. She knew so little about his past, his life with his father's people. Sometimes she nearly forgot his ties to the Shawnee. Perhaps she'd best begin finding out.

Her eyes held his in question. "Remember when you came across me picking berries in the woods?"

He studied her thoughtfully. "The day you asked about my Indian name?"

The bittersweet memory almost made her smile. "Yes, but you wouldn't tell me."

"I knew you wouldn't like it if I did. I'm not sure you will now."

"Now that we're wed, it seems like I should know."

He added another stick of wood to the fire. "Wawilaway. It means 'warrior.'"

She expelled a little breath. "I can see why you held your tongue."

"Does it frighten you?"

She hesitated, ashamed to admit his past frightened her beyond all reason, and that was why she asked him so few questions.

His intensity turned to wry amusement. "How is it that a lady like you married a man whose name you didn't know?"

She smiled. "I knew you as Red Shirt."

"I like that name no better."

"What did your mother call you?"

He grew pensive and looked into the fire as if trying to grasp a memory too long denied him. "I don't remember. But at Brafferton in Virginia, they called me Will."

"Taken from your Shawnee name?" He nodded, and she went on, undeniably curious. "How long were you in school there?"

"Long enough to know I couldn't be the gentleman they wanted me to be. Four . . . five winters."

Winters . . . years? The Shawnee phrasing inexplicably tugged at her heart. "You had no happy memories, then?"

"My happiest memory was the day I left. It might have been theirs too."

She smiled back at him, but there were tears in her eyes. "You went all that way in the wilderness to return to your father? Alone—just a boy?"

"I was used to being alone." He stirred the fire with a stick till it blazed a deep cherry red. "A half blood belongs to no one, red or white, remember."

"You belong to me," she said softly.

His eyes met hers, thankfulness in their depths. "You—and Christ."

His heartfelt words made her ache with regret. He was hers, yes, but she'd once been so blinded by unforgiveness she'd hardly looked at him. How like Pa he was, she mused. Though he had reasons aplenty to bear a grudge, he didn't do so.

He unrolled a blanket and lay on his back, eyes closed. Stirring the broth, she was glad to see him at rest. He'd walked every foot-scalding mile today to ease his lame horse, while she'd ridden the mare. Beneath his frocked shirt, his chest soon rose and fell in the easy rhythm of sleep. Smothering a yawn, she fussed with the fire, but he reached over and caught her hand. The firelight flickered over them with beguiling light as they lay down, nose to nose, clearly delighted with each other.

"Aren't you hungry?" she asked as he kissed the hollow of her throat.

"Only for you," he answered.

26

They were traveling west through river valleys so pristine it seemed to Morrow that no one had ever passed this way before, be it red man or white. The air was so sharp and scented with pine she felt she could open her mouth and taste it. As the weather cleared, the sun struck the ground with such brilliance that Red Shirt painted black smudges beneath her eyes to counter snow blindness. The charcoal and bear grease stung her wind-chapped cheeks, but at last she could look around without wincing.

She noticed he seemed to be circling back now, leaving her for short periods beneath a rock shelter or stand of trees while he retraced their steps on his stallion. Ever watchful, he always seemed one step ahead of her, and at first she gave it little thought. But now there seemed a new tension about him that bespoke danger, and she felt it sharp as a knife's edge.

He returned from his backtracking to the camp they were making and hobbled his horse before turning her way. *"Neewa."*

She looked up from the flint and tinder in her hands, warmed by his calling her wife. But the intensity in his face swept all sweet feelings aside as he took the fire starters from her and returned them to their pouch, enfolding her cold fingers in his.

"We can't make camp here. We must go on."

She searched his eyes and saw a flicker of warning. "But it's almost twilight . . ." *And I'm so tired I can't go any further.*

"I'll have to push you," he told her, his breath a crystal cloud. "You're going to have to trust me."

"I do . . . but—"

"We're being followed by Bluecoat soldiers."

What? Her thoughts began a woozy whirl and she gripped his hands. Men like McKie? Seeking to avenge McKie? Or bent on returning her to the Red River?

"If we continue west, we'll lead them right into the heart of my father's camp. Starting tonight we'll head northeast. The moon is full for travel. I know this land like I know your form and face, but they have no such advantage. By dawn we'll have outdistanced them."

She looked toward her mare, hiding her dismay. The poor animal seemed as tired as she. But they must go on. What choice did they have? Unable to speak, she simply nodded, a prayer for strength already dawning in her heart. *Lord, protect us . . . shelter us.*

On into the moonlit night they rode. Morrow's worry faded to a sharp, cold wakefulness that pushed her beyond the edges of endurance. Toward dawn they took shelter in a cave, a small fire warming them and blackening the damp ceiling. She knew that smoke from an open fire, like their tracks in the snow, might lead the soldiers right to them. While he stood watch, she slept rolled up in his buffalo coat till the sun rode higher in the sky and shed fierce light on a forest that now seemed more enemy than friend.

They'd not yet spoken of McKie. He seemed a part of the past, shed like her velvet dress upon leaving the Red River. Yet she couldn't quite clear her mind of the fact that murder was wrong, no matter the motive. But what would she have done if he hadn't been killed? His death seemed to have delivered her—and Pa—from a net of trickery and treason, as well as avenging the murders committed on the Kanawha against the Shawnee, and even Robbie Clay.

Red Shirt rode close beside her now, no longer leading, his

leg brushing her own. "You can rest. The Bluecoats have turned back."

Strangely, the words brought small comfort. She was too worn to even utter a simple "I'm glad," though she saw the satisfaction in his eyes. Reaching out, he encircled her with one hard arm and brought her off her own horse and onto his. Sideways in the saddle, she lay limp as a rag doll against the bulwark of his body, her head cradled against his shoulder.

His arms formed a hedge around her as he held the reins, his voice already sounding queer and far-off. "Sleep, Morrow, and forget about the trouble."

Morrow awoke to a little glen drifted deep in white mist, the sulfurous odor reminding her of smelling salts. Was she dreaming? Red Shirt helped her down, steadying her till she got her bearings.

"Mineral springs?" she said in wonder.

"Long ago when I was a boy, the Shawnee made camp here. I wanted to show you."

"Pa used to speak of such springs in Virginia."

Weary as she was, she felt the delight of it clear to her toes. Tall stands of cedar and hemlock framed a number of steaming pools, the milky water a froth of bubbles and founts. Turning toward the mare, she fumbled with the tie on a saddlebag and retrieved a pewter cup. Walking to the edge of the nearest spring, she dipped her cup into the bubbling water and drank it down. Its warmth seemed to spread in a languid stream through her stiff limbs, bringing a sudden flush to her face.

He watched her keenly, amusement in his eyes. "I thought you'd want to bathe in it, not drink it."

"I'll do both." Handing him the empty cup, she began removing her shoepacks and leggings, shedding her shift and skirt along with all her inhibitions, finally freeing her hair of its pins.

Poised on the rim of the largest pool, she looked back at him, hair streaming over her paleness like some woodland nymph. Through the mist he regarded her with mingled wonder and desire, and she gave a belated blush, eyes falling to the steaming water. No matter the cold or the danger, she was a bride and he was her groom, and no Bluecoat soldiers bent on destruction could change that.

She was growing tired . . . so tired. And it was becoming ever harder to hide it. What, she wondered, would Pa think if he could see her now? Each new day found her cleaning and stretching beaver plews on willow frames to dry, a snapping fire warming her back as she worked in their temporary shelter. The musky scent seemed to follow her everywhere, staining her hands and clothing, but somehow filling all the uncomfortable corners of her life with the satisfaction of work well done.

Standing on the banks of nameless creeks and streams, Morrow watched her husband wade into the frigid water and set his traps in the shallows, thrusting a pole through the ring end to hold and mark it, then smearing an exposed willow twig with beaver scent taken from the glands of earlier caches. He worked quickly and expertly, and the pile of plews mounted as they made their way north.

Soon she lost all track of time. As the days passed in a whirl of work and weariness, she tried to grasp the goodness in this trial. Although they were no longer heading toward Missouri, they were together. They'd eluded the soldiers. She was no longer the same Morrow who'd left the Red River weeks before. She had a new and wondrous secret . . .

"We're nearing Loramie's Station," Red Shirt told her as if sensing her growing weariness. "We'll rest there and get fresh provisions before heading west."

Loramie's Station. It sounded rough yet heaven-sent. A safe haven. Though they didn't speak of it, their flight from the Bluecoats seemed to wedge its way between them, tainting their joy. She thought of it as she sewed a new shirt for him around the fire, pleased by the satisfaction she saw in his face as he eyed her efforts. But her thread was almost gone, and somewhere along the way she'd lost Aunt Etta's silver thimble.

She paused to rest her eyes, her needle still. "Who is Loramie?"

He looked up from the trap he was repairing. "Loramie is French—a trader."

"I've heard Joe talk of him. He's a loyal friend of the Indians."

"And a bitter enemy of the Bluecoats," he added, saying no more.

She set aside her sewing and lay down on their makeshift bed. The wind seemed to whistle as it shook their small shelter, scattering smoke from the fire to the far corners. He joined her, his rifle within arm's reach. Tonight she was too tired to undress or even unravel her hair from the careless bun she'd made. She simply laid her head upon his shoulder.

The silence deepened, and she heard a lone wolf howl. A thousand thoughts swirled in her head, and she shut her eyes, one hand atop the smooth leather of Pa's worn Bible.

Strengthen Thou me.

Sunlight stole away the stars and sent the moon packing, ushering in an early dawn. When she awoke, Red Shirt had gone to check his traps, but he'd coaxed the waning fire into a cheerful blaze. She left the shelter to relieve herself, leaning against a tree when she stood. All around her the woods seemed to tilt and spin. Why had she walked so far from the shelter? Her mouth was dry as cotton, and she was trembling from head to toe. Even bundled warmly in her winter garb, she felt nearly naked.

With an overwhelmingly helpless feeling, she sank to her knees atop the hard ground, frozen moss and mud beneath her fingers. Despite the near-blinding whiteness of the snow, the edges of the forest began to grow shadowed, then quickly darkened to midnight. Before she collapsed completely, she heard Red Shirt calling her name.

Only an expert horseman could move so quickly, carrying her over such uneven ground her teeth chattered. She came to her senses twice, once when they crossed an ice-edged river and the horse stumbled, and again when the sun seemed almost to melt her and she realized she was burning up with fever. Though she could no longer hold her eyes open, her sense of smell was keen. The odor of tanned furs and lamp oil, coffee beans and tobacco, assailed her.

Equally strange were the voices, the most unusual of them being a man speaking heavily accented English. Red Shirt's voice was clearest of all and unmistakably anguished as he switched from English to Shawnee, then, to Morrow's surprise, into French. In time a woman's soothing voice bridged the darkness. The melodious sounds were like music, swelling like a stirring symphony on every side of her before ceasing altogether.

In time she stopped hearing anything at all, lost in the hellacious heat that soaked her and then made her shiver. Pa seemed to hover at her side, saying her name, soothing her as he'd done when she was small and sick. But where was Red Shirt? Crying out for him only brought the terror nearer and made him seem farther away. Her dreams seemed to taunt her. She was not fit for his wild life, sick and white as she was. She was a burden he'd not dreamed of.

At last she awoke to a glimmer of light shining through a shuttered window. Beside her, Red Shirt was dozing in a chair. The spectacle almost made her smile. He sat arrow straight, head tipped back slightly against the rough wall, arms folded and eyes shut. How was it, she wondered, that even asleep he managed to look wary?

Slowly she sat up, fighting dizziness before swinging her feet free of the feather tick. Beneath her unfamiliar muslin shift, her body felt light as thistledown and her skin seemed to crawl. Only the weight of her uncombed, tangled hair falling to the small of her back was reassuringly familiar.

Before she'd taken two shaky steps, he jerked awake, catching her in his arms. Suddenly he was murmuring endearments in her ear, and his hands were everywhere at once—in her hair, on her bare shoulders, down her back—as if doubting she was truly standing, truly alive.

"I—I thought I was dying," she said, clutching the soft fringe of his frocked shirt as if to stay upright.

"You nearly did," he said.

"Where are we?"

"Loramie's Station."

"How long?"

"Six agonizing sleeps," he told her.

Six days, nights? A sense of the miraculous stole over her. If not for his quick action, she knew she'd have never made it. Gently he settled her back on the bed, and the tide of events slowly came back to her like fragments of a bad dream best forgotten. "You never left my side . . . you were here all along." He nodded, and she rushed on. "But what of our furs—our camp?"

"Loramie sent his clerk to bring them in. But it matters little, Morrow."

He crouched in front of her and brushed back her hair with a rough hand. In turn her fingertips skimmed the smooth line of his jaw, noting the telling shadows beneath his eyes, the striking features more finely chiseled. "Why, you've hardly eaten—or slept."

His intensity softened, and he smiled. "Now I can."

She darted a glance about the room, surprised by the fine armoire that graced one corner opposite a Windsor chair and writing desk, so at odds with the crude wood walls. Beneath her bare feet was a thick gros point rug covering unpolished planking that stretched to a rough wooden door. Bewildered, she looked back at him. "I thought I heard Pa calling my name . . ."

His smile was relieved if wry. "Your father's spirit seemed to hover at my shoulder, demanding to know what I'd done with his daughter."

Her face softened. "Pa never doubted you'd take care of me."

"Loramie's wife made you well. I lost my medicine bag in the river, remember?"

But she was hardly able to recall their frantic flight across the icy water. As she groped about for details, a decisive knock sounded on the door. It swung open, revealing a brocade-clad figure, a bundle of fresh bedding in her arms. For a brief moment it seemed Good Robe stood before them, and Morrow nearly said her name. The woman came forward, followed by a boy with an armful of firewood and another lugging a hip bath.

"Leave your wife with me, and I promise to return her to you by supper," she said to Red Shirt with a surprising familiarity.

He simply nodded and then left without a word, tousling the dark heads of the two boys as they scampered ahead of him. Alone with the strange woman, Morrow felt a trifle tongue-tied as sharp black eyes appraised every inch of her.

"Ah, but you will be a pleasure to resurrect," she murmured in heavily accented English, calling over her shoulder for hot water. Within moments the door opened again, and a trio of girls trooped in bearing steaming buckets. They looked her way shyly, their comely features such a mix of Indian and white blood that Morrow was reminded of Little Eli.

"I want to thank you for helping make me well," Morrow told the woman.

"*Oui, oui.* We simply said our prayers and the Almighty answered," she replied, her slender face creasing in a satisfied smile. She worked around Morrow as she sat on the edge of the bed, supervising the girls as they came and went with their buckets, checking the water level in the tub and adding a handful of something that scented the whole room. Lily of the valley, Morrow guessed. She hadn't had a real bath since her wedding day, if one didn't count the rivers and creeks and mineral springs. But when she stood to undress, her senses seemed to scatter.

The woman left the room, returning with a tray. Morrow tried to hide her surprise at the embroidered napkin, the porcelain teapot with an exquisite china cup, and the plate of tiny biscuits, cheeses, and sweetmeats set before her.

"You spoil me," Morrow exclaimed.

"You are a lady, no? Your husband tells me you are."

Morrow looked down at the cuts on her hands from skinning beaver, thought of the filthy dress she'd had on when she fell into the mud in her delirium. *A lady indeed.* Tears filled her eyes, touched that he'd say so and that this woman was gracious enough to believe him.

Without further ado, the woman began to pour the steaming tea, making belated introductions. "I am the wife of Pierre Loramie. Angelique is my French name, given to me by my voyageur father. I am also called Straight Ahead by my mother's people, the Shawnee."

Morrow looked up. "And the children?"

"All those half bloods you see coming and going are mine as well. They will make their own introductions in time. For now you must simply eat and bathe. There is a bell on the table there, should you need me."

Famished, Morrow sampled each item on the tray and sipped the tea—strong bohea by its bite and flavor—and felt her strength return bit by bit. When she'd finished, she made her way to a window, pushed back the shutters, and peered out on pickets that seemed to impale a leaden sky. A sweeping glance told her she was in a two-story log house that was part of a fortified post. On every side, a winter tracing of trees held back bleak woods as far as the eye could see, evidence that they were in the very heart of the wilderness.

Turning away, she shed the strange shift and stepped into the steaming tub. The pleasure it gave her nearly made her moan. Hot water. Bayberry soap. A stack of soft cotton towels. Within minutes she felt renewed but couldn't see a speck of clean clothing anywhere in the room. Angelique soon remedied that, carrying in an armful of garments and placing them on a chair.

Taking up a comb, the elegant woman began to work, and in half an hour Morrow stood alone before a full-length mirror, shaken to her stocking feet. Once before, she'd had this strange feeling, when she'd first dressed in the clothing Red Shirt had brought her. Now the reflected image was startling in a different way. Her hips and legs were encased in silk stockings and garters and petticoats, her bosom buried beneath a camisole of finely embroidered muslin. Atop everything was a snug dress with faux pearl buttons, the soft apricot brocade overlaid with fragile ivory lace.

Who am I, anyway?

Woozy, she sat down again on the crisply made bed, thinking she couldn't possibly go below stairs. The smells of supper thickened on the air, and she could hear girlish laughter and the clink of cutlery as someone set a table and readied for a meal. She fingered the fine fabric, feeling a bit smothered by the too-tight bodice. There was no doubt she appreciated such fine things. They warmed her with memories of Philadelphia and Aunt Etta's fine dress shop and the old wardrobe in her attic room. But dressed as she was, she looked waxen . . . fragile as eggshell. She *felt* fragile as eggshell. Red Shirt would no doubt be even more careful of her, particularly if she told him what she was now sure of . . .

The door swung open without a warning knock, and he stepped into the room. She couldn't look at him, trussed up as she was, so she looked away, fixing her eyes on a crack in the floor by her right foot. The feather tick gave way as he sat beside her. He tucked in a stray curl that had come free of the ribbon and lace Angelique had woven into her upswept hair. Timidly her eyes skimmed the floor and fastened on one black boot firmly planted just beyond the sweep of her skirts. Next her eye trailed to seamless buckskin breeches before taking in the ruffled cuff of an exquisite linen shirtsleeve.

His voice was low and amused. "What a pair we make, Morrow. The lovesick Métis scout and the beautiful Shemanese princess. At least that's what Loramie called us when we dragged ourselves into this post."

At this she laughed and looked him fully in the face. His hair was freshly washed and hung in ebony strands about his shoulders, dampening his fine shirt. He smelled of bayberry and tobacco and something else she couldn't place. And his eyes, though tired, shone with pleasure.

"I hardly know you," she exclaimed softly, reaching out and touching the wedding band that glinted on his hand.

"I hardly know myself," he said.

"I'm ready to go below," she said with forced eagerness, ignoring the nausea swelling beneath her snug bodice. "I want to meet our host . . . see where we are."

Though he said nothing, she sensed he saw past her pretense

to the exhaustion beneath. But she'd not lie abed a minute longer. Avoiding his eyes, she took in all the details of the charmingly inconsistent room, lingering on the genteel painting above the rough-hewn mantel. An oil landscape, she guessed, like the ones she'd seen in Philadelphia. Who was this Pierre Loramie? Something told her he was as much a puzzle as their surroundings.

Through the cracked door came a sudden burst of childish giggling and French chatter. She looked up and found several children spying on them from the doorway, faces alight.

"Come, Monsieur Red Shirt, and bring your lovely bride. Our dear papa is waiting."

27

Days before, Morrow had been carried into Loramie's Station but had no recollection of it. Now, on Red Shirt's arm, she descended a wide set of steps, marveling at all she'd missed. Her fingers brushed a swirl of pungent greenery tied with gold ribbon along the polished handrail. Bayberry candles glinted abundantly in the foyer below, their scent so pleasant after the stale, shut-in bedroom. She smelled roasting meat—goose, she guessed. And stuffing. Her mouth began to moisten. Across the way a door was open to a dining room, and on the long table was an enormous standing salt and salver of sweetmeats.

A bit awed, she turned to a small man standing at the head of the table. Dressed with French flair, he wore a scarlet silk waistcoat, the silver queue of his hair hanging over one shoulder and—could it be?—falling to his knees. "My name is Pierre Loramie, Madame Red Shirt. Welcome to my table."

She smiled, flattered when he came forward and kissed her hand then introduced her to his other guests. A curious assortment of British soldiers, frontiersmen, and Indians stood at intervals about the room.

Loramie seated her then Angelique. Fleetingly, she wondered where the children were. She could hear their playful voices behind a closed door. Red Shirt sat beside her, his knee brushing her heavy skirt beneath the table. At the head of the table, Loramie bowed his head and said grace—in French—and the words struck a strange chord though she understood little.

As if on cue, two women in crisp cambric aprons brought heaping platters of meat and stuffing, apple tansy, and other dishes she had no name for. The men ate with gusto, speaking a mishmash of Shawnee, French, and English, while the candles smoldered in their holders, nearly overpowering the aroma of the meal with their rich perfume. Everyone seemed in high spirits, making her think it was some sort of French holiday.

Perplexed, she looked at Red Shirt. "What day is it?"

At this, all the chatter at the table seemed to still. Red Shirt turned his head to answer, but another voice drew Morrow's eyes to the end of the table. "To the Shawnee it is merely the Cold Moon, Madame Red Shirt. To the French it is Joyeux Noel. To the Americans it is almost Christmas."

She set her fork down and swallowed a mouthful of meat, trying to contain her welling emotions. They were hours away from Christmas Day. A crushing sense of homesickness stole over her as she recalled her last winter with Pa.

"Tomorrow we celebrate our Savior's birth," Loramie continued as if sensing her disquiet. "After divine service we will meet here to exchange a present or two and partake of another meal that is even finer than this one. We are not so uncivilized that we neglect the Almighty or each other, even on the frontier, no?"

She offered him a grateful smile, glad when the merry conversation around her resumed. Red Shirt joined in, filling her with wonder at his French. On her sickbed she'd heard him speaking such but thought it just a dream. Now little eddies of disbelief swirled inside her as she listened to a man she had known intimately yet felt she didn't know at all.

She darted a quick glance at him, taking in all the little heart-stopping details that made him so handsome. It wasn't simply the elegant English-made shirt or the sheen of hair tied back with silk ribbon, nor the new breeches and boots from Loramie's stores. Here in this room amidst other men, he had a presence, just as Pa had once said. When he spoke, they listened or deferred, and he seemed to know a great many things she didn't, like the status of the war raging in the East, treaties being made and broken, and the standing of other tribes.

Despite all that was going on about them, he was remarkably attentive to her, even now looking at her like she was not Morrow at all but someone else entirely, brought back from the grave, perhaps, and into his arms again. Though he'd said little about it, she knew she'd nearly died since coming to this place. The shadows beneath his eyes told her so, as did the lean lines of his tanned face, made more pronounced in the candlelight.

"What say you, Red Shirt? Will General Hand summon you as interpreter for the tribal council at Fort Pitt this spring?" Loramie's voice rose and silenced the din as he looked down the table. "Supposedly he has dispatched such a request, and a Shawnee courier is even now on his way to your father's village."

Red Shirt took Morrow's hand beneath the table and leaned back slightly in his chair, his profile thoughtful. "I've heard nothing of it until now."

Loramie's face was grave. "Since our great chief and friend Cornstalk traveled the Kanawha in good faith and met with treachery, the violence has been increasing even during so-called peaceable treaty-makings. I must caution against Fort Pitt in the future. If you go, I fear for you, *mon ami*. It seems there were no repercussions for the soldiers who committed such a crime at Fort Randolph, thus the path is prepared for more of the same."

At his words, a volley of voices erupted around the table, but the frontiersman nearest Loramie was the most vocal. "There is a half blood at this very table who righted that particular wrong, or so I've been told. The murdering soldier chief at Fort Randolph is no more."

Loramie's eyes swung to Red Shirt, a knowing smile stealing

over his face. Morrow felt Angelique's eyes on her as if gauging her reaction to so indelicate a subject, but the pressure of Red Shirt's hand settled her. Still, the image of Major McKie's russet scalp seemed to cast a sudden pall over the festivities.

"Ah, so there is justice at the hands of a half blood, after all. I rejoice!" Springing up, Loramie went to an ornate liquor cabinet behind his chair, fumbled in his waistcoat for a key, and opened the door to reveal a dizzying assortment of bottles. "We must celebrate such a victory, however belated. Gentlemen, what shall it be? Brandy? Madeira? Port? *A votre sante!* To your health!"

Every man stood but Red Shirt. In moments their host had emptied two bottles of cranberry-colored liquid into crystal glasses, at last coming around behind them where they sat. Red Shirt reached out and covered the top of his goblet with one hand. "*Nekanoh*, I am not the man I was."

Loramie hesitated. "So the rumors I have been hearing are true. You have buried the hatchet. You are a man of peace."

"I am a murderer and a horse thief," he answered. "But I have been forgiven."

"You have made your peace with God, then," Loramie mused, raising his glass. "Well, *mon ami*, I am glad you did so *after* avenging Major McKie."

Goblets were raised high in a toast, and then the room stilled again, every eye turned toward them. Morrow felt Angelique touch her shoulder and motion her away. She stood up reluctantly, but it was clear the men had matters to discuss and wanted to do so apart from feminine company. She followed her hostess into an adjoining room, smaller but equally bright with candle flame. The children were finishing their meal and looked up, making exclamations of pleasure in French.

"This is Pierre, Josee, Minon, Albert, and Esme." Angelique seemed to glow as she shut the door and studied each face. "And this, my dear children, is Madame Red Shirt."

"*Oui, oui!* The Shemanese princess!" they shouted in unison, making Morrow laugh despite her weariness.

"Now, you mustn't tire her. She will be staying with us until she is well. Perhaps she would like some music. Esme, will you play for us?"

A tall girl in ivory brocade got up from the table and sat down at a harpsichord near a shuttered window. Morrow took a chair, smiling as the smallest girl—Josee?—came near and climbed onto her lap. She melted as the child leaned into her, her plump body smelling of talcum powder, her mouth rimmed with cocoa from her cup. Morrow rifled her dark curls, lost in thought.

The music coming from beneath the hands of the girl across the room was lovely and soft and soothing. Morrow breathed a prayer of thanks to have come to this rough yet strangely refined place after so long a journey. She was sorry when the music came to an end, but after half an hour Angelique urged her to return to her room and rest, excusing herself and herding the children off to bed.

The door to the main dining room was ajar, and Morrow slipped through the opening. The men were now gathered around a crackling hearth in the sitting room opposite, shoulder to shoulder, most with glasses or pipes in hand. Snatches of conversation drifted to her in a variety of languages. She didn't mean to eavesdrop, nor wanted to, particularly when it concerned matters of war.

The tobacco-laden air seemed rife with intrigue and speculation, full of the latest rumblings from across *La Belle Riviere*. Since they'd left the Red River, the Shawnee and their British allies were preparing to raid the settlements again in retaliation for McKie's attacks upon the Shawnee towns. Their planned assault would commence in late summer, when the settlement's crops were most vulnerable, thus creating a lean winter for the Kentuckians. The grim news, related so matter-of-factly, kicked up a whirlwind inside her. Late summer. By then, if her calculations were right . . . if she hadn't miscounted . . .

She took a steadying breath and started up the stairs, torn between telling Red Shirt her secret or tucking it away. Best keep it close till morning. 'Twould make a fine Christmas gift in light of the fact she had none other to give.

Should she . . . or shouldn't she? All through Christmas dinner, nausea rising, Morrow weighed the wisdom of sharing her secret as she pushed her uneaten food around her china plate. She didn't want to tell Red Shirt just yet, but if she tarried, emptying her stomach in a chamber pot would soon give her away. And then how would she explain her reluctance to share such news?

Raising her eyes, she flushed to find him studying her through the haze of candle flame. Astute as he was, might he already know? Feeling feverish, she dropped her eyes to the napkin in her lap. Just this morning at breakfast, Angelique had whispered her startling question, yet it hadn't felt right to confess to her hostess what she'd held back from her own husband.

As if urging her on, the grandfather clock just beyond the dining room struck nine times. Only three hours left till the day was done. But would the gaiety never end?

The snap of a Yule log and glint of candles lent an inviting air to the spacious sitting room they adjourned to after supper. All within was crowded and congenial and exhausting, while beyond the shuttered windows, icicles sharp as saber points hung from the frozen eaves. There'd been a startling absence of war talk today, just feasting and toasting and good wishes, and now, at last, Loramie's guests began to disperse. Soon even their host slipped away, bidding them a merry good night.

Morrow lingered by the fire on a brocade sofa, hands clasped in her lap. Red Shirt sat beside her, looking decidedly out of place upon the stiff sofa, not only dwarfing it but making it seem ridiculously ornate. The spectacle made her smile, and then she almost laughed as he reached up and yanked at the stock binding his neck like a noose. Balling it in a fist, he deposited it in an urn on the hearth.

"Reminds me of Brafferton," he said quietly, unbuttoning his waistcoat.

Bending down, she removed her too-tight shoes, taking a deep breath. The clock in the hall struck midnight, and he moved to put another log on the fire as if inviting her to linger and tell him everything. But the practiced words seemed to stick in her throat. What if the news only made him more careful with her? What if . . . She swallowed down her dismay, hardly able to complete the thought. What if he wasn't happy with the news?

He was reaching into the pocket of his waistcoat, his features suddenly solemn. "Close your eyes."

Did he have a present for her, then? Shutting her eyes, she felt him take her hand and kiss her callused palm. The tender gesture turned her heart over, and a tear slid beneath her lashes. Next he placed something in her hand and closed her fingers around it. A delicious anticipation eclipsed her angst.

"For you," he said, "from your father."

Pa? She opened her hand and looked down at an oval miniature. Instantly she knew whose picture was contained within that tiny silver frame. Ma and Jess. Not Jess as she'd known him but Jess as a baby, small and pink and round, his hair the hue of bittersweet. Their firstborn. Biting her lip, she brought the gift to her breast, too moved to speak.

He leaned nearer, one arm encircling her. "I didn't mean to make you sad—"

She stemmed his words with her fingers. "It means so much . . . even more tonight . . ." She looked down at the miniature again, knowing now was the time to tell him. When she hesitated, he reached into the urn to retrieve his stock and began to dry her face with the soft linen.

"I'm not done crying yet," she whispered with a smile, taking the neck cloth away from him. "I still haven't given you your gift."

"I have nothing for you," he said.

"Oh, but you do. The gift you've given me is the same one I'm giving you."

Setting the stock and miniature in her lap, she took his hands. She could feel the warmth of his fingers through the fine cloth of her dress as she pressed them to her middle. He looked at her, stark wonder in his eyes.

"Forgive me for not telling you sooner. I've known for some time." She gave him a half smile. "Perhaps clear back to the Falls of the Ohio."

"Our first time?" He sounded amazed, even amused.

"If a woman can know such things, yes."

His handsome face held a touch of disbelief—and something akin to grief. Was he sorry? Thinking they'd not make it to Missouri? "I would have brought you here sooner if I'd known."

She shook her head. "It doesn't matter. I'm fine now . . . and ready to leave for Missouri when you are. The baby isn't coming for months yet."

"When?"

"Summer . . . August, perhaps."

"We'll winter here, then," he said with characteristic calm. "Loramie is in need of a hunter and scout."

A shadow of alarm gripped her. "But what about going west?"

"Spring is a better time to travel."

Looking down at the miniature again, she felt disappointment crowd out her anticipation, yet she couldn't deny the wisdom of waiting. She'd been on her feet but two days since the fever and was still weak. And now, with a baby coming . . .

He bent his head till his mouth was warm against her ear. "We'll make our way to Missouri, Morrow. There's plenty of time yet to travel before next winter sets in."

She heard the promise and the pleasure in his voice and tried to smile.

Morrow peeked past the massive oak doors of the trading room. Within the lantern-lit space, she watched as capable clerks transacted business, bartering and trading in furs and English currency. Red Shirt had yet to trade, so she held her anticipation tight, like a child with an unopened package, knowing the pleasure was largely in the waiting. Loramie's Station was more hospitable than any frontier post she'd ever seen. Large parties of Indians from the Great Lakes to the warmer southern climes frequented the post that bordered Loramie's Creek, throwing up temporary shelters just beyond the picketed walls. The distillation of rum and tobacco and smoking meat filled the air day and night, and a festive feeling lingered.

She found their French host charming, shrewd, and breathtakingly blunt. He bore a deep grudge against the Americans who ate up the land as they pushed west, decimating game, bringing disease, and feeding the Indians lies by serving up worthless treaties. And he didn't hesitate to discuss such matters with anyone who cared to do so.

"You listen hard, Madame Red Shirt," Loramie remarked one evening after dinner as they gathered about the sitting room fire. "Where do your loyalties lie?"

She looked up from the handkerchief she was embroidering, realizing she could no longer plead neutrality in the growing conflict. "My father schooled me to consider both sides."

"Wise words. Your dear departed papa was a man of God, no? Principled and unprejudiced? Your husband has told me of him."

"You must know of my brother, then. The Shawnee took him captive nearly fifteen years ago."

He nodded thoughtfully, drawing on his pipe. "If your brother remains with the Shawnee, he is by now more Indian than white. There are many captives willing to stay missing. Do not grieve unduly. I doubt he grieves for you."

His words saddened her, but she noted a telling sympathy in his eyes. Returning to her sewing, she listened to the steady cadence of their voices and worked to stay awake. But the bright fire and the hot cocoa Angelique had served made her feel as lethargic as the calico cat curled up at her feet. She glanced at Red Shirt, now speaking French with Loramie an arm's length away. Lately she wondered if they lapsed into the melodious language to avoid unsettling her.

Since she'd shared the news of her pregnancy, they seemed to treat her like the exquisite porcelain china that graced the shelves of Loramie's store. Though every piece was packed in straw and shipped in metal-banded barrels from France, not all survived the journey. Was that how she seemed to them? Fragile? About to break? The fever she'd survived still seemed to hover—and now there was this unbridled nausea.

"You must rest," Angelique cautioned, urging her upstairs. "Tomorrow is the day you will trade and move into your own cabin."

Morrow tried to summon some excitement for the task ahead.

The next morning, standing in the middle of Loramie's well-stocked store, she was surprised to find she felt as enchanted as a child. An intoxicating blend of things embraced her the moment she walked in. Freshly ground coffee and leather. Perfume and pickling spices. Smoked hams and lamp oil and the feral scent of furs. The beaver plews they'd taken coming north netted a small fortune. Of all the furs, beaver fetched the highest price, bundled and sent East to become fine hats for wealthy colonists and Europeans alike.

"I've never seen finer," Loramie's clerk said as he examined the pelts. "I hardly have to glance at them to know they are your husband's, Madame Red Shirt. Every season it is the same."

"They're more Morrow's than mine," Red Shirt replied, selecting powder and shot further down the wide counter. "She cured them."

Surprised, she looked at him. He'd not shown his appreciation till now, and it warmed her like the potbellied stove at her back.

Taking her arm, Pierre Loramie gestured to row upon row of trade goods. "What catches your eye today? I have fine silks, embossed flannel, vermillion, gartering, ribbon, pinheads, handkerchiefs, and some brocade recently arrived from d'Etroit."

"Might you have a thimble and some thread?" she asked.

"For you, madame, I have more."

Crossing the plank floor, he led her to a lantern-lit corner. There she grew wide-eyed at sewing chests finer than Aunt Etta's own and a rainbow of fabrics she couldn't even name. Elaborate tins held countless spools of bright thread, thimbles, metal needles, and a bounty of buttons.

"I'll take one spool of plain thread, two needles, and one thimble," she said softly, unsure of how the trading transpired.

Loramie winked conspiratorially. "Your husband has told me you are to take anything you like."

Turning, she looked at Red Shirt, who merely smiled while Loramie began displaying his latest shipment of striped cotton, the heavier osnaburg, and delicate silks. Thinking ahead, she selected swanskin and watched as the clerk cut enough for two babies.

"I know you are partial to cocoa," Loramie said, turning to take two tins off a shelf.

She smiled her thanks, already perusing the bins of dried rice and beans, huge barrels of pickles and brined beef, and a selection of books that would have made Pa linger. A final aisle boasted elaborately plumed hats and silk shoes and overdone dresses.

Morrow watched the clerks move their goods across the frozen common, past Loramie's imposing house to the cabin that would be their home till they went west. Soon after, she stood in the middle of the impossibly small room and tried to summon some appreciation for the cane-backed rocker before the stone hearth and the bed in the corner boasting a clean, if less than fluffy, feather tick. Angelique brought over a washbasin and pitcher while Morrow unpacked their belongings from the Red River cabin.

Almost home, she thought, her mind on Missouri. She saw Red Shirt's eyes linger on the thick-timbered beams strung with spiderwebs before taking in every dim corner escaping the lamplight. Though he said nothing, she sensed his dissatisfaction. Was he missing his old way of life? Wanting to be out under the stars? The thought that he might be grieved her. They should have been well on their way to Missouri by now . . .

While he went with Loramie to settle accounts, she finished unpacking. Esme helped make the big bed and set out kettles and pans at the hearth before leaving Morrow alone.

As she bent to take some pewter cups out of a saddlebag, her senses quickened. From far off came a distant yet distinct sound, almost an echo. Long minutes ticked by, bringing the noise ever nearer. The very room seemed to reverberate, reminding her of the steady cadence of regimental drums, full of bluster and warning.

Red Shirt appeared in the doorway. "Redcoats," he said.

Redcoats . . . not Bluecoats. Lately she'd hardly thought of the Americans who'd pursued them beyond the Ohio River. Within the safety of Loramie's Station, she'd begun to feel cocooned from the danger. Their ongoing honeymoon, sweet and hallowed as any should be, had eclipsed the gathering darkness. Did her fear show in her face?

He looked at her, the thunder of the drums between them, and she looked at his weapons by the cabin door. Loramie's words, spoken across the candlelit table on Christmas Eve, returned to her in a haunting rush.

I fear for you, mon ami.

28

Having never lived within the confines of a fort, Morrow was soon wondering how Lizzy and Jemima had managed traipsing to the necessary at the far end of the common and laundering their under things in plain view of so many men. There was no privacy to be had unless the door was barred, and then the boldest Indians and frontiersmen would appear at the windows. Within a few days she'd all but abandoned the strictures of her old Red River routine. Her new life was like a patchwork quilt, bright and colorful but entirely without pattern or order. She quickly learned to keep a pot of stew simmering all day and to show no surprise when someone stopped in to have a bite to eat and a good look at her besides. Soon there was a marked trail to their cabin door and dozens of bewildering reunions.

"I think you know everyone in this fort," she said to Red Shirt with wonder. "Perhaps the whole frontier."

He smiled and his eyes seemed to dance. "Once you asked if I ever stayed in one place. Now you know the answer."

British soldiers, Indians, and frontiersmen gathered round their hearth, filling the air with a thundercloud of smoke as they puffed on their pipes and swapped stories or news. She understood little of the cacophony of languages—English, French, Spanish, and a host of Indian tongues—but all reminded her of Babel.

Sitting apart from the circle of men, she stayed engrossed in her sewing, fashioning tiny garments made of swanskin from

Loramie's store and praying for the child she carried. Sometimes when her queasiness seemed unbearable, she would slip outside to stand beneath the blockhouse eave. There, beyond the post's open postern gate, she could see the glowing campfires along Loramie's Creek and was rewarded with the sweet trill of a fife or a fiddle.

And then, quite suddenly, the torrent of visitors slowed to a trickle.

Slightly alarmed, she turned to Red Shirt. "Is something wrong? We have so few visitors anymore."

"The trading season is simply slowing down," he said. "And your patience has been rewarded with peace."

Peace. That was what she felt in the flickering firelight alone with him in the evenings to come, when they sat shoulder to shoulder and he read from his Bible. The treasured copy was even more worn now, having survived a second immersion in the river they'd crossed on their way to Loramie's. She'd looked regretfully at the water-stained text and had been grateful when their host had offered a new one from his stores.

"Take it with you when you go out on a scout, *mon ami*," he'd said. "It will cheer you when you sit about your campfire and are missing your lovely wife."

Later, as she packed both Bibles in Red Shirt's saddlebags, sneaking in some sweetmeats and other nonessentials from Loramie's store, she prayed unceasingly for his safety. When he first rode out, it seemed she held her breath and didn't exhale till he came back again.

"What do you do out there?" she asked in the inky midnight darkness when she couldn't sleep, knowing he'd be gone again by dawn.

"Ride and read sign and hunt. Sometimes I come across red flag men—"

"Red flag men?"

"Surveyors," he said. "And I send them and their chains and markers back from whence they came."

She realized how dangerous it was, yet she knew he couldn't be shut up in the post. He was earning their keep supplying meat for Loramie's table, at which they were often guests. When he was away, she spent much of her time with Angelique and her daughters, sewing in their brightly lit sitting room. Their shared talk and laughter seemed a living thing—warm and consoling, strengthening and healing.

Often she thought of home, or tried to, but all the little details that had cocooned her there were growing hazy. The view from her bedroom window . . . the leafy richness of the orchard . . . the disarray across the dogtrot . . . the poignant timbre of Pa's voice. Even her treasured, tattered memory of Jess seemed to have fallen to pieces, as if leaving the Red River had broken their last tenuous tie. Yet he was ever in her thoughts as she discreetly studied the men who ventured into the post, hoping and praying he might be among them. But she soon grew disheartened. There were so many bearded, trail-worn, dirty travelers. How would she even recognize him if she saw him? And after so long, how could he possibly know her?

As the snow thawed, Red Shirt's forays led to longer absences. She began to sense a growing restlessness about him when he was within fort walls. Though he never complained, she saw the faraway look in his eyes and feared he was wishing they were on the trail to Missouri. Sitting by the fire without him, she felt the baby flutter inside her and pondered their uncertain future. Even with Angelique across the way and hoards of people within and without fort walls, she felt smothered by aloneness. She tried to pray, but her tangled thoughts took a lonesome turn.

Pa, Ma, Euphemia dead. Jess missing.

And Morrow lost.

Red Shirt had been away for eight days. The first of spring's wildflowers he'd picked for her—pale blue and nameless—had wilted, bent over their vase in colorful disarray. Morrow tried not to look at them as she walked to the postern gates and gazed in the direction he'd ridden out, as if doing so could bring him back to her. Even Loramie seemed tense and restless in his absence. His best scout had gone missing and he could not account for him, and he was a man who liked to account for everything.

Awakening the next morning to a tumbled bed empty of Red Shirt's bulk once more, she felt a gnawing restlessness. Finally, she could stand it no longer. She sat up on the side of the feather bed and waited for the unwelcome rush of wooziness, but all she felt were her cold feet and the miracle of life inside her. Despite her heaviness of heart, the wonder of it made her want to sing. She hummed an old French lullaby that pulled at the corners of her mind.

She dressed in simple calico, reaching for the scarlet cape Angelique had given her and settling it around her shoulders. Quiet as an Indian, she slipped through the front gates in the early dawn, past shelters and arbors full of sated, snoring wayfarers sleeping off their revelry of the night before.

As she walked south along Loramie's Creek, toward Kentucke and the Red River and all the familiar things she'd turned her back on months before, the implications of Red Shirt's absence tugged at her. He'd never been away more than three days at most. Eight seemed a lifetime. Anger crowded out concern and then circled back to simple worry.

Lord, You know where he is even if I don't. Please don't leave me wondering, like I've always wondered about Jess.

The morning was new and clean-smelling, the air threaded with birdsong. Out here God seemed to give her a gift at every turn—a pretty stone, an eagle's majestic flight, a fragile wildflower pushing up through new grass. She stopped and rested on a sun-warmed rock, eyes on a distant river unfolding in its spring rush through the greening valley beyond.

The sturdy pickets of Loramie's Station were no longer visible. She felt a bit foolish for having wandered so far without telling anyone at the fort. There was a real risk in being alone in the wilderness, unarmed except for a small pen knife.

It was past noon when she sensed she was being followed. The hair at the nape of her neck seemed to tingle, and then a horse's soft nickering alerted her. Veering away from the creek, she plunged into the gloom of the woods. There she made herself small, huddling behind a fallen log, suddenly aware she was bright as a cardinal in the scarlet cape. She'd left no trail following the water's gravelly bank, but this was cold comfort. If something happened to her, who would know? Or care? Not Aunt Etta, far away in Philadelphia. Only Red Shirt, she guessed.

Closing her eyes, she mumbled a terrified prayer. When she opened them, she saw a tall shadow leaning against the trunk of the pine she hid beneath. The rush of relief she felt was so acute she was half sick.

Arms crossed, Red Shirt looked down at her, stark displeasure in his eyes. "You came a long way. I nearly lost your trail."

"I wanted to take a little walk, is all . . ."

"Hardly a little walk, Morrow."

She flushed. She hadn't thought of him returning and finding her missing, trail-weary as he was. All his weapons were upon him, his leggings mud-spattered, his frocked shirt torn. He looked leaner, his jaw more whiskered than she'd ever seen, his handsome face almost haunting.

"The cabin was so empty. I just had to be free of the fort . . ." Even as she said it, she realized how selfish it sounded. "I wanted to find you. I thought—when you didn't come back—"

"You thought . . . ?"

"I thought . . ." Her voice broke, and she looked toward the river glinting through the trees. "I thought you didn't want to."

A flash of pain darkened his face, replacing the anger of a moment before. He moved to sit beside her, his shoulder solid and reassuring against her own. Though she worked to stop them, tears began making trails to her chin, and all her pent-up angst of the past months seemed to unleash itself in an irrepressible torrent.

"You should have been in Missouri now like you wanted," she said. "But I've kept you from it. I've been nothing but a burden since we came north. You're used to living free, answering to no one, going where you please. I know how hard it must be for you, living at the fort—"

"How hard it is for me?" The quiet words were edged with disbelief. "I'm not the one grieving a father. I didn't almost die of a fever. Nor am I carrying a child."

Despite his reasonable words, her heart was choked with doubt. She swallowed past the knot in her throat, aware of his eyes on her while hers remained on the river. "Lately I've been wondering if I'm made for this kind of life . . . if I'm the wife you need. Maybe Pa was right. I—I don't seem to weather things well . . ."

Her voice faded, each word seeming to hover between them, the stillness excruciating. A tiny bird lit on a nearby branch, singing with all its might. How she wished she was that bird. *Oh, that I had wings like a dove, for then would I fly away and be at rest.*

He said quietly, "Do you love me, Morrow?"

She turned her face to him in alarm. Did he doubt her love? Did he think all her emotional talk was her way of telling him she didn't?

A humbling realization stole over her. Not once had she ever said she loved him. Not on their wedding day . . . or wedding night. She felt an overwhelming love for him, but the tender words seemed to lodge in her throat.

Reaching out, she took his hand, the golden band a telling reminder of their tie. "I love you. I will always love you . . . more than you know."

His eyes were solemn. "You show me your love in many ways. But you haven't said it till now."

She hadn't . . . but he had. She flushed, thinking of the countless times he'd whispered his love to her, both in passion and in the many practical moments that made up their days. The heartfelt words had formed a hedge around her, shoring her up against all the trouble she'd encountered since leaving the Red River. And he'd kept on saying them even when she hadn't, with no promise she ever would.

"Do you believe I love you, Morrow?"

"Yes."

"Do you believe what the holy words say?"

She nodded, thinking of their Bible reading by the fire.

"Then you know love bears all things," he said.

The fragment of Scripture, so unexpected, so simply stated, gave her pause. *Love beareth all things, believeth all things, hopeth all things, endureth all things.* The simple utterance seemed to cast down all her disappointments and failures, her unmet expectations and fears, and turn them to ashes. How was it, she wondered, that he always managed to condense a matter in so few words and restore reason?

He stood and called for his horse, then bent down and helped her up. Already she was considerably rounded, the baby making her feel awkward. The black stallion came stamping through the brush, snorting as if impatient to be off. She rubbed his nose, glad she'd not have to walk all the way back to the post.

She watched Red Shirt adjust the saddle just for her comfort. Yet another expression of his love, like bringing his horse today when he could have let her find her way back on foot to chasten her for her wandering. She stepped closer and touched his sleeve. He was wearing the linsey hunting shirt she'd made, dun-colored and heavily fringed to wick away water. Her eyes trailed along its masculine lines, thinking of the love in every stitch. He paused and looked down at her, surely unaware, she thought, of the hold he had on her heart.

"I missed you," she said, thinking how cold the bed had been and the way the days seemed to double in his absence.

"And I you," he replied. "I had to go further than I wanted—to meet up with the courier Loramie told us about."

She furrowed her forehead in concern. "The one wanting you to come to Fort Pitt?"

He nodded. "My father asked me to go to Pitt and act as mediator as well. There's a new Indian agent there who seems more honorable than those before him." His eyes flickered over her as if gauging her feelings. "But I sent the courier back to General Hand to say I won't be coming."

The words turned her inside out with relief. She couldn't tell him how much Loramie's warning words had been in her thoughts of late. Or how she'd been haunted by the threat of Bluecoat soldiers when he hadn't come back.

"I won't break the promise I made to your father," he said with quiet conviction. "I won't leave you heavy with child as you're becoming."

Her shoulders relaxed, and the cape she wore slipped to the forest floor. A slice of sunlight through the trees cast a lacy pattern on her calico dress, and she stood in its warmth, pondering all he'd told her. He paused to take her in, his face awash with tenderness. She felt a certain shyness at his scrutiny. Placing one hand on the horse's mane, she prepared to mount, but he made no move to help her. His eyes were on the scarlet cape at her feet. He bent not to retrieve it but to hobble his horse.

"Morrow . . . you're like molasses to a winter-weary bear."

With a sure hand he brought her against him. Oh, but he'd been gone too long. He began kissing her like he'd kissed her beside the Falls of the Ohio, till he took her breath. And she heard herself whispering over and over what she'd so long denied him. *I love you . . . love you . . . love you.* It was like a snow melting inside her, thawing all the hurt and distance between them, forging a new, beloved tie.

It was late when they returned to Loramie's Station. But the scent of spring was in the air, and her world had been righted again. In the lengthening shadows, she saw him looking west and wondered . . .

Lord, please hasten us to Missouri.

29

Half a dozen fiddlers and pipers struck up a brisk reel, and Morrow watched in amusement as a group of men partnered each other with as much zeal as they could muster. The large dusty common had been transformed from orderly and efficient by day to one of rambunctious abandon this April eve. Redcoats and Indians stood smoking and downing the rum Loramie had so generously provided, while intoxicated trappers and traders clogged and entertained. Morrow danced a four-handed reel with Angelique and her daughters, but the girls were soon whisked away to the sanctuary of their rooms as the revelry grew more unrestrained. On the fringe of the crowd, Loramie stood, a pair of pistols in his belt, his small stature belying his imposing reputation. On his watch nothing untoward would happen.

Winded from the dance, Morrow stood with Red Shirt in the shadow of a blockhouse eave. Without a word he put his pipe away and took her hand, leading her beyond the fort's front gates. Fireflies winged about, reminding her of the Red River, of fruit jars and Jess and the long lost days of childhood. A full moon spilled silver light on the cornfields beginning to take shape beyond the fort's east wall, the stalks aligned like rows of soldiers. She shivered, turning to take in his solemn profile, all too aware of the rifle he carried.

"The night—it bears watching," he said, drawing her into the crook of his arm.

"Do you sense something . . . someone?"

"If I did, you wouldn't be here." Raising a hand, he pointed out one shooting star and then another in the midnight sky.

But it was a momentary diversion, and she turned back to him. "Ever since you met with the courier, I've sensed a burden about you. I want to know what weighs you down so."

He shook his head. "So you can be burdened too? No, Morrow. It's simply war talk. Little else."

She watched him as he studied their surroundings and wanted to kiss his unsmiling mouth. "Don't you ever get weary of all the trouble? Do you think it will ever end?"

He drew her closer. "There's no war being waged in Missouri."

Not yet. She studied him solemnly, thinking of the ebb and flow of conversation at the dinner table. "Is it true there's an American officer named Clark pushing further west than any white man before him?"

He nodded, looking down at her in the darkness. "I've seen firsthand the fort he's building at the Falls of the Ohio."

The falls? The breathtaking torrent of water came back to her, along with a rush of recollection so sweet she felt breathless. "The same place we made camp and swam? Our honeymoon . . ."

"Is that what you call it?"

"It fits, does it not?"

He smiled, his teeth a flash of white in the darkness. "*Honeymoon* is too tame a word for what happened between us."

But she hardly noticed his gentle teasing. She felt stung by a suffocating sense of loss at the revelation. The thought of such a place being overrun with soldiers and camp followers seemed a desecration. But there were other things pressing on her mind and heart, and she felt the need to further unburden herself.

"Tonight at supper I heard Loramie mention a prisoner exchange at Fort Pitt."

"It's part of the coming treaty-making there."

She fell silent, thoughts full of Jess.

"Do you want me to go, Morrow?"

She slipped her arms around him, her heart too full to say anything but a simple "No."

"I would gladly go if I thought it might bring your brother back to you. But I made a promise to your father to stay near at hand. And I've told Loramie we're leaving by month's end."

She looked up at him, lips parting in surprise. The words were so welcome—so long awaited—she was speechless with joy.

"If we go now, we'll cross the Missouri after the spring rush and be in a cabin of our own before winter sets in."

"I'm ready to go now, tomorrow."

Smiling again, he gave a playful tug on her kerchief. "A fortnight is soon enough. There are still provisions to gather—horses, medicines. I need to consider the best routes for travel."

Warming to the anticipation in his voice, she shut the thought of Jess away. In two weeks' time, when she could still travel comfortably, they'd leave this dusty, crowded place. They'd go west to make a home of their own. *Home.* Surely there was no sweeter word than this.

The following days were spent readying for the journey, selecting the best horses to take them west, taking stock of supplies, medicines, food. Queasiness gone, Morrow felt better than she had in months. Stronger and more settled. Lighter in spirit. Trapper Joe's parting words returned to her over and over like a song she never tired of singing. *Prime country for hunting, prime country for living.* Already Missouri felt like home to her, and she sensed Red Shirt's excitement was as keen as her own.

Three days before their departure, Surrounded by the Enemy arrived on his way east, a hundred or more Kispoko warriors in his wake. They stood just beyond the fort's postern gate in the swirling dust of late spring, their tawny bodies glistening with bear oil, their mounts tossing their heads and stamping the ground as if aware they were part of an important procession. Loramie greeted them on the grassy plain, Red Shirt with him. Morrow followed at her husband's urging, more than a little awed, mindful that this was likely the last time she'd see the man who'd forged such an unlikely friendship with her father.

Surrounded took her by the shoulders, looking down at her from his impossible height, a slight smile warming his face. "I wish that I could return by way of the Red River and bring your father to you. It would be good for him to see you so content and soon to bear a child." The English words—seeming rusty with disuse—were interspersed with Shawnee yet so full of feeling they brought tears to her eyes.

She stood by Red Shirt and watched the procession move east in a great swath, feathers fluttering and silver flashing. Though they lacked war paint and were en route to a customary council, their faces were grim and they bore all the weapons of war. Watching them leave, she felt a profound welling of relief that Red Shirt remained behind. Yet she wondered . . . deep down, did he want to go?

She saw the grim set of his mouth, the little sun lines about his eyes that creased in concern as the last man faded into the distant tree line. But her thoughts were already turning to Missouri, far away from war talk and treaty-making, well beyond the summons of American officers and Indian agents. She was only too glad to resume packing.

Red Shirt turned to her amidst the chaos of the cabin and studied her as he'd not done for days, distracted as he'd been with the Missouri trip. "Morrow, I thought you beautiful before. But now . . ."

She flushed, her hands self-consciously covering her bulk. "I'm only beautiful to you."

Almost overnight it seemed she'd blossomed as wide and pink as the wild roses scattered across the river bottoms. For a fleeting moment, she saw concern darken his eyes. Was he wondering if she was up to the trip, if she could travel so far, heavy with child as she was becoming? Turning away, she resumed packing. Nothing must get in the way of their leaving. *Nothing.* She, most of all.

Morrow spent her last afternoon at Loramie's Station along the creek with Josee. The day was almost summerlike, the heat ratcheting up as if driven by some devilish hand. Come morning they would leave for Missouri in a swirl of dust. She was all but counting the hours, nearly bursting to begin, though the trail west would be all ablaze. But better that than ankle-deep in mud, she guessed. For now she tried to savor the cold water and carefree play erupting all around her. With a shriek, Josee splashed about with the children of trappers and Indians, the boys clutching miniature bows and arrows, the little girls bearing miniature cradle boards with rawhide dolls upon their backs.

Watching her charge at play in the water, Morrow hardly noticed the commotion at the front gate. But in time her eye was drawn to the ponderous procession of horses stirring the dust and one lone stallion pulling a litter. They moved slowly, the fine mounts stripped of all the accoutrements the Shawnee were known for—flashing silver and brightly colored cloth and fine leather. How different they looked from Surrounded's proud party two days before. These were horses of sorrow, of mourning.

Sweat beaded her brow, coursing from her hairline in itchy trickles as she stood and brushed the dust off her muslin skirt. Since early afternoon, a steady stream of frontiersmen and Indians had passed through the gates to trade. It was a day like any other, save the unusual heat. Red Shirt was not out on a scout but inside the post with Loramie, looking at maps of the Missouri territory and finalizing the best routes for travel. Glancing at the watch pinned to her bodice, she realized it was nearly suppertime and remembered Angelique liked the girls to bathe and dress beforehand.

"Josee," she called, her eyes on the shimmering blueness where Loramie's youngest daughter played. "We need to return to the fort. 'Tis nearly time for supper."

She glanced again toward the post's gates, but the Shawnee had disappeared behind the tall pickets. The Shawnee horses she'd seen moments before now stood outside without their riders, though the one bearing a litter had disappeared within. Loramie was hurrying to a far blockhouse, hardly giving her a glance. A deep dread clenched her insides as she sent Josee into Angelique's waiting arms and began the short walk to her cabin.

When she neared the largest blockhouse, she heard men's voices. The wind gusted and sent a skiff of dust through the open doorway, drawing her attention to the scene inside. A dozen bare, tawny backs kept her from seeing the heart of the ordeal, but the voice that reached her was Red Shirt's own. Though he spoke Shawnee, it lacked the melodious quality she'd come to know. He seemed to be stumbling over his words, each syllable aggrieved.

She stepped over the threshold, and the distillation of sweat and dust and bear grease nearly nauseated her. For a few moments she struggled to adjust to the dimness after the sun's brilliance, and then the shadows assumed familiar forms. Surrounded lay on a military cot, Red Shirt beside him. A British surgeon hovered, his shadow dancing in the light of a tin lantern.

Red Shirt's voice was the only sound in the suddenly still room. "Father, do you know where you're going?"

The reply was a long time coming. "It is very dark over there," Surrounded finally said.

"It doesn't have to be," Red Shirt answered.

She heard the catch of sorrow in his voice, and her heart swelled. Breathless, she leaned against the rough log wall and simply listened as Red Shirt switched to Shawnee. Angelique came to stand beside her, whispering the translation in her ear. Red Shirt was repeating Pa's poignant words of the past. Of death being a new land, a new life. A beginning, not an end. Light, not darkness.

Angelique was silent now, as if she could no longer grasp the interchange between father and son. Confused, Morrow looked across the room at Loramie. Even in the shadows, there was no denying the alarm spelled across his thin face. His eyes held a warning—a flicker of disbelief and profound dismay. The voices hushed. Time seemed to have frozen still right there in the suffocating heat of the blockhouse. The Shawnee in front of her stood like stone. Finally Loramie came to her and took her outside, where the flies buzzed and the sun beat down on her stooped shoulders.

Surrounded by the Enemy was dead, Loramie said. His horse had thrown and trampled him after only two days' travel to Fort Pitt. As he lay dying, he cried out for his son and asked for forgiveness.

For killing Ma and Euphemia and taking Jess.

Overwhelming anguish took hold of her, and she clamped a hand over her mouth to keep it from spilling out. Before she could turn away from Loramie, Red Shirt stepped outside, his dark eyes fastening on her at once. The distress on his face was beyond anything she'd ever seen, and she felt as tenuous as shattered glass.

"Morrow . . ."

She shook her head in denial, clutching her handkerchief tight as if it could ground her. He took one step in her direction, and she folded like a paper fan. Bending down in the dust, he gathered her up and took her inside their cabin, kicking a stool and crate out of the way. Sitting in the cluttered room, he held her and told her what she had no wish to hear.

"My father is dead, Morrow. There was some trouble with the horses and he fell." He swallowed hard, his hand a bit heavy as he stroked her hair. "He confessed some things—"

"I know . . . I heard . . . heard it all." *All.* The simple word encompassed a bottomless pit of hurt and loss. She sensed his struggle as he weighed how much to say—to hold back.

"He asked your father to forgive him . . ."

Oh no . . . She felt all the blood leave her face. The thought of Pa hearing such a confession, having to forgive something so terrible and irreversible was beyond understanding . . . beyond bearing.

"Your father forgave him. But neither he nor my father wanted us to know."

Her voice broke. "Why?"

"They didn't want to destroy the love they saw between us."

She was weeping now, grieving Pa all over again. "I'd rather not know—not now."

"He was afraid we'd learn the truth another way. From the warriors who were with him that day."

She shook her head, shaking now, nearly sick. "How could he keep coming to the cabin . . . pretending to be a friend—"

"Morrow, my father was grieved by what he'd done. When he came to know your father—his God—he saw the evil in his heart and was ashamed."

The truth trickled over her bit by bit, ushering in a blessed numbness. She simply sat and listened dully as he said, "My father wanted to bring your brother back, but too much time had passed. He only remembers telling the other warriors to take him north after the raid on your cabin."

Something inside her was extinguished at the revelation—a tiny flame of hope kept alive since she was five. *Jess.*

She couldn't breathe and pushed Red Shirt away. He released her reluctantly, a shadow darkening his face. He'd just lost his own father. Surely she could understand that. But she couldn't offer any sympathy—nor hear any more of what Pa had never meant for her to know.

"Morrow . . ."

She turned her head, unable to look at him, to handle both his pain and hers. As she stepped away, Loramie came to stand between them, uttering things about preparing the body for burial at the nearest Indian town in keeping with Shawnee custom. Red Shirt left and she was glad to see him go, glad when Angelique took her into their house to the upstairs room where she'd been so ill the past winter.

Red Shirt returned the next morning, face drawn and eyes bloodshot. But he stood stalwart before her, following her with his eyes while she did the most menial tasks to avoid him. Finally he said, "Morrow, I must go . . . to Fort Pitt."

What? She whirled to face him, the words like a physical blow. Grasping the back of a chair, she fastened her eyes on his grieved face.

"I'm not asking you to understand—nor can I explain it to you."

"But—"

"I don't want to leave you nor break the promise I made to your father. Loramie has warned me against going as well—"

"Then why would you?" She grasped the chair harder, amazed at his calm. "You're going because your father asked you to . . . as he lay dying . . ."

"Not my earthly father, Morrow." He hesitated, the tense silence between them lengthening. His tired eyes held hers steadfastly and seemed to demand something of her. "Has God never asked you to do anything?"

"W-what has God to do with this?" She was so angry she felt the tick of her pulse in her forehead and wrist. She groped about for words as hurt and confusion filled her. "You might not come back—our baby may grow up without a father—"

"I feel I must go. I've felt it for some time now."

Had he? And he hadn't told her? "Something terrible is going to happen—I can sense it . . ."

She turned away, thoughts of McKie and Bluecoat soldiers swirling in her throbbing head—thoughts so dire she felt she hovered on the brink of some terrible darkness. Yet no matter how she cried and stormed and questioned, she knew he wasn't turning back. Every sun-hardened line of his face was so resolute it seemed he was simply going to Missouri.

Just beyond the cabin's open door, one of Loramie's sons was readying Red Shirt's horse. She could hear it snort and see the dust kicked up by its prancing. This was the same black stallion Surrounded had given Pa years before, and the sight only deepened her grief.

"Morrow, look at me." Gently he turned her around to face him, taking hold of her shaking shoulders. But his touch, once treasured, now made her stiffen. Why did he remind her so of his father, when he hadn't before? Resentment rose up hard and strong and stung her.

"I need your prayers for the trip ahead of me."

He bent his head till it rested against hers, their warm, salty tears mingling. She wanted to pull away, yet something inside her seemed to burst at his tenderness. With a broken cry she flung her arms around his neck.

His arms tightened about her. "I need to tell you something else."

She shook her head and placed trembling fingers to his lips. "No—please—don't say it."

"You need to know that I've made provisions for you, that you won't be alone." He swallowed hard, jaw tightening. "If I don't come back, Loramie will take care of you . . . and our child."

If you don't come back? But what is life without you?

She started to speak, to say the words, but couldn't. They stayed buried beneath all the hurt in her heart, tainted with regret and confusion and grief. Nor could she say the only thing that really mattered . . .

I love you. I will always love you. More than words can say.

He framed her face with his hands, wiping her tears away as soon as they spilled over. "Morrow . . . my heart is on the ground." The simple Shawnee phrase rent her heart. She simply bent her head as he whispered, "Remember how much I love you. Remember love bears all things."

30

Loramie and Angelique insisted she stay with them and not return to her cabin. In the confines of her upstairs bedroom, she lay atop the feather tick, the heat pressing down on her like a blanket. Her nightgown clung to her skin, accentuating her swelling middle. Tonight the baby began to kick up a storm inside her womb, and she swallowed down the fiery bile that seemed to burn a hole in her. The plaintive call of a dove beyond the shuttered window, lonesome and low, seemed to echo the emptiness in her heart.

She tried to think of other things—anything—to keep dark thoughts at bay, but her mind kept returning to Surrounded. She wondered how so expert a horseman could have fallen and died. Most of all, she wondered why he and his warriors had happened upon the Red River cabin so long ago and wreaked such destruction. What had been in Pa's heart when he'd heard Surrounded's confession? How well he'd hidden it from her.

In the following days, Loramie reassured her of Red Shirt's promise to send word of the goings-on at Fort Pitt, and so they waited, looking for a cloud of dust that would announce the promised courier. But as the days lengthened with no word, Morrow looked with dismay at all they'd readied for Missouri now gathering dust inside their shadowed cabin. Her thoughts and feelings were adrift like a leaf in a river's current, restless and unpredictable, never settling.

Lord, please let no harm come to him. Hasten us to Missouri. Before it's too late.

Slowly Morrow trudged to the creek that lay like a limp blue ribbon between dusty brown banks. Josee had forgotten her doll earlier that day, and now at dusk Morrow retraced her steps toward the spot marked by tall reeds and cattails where Josee had played. Pausing to catch her breath, Morrow watched fireflies stud the sticky air. What was in the mind and heart of a little half-blood girl, she wondered, to make her miss such a homely doll? Josee had other dolls, some so fancy they bore porcelain faces and miniature silk dresses like the ones buried in the wardrobe of Morrow's old attic room. But the misplaced one was her favorite, with its beaded doeskin tunic and tiny moccasins.

At last Morrow stumbled upon the lost treasure partially submerged in the creek, its clothing darkened to black, the horsehair braid unraveled. Sitting down in the grass, she began to plait the ebony hair. It was peaceful here at the north fork of the creek, without the myriad arbors and shelters further south, and peace was what she craved. She hardly noticed the shadow looming over her.

"Miz Morrow, that you?"

She felt a rush of surprise, then overwhelming joy. She nearly couldn't speak. "Joe?"

He stood looking down at her, the brim of his beaver felt hat pulled low against the waning sun. "It's me all right."

She jumped up as fast as her bulk would allow, the doll forgotten, and flung her arms around his dusty, tobacco-scented neck. He supported her with a wiry arm, his voice almost soft. "I've been wonderin' where you and Red Shirt went. When I rode 'in to trade a few minutes ago, I couldn't believe my eyes seein' you sittin' here in the grass with a doll. Reminds me of when you were little and your pa would take you out to the fields so he could work."

The bittersweet memory made her smile despite her tears. "Oh, Joe, I can't believe it's you. How are Good Robe and Little Eli?"

"Fit as fiddles in that fine cabin of yours. Only thing wrong is that you and your pa ain't there." Sorrow weighted his tone, but he cleared his throat and continued on. "But it's about to get a mite crowded. Come winter we're to have another."

"That's wonderful news. There's nothing like a baby coming."

He eyed her thoughtfully. "Care to tell me what's goin' on with you?"

For one moment she hesitated. How could she possibly explain all that had happened when she didn't understand it herself? "We've been living at the fort since Christmas. Red Shirt's scouting for Loramie. We'd hoped—planned—to be on our way west by now. But Surrounded died suddenly, and Red Shirt decided to go to Fort Pitt for that important council."

No surprise crossed his face. "Seems safer to head to Missouri territory."

She simply nodded as fear gained a fresh foothold in her heart.

"How long's he been gone?"

"Six weeks or so."

"He should be back soon, and then you'll be on your way west."

Was it her imagination, or did he look as doubtful as she felt? "Have you heard anything about the council at Fort Pitt? Anything at all?"

"Just hearsay. Supposed to be the most important treaty-makin' to date. All the Shawnee septs sent their chiefs and a good many warriors in case there was any tomfoolery."

"I thought Red Shirt would be back by now."

"It'll likely take a bit longer given that prisoner exchange."

"I keep hoping—praying—he'll be here before the baby comes."

"He might yet. But all that treaty-makin' takes time, though I can tell you in a few words what takes up those Fort Pitt commissioners' days." Leaning over, he spit a stream of tobacco juice into the tall grass. "Them Bluecoats promise to stay on their side of the Ohio River and beg the Shawnee to do the same. Attacks on river travelers are forbidden. The Shawnee promise to abide by the rules of trade. Then there's the passin' of the pipe, the long speeches, the translatin', and finally the feastin' and drunkenness." Seeing her concern, he added, "But you can bet Red Shirt is a lick too smart for the latter."

"I've always wondered what went on but was afraid to ask."

"Here lately them commissioners have added another thing or two. They're insistin' the Indians return any captives. And then there's some nonsense about punishin' any Shawnee or white man who does violence to the other."

Morrow grew quiet, her eyes angled east. Did he know about Red Shirt and McKie? Perhaps Pa had even told him of Surrounded's confession . . .

He eyed her with a sudden grin. "Now I want to hear about you—and that baby."

Forcing lightness into her tone, she wrapped her arms about her burgeoning waist and said, "Look at me—big as a barn. I'm surprised you recognized me."

"When you due?"

"Another month or more."

"Miz Morrow, you'll never make it."

She pushed the worrisome thought aside, a bit wistful. "Tell me about Kentucke, Joe. How's Lizzy? And Jemima?"

He scratched his beard. "Jemima married a soldier by the name of Kincaid a while back. They're still livin' at the fort. Abe's been put in charge of the militia. He and Lizzy are hopin' to move over to Tate's Creek come fall." He reached for another twist of tobacco. "Lizzy asked after you."

Hearing it, she felt a twist of sentiment. Unlike Jemima, Lizzy had stayed true till the end. She longed to know more but was hesitant to ask. Some things, she guessed, were better left unspoken.

With a complaint about his rheumatism, Joe got up slowly and hobbled to where his horse grazed in deep timothy and clover. Untying a saddlebag, he retrieved a letter and passed it to her. One glance at the indigo wax seal assured her it was from Philadelphia.

"Been carryin' it around for months now, wonderin' if I'd ever see you again."

She broke the seal and opened the once-crisp foolscap, surprised to find it so short. Just a few telling lines, all of them heavy with regret and disbelief, dwindling down to a final, stiff conclusion.

> Should you decide to leave the life you have chosen, my door remains open to you and any mixed-breed children you may have. Philadelphia boasts a charity school where they might board and obtain an education to make them fit for civilized society.
>
> Your loving aunt, Etta

"Thank you, Joe," she said, wondering if he could see the hurt she tried to hide. Till now she'd thought Aunt Etta might welcome her if her fears were realized and something went terribly awry at Fort Pitt. But this letter . . .

They sat in silence for a time, the only sound a few distant, barking dogs and the wind laying the grasses low. A sliver of moon had risen, reminding them another day was done. For a moment the evening was silver and tranquil and serene, and she felt somewhat solaced.

"I believe I'll stay on at Loramie's for a spell," Joe told her with a wink. "Good Robe will tan my hide if I leave without knowin' if you've had a boy or girl."

She squeezed his arm in thanks and said with a tremulous smile, "I don't think you'll have to wait much longer, Joe."

Morrow bent over to peer into the sapling shelter where Trapper Joe was camped along Loramie's Creek. But a cold campfire and some turkey bones were all she saw in the small square of shade. Panic rose up and seemed to snuff out all common sense, and she bit her lip hard to keep herself in check.

Oh Lord, where is he?

She'd been so sure Joe was near at hand for this very day, this very hour. When a scout had brought the terrifying news but minutes before, her only thought had been to get to Joe. Although Loramie had turned a deaf if sympathetic ear to her plea, Joe would not, she felt certain. A sudden rustle in the grass made her turn. *Joe!* He eyed her warily as if he already knew what she wanted.

"Oh, Joe, there's been some trouble at Fort Pitt—Red Shirt's been wounded." She stumbled over the words in her angst, and he simply stared at her as if trying to piece it all together. "A scout just brought word he's been taken to Mekoche Town. How far away is that?"

His sandy brows knit together. "Half a day's hard ridin' if the rider ain't with child."

"I want you to take me there." Even as she said it, she was aware of a strange pressure about her middle like a belt squeezed tight.

Oh Lord, not now . . . not yet.

"How bad's he hurt?"

She lifted her shoulders in a shrug and started to cry. Then and now the courier's lack of details left her breathless. Angelique had taken her upstairs before he'd finished telling all his news so that only Loramie remained below to hear what had unraveled upriver.

"We can go right now if you want to," Joe said, sympathy softening his tone.

Without another word, he started for the fort and soon returned with her mare, saddlebags stuffed with provisions and water. She looked at Dollie and braced herself as Joe helped her mount. Once in the saddle, she felt all the blood leave her face. He stood looking up at her as if waiting for her to change her mind—or for Loramie to come out of the post's gates and stop them.

But they were soon heading east—he on a big bay horse, she following near enough to be his shadow. She kept her eyes fixed on his narrow back, the grit of dust in her mouth, a beloved Scripture dawning in her heart. *Love beareth all things.* The words lay like a lintel on the doorpost of her mind, keeping her from dissolving completely.

Heat shimmers rippled across the wide, sun-scorched valley. She could smell the wild honeysuckle, a poignant reminder of the lonesome graves she'd likely never see again. On and on they rode, and it seemed some unseen hand was helping keep her in the saddle. As they plunged deeper into the woods, gnats and mosquitoes gnawed at her, and her horse shied from a rattlesnake lying on a rock at the first creek they crossed.

Joe slowed to ride beside her, handing her a canteen of water. "We're halfway to Mekoche Town."

Only halfway? Oh Lord, help me with the other half.

At noon they stopped to rest, but the heat of the woods was as suffocating as the treeless prairie. In late afternoon, her thoughts in a tangle over Red Shirt, she leaned into the mare's mane, nearly falling to the ground. The heat was making a mess of her, unraveling her braids, streaking her skin with sweaty fingers and deepening the heat of her sunburned skin.

"Joe, I need to walk," she finally said, thankful when he slid off his horse and helped her down.

"That's all right, Miz Morrow. We're nearly there."

In minutes they came to a small bluff overlooking an Indian encampment. She stood on unsteady legs and marveled at the scene spread before them. Like a painting it was, nearly perfect, the valley deep green and untrammeled, the river a brushstroke of blue. Bark shelters dotted both banks, and the great number of them took her breath. Red Shirt was here . . . somewhere. And this was where their baby would be born. Though she'd managed to hide her distress thus far, the pain nearly brought her to her knees as they picked their way down the grassy hillside.

Please, Lord, I don't want to give birth in an Indian town.

The irony was overwhelming. She was going to produce life amongst a people she associated with death. Never in her wildest imaginings had she considered this. Till now she thought her baby would be born within the familiar walls of Loramie's Station, Angelique at her side. Not here amidst such strange people and stranger surroundings. But what choice did she have?

Their arrival was causing a stir she'd not reckoned with, but she supposed a pregnant white woman and a grizzled trapper were a strange sight. A tall Indian came forward to greet them, a great swell of coppery faces in his wake. Joe began speaking in Shawnee, and Morrow swallowed her impatience over their prolonged interchange. As she waited, a cluster of half-naked children swarmed her like swirling brown butterflies, brushing her face and hair and hands. Had they never seen a white woman before? She smiled, but they ran away as if playing a game, eyes shiny as black beads, each small face alight.

Finally the Indian gestured for them to follow. Morrow moved slowly, wondering where Red Shirt was . . . how badly he was hurt.

The camp was far larger than Loramie's Station and seemed to pulse with a different sort of life. They passed a great council lodge and a cluster of log houses along a dusty path, and she stared in bewilderment at some cows grazing behind a brush fence. A few more agonizing steps and they came to the western rim of the camp, where a sturdy shelter rested beneath some cottonwood trees.

Joe motioned her inside. As she pushed aside the hide door flap, a cold hand clenched her heart. There, just ten steps away, lay Red Shirt on a pallet in back of a weak fire. She clasped a hand over her mouth to keep from crying out in alarm, glad Joe and the Indian remained outside. The smell of herbs and plants seemed to swirl around her and slice the very air with their sharpness.

His eyes were closed, his face free of pain. Cuts and scratches marred the smooth skin of his upper body, and one particularly deep gash across his thigh made her wince. Her eyes fell on the cloth bound tightly about his waist, the bloodstained bandages resurrecting a memory of his wounded shoulder. For once his hair was disheveled and devoid of gloss. Even his skin, normally supple and sun-darkened, seemed faded. He wore no shirt, but his leggings and loincloth were stiff with spattered blood.

With a groan he moved and flung out his arm, striking her thigh as she bent over him. Sweat beaded his brow, and she rued the stifling stillness of the lodge. Spying a bowl of water and a cloth, she knelt and began wiping his face, her eyes roaming every inch of him.

Even on his back, his strength sapped, he took her breath away. Placing a hand upon his perspiring forehead, she mouthed a plaintive prayer almost absurd in its simplicity. *Lord, please help him . . . help me.* Unable to sit upright any longer, she lay down on the unfamiliar bed beside him. Suddenly, miraculously, her own cramping eased. In moments she succumbed to exhaustion, her senses filled with the humid scent of herbs, and didn't awaken till she heard her name.

"Morrow . . ."

Her eyes fluttered open, and for a moment she forgot just where she was. *Red Shirt here . . . Red Shirt hurt.* His face was so near her own, she felt his breath on her cheek.

"Morrow." His expression held a look of wonder, as if he might be dreaming.

She smiled and smoothed back his tumbled hair. "You look at me like I'm an angel from the Otherside world." When his face darkened with concern, she said, "I came with Joe as soon as I heard."

"Joe?" He reached out a tanned hand, the back scratched and bloody, and rested it on her middle.

"We've not been here long."

"I didn't want you . . . to know." His words were slightly slurred and his eyes had lost their keen edge. Had he been given some of the healers hanging above their heads?

"Say nothing," she murmured, throat tight. "Save your strength. I'm praying for you."

His eyes seemed to clear. "Your prayers spared my life." With studied effort, he rose up and pulled her nearer. "You came . . . so far."

She tried to smile, hardly believing she had. "I'd do it all again. For you."

They both slept, the feverish day rushing toward twilight. Morrow awoke to the smell of succotash and saw skewers of roasted meat on a large wooden platter. Someone had placed the food just inside the door flap—but who? Thoughts swirling, she lay still till Red Shirt stirred, the pain and pressure in her womb returning with a breathtaking intensity.

He awoke and attempted to sit up, but almost immediately the bandages turned scarlet. Neither Joe nor the Shawnee were in sight, though she looked anxiously through the doorway. Spying clean cloths, she tore them into strips, rewrapping his waist as tight as common sense allowed. The sight of so much blood chilled her, almost made her sick. Her face must have mirrored her distress, for he stilled her trembling hands, his concern for her etched across his face.

"Morrow, I'm all right."

"Are you hungry . . . thirsty?"

He nodded and laid back, a rolled-up blanket beneath his head. She struggled to get up again, barely able to bend over to retrieve their meal. Handing him a skewer of meat, she wondered if he ate just to please her. He took two bites before reaching for an earthenware jug. When he uncorked it, he smelled the contents and grimaced.

"It was rum that started the trouble at Fort Pitt."

Wary, she sank down beside him, handing him her canteen of water.

He took a drink, his expression rueful. "When the Shawnee delegation arrived for the treaty, the chiefs refused to go inside fort walls. They wisely insisted that the meetings take place on the plain beneath the fort. I didn't realize that some of the warriors were riding horses stolen from the Kentucke settlements, but some of the soldiers did. One Bluecoat swore he would get the animals back if he had to scalp every Indian to do it. That's when the trouble started."

"Before the treaty even began?"

He nodded. "The new Indian agent had the ague and couldn't be present. Some of the chiefs took this as a bad sign and became restless. In order to pacify them, the officer in charge began distributing rum. When I warned the chiefs not to drink, the Bluecoats became angry. One saw my ring and decided it must have been taken in a raid along with the stolen horses."

She glanced down in surprise. Pa's gold band was missing from his hand. In her concern for him she hadn't noticed, and now she felt a sudden emptiness.

"They took the horses—and the ring." He paused, his eyes clouded with pain as he related the details. "When some of the Shawnee refused to cooperate and give up the horses, the commissioners decided they would take four chiefs hostage till they did."

Alarm filled her. "What happened next?"

He lay back, favoring his wound. "The chiefs began murmuring about what happened to Cornstalk and his men at Fort Randolph on the Kanawha. Some of the younger warriors began rounding up the stolen horses the Americans were trying to take back, and fighting broke out."

She could well imagine the mayhem and suppressed a shudder. "You could have been killed."

"Some were." He studied her as if weighing whether to say more. "Shortly before the fighting began, Captain Click asked about you. He was acting as mediator for negotiations and talked to me for a time."

Dismay trickled through her, though she knew Click to be an honorable man. The summer he'd returned her to her father from Fort Pitt had earned him a fond place in her memory. "What did he say?"

"Joe had told him of your father's passing and that you'd gone west with me."

Her forehead creased in concern. "Is that all?"

"I don't think he believes you went willingly."

She stared past him, the implications slowly dawning. "Was he hurt in the fighting?"

"With the smoke of the guns and all the confusion, I couldn't tell."

She looked away, fear pulsing through her.

He said quietly, "I won't hide the hard things from you, Morrow. The truth needn't make you fearful. Just prayerful."

She rested a hand atop her swollen middle, ashamed. Her

faith was so small and seemed to have shattered at Pa's passing. Here she was, picking up the pieces, trying to mend her faith with threads of fear. Fear of the future. Fear of losing him like everyone else she'd loved. Fear of never making it to Missouri. Fear of men like Captain Click coming to take her away from her new, bittersweet life.

She looked at his hand without its wedding band, wondering why the soldiers would take something so small, so insignificant. Truly, their greed knew no bounds.

"What about the prisoner exchange?" Her voice was so small, so hopeful, he seemed reluctant to say more.

"The Shawnee kept their prisoners downriver, waiting to see how the treaty-making progressed before bringing them in. When the trouble started, the captives ran away. Most of them had been with the Indians so long they didn't want to be part of the exchange to begin with."

Strangely, this didn't surprise her. "How did you possibly make it to Mekoche Town, wounded as you are?"

"We canoed partway down the Ohio. I was all right till the wound began to fester. I tried to make it to Loramie's but got no further than this."

She bit her tongue to keep from pronouncing the trip a disaster. Did he still feel God had called him to go? And for what purpose? He'd gained nothing but an injury and the ire of American soldiers. The time they'd lost en route to Missouri was unrecoverable. And now she was ready to give birth, further delaying them.

Forgive me, Lord. It might have been so much worse.

Still, her disappointment was so profound she was hardly aware of the slap of the door flap behind them. Joe entered with an unfamiliar Indian, this one so old his mahogany features were nearly obscured by wrinkles.

A satisfied smile spread across Joe's face. "Miz Morrow's good medicine."

"The best," Red Shirt said. The Shawnee began examining his wound, taking down some herbs from the sapling frame overhead and mixing them with water. Morrow watched as he applied a thick paste, rewrapping Red Shirt's side just as she'd done, but with far greater finesse.

His old eyes roamed the room before resting on her. Voice low, he spoke directly to her while Joe translated. "You look in need of the aunts. I have told them of your coming."

With a knowing smile he withdrew, Joe in his wake, leaving her to wonder what awaited her. "Aunts?" she echoed, looking at Red Shirt.

"Shawnee midwives," he said.

She said nothing to this, wondering if he sensed her deep dismay at giving birth in such a place. Spying his pipe, she stood awkwardly and crossed the shelter. As she bent to retrieve it, she felt a little twinge. The ungainly movement seemed to release a rush of water, soaking her bare feet and the dry earth floor. She flushed, sure it meant something momentous. The baby seemed to turn sharply and settle, and a tremendous pressure nearly brought her to her knees.

"Morrow, what is it?"

"I—the baby—"

"Is it time?"

Their eyes locked. She was feeling a dozen different things—could he sense them? Elation. Awe. Alarm.

Slowly he got to his feet, coming to put his arms around her. "Don't be afraid," he said, smoothing back the wayward wisps of hair that had escaped her pins. "I won't be far away." She looked up at him, finding his eyes warm with amber light. "Remember, Morrow, God is near . . . even in a Shawnee town."

At this, she tried to smile. Looking up toward the smoke hole, she felt the heaviness of the air and smelled the coming rain.

Oh Lord, watch over my baby. Help me to be brave.

31

Was this the valley of the shadow of death? Twice before the darkness had nearly claimed her, both times by fever. And now by childbirth. She remembered so little after it all began, just the door flap fluttering like a flag as wind and rain collided, drawing her mind beyond her swollen body. Red Shirt left and a woman came to be with her, the fringe of her doeskin tunic swaying, her ebony braid snaking over one shoulder. Up and down her arms were a number of silver bangles that flashed in the firelight.

Round and round the woman walked with her as the pains ebbed and built to a breathtaking intensity. When she wanted to sit, the midwife kept her on her feet, occasionally offering small sips of water and murmurs of encouragement. At last she lay down, the taste of blood on her tongue. She'd bitten her lip to keep from crying out, but it was becoming more of a burden to stay silent. There was just pain upon pain with no rest in between, and then a great burning seemed to consume her.

I cannot go on.

When daylight spilled into the shelter, the rain eased. Everything smelled wet—clean—but she hardly noticed. An infant's lusty wailing shattered the stillness, and she realized suddenly, bewilderingly, that she was alive. The Indian woman was tending to her baby boy, examining every plump part of him as he wriggled and fussed. Already she ached to hold him, her eyes caressing every unfamiliar part of him as the woman cut the cord and cleaned him, applying a light coating of oil to his dusky skin. And then at last she handed him over.

Awe suffused every part of her as she brought his warm bulk against her chest. He quieted and looked up at her, his fat face remarkably expressive, his eyes flecked with amber light, alert as his father's own. But his hair . . . it wasn't black as night as she thought it might be, but a deep, startling red—bright as a candle flame.

Just like Jess's.

A low fire barely illuminated the bark walls of the *wegiwa* where Morrow lay in the summer twilight. The thankfulness she felt at having survived the ordeal was profound, but her body felt broken, beyond repair. When Red Shirt entered, she struggled to sit up but couldn't. He knelt beside her in the shadows, his eyes more on her than on the bundle in her arms.

Reaching out a hand, he smoothed her unkempt hair, his eyes worn with worry. "You labored a long time. Near the end I thought—"

"I'm all right," she reassured him, lowering her head to look at the only thing that mattered. The baby, sleeping now, was nestled in the crook of her arm.

With a tired but triumphant smile, she offered him their firstborn. He took the bundle a bit clumsily, the blanket falling open to reveal their sturdy son. Eyes shimmering, he smoothed the damp hair and outlined a dusky ear with his finger. She looked from the baby to him, moved by the telling emotion she found in his face.

"He looks like you," she said.

His voice was an awed whisper. "All but his hair."

She couldn't keep her eyes off their son—he seemed as near perfect as anything she'd ever seen. Taking him back, she breathed in the just-born scent of him and kissed his wee nose. He blinked then sneezed, and they laughed. Opening his mouth wide, the baby yawned, and she caressed his cheek, inspecting the tiny pink gums.

"I think he's worn out, same as me," she said. She pulled her eyes away from their son to look at him. "Now . . . close your eyes."

His face held a question, but he did as she bid. Carefully she laid the baby down, bringing the bundle hidden on the other side of her into the light.

"Look," she whispered.

He blinked in disbelief, every bit as amazed as she'd been when their secondborn had slipped into the midwife's hands. Nature's afterthought.

Speechless, he passed a hand over his eyes. She said nothing for the catch in her throat, just handed him their daughter. He cradled her head in one hand with a surety that made Morrow marvel. A haze of black hair covered her tiny scalp, and her features were delicate as a doll's. Looking into her violet eyes, Morrow felt she was looking into her own.

"She's small," Morrow said softly, a note of lament in her voice.

His eyes roamed over her in careful appraisal. "She's simply little like you."

"I wish she'd cry."

He smiled wryly. "Our son seems to manage that for the both of them."

The loud howls that had begun more like a kitten's mewl moments before intensified. She gathered her firstborn up a bit awkwardly and cradled him, murmuring in his ear till he quieted. Never had she imagined having two babies. The wonder of it pierced the thick layer of her exhaustion, and she felt a startling pride and pleasure.

He looked up from the baby in his hands, taking in her tired eyes and disheveled hair. "You need to rest. The babies need to rest."

Bending his head, he kissed each infant drifting toward sleep. As she closed her eyes, she felt Red Shirt's hand on her head. Though he said not a word, she knew he was praying for her, for their babies, for their uncertain future. Through the smoke hole above, the sun was shining. It seemed, for a few precious moments, that there would never be trouble again.

For several days following the births, Morrow slept, both babies in arm, every need tended to by the Shawnee midwife. Though elated, she was very weak, her condition causing Red Shirt a great deal of concern. He seemed to watch her warily, just as he'd done when she'd recovered from the fever. But she made light of it, caught up in the newness of being a mother. When her milk came in, she marveled at her son's appetite, then fretted when her tiny daughter couldn't nurse.

"She is too small to suckle," the midwife told them, producing a reed with which to feed the baby. "Many times a day she must eat. When she is stronger, she will nurse like her brother. It is good that he is so *meshewa* and will take much milk."

Though she longed to return to the familiarity and comfort of Loramie's Station, their time in the Shawnee town stretched on as long as the late summer days. Twenty, by Morrow's count. Yet she felt a deep contentment as both babies seemed to thrive. Although Red Shirt's wound was healing quickly, her own recovery was slow. They spent much of their time in the shade of a willow arbor outside their *wegiwa*, the late summer trees rustling in an ever-present wind. Joe would often join them there, badgering Red Shirt to play endless rounds of *sheguonurah*, or stones, a Shawnee game requiring considerable strategy.

In the evenings, Joe would amble off in search of a new opponent and some *kinnikinnik*. Alone with Red Shirt and their babies, Morrow felt his pride when he looked at them, and it made her heart swell. She studied their son now as he slept, one tawny thumb wedged in his mouth as he lay curled on his side. Alongside him was his sister, her hair damp and wispy from the heat, violet eyes shut.

"We must name her," Red Shirt said.

Morrow met his eyes and felt a strange reluctance. It seemed that heaven had let them borrow her for only a time and might take her back if they held on to her too tightly. "She reminds me of a rose," she finally said. Truly, their daughter resembled a tiny rosebud, her skin a dusky pink, her delicate features as tightly furled as her fists, the sweeping black lashes shuttered in sleep.

"Why not call her that?"

"All right," she said. "But she's so small I think she'll just be Rosebud for now."

He looked toward their son as if considering him next, but surprised her when he said, "Morrow, are you strong enough to travel?"

She nodded despite her doubts, one hand trailing to their little daughter on the blanket beside her.

"We leave for Loramie's at first light," he said.

Loramie's . . . and then Missouri? "The babies should make the trip well enough. 'Tis not too far."

He looked at her in the lengthening shadows, his eyes weary and red-rimmed. Studying him, she felt a little start. Why hadn't she noticed how tired he was—how tense? He'd seemed so preoccupied of late while she'd been consumed with the babies. Perhaps being in a Shawnee camp was resurrecting his old life, deepening his grief over his father. Or was there more trouble brewing after the fracas at Fort Pitt?

"We can't stay here any longer." He hesitated, and she could see his jaw tighten in a way that revealed his inner turmoil. "We need to move on like we planned."

She looked down at their babies—so new and vulnerable

they made her heart ache. "You're not telling me everything. Something is wrong. I can sense it."

Their eyes met, and his shimmered like a dark pool. "I'm leaving for Missouri as soon as you're settled at Loramie's."

"You're going on without us?" The words were an alarmed whisper on the warm air.

"When I file our claim with the Spanish government and finish our cabin, I'll return and take you there."

She felt a chill and groped for words, trying to find reason in what he said. But it made no more sense than when he'd left for Fort Pitt. Was God telling him to go once again? Concern gripped her as she struggled to stay calm in the face of another setback.

"The winter will be a hard one. There's not as much game as there used to be. I can't have you with me when the babies are so small. Loramie's is the only safe haven."

"But if you go so far away . . ." Her voice broke, and she looked down in confusion, her feelings in such disarray that all her heartfelt words scattered.

"Morrow, look at me."

But she couldn't. The sting of his leaving, of his not telling her till now, hurt more deeply than anything that had gone before. "You're leaving me at Loramie's because I'm weak—a burden."

"I'm *taking* you to Loramie's because I want you to be safe."

The patience in his voice was fraying, and she knew she was stretching the very seams of it, yet she continued in a little rush, "As long as we have food—shelter—we'll follow you anywhere."

"There's more that you don't know. It's no longer safe for us to stay here. The Bluecoats are threatening to invade the middle ground and burn more Shawnee towns after the trouble at Fort Pitt." He took up the stick to stir the ashes again, and the fire in his eyes seemed to skewer her with their intensity. "We leave for Loramie's at first light. That is all I have to say."

32

The pickets of Loramie's Station seemed edged in gold as the sun slid west and ushered in a warm August twilight. Morrow rode toward the tranquil scene on her mare, the twins snug against her in a soft cloth sling. Ahead of her was Red Shirt on the black stallion and Trapper Joe alongside him on his bay. The dry grass rustled beneath the horses' hooves, and the fading scent of summer perfumed the air. On the shadowed plain outside the open doors of the station were even more shelters than she remembered, fires flickering like fallen stars upon the ground. Her relief at arriving safely was tainted by one joy-stealing thought.

Is Loramie's Station any safer than a Shawnee town?

Within the post's dusty confines, Loramie greeted them more like family than friends, insisting they stay at the house rather than return to their cabin. Angelique led the way upstairs to their former room, her daughters hovering as Morrow lowered the babies into a waiting cradle's cocoonlike folds. Rosebud lay quietly and didn't make a sound, but her brother waved fat fists and his dark eyes seemed to snap.

Angelique chuckled. "That one will be climbing out of his cradle before the Cold Moon."

Morrow tickled his bare belly, and he kicked a leg, coming free of his wrap. "My little son has wrapped me round his finger since I first set eyes on him."

"Have you named him?"

"Not yet," Morrow said, thinking of how distracted they'd been. "We haven't been able to agree on a name. And with all the trouble . . ."

Angelique's smile faded. "*Oui, oui,* but the trouble is far from here." She turned away, calling for a serving girl to bring up hot water and refreshments.

In the days to come, Morrow would watch from her upstairs window as Red Shirt disappeared into their cabin across the common to sort through what he would take west. Despite his impending departure, she continued to pray he'd change his mind. As August moved into September, she thought he might. Not one word did he utter about leaving. For a time he took up scouting again, though he was never gone for long, always returning to them at day's end to eat in the ornate dining room and make much of the twins. Could it be he found it as hard leaving her as she did him?

But their idyll was not to last. Inexplicably she sensed a change coming. Even the babies seemed to grow restless. During dinner one night, she could hear their cries through the paneled wood walls, though Esme tried to quiet them. Leaving her plate unfinished, she hurried upstairs to nurse them, and Red Shirt joined her soon after. Stripping off his fine shirt in the stifling room, he sat on a fragile Windsor chair beside her a bit uncomfortably, even warily, as if he doubted its fine lines could hold him.

"It's time we christen our son, as the English say," he told her, taking the squirming boy from her though he grunted a protest. "The Shawnee are beginning to call him Boy With No Name."

She smiled and tied the strings of her shift closed, studying father and son in the light of the sconce on the mantel above. The similarities were startling, from the golden-brown hue of their eyes to the stubborn slant of jaw. "He's so like you," she said, "that if we named him anything else, it would be wrong."

He looked thoughtful. "I think we should call him Jess."

The heartfelt words sent a river of warmth through her, and she said, "I think Pa—and Jess—would be pleased."

Passing her their sturdy son, he gathered up their daughter. She awoke with such a pathetic little mewl they both laughed. Bringing her near, he smoothed the heat-dampened hair atop her head, and she regarded him with eyes that had darkened to indigo. Watching them, Morrow felt a shaft of joy thrust through her turmoil. Here in this room at day's end was all she held most dear . . . yet soon Red Shirt would leave them.

Scraps of an earlier conversation, most of it disturbing, returned to her now in the heat and stillness of the bedroom. At dinner, all the details previously denied her had been laid out like cards on a table. Come morning, Red Shirt would head west. Though the Spanish claimed exclusive rights to the Missouri territory, the ties they boasted of were mere spiderwebbing, Loramie said. Few Spaniards were there, and only a scattering of French and Indians. Settlement, he assured them, was wide-open.

Loramie's manner, usually one of contagious *joie de vivre*, had seemed almost sullen in the candlelight. "Although the Americans have only threatened to torch more Shawnee towns, I have heard rumblings the whole of Ohio will soon be filled with smoke."

Joe grimaced and looked up from his plate. "I misdoubt they'll cross the Ohio like they're thunderin'. Even with reinforcements comin' from Virginia, Kentucke's got precious few men with the war blazin' in the East."

"'Twould be a fine time for the British and their Indian allies to sneak across the Ohio and take back the Kentucke territory," Loramie mused. "But I have heard they sit in their camps like drunken dogs and do nothing."

"Maybe neither side will move and there'll be peace," Joe said, looking doubtful.

"My concern is this colonel called Clark," Loramie told them, emptying his wine glass.

"Aw, Clark's too busy at the Falls of the Ohio to make trouble this far north," Joe said. "At least with winter comin'."

Loramie nodded thoughtfully. "Fortunately, making war in winter is a miserable affair—the only point of agreement between the Americans and us—so we will likely rest easy till spring. But I have been thinking of taking Angelique and the children to d'Etroit for safekeeping next year until I can determine what the Bluecoats will do."

"I knew there would be trouble after the failed treaty at Fort Pitt," Red Shirt said.

Loramie nodded again and motioned the serving girl forward to pour more wine. "Such a fracas did not endear the Shawnee to the Americans. They now have even more reason to drive the Shawnee out of their Ohio homelands. And I have heard more troubling news. It seems some of the Shawnee have crossed over to the Americans and become spies and scouts."

Red Shirt nodded. "Rum is a powerful weapon."

"Sadly, it is so. But no one likes a traitor—not even the Americans—and that is what these turncoats have become. Once they have led the soldiers to the Shawnee villages, the Bluecoats will likely be rid of them and refuse to pay them in trade goods and spirits."

"I'd best get home before I get caught in the middle of the tussle," Joe said, throwing his napkin down. "I've been gone so long Good Robe likely thinks I ain't comin' back."

Lying atop the feather tick, Morrow tried to empty her mind of the troubling talk at dinner. Beside her, the babies' gentle breathing, synchronized even in sleep, solaced her a bit. She stirred as Red Shirt got up and crossed to the open window and pushed the shutters aside. Cool air threaded through the stale room. Though autumn, it was still hot as a kiln. Spring seemed years away . . .

She watched him lean against the rough window frame and look west, unaware of her scrutiny. Moonlight limned all the pensive lines of his striking face, and her heart squeezed tight. Was he thinking of his father? Leaving at first light? Crossing the Mississippi before the first snow? Was he wishing he was outside, under the stars, away from this breathless room smelling of dried lavender and dust and babies? She remembered how he'd once stood by her attic window, looking down on McKie and his men that winter's eve. When he'd left, she'd feared he'd never come back, but after long, lonesome months, he had. Would God return him to her once again?

When at last he lay down, he reached for her, one hand brushing the dampness of her face. "Morrow, are you crying?"

Unable to answer, she felt the mattress move beneath his weight as he gathered her up in his arms. She placed a tentative hand on his bare skin, relearning the wide lines of his shoulders and the smooth slope of his chest. They'd not come together in so long he seemed oddly unfamiliar. When he kissed the hollow of her throat, she shivered, her need of him scattering her senses. But she lay back in the crook of his arm, willing her body to heal, tamping down her heartache.

He ran a hand through her unbound hair. "When I come back, there will be time for us."

If you come back.

Tonight, in this stifling room, was all they had. The brevity of it broke her heart into little pieces and made her reckless. She needed him—all of him—if only for the little time left to them. She needed the memory to hold on to till spring.

She turned her face to him. "Just one kiss."

She sensed him smile in the darkness. "Morrow, there is no such thing."

Her voice was a beguiling whisper. "Just . . . one."

A gust of wind slapped the shutter against the wood wall, and Rosebud startled, letting out a little cry. Reaching a hand into the cradle, Morrow rubbed her bare back till she settled. The babies had just been fed—surely they'd sleep.

Before she turned back to him, he was reaching for her again, his raw strength making her feel doubly fragile.

"One," he whispered.

He took his time, his mouth moving along the damp wisps of her hairline to her ear. Breathless, she freed his hair of its leather tie till it spilled like a black waterfall onto the thin fabric of her nightshift. Oh, but she'd forgotten how sweet he could be . . . how unerringly gentle, even gallant.

She felt like a bride again and shut her eyes, remembering how he'd held her that very first time, beside all that rushing water. Only now, with time against them, it was sweeter still.

33

Morrow unlatched the shutters, peering past the frosted glass to take in the swell of slopes to the west with their bright dusting of snow. Somewhere out there beyond the icy Mississippi River was the place called Missouri, and further still stood the Shining Mountains. But here, in her upstairs room, the twins were making their musical baby noises from the snug confines of their cradle near a crackling hearth, and all was warmth and comfort and peace.

Oh, Red Shirt, where are you on such a cold morning?

Resting her forehead on the frosty pane, she breathed a prayer just as she'd done every morning since he'd left in September. Now that it was December, she felt prayer was all that tethered them, that it might be the only thing that brought him back to her. Having made amends with her hurt over his leaving, she admitted he'd been right to bring them here. Loramie and Angelique spared nothing for their comfort and happiness, treating her like family, keeping her with them at the house instead of the lonesome cabin. She'd even assumed a place in the trade room, overseeing all the sewing goods from d'Etroit.

Without Red Shirt, her days were relentlessly the same. Leaving the twins with Angelique and her daughters, she went to work every morning save the Sabbath. As she opened crates of cloth and needles, scissors and sewing chests, her heartache was softened somewhat. She was glad to be useful. Busy in the big timbered room with its rich aromas, she kept a discreet eye on the men who came to trade, always searching for some semblance of Jess in their bearded, intense faces. Sometimes it seemed they eyed her more intently than she did them, and she felt chilled by their brazen scrutiny. To be less conspicuous, she wore simple wool and subdued her hair in a severe knot.

But the day came when Loramie took her aside, a wary light in his keen eyes. "Madame Red Shirt, you are—ah, shall I say, *not* a plain woman. Since your coming, the success of our sewing goods has increased tenfold, and for that I am grateful. But only this morning I have had two more offers for your hand."

Surprise—and a decided flush—swept across her face, and she fanned her hands over the heavy dress that draped her rounding middle. The glint of gold on her wedding finger caught the lantern light, reminding her of Red Shirt's missing ring.

Loramie forged ahead as tactfully as he could. "It matters not that you are *enceinte* and tightly wed. These hungry frontiersmen and Indians look no further than your lovely face. Your husband, I fear, would not be pleased with the arrangement. So, *chère* Morrow, I must close the curtain on your tenure as my clerk, however profitable it has been to us both."

His gentlemanly phrasing elicited a slightly sheepish smile from her, and she said as gracefully as she could, "I think I hear my babies crying."

But at five months, they rarely cried except when hungry, doted on as they were by Angelique and the children. She guessed she didn't need the distraction of the trading room, truly. She was tremendously content with the twins, nuzzling their velvety necks, kissing their plump fingers and toes, nursing them, and napping with them till time was lost to her altogether.

She'd written Aunt Etta of their birth but received no reply. She considered writing Lizzy but feared where that might lead. Perhaps it was best if no one knew she was in this far-flung post. And so now, in the dwindling days before Christmas, as snow piled high against the pickets, she kept to the family's quarters, counting the days till spring and wishing Red Shirt was back. When he came, his wee son and daughter wouldn't know him, or he them. And now, this new one . . .

She was at her window again, looking west, night falling like a curtain over the land. The winter air was so bitter the occasional snap of a tree split the air like musket fire. It was only this she thought she heard as she drew the shutters closed. But the pop and snap sounded again—and again—and when she peered past the shutter a second time, the far pickets of the entire west wall seemed to melt away. Her eyes ricocheted about as she tried to make sense of what she saw.

Below, scattering like ants on the common, were Loramie's clerks and housekeeper and guests. And flooding through the post's gates were a great many men—Bluecoats?—and a great many Indians. The Americans hated Loramie—and he them. Were they now storming his post? Whirling, she began scooping up her sleeping babies, only to lay them down again in her panic and confusion to search for their slings.

Trembling, she arranged Rosebud across her breast, just above her swelling waist, cinching the calico sling in a double knot. From below she could hear Loramie's frantic shouting and the high-pitched screams of his daughters. *Minon? Esme?* Hysteria began rising inside her like steam from a kettle. Rushing to the door with both her babies, she nearly collided with Angelique as she swept into the room. Her usually placid face was tight with fright as she took Jess from her.

"Come quickly, we must take the back stairs!"

The hall outside was dark, the sconces extinguished by a furious draft. Morrow's senses felt singed with the stench of burning fabric and furs, wood and trade goods. Billows of smoke swept in like a tide and soon separated them. Panicked, choking, Morrow called out for Angelique, but her cries were lost as a series of explosions erupted deep inside the post. Had the powder magazine met the fire's fury?

She stumbled out the door into the slush of the common, where the heat of the fire melted any remaining snow and speckled her face and neck with sweat. A herd of horses stampeded past, and she hugged a wall, her thin slippers sinking deep into icy mud. Terrified, she took in yet another fire-eaten wall.

Where was her little son? Angelique?

She could see soldiers looting and fighting among themselves, carrying trade goods beyond the inferno's reach, swinging swords at any who tried to stop them. Her mind began piecing words together in a terror-riddled prayer. *Father . . . help us . . . spare us.* Before the words left her lips, an Indian emerged from the smoke and shadows, the tails of his Continental coat flapping around mud-spattered leggings. He fastened his eyes on her, his face so ravaged with hate it seemed to wound her.

He was but one of several Indians who surrounded her in a nooselike circle. She blinked, trying to make sense of his face and form through the smoke. Hadn't she seen him days before in the trade room? Hadn't she seen them all? Their eyes were fixed on the sling across her breast, and she hugged Rosebud tighter, fearing they might tear her away and fling her against a burning post. With one lithe movement, an Indian grabbed her wrist and pulled her to a waiting mare.

The horse shied, but he jerked its bridle and manhandled her into the saddle, nearly spilling Rosebud from her sling. The tawny men surrounding her turned and mounted skittish horses of their own, clearly anxious to be away from the destruction they'd made. The Bluecoat Indian rode at the front, a jug of rum tipped to his lips. Around her fanned several warriors. Terrified, she wondered if they were Shawnee turncoats, perhaps American spies and scouts. All were dressed warmly in buckskins and buffalo robes and beaver hats.

Thoughts rattled around her head like spent musket balls. Where were they going? Why? On such a night it seemed more fool's errand than battle plan. But they went boldly down the frozen valley, carrying pitch-pine torches. Once she looked back to see a furious column of black smoke rising like some evil offering, a great funnel of swirling spark and ash, the flourishing finish to Loramie's Station. Her heart couldn't hold it all, and she hung her head, numb with disbelief.

In time they came to a nameless river that uncoiled like a mud-covered serpent. They put her in a bull boat with two men who paddled, then crossed at the river's narrowest point. She sat rigid as if doing so would keep her fraying emotions in check. The choppy water bore chunks of floating ice, and the occasional spray from the paddles reminded her of how little she wore. Just a wool dress and worthless slippers. Her feet were wet, benumbed. But at least Rosebud was snug in a swanskin nightgown and a little lace-edged sleeping cap, her feet bound in fur-lined shoes.

Thoughts of her little son—his sweet, milk-sated smile, the dimpled hands that pulled at her bodice, the sounds he was beginning to make in French and English—burned like a hot ember in her breast. He was so small and it was so cold. Had Angelique made it out of the burning post? As Morrow's eyes filled and overflowed, she felt a rough hand push her out of the boat, and she was surprised to see fresh horses on the opposite shore.

Amidst all the jostling, Rosebud awoke and began to cry. With shaking hands Morrow fumbled with the lacing of her dress so she could nurse, so cold she felt she'd turned to ice. Rough hands helped her mount another mare, and someone draped a buffalo robe about her. Toward dawn one man shoved a canteen of water at her, but when she refused it, he gestured to his tomahawk. Dumbly she stared back at him, wondering why he'd even offered. She had no ally among these men.

That first night, her chief captor sat opposite her across the fire, eyes on the sling as he ate a piece of roasted meat. "I will kill the child if it cries."

The threat jerked her awake, but she held her tongue, bent on protecting her baby at all costs. The other warriors were watching her—and watching him, as if anticipating what he might do to her. Looking away, she swiped her nose dry with the edge of her dress sleeve. She'd taken a cold and was still feeling its ill effects, head throbbing and throat raw.

One warrior crouched beside her and dropped a piece of jerky and some kernels of parched corn in her lap. She nearly refused them but knew she must keep up her strength, if only for Rosebud's sake. Each bite threatened to come up, so she chewed slowly, tamping it down with sips of water. Though the fire burned brightly, she felt she'd never be warm again.

As the night grew longer, a guard was posted and the men rolled up in buffalo robes, feet to the fire. She was tethered to a lanky brave, his eyes slits of contempt in his leatherlike face. Cocooned in the robe, she drew Rosebud closer, letting her nurse at will through the long, near-sleepless night. In the morning she was too tired to sit on her horse, falling asleep in the saddle before they'd made much time. Circling back, the Bluecoat chief slapped her on the leg with his whip. The sting of it jolted her awake and made a bloody welt under her dress, but it kept her alert mile after miserable mile.

Miraculously, Rosebud slept, never making a sound. She was heavier now, all rolls and dimples, so unlike the fragile baby at birth, and her bulk made Morrow's neck and back sore where the sling cut across. But somehow, strangely, Rosebud seemed a sort of buffer between Morrow and these men. Wicked as they were, they seemed reluctant to lay a hand on her. She sensed a skittishness about them as they traveled. Often she caught them looking over their shoulders as if fearful of being followed, and this gave her comfort.

But as the hours unwound, they seemed to grow more confident, emboldened by the flasks they passed around. The smell of rum was near constant now, and she shook her head when her guardian offered her some, though she wondered if it might help warm her. Snow and ice crusted their blankets one morning, and as the daylight dwindled, it became so cold they had to make camp in a cave above a frozen slip of creek.

Oh Lord, where am I? Who are they? Where are we going?

To keep her spirits up, she began to sing. She crooned a French lullaby no more than a whisper in Rosebud's ear, unsure from whence it came. Perhaps Ma had sung the same to her or Jess or Euphemia. It seemed to solace Rosebud and settle her to sleep. Morrow tensed for another slap of the whip to shush her, but the men seemed oblivious to her murmurings in their haste south.

Soon she lost track of time. How many days, nights? She ached for Red Shirt, craved her son's sweet smile. The mere memory of them, blurred though it was by exhaustion, made her weep.

"You are slowing us. I don't know what to do with you."

Half-asleep, she straightened, her back pressed against another damp cave wall. The Bluecoat chief stood over her, reeking of rum. The other men were asleep, or pretending to be. She said nothing, so weary she felt sick. Was this how it had been when Jess was taken captive? Desperate? Exhausted? Without hope?

"Colonel Clark is waiting for you. I would kill you otherwise."

Colonel Clark? She seemed to recall something about his being at the Falls of the Ohio. But her exhaustion and fear were so profound the details blurred to nothingness in her brain.

He continued, his face hidden in shadows. "You will bring me a fortune in trade goods, perhaps a new horse and musket. And plenty of rum. The child is worthless but seems to keep you quiet."

Worthless. The gibe loosened her tongue. "What do you want with me? I mean nothing to you."

He snorted and stepped back, taking out the flask again. "Perhaps you are not as stupid as most white faces. You are right in saying you mean nothing to me. But you do mean something to the soldier chief Clark. He has come into Kentucke to make the Shawnee abide by the treaty terms and return white captives."

"I'm no captive."

"Captain Click says you are. I was with him at the Fort Pitt treaty-making. He found out you were at Mekoche Town and then at Loramie's Station."

Captain Click? Did he truly think she'd married and gone north against her will? Her mind leaped back to their journey downriver some two years past. She'd been all lace and ribbons then, looking like a Philadelphia lady. Was it any wonder he doubted she'd wed a half-blood scout?

Spirits ebbing further, she looked again at the warrior before her. She knew better than to try to reason with him, but a biting resentment spurred her on. "Colonel Clark will learn the truth."

"I will listen to no white woman," he spat, finishing the flask and sinking down opposite along the wet cave wall. For a time it seemed he brooded, his head tilted toward unconsciousness or sleep. Her guardian slept beside her, but the familiar rawhide tug that usually bound them didn't rub her wrist raw tonight. He'd forgotten to tether her.

Slowly, she glanced out of the mouth of the cave. The world was white, the wind howling like a wolf. She might escape if she dared. But where? And what of Rosebud asleep at her breast? The sour-milk smell of her was nearly overwhelming, and her bottom and thighs were red-splotched from a rash. Morrow had been unable to keep Rosebud clean, but under their guardian's watchful eye, she sliced off pieces of an old trade blanket with a knife to keep her dry. Her violet eyes were open now, absent of all joy. She seemed to study Morrow with the intensity of her father, reminding her of Red Shirt in every striking line of her little face.

Swallowing back a sob, Morrow began to hum again, and the long-lashed eyes drooped shut, the tiny pink mouth opening to emit a ragged breath. Rosebud had caught a cold that seemed only to worsen in the chill. Her tiny hands clutched at her mother's filthy bodice, now soiled with mud and stiffened by milk. Bending her head, Morrow's tears fell on her flushed face, her lips moving silently.

Yea, though I walk through the valley of the shadow of death, I will fear no evil . . .

They were in the belly of a blizzard now, so white it hurt her eyes. To fight snow blindness, the men slashed black paint beneath their eyes. Morrow remembered how Red Shirt had done the same—tenderly—planting a kiss on her cold lips when done.

The Bluecoat chief continued on, his stamina staggering. She could no longer feel her fingers or her toes, and she worried without end. *Rosebud . . . always Rosebud.* Her breathing seemed labored, and she'd not so much as whimpered since dawn. As Morrow placed a frigid hand against Rosebud's soft cheek, her fingers felt stung from the heat of her face.

The mare Morrow rode became lame and was shot, so she was hefted behind her guardian. His bulk sheltered her from the bitter bite of wind and hedged the baby like a wall. Soon after, she saw smoke and heard the roar of water not yet frozen by winter. A ghostly memory returned to her, beloved and bittersweet. *Could it be?* Wasn't this the same place she and Red Shirt had first come together, conceiving the baby she now held? The sight of pickets made her insides ache, as did the ugly stumps littering the once lovely island just below the falls. This was the wilderness beneath the white man's hand. But it wasn't at all as she remembered, and she shut her eyes to block it out.

A warrior at the advance of the column hoisted a stick with a white rag high in the air in case some hasty soldier mistook them for hostiles. The gates swung open with a groan. Once inside the garrison, she stumbled off her horse and onto her knees, snow covering her with furious flakes from her bare head to her frozen hem. There she sat and rocked Rosebud and made a spectacle of herself before the gathering soldiers. They regarded her with solemn eyes in the gloom of twilight and made no move toward her.

"Is this the preacher's daughter?"

The voice behind her was distinguished, even aristocratic, and held more than a hint of command. In answer, one brave jerked her to her feet, turning her to face the man she guessed was Colonel Clark. He stood tall in his fine Continental coat, dwarfing the gawking soldiers surrounding him.

"Well, don't leave her standing in this weather! Take her inside at once," he bellowed, squinting in the bitter wind. "Is that a baby? Good heavens, the woman looks frostbitten. Call for Dr. Clary."

Making haste, an orderly led her into a blockhouse and up some stairs where a bath and bed waited. Morrow struggled to make sense of the dimness after the blinding whiteness of the snow. There, upon the landing, a plump black woman regarded her with wide eyes and reached for Rosebud, but Morrow wouldn't release her.

"Now don't you pay me no never mind. It's only Hester here to help you and the babe, iffen you let me." Her voice was so kind that Morrow felt a thawing, wooed further by the steaming tub Hester gestured to near the hearth. "It was a heap of trouble totin' all that water for what should have been a fine bath for Colonel Clark. But you needs it a sight worse than him—and all my hard work ain't gonna go to waste."

Never had anything looked as fine as the steam rising off the tub's top like a coveted cup of tea. Numb, Morrow stood as Hester stripped off her soiled clothes and took Rosebud from the filthy sling. "Well, ain't she a purty thing. And those eyes! Ain't no Indian baby ever had eyes like that."

She set Rosebud on Morrow's naked knees in the tub, chuckling as she came wide awake and splashed and kicked. The water swirled around them, stinging Morrow's skin and melting away the dirt. Taking out a bristle brush, Hester began to scrub them with soft soap, thoroughly but gently. "Ain't gonna let Dr. Clary see you till you gets cleaned up. Now close your eyes and hold that baby high while I rinse you off."

Afterward Hester took Rosebud and laid her on the bed, swaddling her while Morrow waited in the hip bath. The sight of an Irish linen dress gave her pause. It was for a small woman with an impossibly small waist, but Hester fixed that too, untying the blue sash so that it fell unhindered about her blossoming body. "You sit here by the fire and nurse yo' baby while I get you some victuals. It ain't much, just soldiers' fixin's. The doctor'll be here shortly."

Morrow obliged, her back to the fire. Rosebud nursed hungrily, her little smacks belabored as she coughed and sputtered. When Hester delivered the promised plate, Morrow fell on it as if famished, scraping up the venison and gravy with a large spoon and eating three biscuits in as many minutes. She drank the hot cider down, marveling at the peculiar taste before she realized it was laced with whiskey.

"It'll shore you up and ease the baby's breathin'," Hester said. "Now I think I hear the good doctor on the stair."

The doctor entered, reeking of snuff and rum. Dare she trust him with Rosebud? But he took her with practiced hands, examining her gently from head to toe. "A bad cold, 'tis all," he announced, handing her to Hester to rock by the fire. The doctor turned to Morrow next, examining her hands and feet. The tips of her fingers were slightly discolored, and she'd yet to feel her toes.

"You've come close to frostbite. By jigs, but you've barely escaped it. You need rest—a great deal of it," he pronounced, shaking his head warily. "I told Colonel Clark 'twas madness to bring a woman here in such weather . . ."

He soon took his leave after instructing Hester about the medicines he'd left. She began to hover again, turning down the bedcovers and placing a warming pan between the sheets. Morrow didn't bother getting undressed, just lay down and pulled the bedding over herself and Rosebud, her damp head on the feather pillow.

Hester clucked. "Go on and get to sleep. You'll need yo' rest so you can face Colonel Clark in the mornin'."

34

In the cold light of midmorning, Morrow was ushered into an austere office in an adjacent blockhouse. She realized Colonel Clark had given up his bed for her—and his bath as well. But this speck of generosity in no way removed the sting of what he'd done in bringing her here. A bitter storm brewed inside her at the thought that this man had separated her from her little son, leaving her to wonder where he was . . . *if* he was.

Colonel Clark rose from his desk when she entered. The stale room stank of tea and whiskey, leather and gunpowder. A knot of officers turned to look at her, their worn, wrinkled uniforms a striking contrast to their clean-shaven faces. They didn't glance away even when her eyes skimmed over each one, dismissing them without expression. Somehow she remembered her manners, thanking the colonel for the chair he offered her and then the tea he poured to ward off the room's chill. The hearth fire directly behind him seemed to hold no warmth, though it looked robust enough to set the whole garrison on fire.

She tried not to study him, but he was a curious sight, young for an officer despite his air of authority. His hair was a rusty red, his heavy brows a dash of white, and she fancied his eyes were a washed-out green, but when he looked up at her, she found them fiercely blue.

"I trust you and your baby passed a peaceful night," he said, passing her a china cup so at odds with their rough surroundings.

She nodded warily, holding the cup away from Rosebud, who slept in the crook of her arm. Somehow she'd thought he'd meet with her alone. She felt ill at ease with these other men and was thankful Hester remained standing behind her.

The towering commander took a seat behind a desk cluttered with papers, a compass, and a spyglass. She felt a nudging to try to sway him with the considerable charms that Jemima once claimed she had, but doing so seemed deceitful somehow. Desperate as she was, she'd plead her case honestly or not at all.

She took in the shadowed corners of the room and wondered where the Bluecoat chief was who'd brought her here. His lies had already done their damage, she guessed, and she wondered how much trouble she'd have unraveling them. She looked straight at the uniformed man before her and said quietly, "I want to tell you the truth about my leaving Kentucke."

He looked up, surprise softening his clean-shaven face. Had he wanted to lead? Did he expect her to be a mouse? Cowed by her supposed captivity? Running a hand through his hair, he nodded and gestured for her to continue.

She swallowed, distracted by the clock on the mantel behind him, unable to recall what day it was. Was Red Shirt already on his way back to Ohio? Would he ever be able to find her? She had no idea how long ago she'd left Loramie's. Days? Weeks?

"I'm not a captive, Colonel Clark, no matter what you've been told."

He looked at her with unflinching eyes. The men about the room moved closer, obviously intent on hearing what she had to say. Colonel Clark cleared his throat. "What is your name and who is your husband?"

She felt a tremor of unease. Looking into his weather-hardened face, she sensed he already knew. "My maiden name is Morrow Little. My husband's name is Red Shirt, a half-blood Shawnee."

"One of the warring sept? And a British scout to boot?"

She set the teacup down on the edge of the desk, not trusting her trembling hand. "He's a man of peace now and has been for some time. We were wed a year ago by my father, who was a preacher in the Red River settlement."

His eyebrows rose, but his gaze remained steadfast. Two officers took chairs on either side of her. Another man—one she'd overlooked when she entered—moved to stand by the hearth just in back of the colonel but in her line of sight. He wore the garb of the woods, a long linen hunting shirt and buckskin leggings, his hair plaited and clubbed in Indian fashion. He reminded her of Captain Click . . .

"Is that your wedding ring?" Colonel Clark asked, eyeing her hand.

She looked down at the narrow band, the Celtic cross catching the light, and remembered that soldiers had taken Red Shirt's. "'Twas my mother's before me."

"Is she still living?"

"She was killed by Indians long ago. My father died of consumption last year."

"After wedding you to the half-blood Shawnee?" A sliver of a smile touched his face, and she shifted uneasily, realizing he didn't believe a word she was saying. Had her captors been so convincing, then?

He leaned back in his chair, never taking his eyes off her. "Surely you have some Kentucke kin."

"No . . . just an aunt in Philadelphia."

This seemed to trouble him, and he looked at Rosebud pensively. Was he wondering what to do with her and her baby? Thinking no white man would want her—and no relative?

Reaching past the inkstand on his desk, he took up a document, untied the leather string, and unfurled it. "I wish to acquaint you with Article 3 of the last treaty made with the Shawnee, Miss Little."

His use of her maiden name stung, as it seemed to slight her marriage, but she simply looked down at Rosebud and waited.

"'If any Indian or Indians of the Shawanoe nation shall commit murder or robbery or do any injury to the citizens of the United States, that nation shall deliver such offender or offenders to the officer commanding the nearest post of the United States, to be punished according to the ordinances of Congress.'" He paused. "Do you remember a Major McKie, Miss Little?"

Oh, please no . . . not McKie.

The name stirred a deep well of worry inside her. She forced herself to look at him, to meet his hard eyes. "I do."

He leaned back in his chair. "I've been informed that this officer was murdered by your husband in violation of this very treaty. The Shawnee scout in my employ—a man who calls himself Talks About Him—is merely acting in accord with Article 3 to deliver the offender to the officer commanding the nearest post. That would be me, you understand."

Is this where her Shawnee captor had gone? To search for Red Shirt? Or lure him here by telling him where she was?

She swallowed, panic flooding her. "My husband is not the man he was."

"Is he not a murderer?"

Unbidden, Red Shirt's poignant words at Loramie's came rushing back to her. *I am a murderer and a horse thief, but I have been forgiven.*

She clutched Rosebud tighter. "My husband is no guiltier than Major McKie, who killed a peaceful Shawnee chief and his men along the Kanawha." Though her voice seemed to warble with every word, exposing her turmoil, she pressed on. "Must I acquaint you with your own treaty articles, Colonel Clark?"

Remembering what Joe had told her, she reached out and took the document from him with a trembling hand, scanning the paper through tear-filled eyes. "'In like manner, any citizen of the United States who shall do an injury to any Indian of the Shawanoe nation shall be punished according to the laws of the United States.'" She paused and looked at him. "I recall Major McKie's punishment being more a promotion, Colonel . . . and I dare any man in this room to argue otherwise."

The ensuing silence was sharp as glass. Not an officer stirred. No one seemed to breathe. Every eye in the room was upon her, but none so fixed as Clark's. She felt she was fighting for Red Shirt's honor—his very life—with words.

The red-haired giant across from her smiled a tight little smile and took the treaty paper from her hand. "Ah, Miss Little. What a clever little minx you are. I do seem to recall some trouble along the Kanawha. And perhaps Major McKie has received his punishment in full. But your husband . . ."

She said nothing, her thoughts whirling, scattered, like wind-blown leaves.

He continued quietly. "I don't have the manpower to hunt for half-blood offenders. Not with a war on. The tactics we use to bring criminals to justice must be particularly ingenious here on the frontier, thus the raid on Loramie's Station. We've killed two birds with one stone—ridding the Ohio territory of an American enemy and rescuing you. Now I can turn my attention to other matters. I am told your husband is quite clever, extremely elusive, and rarely lets his guard down, except, perhaps, where you are concerned."

What could she say to this? Except pray Red Shirt would not come for her?

Rosebud awoke, and Morrow brought her against her shoulder, sensing she might cry. She breathed in her daughter's soft scent and felt smothered by helplessness. Did her anguish show? Surely it did, for Colonel Clark leaned back in his chair and said a bit less forcefully, "I had not thought to kill your husband, just question him."

Her voice turned entreating. "What if he doesn't come?"

"Oh, he'll come. And when he does, we will . . . parley."

Oh, but he was smooth as butter, she thought. Their eyes met, but he was the first to look away. The danger she'd felt upon coming here seemed to quicken, and she felt as helpless as the baby in her arms. In this cold room with this cold man, her hopes seemed little more than ashes. Clearly, Colonel Clark's mission wasn't to listen to half bloods or Indians, or to those defending them, just be rid of them. This was why his garrison was standing on lands secured by treaty for the Shawnee.

She looked down at Rosebud, who gave her a sleepy smile. One chubby hand grabbed at the kerchief of her borrowed dress, just like her brother had often done. The memory nearly shattered Morrow's composure. In a heartbeat the room became a blur of timber, erasing the buckskin-clad man before the hearth, and the colonel as well. Finally she felt Hester's hand on her shoulder, telling her it was time to go.

Upstairs she gave way to her fear and exhaustion, rocking Rosebud and crying as she sat before the fire. Hester padded away on soft feet, leaving her to sleep, but she couldn't close her eyes. Crossing to the window, she looked out on a crude scaffold made more hideous by gentle swells of snow. Red Shirt would come, and they would make an example of him. The love that tethered them—and the truth—would bring him to this once beloved and now terrible place. And she was captive till he came.

The days passed, and she was imprisoned in the blockhouse, the view of the gallows blocking the beauty of the surrounding forest. 'Twas nearly New Year's, Hester said. Morrow had been at Fort Clark a fortnight, but it seemed far longer. The blizzard that had brought them there had been washed away by a warm wind.

She placed a hand on her swelling waist, feeling life within. What had begun as a faint fluttering was now an unmistakable nudge. Truly, there was no such thing as one kiss. She was now tired enough and plump enough to prove it.

Hester kept her company by bringing her meals and tea, fussing over Rosebud, washing Morrow's clothes, and doing her hair as if she was the colonel's lady. "Colonel Clark is sure taken wi' you," she said. "Neither man nor beast ever talks back to that man, but you shore put him in his place over that bad business at Fort Randolph. And lo and behold, I think he liked it. But for one little thing."

Morrow looked up from nursing Rosebud.

"He just can't figure out why a beautiful woman like yo'self would settle for a savage."

The slight wasn't surprising, and she said nothing, just asked if she might borrow a Bible. The thought that Pa's had been destroyed in the fire at Loramie's grieved her as much as the lost miniature of her mother and Jess. But this was nothing when weighed against her other losses. Day and night her son's small, startled face returned to her as it had been just before the smoke and darkness separated them. What if she never saw him again? The bruising thought seemed to push her toward the edge of some terrible, irreversible darkness, and she grew more afraid.

Oh Lord, keep Red Shirt away from here, even if it means I never see him again. And bless my little son, wherever he is . . .

It was New Year's Eve when Hester came to fetch her. Colonel Clark had requested her company at the holiday dinner. Would she join them? Her heart sank, and she was loath to leave the hearth fire. A fiddler played across the common, and she smelled roast beef and chestnuts but had no appetite.

"Perhaps just go and have a little toast," Hester urged. "It might do yo' cause some good."

Her cause. Was it a lost cause, she wondered?

She entered the candlelit space that served as a dining room, and an officer seated her in a cane-bottom chair by the hearth. Despite her reluctance to give up her daughter, the soldiers passed Rosebud around, marveling at her amazing eyes and making much of her daintiness. Hester had dressed her in a bit of finery—a little red bonnet trimmed with ribbon and a white flannel gown. Where she'd gotten such things Morrow could only guess, though there were a few camp followers here, mostly wives and children and sweethearts of those in the army. Colonel Clark asked her for a dance, but she declined, wishing she had a fan to hide behind.

Numbly, she sat, hands folded in her lap, wanting Rosebud back. Gradually she became aware of someone watching her from a corner. The lone frontiersman? He'd been present when she'd had words with Colonel Clark in his office days before, but she'd forgotten about him since. She couldn't get a good look at him for the press of people and the haze of tobacco smoke, and he soon disappeared.

As the smell of spirits grew stronger, she felt nearly pricked by the soldiers' bold stares. Amidst the stomp of the music and dancing, her mind began to drift. The new baby she was carrying made her so tired, and she simply wanted to go to bed.

At last, after a nod from Colonel Clark, Hester took her back upstairs and then left again. Morrow could hear the frolic through her shuttered window, and the merriment only deepened her melancholy. Without bothering to undress, she lay down, Rosebud asleep in her arms. In moments she'd drifted off, only to come awake when the clock below struck nine times.

Groggy, she looked toward the flickering fire, wondering who had replenished it without her waking. When a shadow shifted in the corner, her breath caught. Behind the door, rifle in hand, was a man. She sat up hard against the headboard, hugging Rosebud closer. But he put out his hand as if to soothe her, and the simple gesture set her at ease.

"Don't be afraid." His voice was low, and he stepped into the firelight. "I'm here to help you—if you want me to."

If? She was already on her feet. "Y-yes, but how—when?"

"Tonight. Now."

She began putting on her borrowed shoes and gathering up Rosebud's blankets and her own few things. He moved to the window, then to the door again, ever-watchful. She felt a tremor of alarm. This was the same frontiersman she'd first seen standing in Clark's office and then at the frolic earlier that night. Could she trust him?

"Who are you?" she asked, trying to better see his features.

"I'm a scout—and interpreter. I'll try to take you to your husband."

"But why—why would you even want to?"

He put a finger to his lips. The sweet strains of fiddling increased. She could hear raucous laughter across the way, fueled by an abundance of rum. He beckoned for her to follow and she did, down the blockhouse steps, pausing briefly at an obscure door while he draped a buffalo robe around her shoulders. Just beyond the unmanned sally port, two horses waited, loaded and ready to go. Wonder washed over her as he helped her into the saddle.

She felt a swell of panic as Rosebud awoke and began to fuss. Quickly she unlaced her bodice, rearranging her so she could nurse as she lay against Morrow's thudding heart.

Into the forest they went, the pickets receding in mere moments as the woods swallowed them whole. Was there no lookout? No guard?

He looked back at her over his shoulder. "We'll have to travel a far piece tonight."

"Fine," she breathed, careful to stay directly in back of him. She murmured a prayer of thanks that she and Rosebud were rested and well fed, thanks to Hester's care. Indeed, she felt she could go miles even in the cold, buoyed by one reassuring line of Scripture that came suddenly to mind.

Thou preparest a table before me in the presence of mine enemies.

35

The full moon seemed ordained for travel, filtering through the trees and making a path for them where there didn't seem to be one. Rosebud had ceased her fretting, and the laxness of her body assured Morrow she was asleep. Her guide kept to the creeks as they climbed higher, leaving little trail. She felt a confidence in him she couldn't fathom, or perhaps it was just profound relief to be free of the fort. The dark image of the gallows was receding with every step.

When the moon dipped so far to the west they couldn't see, they made camp. He kindled a fire, put a skin on the ground, and gestured for her to sit down. She did as he bid, wanting to pepper him with questions, yet sensing she'd best wait. Weary, she watched as he heated water and made some gruel.

"Why not give your baby some?" he said, passing her a wooden bowl and spoon.

Surprised, she looked down at Rosebud. Her wide, searching eyes seemed to take everything in as she sat in Morrow's lap. Blowing on a spoonful, Morrow fed her gingerly, almost smiling when she spit some out and then swallowed the rest, opening her mouth for more.

"You're a fine cook," Morrow told him.

"It's the molasses," he said with a knowing smile.

She took a taste and continued feeding Rosebud, amazed at her appetite. He spooned more gruel into her bowl and reminded her to take some for herself. "I had a wife once . . . a baby girl."

Once. The haunting word hung between them and forbade further questions. Morrow looked at him carefully between bites. "Is that why you're helping me?"

He nodded. "That, and the fact I believe you told Colonel Clark the truth."

Tears stung her eyes. "He didn't believe me."

"Clark's a fine soldier, but he's no friend to the Indians." He leaned back against the rough bark of a pine. "I was at Fort Pitt last summer when the trouble started with the Shawnee. I remember your husband right well. He's a half blood, talks as well as a white man, carries himself like a Kispoko chief."

At this, she felt a strange kinship but said nothing.

He went on quietly, respectfully. "How'd you come to be at Loramie's?"

She hugged the buffalo robe closer. "Pierre Loramie is a friend. My husband thought we'd be safer there till spring."

"Just you and your baby girl?"

"I have a son—they're twins." Her firstborn's little face rose up in her mind, but she shut it away. "We were separated when the post burned. Loramie's wife had him. I don't know what happened to them."

He nodded thoughtfully. "It's likely Loramie and his kin—and your son—made it out safely and fled to the nearest Shawnee village." He added, "Clark's intent wasn't to kill Loramie, just deprive the Indians of an ally and destroy his post. But he means harm to your husband, and I need to know where you think he is."

Her face turned entreating. "Why is he singling out Red Shirt?"

"Your husband's well known on the frontier. Clark means to make an example of him. Or maybe you didn't know Major McKie was a cousin to Colonel Clark?" At her surprise, he said, "Both are from old Virginia stock. Caroline County. Besides, an officer doesn't take kindly to another officer being killed, family or no."

Despite his openness, she felt a bite of distrust. Just how much should she tell him? "Red Shirt left Loramie's in September and went west . . . to make a home for us in Missouri. He was going to come back and take us there."

"West is where I'm headed now that my enlistment's ended." He took a clay pipe from a saddlebag, face pensive. "By now your husband would have heard of the raid on Loramie's. And if he's half the man I think he is, he's near here—or soon will be." He looked away from her to the woods, as if expecting Red Shirt to materialize in the shadows. "I figure we'll head west on the buffalo trace. If your husband's coming east, he'll likely take that trail. Even if he doesn't, he's sure to find us eventually. The Shawnee are master trackers, as you know."

The reassurance filled her with relief, then raw alarm. "But what if Colonel Clark sends someone after us?"

His eyes narrowed. "Like Talks About Him, you mean?"

She could only nod, terror overtaking her.

"Then we'll just have to pray that Red Shirt finds us first."

All around them, dawn edged the forest in pale yellow light, and she looked about, feeling the need to be on her feet and put as much distance between them and Clark's men as they could. She couldn't rest till they found Red Shirt. But the impossibility of it all tamped down her hopes and turned her teary. How in the middle of such a vast wilderness would they cross paths? The timing had to be perfect . . . providential.

Standing up, she gathered the dirty bowls and cups to wash in a nearby stream after handing Rosebud to her guide. As soon as she turned away, she sensed she'd erred. Might her baby bring back memories of all he'd lost? But another glance told her he was pleased to hold her, maybe a bit surprised that Morrow had given her over. And Rosebud was making much of him, fists full of his fringed shirt, smile coy. Reassured, Morrow did the dishes, splashing icy water on her face to collect herself before rejoining them at the fire.

"You said your pa was a preacher?" he asked as she sat back down. "That you lived on the Red River?"

She nodded. "Are you familiar with that part of Kentucke?"

"I've been there," he said, face reflective. "A long time ago." With a yawn, he stood and reached for his rifle. "We'll travel a few more miles before making camp and you can sleep. I want to be heading west on the trace by noon."

She determined to oblige him any way she could, since she'd still be staring at the gallows if he hadn't taken time to trouble himself with her. The fact that he'd come to her aid still stunned her.

She studied him discreetly as he readied the horses, wondering what it was about him that seemed familiar. Why, she didn't even know his name. But it hardly seemed to matter, desperate as she felt, her every waking thought consumed with survival. They'd be on the trail a long time, likely. Plenty of time to ask questions and find answers. Whoever he was, she felt comfortable with him, unafraid to be who she was, unashamed of her Shawnee tie. With Colonel Clark, she'd read the recrimination in his cold eyes whenever he looked at her. But this man, dressed like a savage himself, was empty of all accusation.

They made it to the trace before noon, and as he'd promised, they rested. She watched in surprise as he constructed a temporary shelter of cedar boughs as effortlessly as Red Shirt might have done. Out of the weather, her feet to the fire, she slept, Rosebud's nursing hardly rousing her. He liked to travel at night, and mercifully, the moon was most obliging.

They were on the trail again by twilight, and it seemed like they stood on top the world, traversing the bony back of first one ridge and then another. How many days had it been? She shrugged the thought away. Keeping track of the time only deepened her despair. Where was Red Shirt? Why hadn't he come? Perhaps he had. In her mind's eye, the pickets of Fort Clark were as menacing as the soldiers' bayonets. And the colonel . . . he didn't seem the type to simply let her leave. Was he even now following?

"We'd best stop here," her guide said abruptly. "The weather's fixing to change, and I don't want to have to fight the wind to make camp."

He led her into a cave with a pine knot torch, and she stood at its entrance and stared down a great cavern that dripped incessant tears. But it was shelter, out of the wind and rain. Once he'd settled her by the fire, he went hunting, returning with a turkey. She nearly salivated at the sight, hungry for fresh meat instead of jerky. While it roasted on a crude spit, he took up his rifle and gestured for her to be completely still. But she couldn't stop Rosebud's cooing. Frantic, she placed a light hand over her daughter's smiling mouth, blowing into her face to get her attention. The effort only made Rosebud shriek louder. *Dear Lord in heaven.* Morrow had never seen so agreeable an infant in the face of danger and deprivation. At any other time she'd be proud.

Beyond the cave, a shot sounded, and wary eyes fastened on her, her guide's gaze communicating a dozen different things. The sound reverberated for long moments, chilling her with its crisp finality. As he edged closer to the entrance, fear swept over her like a fever. On shaking legs, she retreated toward the back of the cave, where the fire sizzled and the smell of roasting meat thickened in the damp air and threatened to expose them.

For a panicked moment, she nearly gave in to stomping out the fire with her foot. He disappeared from sight, then returned when the turkey was so succulent it fell off the bone. But his demeanor forbade any talking, and she served him in silence, knowing he needed the strength of a meal and the fire's warmth even as her unasked questions created an ache in her chest.

As he ate, rifle at the ready, he never took his eyes off the cave entrance. She sat beside him, in too much turmoil to take even one bite, and he finally whispered, "We're being followed. Whoever it is brought down a deer with that shot you heard, but I couldn't get close enough to see who it was. Our trail is pretty cold, but they're getting closer. Best stay here till I can figure out who it is."

His intensity only fueled her angst, and she turned the facts over in her mind. A lone hunter? Talks About Him? *Oh, Red Shirt, where are you?* She bent her head and prayed, then ate what she could. Beside her, Rosebud was cooing again and had found her stocking-clad feet.

"I think everything will turn out all right," the man across from her said quietly, passing her a canteen of water.

She nodded and tried to smile, her eyes returning again and again to the cave entrance, where a fine fog hovered like a white curtain. Her voice was a broken whisper. "I can never repay you for what you've done."

He seemed to color slightly and lifted a hand to remove his hat. The sight of the beaver felt resurrected a host of memories. Pa had had such a hat, though they were common enough on the frontier. She could view her guide plainly from beneath the brim's shadow and now assessed him in one sweep. Rusty hair that might have once been red. Cool blue gray eyes. He was long and lean as leather string. A bit older than herself, she guessed.

When she dropped her eyes, she felt him studying her as well, but it wasn't the way a man studied a woman he found pretty. He seemed to look past her appearance, beyond the soiled Irish linen dress and borrowed shoes, as if trying to place her.

"I keep thinking I've seen you before," he said. "But I disremember."

She brightened. "I feel the same."

"Any ideas?" he asked.

Befuddled, she shook her head and began to hum a lullaby, rocking Rosebud where she sat, the firelight dancing on the damp walls. Across from her, he sat with his buffalo robe about his shoulders, eyes on the cave opening, rifle in hand. She stopped her humming, afraid the barest echo would alert the enemy. On the other hand, might it bring Red Shirt back to her?

Rosebud looked up, her wee mouth puckered as if the silence nettled. Morrow crawled into her bed of blankets, holding her daughter close. The fire shifted and settled, and she closed her eyes, a prayer already forming on her lips. She had a family . . . another baby on the way. She ached for her former life, unsettled as it was. Having blessed her so abundantly, the Almighty wouldn't let it end. Would He?

36

On the third day they left the cave behind. The woods seemed weighted with silence, as if they were the only living souls in the entire wilderness. Morrow felt blindingly disoriented. If not for this man, she wouldn't even know where she was. Hemmed in by dense forest, unable to get her bearings, she fought the urge to cling to him more closely. Even the birdsong was suspended and the gloom of the day was unrelieved, as were her spirits.

"It's going to storm," her guide said, studying the sky. "Temperature's dropping, and we'll likely see snow by morning."

They'd stumbled onto a half-face camp on the side of a ridge, abandoned by trappers, and he proceeded to build a fire. She worked as best she could helping him unpack the horses, Rosebud growing heavy in her sling, while he made supper from the provisions at hand. When they were seated in the shelter, she served him and herself, smiling her appreciation when he said, *"Takuwah-nepi."*

Bread water. The meal Red Shirt had made when they'd first been on the trail. The memory only deepened the sadness inside her. She began feeding Rosebud and said, "You know a lot about the Shawnee."

"I lived with them for a time. Married a Shawanoe woman."

Surprised, she took another bite of the gruel he'd laced generously with molasses, thinking of the tender care the Mekoche midwife had shown her. "I suppose there's much to admire about them—the Shawnee, I mean."

He nodded. “Intelligent. Brave. Eloquent. Tolerant of whites who want to learn their ways. It’s a shame it’s so one-sided.”

She thought of Colonel Clark and McKie and all the Indian haters she knew. But for Pa, she’d have been among them. “How old was your little girl?” she dared to ask, not looking at him.

He hesitated, eyes on the fire. “Nearly two. She died of smallpox, same as my wife.”

“I’m sorry.” The words, though heartfelt, seemed woefully inadequate.

“You’re no stranger to suffering yourself from the sound of it. Didn’t you say your father died last year?”

She nodded. “Pa had consumption. My mother and sister died years before in an Indian raid . . . and my brother was taken captive. Pa tried to find him, participate in a prisoner exchange, but nothing ever came of it.”

“Sometimes white captives want to stay missing,” he said simply.

She nodded, wiping Rosebud’s mouth. “I’ve heard the same.”

“Was it Shawnees who killed your ma and sister . . . took your brother?”

She hesitated, thinking of Surrounded. “Yes.”

He eyed her thoughtfully. “How’d you come to make peace?”

“My father made peace with them. One winter he took in a sick Indian boy during a blizzard and nursed him back to health. He turned out to be the half-blood son of a chief. After that the boy and his father kept coming back. Pa thought they might know about Jess—”

“Your brother?”

She nodded. “He was a few years older than me, about ten when he was taken. For a long time I couldn’t forgive the Shawnee for what they’d done. But Pa . . .” She hesitated, feeling the familiar lump thicken in her throat. “Pa refused to hold a grudge. I wanted to be like him, but it took time.”

He nodded slowly as if understanding all she couldn't say.

"I heard you singing to your baby last night. Are you French?"

"My mother was, but I don't remember much about her. I guess I'm thinking of a song she sang to me."

"You've forgotten the last line," he told her, setting his bowl aside. "It goes like this." He sang a few words in perfect French, stunning her with his fine baritone.

"H-how did you know?"

He shrugged. "I've lived among the French all my life—traders and trappers and their wives up around Vincennes. I know a few ditties, most of them unmentionable."

She stared at him openly now, though he seemed not to notice, busy as he was assembling shot and powder. Something about the angle of his jaw, the way he held his mouth while speaking, the smile that was bewilderingly familiar . . .

She swallowed down her inhibitions and heard herself say, "What's your name?"

The rough hands that cleaned the fine rifle stilled. "Louis."

Louis, or Lewis? First name, or last? She felt a stinging disappointment and began fussing with Rosebud, folding a length of linen and swaddling her bottom before tying the ends off. She wished he'd tell her more about himself and satisfy her curiosity, but he'd put on his hat, and the simple gesture seemed to build a wall between them. He kept busy with his rifle, his actions telling her he was about to go hunting. When she looked up again, he was handing her a weapon. The flintlock pistol gleamed silver in the firelight, its handle smooth and worn.

"Know how to shoot?" he asked. When she shook her head, he said, "Time you learned how. I've loaded it for you. All you have to do is cock this here and pull the trigger."

She marveled at the weapon's strangeness, praying she'd have no occasion to use it.

"I'll be back before long, hopefully with a bear or buffalo. We need fresh meat and can jerk a bit for the rest of the trip. If you see a panther or anything that spooks you, don't hesitate to use it." His warning gaze slid into a grin. "Just don't shoot me."

She merely nodded and held Rosebud tighter, backing up further into the shelter. At the sight of his retreating back, she felt a sharp, cold lonesomeness.

When he'd reached a tall cedar almost out of sight, he turned back to her, his deep voice cutting through the twilight. "You stay put—don't even twitch—till I come back."

You stay put—don't even twitch—till I come back.

The words seemed to echo across time like the skimming of a rock on a murky pond, each word a ripple, resurrecting memories of a different place, a different life. They were Jess's words, the same ones he'd uttered on the banks of the Red River when the Shawnee first came. The last words she'd ever heard him say. She lay Rosebud down and scrambled out of the shelter after him, bewildered and disbelieving.

The cedar where he'd been standing stood stalwart, its graceful branches brushing her as they swayed in the wind. But he was gone, and there was no sense running after him. The snow he'd predicted was already erasing his tracks, falling and swirling in a lovely winter's dance that nearly made her forget where and who she was. For a few moments, she was five again, standing alone on the riverbank with what was left of her shattered life.

The sound of Rosebud's cooing pulled her back. She returned to the shelter, praying that Louis—for that is what he'd come to be in her mind—would find his way back. All she had to do was stay put and feed the fire at the front of the shelter. There was no moon tonight, but it didn't seem to matter, for the snow was bright as a lantern even with the last of daylight snuffed out.

He giveth snow like wool: he scattereth the hoarfrost like ashes.

Just when it seemed her hope was spent, God had sent the snow. The trail of man or beast was plain for all to see, though in this unending forest it seemed of little consequence. Yet might it lead Red Shirt to her? Or her to him? She dismissed all other terrifying possibilities. The pistol lay beside her, and she eyed it as she held Rosebud. Surely even a panther had sense enough to take cover on such a night.

After a time she fell asleep, pulling the buffalo robe close about her. But her dreams were disturbing, confused. She jerked awake at the report of a rifle.

The world she awoke to was not the one of an hour before. Just beyond the mouth of the shelter, the snow lay calf-deep. Her gaze traveled from the dwindling fire to the far cedar, where she saw a man. Not Louis. The shadow was too tall and moved in an altogether different manner. One of Clark's men? Talks About Him?

Panic rose up and seemed to smother her. Something told her he'd not take her captive again but would kill her. Shaking, she held up the gun. The cold metal seemed to hurt her hand.

Father, forgive me.

For Red Shirt she did this. And her babies.

When he was within twenty feet of the half-face shelter, she cocked the gun. It snapped in the cold, inviting her to finish. She held it with both hands to quell her trembling. Closer and closer the shadow came till it stood between her and the fire.

"Morrow?"

With a cry she dropped the pistol, and it went off with a flash, blinding her. Warily, Red Shirt bent over and began to make his way toward them, while Rosebud cried with such ferocity it seemed to shake the very shelter.

She'd almost killed him.

When he touched her, it seemed to unleash an avalanche of emotion. All her angst and exhaustion came crashing down and took her breath. Sobbing, she felt him take her in his arms, murmuring things she thought she'd never hear again.

"*Neewa,* what a welcome." His voice was bemused, disbelieving.

"D-did I h-hurt you?"

"No . . . you're a poor shot."

Rosebud howled louder, ending their exchange. Red Shirt took her and held her close, smoothing her silky hair, blowing gently on her face to quiet her. She stilled and raised her head to look at him. For a long moment, she took in every aspect of his firelit form before smiling shyly and reaching up to touch his cheek and chin. Looking on, Morrow's heart turned over. Though time and trouble had separated them, Rosebud seemed to know it was her father.

His eyes were damp, full of things he couldn't say. For a time they just sat where they were, huddled together, his strengthening presence settling them. Soon Rosebud's eyes closed and she drooped against him, her tiny fingers entwined in the fringe of his hunting shirt. Carefully he wrapped her in a trade blanket and put her down.

He drew Morrow closer, taking in her disheveled hair and tear-streaked face. "You knew I would come."

"I—I didn't doubt you, but it's not safe. Clark is looking for you—for me—"

"No, Morrow. Clark and his men never left the fort."

His reassuring words failed to burrow beneath her exhaustion, and her voice broke. "But our little son—and Angelique and Loramie—"

"They're just a few leagues from here. When Loramie's burned, they fled to the nearest Shawnee town. I've seen them myself, and all are safe and well, though our son is missing you."

She simply stared at him, trying to take it all in. Thankfulness flooded her, and she shut her eyes, a bit disbelieving that Clark had given up the chase. Could it truly be over?

He stroked her hair, his mouth near her ear. "Did anyone hurt you—the baby?"

"No . . . and the one I'm carrying has come to no harm," she said in a little rush.

His hand stilled in her hair.

She whispered, "Perhaps it's too soon to be bearing again . . ."

"Soon? You're still not strong—"

"I'm stronger than I look."

"You're not strong, just stubborn. We've had this conversation before."

She laid her cheek against his shoulder. "You say I'm not strong, yet I've just come a hundred or more miles to a strange fort in a near blizzard, with a baby in my arms and another inside me, with little to eat, not knowing if I'll ever see you or my little son again. And here I am on the run again . . ."

She sensed he was smiling, though the shadows hid him. "Tomorrow we'll meet up with the party I'm traveling with and head west."

But her thoughts were leaping ahead—to her little son waiting for them, and Louis. "I've met a man—a guide. I owe so much to him—he took me from the fort. Colonel Clark wanted to lure you there—"

"I know. This man—Louis—killed a buffalo near our camp tonight and is there now, sharing his meat. He told me you were here . . . how you came to be together."

"So we're . . . safe?"

"Safer than you've ever been—and almost to Missouri."

"I wish we could leave tonight."

"Tomorrow will be soon enough."

He was smiling now, his joy so plain it spilled over to her as she leaned against him. He loosened the remaining pins that held back her hair, unraveling its length with one hand till it covered her shaking shoulders like a shawl. "Go to sleep, Morrow, and forget about all this trouble."

She smiled, her whispered words weary but rife with relief. "What trouble?"

37

As they traveled to meet up with Louis the next morning, Red Shirt explained that he'd been on his way back to her, not wanting to wait till spring, sensing there might be more trouble brewing in the middle ground. When he was within a day's reach of Loramie's Station, he'd learned that the post had been destroyed and Loramie and his family had fled to the nearest Shawnee town. Indian scouts told him they'd seen Shawnee turncoats taking a woman and baby south toward the Falls of the Ohio. He was soon on his way there, intersecting with Louis as he was hunting. Despite everything, Morrow's prayers had been answered, and she was nearer Missouri than she'd ever been.

Now she stood in the midst of a dozen frontiersmen and Indians, a small remnant from Loramie's Station who would accompany them west to Missouri. Her longing to be on the trail was nearly overwhelming as she watched Red Shirt prepare her horse for travel. She began fashioning a sling for Rosebud out of some stroud in Louis's provisions, speculating on the trip before them.

"How long will it take to meet up with Loramie's party and see our son?"

"A few days or so," he told her, adjusting the saddle. "We'll go slowly. I don't want you—or the babies—to have trouble."

"What made Loramie decide to go on to Missouri with us rather than d'Etroit?"

"He said a new land needs a new trading post. And it's far beyond the reach of the Bluecoats."

They rode west single file through a great cathedral of trees, Red Shirt leading, she in the middle of the procession, and Louis riding directly behind on his sorrel horse. Often Red Shirt would circle back to see how she fared, taking Rosebud for a time so she could rest. Their prayers for fair weather prevailed, and the sky above was a stunning ice blue. Dressed in shoepacks and a buffalo coat, she was able to stay warm enough, and they made rapid progress. Any weariness was replaced with excitement the closer they came. Soon she'd hold both her babies in her arms . . . sit by the fire with her sewing . . . laugh with Angelique and her children.

For now, the monotony of cold nights about the campfire was relieved by laughter and storytelling. The men regaled each other with hunting exploits or other feats of valor, softened, Morrow thought, for her benefit. Seated between Louis and Red Shirt, she smiled at their bravado, wondering what Louis thought of all the big talk. In his quiet, soft-spoken way, he told a few stories of his own that proved every bit as interesting as theirs.

He'd traveled far, knew the middle ground of Kentucke and Ohio as well as they, had even wintered with the Cherokee to the south and the Sioux to the west. He spoke half a dozen Indian languages and was considering opening a trading post toward the Shining Mountains. Upon hearing this, Morrow felt a sudden sadness. He would move on, then, once they came to Missouri, and she'd be left with a hoard of unasked questions begging for answers.

Turning to him in the firelight, she spoke in a whisper. "Don't you have any family?"

Louis looked at her thoughtfully. "A sister."

"A sister," she echoed. "Is that all?"

He chuckled and took a buffalo rib from the fire's spit. "You want me to make up some kin, invent a few names, maybe?"

She smiled at his teasing. "I just don't like the thought of you all alone, is all."

"Maybe I like being alone."

"Have you ever thought of marrying again—having a family?"

He smiled. "Sounds like you have somebody you'd like to tie me to."

She could hardly see his face for the generous brim of his hat and didn't know how far to tread. Thinking of Esme, she dared. "As a matter of fact, I do."

"And who might that be?"

"Come with us and find out," she said.

Leaning back, he tossed a bone to a frontiersman's dog. "I plan on seeing you safely settled . . . but I can't guarantee anything beyond that."

"I can never repay you for what you've done for us," Morrow said again.

He merely nodded, taking out a pipe and packing it full of tobacco crumbles. She reached into the fire for a twig with which to light it, and he thanked her, looking pleased.

Red Shirt was watching them, Rosebud asleep in his arms, her dusky head half-hidden beneath the red cap Hester had given her. Taking the baby from him, Morrow retreated into a sapling shelter, leaving the men to smoke. Stretched out on the makeshift bed of trade blankets, she was still able to see the goings-on about the fire. Louis's profile was etched clearly against the backdrop of the burnt-orange flames, but it was her father's face she saw beneath the brim of his felt hat, before time and grief had done their work. Or was she simply wishing it was so?

Turning over, she hugged Rosebud closer and tried to sleep. Red Shirt soon joined her, his voice low and contemplative. "What do you know of Louis, Morrow?"

The pointed question nearly brought her upright. She turned

toward him, thinking of what she'd gleaned since they'd been together on the trail. "I know his name. He's buried a Shawnee wife and child . . . served as scout and interpreter for Colonel Clark . . . has a sister. Why do you ask?"

"I see your father in his face."

She expelled a tense breath. "The other night, when he left to hunt, he spoke the same words Jess spoke when I last saw him."

He hesitated. "Why don't you ask him?"

"Ask if he's Jess? I don't know if I could."

"It's a simple matter," he said quietly. "He will say either yes or no."

"If he is Jess, I think he might not want to be found."

"Why? Because he told you his name is Louis?"

Louis. What was Jessamyn's full name? Pa had scrawled it in their family Bible, but it had been destroyed when the Shawnee—Surrounded—came. Though she'd tried to dredge it up over the years, the memory was denied her.

She peered into the darkness as if it held the answers she sought. "So much time has passed. If Louis is Jess, perhaps he's content to see me, know that I'm all right, and then go about his business."

"And you? Are you content with that?"

"No." The word was emphatic though softly spoken. She'd not been content for fifteen years, ever since he'd turned away from her on the riverbank. But if Jess was out there, smoking about the fire, he was hardly the boy she remembered.

Red Shirt reached for her hand. "Perhaps it's not as simple as it sounds."

She said nothing more, just lay back and listened to his deep, even breathing once he was asleep. 'Twas simple, truly. But she simply lacked the courage to ask.

Red Shirt led Morrow's mare to the front of the procession so she could be the first to see the camp scattered along the icy expanse of the Mississippi. It was twilight, and a gauzy haze hung about the shelters from the many fires, the snowy mountains in the distance a deep, ice blue. As they drew nearer, dogs began barking and people started leaving the warmth of their shelters to welcome them, Loramie leading. At his warm greeting, Morrow could hardly keep herself in check. There were many familiar faces here, most of them from Loramie's Station, and all seemed well and safe. Anxiously she looked around for sight of her little son.

When she finally spied Angelique, her daughters in her wake, she passed Rosebud to Louis. Morrow's heart swelled then tightened as Loramie's wife stopped an arm's length away. In her arms was Jess. Stout and handsome, he regarded her with solemn eyes that were the same unmistakable shade as his father's. His hair was damp, and it curled and waved in bright abandon atop his head. But his lower lip puckered slightly, and she thought he might cry. Smiling through her tears, she simply held out her arms to him, aware of Red Shirt and Louis looking on. But Jess turned his little face away and buried his head in Angelique's neck.

"Your mother has come back and wants to see you," Angelique said to him gently. "And I must tend to my own children."

Morrow murmured her thanks and took him, grieved at the taut resistance in his little body. She cradled him under her chin, the soft weight of him like a healing salve. Still, he turned away from her.

"He will not be so particular when he is hungry," Loramie said wryly, and Angelique laughed.

Morrow bent her head and whispered into his ear. Would he remember the old French lullaby? He raised his head and looked at her, one plump hand resting on her cheek. At his touch she dissolved, turning away so the others couldn't see her struggle.

"You've grown so big since I've been gone," she whispered, kissing his head and cheek, his chin. He opened his mouth, and she spied a single tooth, a tiny pearl on his lower gum. "I see that Angelique and the girls took good care of you."

Her chatter seemed to settle him, and he grabbed at the soiled kerchief of her dress. She glanced longingly at the shelters, wondering which was their own, wanting to be alone with him and rest. As if sensing her disquiet, Red Shirt took her elbow and guided her to the one that would house them till the river thawed and they could cross into Missouri territory.

As she entered in, her eyes fastened on an upraised bed and cooking vessels and sewing baskets scattered all around the shelter, with a welcoming fire at its heart. Someone—Angelique?—had done an admirable job of trying to make the place comfortable. In the quiet Morrow and Red Shirt stood, their little son looking from one to the other of them as if trying to determine where they'd been for so long. Raising his arms, he reached for his father, and Morrow released him reluctantly.

Sitting on the edge of the upraised bed, she watched Red Shirt laugh and toss Jess into the air, toward the smoke spiraling out the smoke hole. He shrieked with delight as his father continued their game. Red Shirt glanced at her, and she wondered if she looked as bedraggled as she felt. His voice was edged with concern. "You need to rest."

"But Loramie mentioned a feast . . ."

"The girls can take care of Rosebud while you stay here with Jess."

"But Louis—"

"Louis isn't leaving yet," he said. "Not till morning."

The news brought a queer hurt. She could hear the celebration already starting outside their door and marveled that everyone else seemed in the mood to take part. Looking down at her hands, she twisted the wedding ring around her finger absently. She must talk to Louis tonight. There was no sense in putting it off any longer. If she tarried, he might be gone. But even now her lids felt leaden, and she was sliding toward sleep.

"Ma-ma."

She looked up to find her little son stretching out his plump arms to her, finally saying the one word she'd longed to hear. She took him, her heart stilling when he laid his head upon her shoulder and began pulling at the lacing of her bodice. She felt the warm release of milk even before she'd settled him on the bed beside her. Her last thought as sleep descended was that Louis would be leaving. But the warmth of her baby son—and then, later, Rosebud and Red Shirt—hemming her in and making her feel safe and warm and tremendously content, pushed all thoughts of goodbye aside.

38

Morrow came awake to find both babies sleeping soundly in the valley of bedding between her and Red Shirt. Rosebud was tucked against the hard expanse of her father's bare chest, just as their little son nestled against her. Her eyes shifted from the crackling fire to the smoke hole and then the blue sky. *Almost to Missouri*, was her first relieved thought, and her second was simply, *Louis*. Placing a hand over the baby tumbling inside her, she sat up, wondering where he'd passed the night. The feasting had gone on till the wee hours, though she'd been asleep through most of it, rousing only to nurse the twins or watch Red Shirt feed the fire. Louis was an early riser, she remembered. Might he have already left?

The thought was so startling she pulled on the dirty linen dress as fast as she could, spying her soiled shoes near the door. With renewed vigor, she ducked past the door flap into the chill morning. Though a scattering of shelters were in the way, she could still discern a few winsome twists and turns of the river called Mississippi and hear the musketlike crack of ice thawing within its frozen banks.

Please, Lord, don't let him leave, not without saying goodbye.

It seemed no one else was up except the customary scouts, so she simply stood, taking in every detail she'd missed in the twilight when they'd ridden into this unfamiliar place. Twenty or so temporary dwellings. A stomp ground and fire pit nearer the river. Spits and trellises for smoking meat. A work area for canoe-making rife with wood shavings and sundry tools. A scattering of skeletal trees, mostly elm and oak and beech, frosted white. And then the corrals where fifty or more horses were milling . . . and Louis leaning against the enclosure.

Her heart seemed to double its cadence. Was he looking for his horse? Shrugging a blue trade blanket around her shoulders, she started in his direction, walking briskly at first and then slowed by a tongue-tied shyness. The nearer she came, the more upended she felt. The tilt of his hat—the decisive set of his whiskery jaw—seemed to bring a hundred heartfelt things to mind of her old life and the father she so fiercely missed. When she was just a stone's throw away, he turned toward her but gave no greeting, just fixed her with tired eyes that were red-rimmed and steady and sorrowful all at once. He wore the same greasy, begrimed hunting shirt he'd had on the day before and looked sorely in need of sleep.

She said the first thing she thought. "Haven't you been to bed?"

He rubbed his jaw. "No, Morrow. I've been up all night wondering what to say to you come morning. And now that it's morning I still don't know what to say."

She swallowed past the lump in her throat. "Are you leaving?"

He took off his hat and gave it an agitated twirl. "You think I'd go without saying goodbye? I did that once before, remember, a long time ago. And I've hated leave-takings ever since."

Jess.

Their eyes locked and held, warm as an embrace yet disbelieving. She watched as he removed something from the small buckskin pouch at his waist. When he placed Pa's wedding ring in the palm of her hand and wrapped her fingers tight around it, she began to cry.

He put his arm around her, face pensive. "I don't remember everything about our home on the Red River, but I do recall that Celtic cross. And you're the picture of our ma."

She studied him through her tears. "You look like Pa."

"I'm glad of that. I remember him being a fine man—a fine father. But I bet he never reckoned his wedding ring would lead me to you."

She swiped at her damp face with the edge of the trade blanket. "Only the Almighty could have arranged that."

He nodded. "The soldiers took that ring and meant it for evil, but like Scripture says, God meant it for good."

"You were there when it happened?"

"Right there at the treaty table, translating alongside Red Shirt. I took the officer in charge aside and told him it belonged to my kin, and he gave it over straightaway. And then when you came to Clark's fort, I saw you wearing Ma's ring. There's no mistaking the design. I've never seen a set of rings like it."

"You call yourself Louis, but I knew you as Jess."

He smiled. "Jessamyn Louis Little."

She looked down at her own band, the little cross glinting in the dawn, and a bittersweet sadness swept through her. "I wish Pa could be here. He never stopped looking for you—wanting you home."

"I never forgot him—or you." He looked away from her and squinted into the sunrise. "I was there when the Shawnee killed Ma and Euphemia. I don't know why they let me live or took me north to the Indian towns. An old Shawnee couple whose son had died adopted me. After a while they became my family."

Family. She felt no hurt at his confession. His ties to the Shawnee were every bit as unusual as her own, and she simply nodded in understanding. "I guess you'll be leaving now." As hard as she tried to stop it, her voice gave way, and his arms encircled her again.

"No, Morrow. I've been roaming a long time and want to settle down. Finding you is like coming home to me. Lord willing, I'll cross into Missouri and live near you in a cabin of my own."

At his words, it seemed a small sunrise was dawning in her breast and all her weariness was washed away. She became aware of a tall shadow behind them and turned. Red Shirt stood looking at them, the twins in his arms. They were almost home. Almost to Missouri.

But home wasn't a place, she was coming to realize. Home was family. Home was right here, right now. With these God-given people.

Laura Frantz credits her grandmother as being the catalyst for her fascination with Kentucky history. Frantz's ancestors followed Daniel Boone into Kentucky in the late eighteenth century and settled in Madison County, where her family still resides. Frantz is a member of the Kentucky Historical Society, American Christian Fiction Writers, and Romance Writers of America, and is the author of *The Frontiersman's Daughter*. She currently lives in the misty woods of Port Angeles, Washington, with her husband and two sons. Contact her at www.laurafrantz.blogspot.com or LauraFrantz.net.

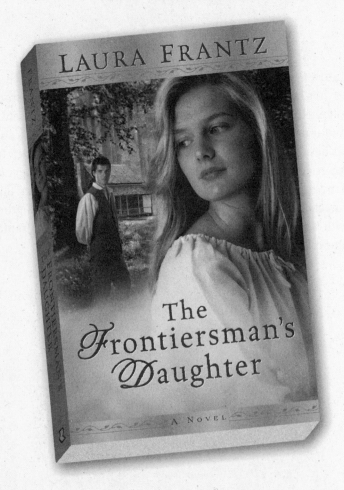

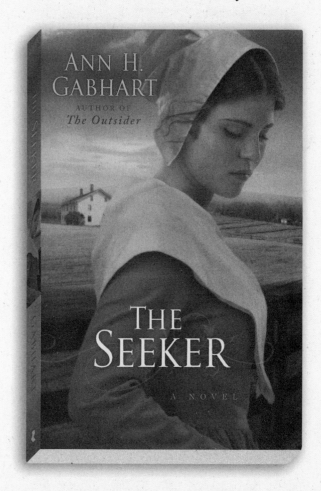

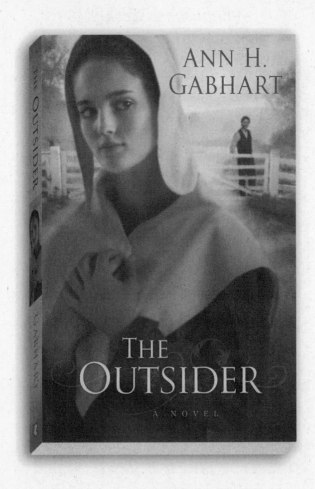

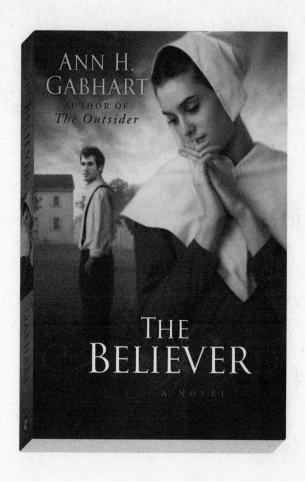